SNOWBOUND WITH A BILLIONAIRE

BY
JULES BENNETT

MILLS
BOON

Published in Great Britain 2014
by Mills & Boon, an imprint of Harlequin (UK) Limited,
Eton House, 18-24 Paradise Road, Richmond, Surrey, TW9 1SR

© 2014 Jules Bennett

ISBN: 978 0 263 91457 3

51-0214

Harlequin (UK) Limited's policy is to use papers that are natural, renewable and recyclable products and made from wood grown in sustainable forests. The logging and manufacturing processes conform to the legal environmental regulations of the country of origin.

Printed and bound in Spain
by Blackprint CPI, Barcelona

National bestselling author **Jules Bennett**'s love of storytelling started when she would get in trouble as a child and would tell her parents her imaginary friends were to blame. Since then, her vivid imagination has taken her down a path she'd only dreamed of. And after twelve years of owning and working in salons, she hung up her shears to write full-time.

Jules doesn't just write Happily Ever After, she lives it. Married to her high school sweetheart, Jules and her hubby have two little girls who keep them smiling. She loves to hear from readers! Contact her at authorjules@ gmail.com, visit her website, www.julesbennett.com, where you can sign up for her newsletter, or send her a letter at PO Box 396, Minford, OH 45653, USA. You can also follow her on Twitter and join her Facebook fan page.

This book is for Allison, who is so much more than my niece—you're my friend, my sounding board and my kids' role model. Every day you continue to inspire me. Even through all of life's obstacles, you rise above and I'm blessed to have you in my life.

One

Max Ford maneuvered his rental car carefully through the slushy streets. Granted this old, dirty snow lining the thoroughfares was nothing new to Lenox, Massachusetts, for the month of February, but it was quite a jump from the palm-draped avenues he was used to back in L.A.

He hadn't been back to Lenox in years and hadn't driven in snow in even longer, but, as he eased off the gas, he realized he'd missed doing this. Shooting a scene for a movie in the snow wasn't the same as spending time off enjoying the pristine white surroundings. Besides, usually when he would shoot a winter locale, it was with man-made snow and not the God-given kind.

Since Max had grown up here, Lenox would always hold a special place in his heart. The population may be small, but the bank accounts of the residents were anything but. The sprawling estates had stood for decades; some were main residences, others second homes.

The two narrow lanes wound through town, and, just as Max rounded the last turn, he spotted a car off the side of the road, its back end sticking up out of a ditch. The flashers were on, and the back door opened. The afternoon sun shone through the car windows, revealing a woman—

bundled up with a stocking cap over her head and a scarf wrapped around her neck and mouth—stepping out.

Instinct told him to slam on his brakes, but he was born and raised on the East Coast and knew better.

Carefully easing his car off the road just ahead of the wreck, Max left the engine running as he stepped out into the frigid temperatures. Damn, that biting cold was something he hadn't missed.

Since he'd come straight from L.A., he didn't exactly have the proper shoes to be trudging in the snow, but there was no way he would leave a woman stranded on the side of the road. Granted he was only a mile from his destination and could've called someone, but that wasn't the type of man he was raised to be.

"Ma'am," he called as he drew closer. "Are you all right?"

He wondered if she'd hear him over the howling wind, but when she froze at his voice, he assumed she'd realized she wasn't alone.

The woman in a long, puffy gray coat turned. All Max could see was her eyes, but he'd know them anywhere. Those bright emerald-green eyes could pierce a man's heart...and once upon a time, they had penetrated his.

"Raine?"

Her eyes widened as she reached up with a gloved hand to shove her scarf down below her chin. "Max, what are you doing here?"

It was too damn cold to be having a discussion about anything other than her current predicament, so he asked again, "Are you all right?"

She glanced over her shoulder, then back at him. "I'm fine, but the car is stuck."

"I can give you a lift," he offered. "Where are you going?"

"Um...I can call a friend."

Max nearly laughed. Were they really going to argue about this? It was freezing, he hadn't seen her in…too many years to count, and he really wanted to get to his mother, who was recovering from surgery.

"Seriously, just get in the car and I can take you anywhere," he said. "Grab your stuff and let's go."

Raine hesitated, holding his gaze as if she were contemplating waiting in the snow for another ride instead of coming with him. Granted they hadn't left things on the best of terms…. No, they had actually left their relationship on very good, very intimate terms. It was after he'd left that something had happened. And he had no clue what that something was because the last time he'd seen her, they'd been in love with plans for a future together.

Still to this day, thinking back on that time in his life left his heart aching.

But now was *not* the time to consider such things. Raine needed to get in, because who knows how long she'd been out here in the freezing cold, and she needed to call a wrecker.

"All right," she conceded. "I have to get a few things first."

She turned into the backseat and seconds later she faced him again, this time with a…baby carrier?

Whoa! He totally wasn't expecting her to have a baby in tow. Not that he'd planned on running into her like this at all, but still…

"Can you hold this?" she asked. "I need to get the base out and strap it into your car."

Base? He had no clue what a *base* was considering the only thing he knew about babies is that he used to be one. Max reached for the handle of the carrier and was surprised how heavy this contraption was. He didn't see the baby for the large blanket-looking thing with a zipper going up the middle. He supposed that was smart, seeing as how the wind was wicked cold right now, and keeping the baby as warm as possible was the best idea.

In all honesty, the idea of Raine with a baby was what really threw him. She was probably married, because a woman like Raine wouldn't settle for a child without having the husband first. And that thought right there kicked him in the gut. Even after all this time, the mental image of her with another man seemed incomprehensible. He had to chalk it up to the fact he'd had no closure on their relationship, because he refused to admit, after years of living apart, that he still had feelings for this emerald-eyed beauty.

She lifted some gray plastic bucket thing from the backseat and started toward his car. He assumed that was his cue to follow.

Max held the handle with both hands since there was no way in hell he'd take a chance dropping what he assumed to be a sleeping baby. Not a peep was made from beneath the zipper. Surely the child was okay after that accident. Her car was barely off the road but enough that the front end was kissing the snow-covered ditch.

Once Raine had the base in, Max carefully handed over the carrier. With a quick click, she had the baby in the warm car and had closed the door.

"I have to get the diaper bag and this gift I was delivering," she stated. "Go ahead and get in...I'll be right back."

"I'll get your bag." He stepped in front of her as she tried to pass him. "It's too cold and you've been out here longer than me. Is everything in the front seat?"

She nodded and looked so damn cute with snowflakes dangling on her lashes, her face void of makeup...just like he'd remembered.

Not waiting for her to protest, Max turned back to her car, cursing the entire way. Cute? He was now thinking she was cute? What was he...five? So they shared a past. A very intimate, very intense past, but in his defense, he hadn't seen her in nearly fifteen years. Of course old feelings were going to crop up, but that didn't mean they had to control his state of mind—or his common sense.

He jerked on her car door's handle and reached in, grabbing the pink diaper bag and a small floral gift bag. Who the hell delivered a gift when the roads were quickly becoming a sheet of ice? With a baby to boot?

Max slid back behind the wheel of his rental, cranked the heat as high as it would go and eased back out onto the road.

"Where am I taking you?" he asked.

"Um…I was on my way to see your mother."

Max jerked in his seat. "My mother?"

Raine barely looked his way before she focused her eyes back on the road, a place he should keep his.

"I swear I had no idea you were coming in today," she quickly told him. "I mean, I knew you were coming, but I didn't know exactly when that would be. If you'd rather I not go…I can come another time."

She was going to see his mother? Things certainly had changed since the last time he'd been in Lenox with Raine and his parents. The way he and Raine had fought to be together, defying both sets of their parents…and it all was for naught.

He cast a quick glance her way, noticed how she kept toying with the threads fraying off the hem of her coat, her eyes either staying in her lap or staring out the window. Why was she so nervous? Was it him? Was she mentally replaying every moment they'd spent together, just like he was? Was she remembering that last night they'd made love, and the promises they'd made to each other? Promises that he had fully intended to keep, not knowing she'd never hold up her end of the deal. Is that what had her so on edge?

"Why are you visiting my mother?"

Raine's soft laugh filled the car. "A lot has changed since you were in Lenox, Max."

Apparently…and since she had pointedly dodged his question, he assumed that was code for "none of your business." And she was right. Whatever she was doing *was* none of his concern. Once upon a time they knew every single detail about one another, but that chapter had closed. They were all but strangers at this point. Could this last mile be any longer? Thank God the drive was in sight.

"I didn't know you had a baby," he said, trying to ease the thick tension, but once the words were out, he realized he sounded like an idiot. "I mean, I assumed you had a life. I just never… So, how many kids do you have?"

"Just Abby. She's three months old."

"Do you need to call your husband?"

Way to go. Smooth, real smooth. Could I be any less subtle?

"No," Raine replied. "I'll call my friend when we get to your mother's house. He can come pick me up."

He? She was calling a male friend and not her husband.

Max mentally shook his head and scolded himself. Still this was none of his business.

He turned into the long, narrow drive. Straight ahead sat his childhood home, now his parents' second home, where his mother was waiting inside recovering from surgery. She would soon begin radiation treatments in town. Thankfully the doctors discovered the lump very early, and chemo wasn't needed.

Max had no clue how she'd look, but he knew he needed to be strong, and being thrown off by seeing Raine couldn't hinder his plans. His mother had to take top priority right now…. God knows his dad wouldn't man up in this situation.

The sprawling two-story colonial-style home always dominated the flat acreage surrounded by tall evergreens. Max loved growing up here and had been fortunate to have been adopted by Thomas and Elise Ford. He never knew his biological parents, and, even though he'd rarely seen eye to eye with his father, he knew there were much worse scenarios he could've entered into as an orphaned baby.

Max pulled in front of the house and killed the engine. "Why don't I take your diaper bag and gift?" he offered. "I'm not comfortable with that carrier…unless you can't maneuver it in the snow."

Raine glanced over at him and laughed. "I've been doing just fine for a few months now, Max. Longer than that before Abby came along."

She got out and closed the door. Her quick jab wasn't lost on him, but he had no idea why she was bitter. She was the one who'd dissed him when he'd gone to L.A. Destroyed any hope of sharing his life with her. And in his rage, after realizing she didn't want him, he had nearly got himself killed.

When he stepped from the vehicle, he noticed she was getting the carrier out, and also had the gift tote and her diaper bag dangling from her arm. Apparently this Raine was a bit more independent and stubborn than the old Raine. Who was he to argue?

He followed her up the steps, careful to stay close in case she slipped. By the time they reached the wide porch, they were stomping the snow off their feet. Max moved forward and opened the door for her, gesturing her in ahead of him.

If she was going to insist on carrying everything even though he'd offered, the least he could do is get the door and be somewhat gentlemanly.

The grand foyer looked exactly the same as when he had left home at eighteen. There was never a need for him to return to this home, because, as soon as he'd left for L.A., his parents had hightailed it to Boston.

His father had always loved the Boston area and thought it would make good business sense to branch out his pubs by starting a second in a larger city. Now his father had a chain of restaurants, and Max still wanted no part of the family business.

The wide, curvaceous staircase dominated the expansive entryway, allowing visitors to see all the way up to the second-floor balcony that ran the width of the entryway. A vast chandelier suspended down from the ceiling of the second floor, the lights casting a kaleidoscope of colors onto the pale marble flooring.

Raine was just unzipping the blanket mechanism covering the carrier when his mother came into the foyer. Max didn't know what to expect when they finally came face-to-face after her major, life-altering surgery, but relief quickly settled in when Elise Ford rushed forward and launched her petite little frame into his arms.

"Max," she said, looking up at him with beautiful blue eyes. "I'm so glad you're here. I hate to pull you away from your work, though."

He was careful how he returned her embrace, knowing the left side of her body was tender from surgery.

"I would drop anything for you, Mom. Besides, I don't start another movie for a couple of months, so I'm all yours." He smiled down at her, soaking in the fact that his mother had been diagnosed with breast cancer, but, had not only fought it, she'd beaten the odds and won. "I can't believe how great you look."

She laughed, swatting his chest. "What were you expecting? I'm sore, and I definitely have my moments where I'm feeling run-down and tired, but today is a good day. Not only is my son home, he brought a beautiful girl and a baby with him."

Max turned to see Raine directly behind him, cradling a swaddled, sleeping baby. While his eyes were drawn to Raine, his curiosity made him look down at the child, wondering what life his ex was leading now. Apparently she'd gotten all she'd wanted out of life: husband, baby, probably that farm of her grandmother's she'd always loved.

"Oh…" Elise moved past Max and sighed. "Look how precious she is. Nothing sweeter than a sleeping baby."

How were babies always instant magnets for women? What exactly was the draw? Baby powder? Slobber? What?

As Max watched the maternal love that settled into Raine's eyes, the softness of her features, the tender smile, he couldn't help but be jealous of this baby.

Perhaps that thread of jealousy stemmed from his lack of being that loved at such a young age…but he didn't think so. Max knew his jealousy had sparked because he once had that same unconditional love from Raine…until she'd broken his heart. So why was he upset? Had he seriously not learned his lesson the first time he got entangled with this woman?

"May I hold her?" his mother asked.

"Are you sure you're up to it?" Raine replied. "I don't want you to hurt yourself."

Elegant as always, his mother waved a hand through the air and smiled. "I'm perfectly fine to hold a little baby. My surgery was two weeks ago. Take your coat off and stay a while, anyway. It's too cold to be out on a day like this."

Raine handed over the baby and made work of removing her coat. Max should've done the same, but he was too busy watching Raine shed her scarf and gloves. When she pulled the crocheted purple hat off her head, she ran a hand over her auburn curls, as if she could tame them. He missed seeing that hair. He remembered running his fingers through it and feeling its silky softness. Truth was, he didn't know he'd longed for such minute things about her at all until just now.

"I need to call my friend to come get me," Raine told his mother. "My car is in a ditch about a mile away."

Elise gasped. "Oh, honey. Are you all right?"

Raine nodded. "I'm fine. Abby's fine. Just scared me, but I was getting ready to call someone when Max pulled up."

His mother turned to him. "Good timing."

Wasn't it just? Fate hated him. He was positive of that. Otherwise he wouldn't be here in his childhood home, with his high school sweetheart and his mother, who had not exactly fought to keep them apart but had expressed her opinion that their teenage relationship wasn't the best move.

Max didn't know what had happened between these two women over the years, but apparently his mother and Raine had made some sort of truce. Hell, he really had no clue what was going on. Even in the times he'd visited his parents in Boston, his mother hadn't mentioned Raine after his first few visits.

Max pulled off his coat, hung it by the door then crossed to Raine. The last thing he wanted to do was get close enough to smell her sweet floral scent or, God forbid, touch her. But, being the gentleman his mother had raised him to be, Max reached for her bag and helped her out of her ratty coat.

"Oh, thanks," she said, not quite meeting his eyes. "If you'll excuse me, I'll make that call."

Raine slipped to the other room, pulling her cell from her pocket. Max turned to his mother who was making some silly faces and equally goofy noises for the baby.

"What on earth is going on?" he asked in a strained whisper.

Elise glanced over and smiled. "I'm holding a baby and visiting with my son."

"You know what I mean, Mom. Why is Raine so welcomed here now, and why are you holding her baby like she's your very own grandchild or something?"

Okay, poor, poor choice of words there, but he was damn confused.

"Raine called me and asked if she could drop something

off," his mother explained. "Of course, I knew she had had a baby, and I've visited with Raine several times over the years when your father and I would come back to Lenox. Trust me when I say, Raine isn't the girl she used to be."

But he liked the girl she used to be. Liked her so much he'd intended on marrying her, making a life with her.

"So you and she are what? Chummy now?"

Raine stepped back into the room and reached for the baby. "Thanks for holding her."

"Oh, it's not hardship holding something so precious," his mother said. "Did you get in touch with your friend, dear?"

"He wasn't home."

Max rested his hands on his hips. Fate absolutely hated him. He'd been home ten minutes, and already he felt as if he was being pushed back into his past, forced to face feelings he simply wasn't ready for.

And before he could think better of it, he opened his mouth. "I can run you home if you want to call a tow truck to pull your car out."

Raine's eyes locked onto his. "Oh, that's okay. I'll call someone else. First I want to give Elise a gift."

"A gift?" his mother asked, clasping her hands together. "Oh, if it's some of that honey lavender lotion, I'm going to just kiss you."

What the hell was happening here? At one time his mother and Raine were at opposite ends of the spectrum, and he was being pulled in both directions. Now he had just entered a whole new world where the two women were clearly the best of friends.

"I knew that scent was your favorite," Raine said, holding up the floral gift bag in one hand and securing the baby against her shoulder with the other. "And I thought you deserved to be pampered."

His mother took the bag, shifted the bright pink tissue

paper and peeked inside. "Oh, the big bottles. Thank you so much, Raine. Let me just go get my purse."

"Oh, no," Raine said, shaking her head. "These are on me. I had planned on bringing you some food as well, but Abby was up all night fussing, and I didn't get to make anything today, because we napped."

Max couldn't take all this in. The baby, the odd bond his mother and his ex seemed to have, and the fact they were totally comfortable ignoring him. He'd been in Hollywood for years, the industry and media swarming him everywhere he went. Yet, here in his childhood home, he was suddenly an outsider.

"Oh, darling," Elise said with a smile. "Don't push yourself. I know you're busy. And now that Max is here, he's more than capable in the kitchen. Besides, I believe my home-care nurse prepared some meals for me before she left."

Max was thankful his mother had hired a nurse and that she'd been able to stay until he could arrive. Apparently his father was once again a no-show in the family when he was needed most.

"Raine," he chimed in. "I'll take you home when you're ready."

Her eyes drifted back to him, and she sighed. "Fine. I need to get Abby home anyway and feed her. I hadn't planned on staying gone long, and I walked out the door with the diaper bag but left the bottle on the counter. And the roads are getting worse."

"Darling," his mother said, placing her hand on Raine's arm. "Please don't feel like you have to do anything for me. Max and I will get along just fine. Visit all you like and bring this precious baby but don't bother with anything else."

Raine's smile was soft, almost innocent as her green

eyes twinkled. "Elise, you're one of my best customers. I'm happy to help."

"You take care of this baby and your other customers first," his mother chided. "I'm seriously feeling good. My radiation treatments start in two weeks, and Max can do whatever I need."

The old Raine would've done anything for anyone. She'd always put others first. Max was glad to see she was just as selfless, just as caring. And it warmed him even more to know that, after everything Max's parents had done to keep him and Raine apart, she could put all that aside and forge a special relationship with his mother.

Raine hugged Elise and strapped the baby back in the carrier. Once they were all bundled up again, he carefully escorted her to the car. He kept a hand hovering near her arm, careful not to touch, but it was there in case she slipped.

The baby started to fuss a little as Raine locked the seat into place, but she unzipped the cover and replaced the pacifier. Instant silence. How did she know exactly what to do? The whole concept of consoling a baby was totally lost on him. Thankfully his social scene the past decade hadn't revolved around children. Some people were natural nurturers, like his mother and Raine. Others, like his father, were not. And even though they weren't biologically related, Max had somehow inherited the not-so-caring trait.

As he pulled out of the drive, he glanced over at Raine. All that gorgeous red hair tumbled from her hat and down her back.

"Where do you live?" he asked, assuming she'd moved out of her parents' home.

"My grandmother's farm."

Max smiled. Raine's grandmother was a woman like no other, and it didn't surprise him that Raine had moved into the historic farmhouse. More than likely she had it overrun with goats, chickens, horses and a giant garden. That had always been her dream.

They used to laugh about it, because Raine had always tried to figure out how she could get all of that in L.A. But she'd assured him that she was willing to try, because she loved him more than this old farmhouse.

Perhaps that was what held her back, kept her distanced from him when he left, and compelled her to ignore his phone calls and letters.

Max passed the spot where her car was still stuck in the ditch. "You going to call a tow truck before it gets dark?"

"I'll call when I get home," she told him.

"Do you want to talk about this?"

She glanced his way. "*This* meaning what? Because if you're referring to the past, then no. If you're referring to the freezing temps, sure."

A muscle worked in his cheek. "Always running from uncomfortable topics," he muttered.

"Running?" she asked, her voice rising. "I've never run from anything in my life. I'd choose better words next time. Or is it too hard when someone hasn't written them for you?"

Max sighed, turning onto her street. The car slid a bit on the icy patch, but he eased the wheel in the opposite direction and righted the vehicle.

Raine was in a mood. Welcome to the club because, now that the initial shock of seeing her again had passed, he could feel all those old memories stirring up inside of him.

"I don't want this to be uncomfortable for either of us," Max said. "It's apparent that you and my mother are…closer than you used to be. But I'll be here for a few months, and so you and I are going to see each other."

Raine turned and faced the front again, her hands twisting in her lap. "The past is dead to me, Max. I have different priorities now, and I don't have the time—or the inclination—to dredge up old memories of that teenage lust we shared."

Ouch. Lust? He'd been head over heels for her, but, with her declaration, there was no way in hell he'd admit that now. She had made her feelings about that time very clear, and he wouldn't beat that dead horse.

Max turned onto her drive and barely suppressed a gasp. The old white sprawling two-story home had definitely seen better days. The stained roof needed to be replaced, paint had chipped off several of the window trims, the porch that stretched the length of the home was a bit saggy on one end, and, from the looks of things, no one had shoveled the snow off the walk.

"Just pull around to the back," she said.

Keeping his mouth shut about the obvious needs of her home, Max eased the car around to the side where a very small path had been cleared from the garage to the back door. The red handle from the shovel stuck up out of the snow, where she'd obviously left it for future use.

"Thanks for the ride."

As Raine jumped out, Max did, too. He opened the back door as she came around, and in seconds she'd unfastened the carrier. Max reached for it before she could grab the baby.

"Let me have her, and you can remove that base," Max told her.

Because it was cold and she knew way more about that contraption than he did, Max started toward the cleared path, watching his steps carefully because he wouldn't dare drop this baby.

Raine came up behind him with her keys and the base. He let her pass to unlock the door, but she blocked the entryway. After easing in, and setting down the base and her purse, she turned back to take the carrier.

"Thanks for the lift home."

Her eyes darted away from his, to the baby, to the snow swirling around them, anywhere but on him.

"Do I make you nervous?" he asked gruffly.

Now she did meet his gaze. "No. You make me remember, and that's worse."

He stepped closer, near enough to see those gold flecks in her bright eyes. "Is remembering so bad?"

"For me it is, maybe not for you." She shifted, holding the carrier between them as if to use the baby as a shield. "I'm not the same person I used to be."

"You're still just as beautiful."

Raine rolled her eyes. "Surely you don't think during the brief time you're home that you can just pick up where you left off?"

"Not at all." But damn if some of those old feelings weren't right there at the surface. "We're both different people, Raine, but you're still stunning. Is it wrong of me to say so?"

"It's wrong of you to be watching my mouth when I talk," she said.

Max grinned. "Just doing a little remembering of my own."

Raine gasped, and Max couldn't suppress his laughter.

"I'll let you get inside," he said. "It's too cold to be out here with that baby."

Just as she started to turn, he called her name.

"What?" she asked on a sigh.

"See you tomorrow."

He walked back to his car without waiting on her to sputter a response or narrow her eyes at him. There wasn't a doubt in his mind she wanted to be left alone, but he just couldn't. Raine had an underlying vulnerability, and like a fool, he couldn't ignore the fact they shared a past and he wanted to know what happened after he left.

Even after all these years apart, all the blockbuster films, all the starlets on his arm and all the lavish parties, Max never felt so at ease, so…comfortable as he did with Raine. He honestly had no clue their past could come back at warp speed and take control over his emotions.

These next few months may be spent caring for his mother, but he sure as hell was going to have an interesting time with the beautifully sexy Raine Monroe.

Two

Raine all but sank against the door. Her heart was so far up in her throat she thought she was going to be sick.

The irony was not lost on her that, when Max had left years ago, she'd been so ready to be his wife and the mother to his children; yet, when he returned, she actually had a child.

But too many years had passed between. A lifetime, really. She'd lived through hell and was still clawing her way out. Her bank account was laughable, and her father was trying to play matchmaker with one of his minions.

Added to that, there was some sort of holdup with Abby's adoption. Raine never could get a straight answer from her lawyer, who was equally frustrated at the untimely manner of the judge. Everything should've been finalized by now.

Other than all of that, her life was great.

Or it was until Max Ford had found her at a humiliating time when she'd wrecked her car thanks to a patch of black ice.

Raine shivered against the memories and the chill that had followed her inside. The Weather Channel update was calling for more snow, and this was just the start of several days. They hadn't officially called it a blizzard, but they were talking in feet and not inches.

She'd have to go check on her chickens and her goats before it got too bad. Worry gnawed away at her, despite the fact that they were each in their own barn, and they had all the necessities an animal could need to endure rough elements. They even had a small built-in hatch to come outside, if they so chose. She loved owning such disciplined, albeit sometimes overly friendly, animals.

At least if she was snowbound, she could finish working on the new lotions for the Farmer's Market next month. Raine was so excited that spring was right around the corner. Each day brought her closer to her favorite time of year, when she could sell all her goods at the market, meet new customers and chat with old ones.

Her finances always dipped in the winter, and she had to really watch her budget. Spring and summer were much more prosperous. Hopefully by next winter her online store would be even more popular, and she would feel more comfortable with her bank account.

Raine had gotten such great starts of cherry tomatoes, lettuce, kale, a variety of peppers and a few types of beans. Indoor winter gardening was quite different, but she had no choice except to take the extra effort to make these plants thrive inside. This was her livelihood and all that was between her and begging her parents for that money they'd taken away when she had refused to live by their haughty standards.

The vegetables were almost ready for the market next month, so all she needed to concentrate on now was making her soaps and lotions to prepare nice, cheerful gift baskets.

But first she had to get Abby sleeping through the night.

Mercy sakes, she had a whole new level of respect for single parents. This all-important job was most definitely not for wimps. But she wouldn't have it any other way. She loved this baby, and her heart had ached nearly a year ago when her cousin, Jill, had come to her and said she was considering an abortion.

Raine couldn't let Jill feel trapped into a decision she wasn't ready to make, especially since Raine had once been in Jill's shoes. Living as a teen with parents who had higher expectations had certainly taken its toll. Of course, their circumstances weren't exactly the same. Jill was in college and just not ready for a baby, whereas Raine had been fresh out of high school and had just had her whole world torn apart. When Raine had discovered her pregnancy, Max had just recently left, and she'd felt so alone. Her parents had been less than supportive, so there was no way Raine would let Jill go through this without a friend and family member to lean on.

When Raine had mentioned adoption, Jill warmed to the idea. And when Raine had offered to be the one to take guardianship, Jill had wept with relief and delight that her baby could live in a loving home.

The scenario seemed so simple looking back now, but for months there were tears and prayers, moments of panic and indecision, hours of contemplation and ultimately pure happiness. After the birth, Jill had returned to school and settled back into her life. She kept in touch with Raine, but said she'd keep her distance for a while so Raine and Abby could bond.

Raine knew absolutely nothing would replace the baby she'd lost years ago. But she loved Abby with every fiber of her being. There was nothing Raine wouldn't do for Abby, no sacrifice she wouldn't make.

Which meant she would do whatever it took to ensure that the little girl's future was secure. But that was easier said than done, since Abby's adoption was still in limbo. All the legal paperwork had been put into place long before Jill ever delivered, so what could possibly be amiss here?

Frustration threatened to consume Raine, but she focused on the here and now. The adoption would go through…eventually. She wouldn't allow any other outcome.

Raine bent down, unzipped the cover over the carrier and unfastened Abby from her seat. Her sweet little bundle was still napping. Raine had always heard the advice "Nap when your baby is napping," but she'd never get anything done if that's how she lived her life.

And who could nap now? Max Ford, Hollywood icon and most eligible bachelor, was back in town. He couldn't get out of Lenox fast enough when he'd turned eighteen, and the tire tracks were still smokin' after he'd landed his first role. Everything had fallen into place with his lifelong goals.

She recalled hearing that he'd been in a severe motorcycle accident not long after he'd gone to L.A., and at that moment, Raine had ached to be by his side. But she quickly realized that, if he'd truly wanted her with him, he'd have sent for her as promised.

And if she'd thought hell was when he had left and didn't contact her, it was the entire year after that which had scarred her for life.

Bitterness threatened to bubble up. He'd gotten all he'd ever wanted—without so much as a wave goodbye. But when she looked to the sleeping baby in her arms, how could she be upset that her life had turned out to be less than what she'd expected?

If she'd gone to L.A. when he did, she wouldn't be here now…and being there for Jill and raising Abby as her own was the most important task of her life.

Kissing Abby on the forehead, Raine walked through the old house and headed upstairs. Once she laid the baby down, she could call the tow truck. Hopefully her car was drivable when it was on all four tires again, because if there was any damage, there was no way she could pay for it.

But even if there was damage under the hood, she'd think of something. She'd been doing a lot of praying since Abby had come into her life. Every decision made wasn't just for Raine anymore. Life may have been easier before, but it sure had been empty. Now she was filled with such a sense of joy and purpose, and it was due in large part to this precious little girl. As she lay Abby down in her crib, she made sure to place a very thin blanket over her legs to keep her warm. Raine tiptoed out of the room and went into her bedroom to call a tow truck.

But all she got was the receptionist who indicated all the drivers were out on calls from all over the county, and they'd put her on the list. Which was fine with her. She wasn't going anywhere tonight anyway, and her car was off the road, so unless another driver went off the road and slammed into it, all was well.

Raine put on a kettle of water to boil. She may be the only person left living under the age of sixty who still used a tea kettle and boiled water the old-fashioned way. She knew she was old-fashioned in pretty much everything, which was probably why she had no man in her life. But in all honesty, Raine didn't mind being labeled as "weird" or "hippie" or her absolute favorite, "tree hugger."

So she liked to use her own herbs, grow her own veggies, and make organic lotions, soaps and other feminine products. Did that really make her stand out so much? All this processed stuff was killing people, and she wanted better for her life, her baby.

Which was just one more area where her parents thought Raine was being difficult. They simply didn't understand Raine's need to grow organic and make a little more effort in being healthy.

Her parents were more concerned about driving the

flashiest cars, keeping up country-club appearances and being on the right board of commissioners at said country clubs.

Maybe men were just thrown off by Abby. Some men weren't all that comfortable around children.

Like Max Ford. She hadn't missed those wide, terrified eyes when he'd first caught a glimpse of the carrier. Oh, he'd been the perfect gentleman and had helped her, but she knew men like him, who, at the first sight of spit up or a smelly diaper, would turn tail and run.

Not that Max needed any reason to run. He'd had a life planned with her; yet he still had found something more appealing, and instead of facing her, he had avoided her.

The man was used to winning awards, filming epic movies and smiling that knee-weakening grin for the cameras.

The tea kettle's shrill whistle cut through her thoughts. Why did he have to come back here? Why did she have to run into him right after she had driven her car into a ditch? And why on earth was she allowing past emotions—and unsettled feelings—to ruin her evening? Lord knows she had other things that she needed to focus on.

Just as she grabbed her favorite flavor of tea from the crock on the counter, her cell rang. Raine pulled the phone from her pocket and resisted the urge to groan…as she did each time she saw the number pop up on her screen.

"Good evening, Mother."

"Loraine, I'm calling to let you know the luncheon I had planned for tomorrow has been postponed."

Raine didn't sigh, didn't roll her eyes—okay, in her head she did—but she refrained from physically doing so, because she knew the gesture would come through in her tone.

She found her favorite mug for drinking tea. A tacky one with a hot, hunky man draped around it. When filled with hot liquid, his clothes disappeared. Who needed a traditional tea cup and saucer?

And if her mother forced her hand at this ridiculous luncheon, the mug might make an appearance.

"Mother, I hadn't planned on coming, remember?"

"Oh, darling, of course you'll be here. I mean, really. When are you going to stop being so stubborn?"

Raine opened the small cabinet above her stove and pulled out the bottle of whiskey she kept on hand for emergencies. And talking with her mother was most definitely an emergency.

"Let's not go through this again, Mother," she pleaded as she poured a dab of liquor into her hot tea. "We've agreed to disagree. You don't like my social life. I don't like yours."

"You don't have a social life, Raine!" her mother exclaimed. "I don't understand why you won't get out a little more, get a job, go back to college for heaven's sake. Let someone else adopt that baby. It's not too late to back out."

Not even an option. No way was anyone else going to adopt Abby. Raine never dreamed the adoption process would take this long, but even if it took ten years, she wasn't letting go of this beloved child.

She'd already lost one baby and was blessed enough to have been given a second chance at motherhood. Abby was a precious bundle that tucked so perfectly into Raine's life.

"Mom, I have to go check on Abby."

"If you're so insistent on keeping her, the least you could do is let me see her," her mother said with a huff.

That was a worry Raine had wrestled with, and one that had kept her up many nights. Raine had always heard the saying "It took a village to raise a child," but she just wasn't sure she could allow her mother's influences to trickle down to Abby.

"You've seen her, Mom," Raine said defensively, then took a sip of her tea, welcoming the burn as it slid down her throat.

"Not enough. She needs to know her place in this family, Raine."

Setting the china cup down, Raine took a deep breath so she didn't explode. "Mother, she's three months old. Her place right now is as my child. Nothing more."

"I didn't call to argue. The luncheon has been rescheduled for next Saturday, and I expect you and Abigail to attend."

"Her name is Abby, Mother."

"Abigail is more dignified."

"But that's not her legal name, so if you refer to her again, call her by the name I chose for her."

Her mother sniffed into the phone. "I don't know where I went wrong with you," she cried. "I just want what's best."

"For whom, Mother? Best for me, or best for you and your social status?"

Silence settled in on the other end of the line and Raine knew she'd gone too far…again. This is how nearly all of their calls went, and in the end Raine always felt guilty and mentally drained.

"I'll talk to you later, Mother."

Raine hung up and rested her palms on the edge of the chipped countertop. Why did she let her mother get to her? For twenty-eight years the woman had tried to make her feel like an outcast, and the majority of that time she'd succeeded. The only person who'd ever really understood her had been her grandmother; but when she had passed eight years ago, Raine had been truly alone.

The wind picked up outside, rattling the old windows. She took her cup and headed to her favorite room of the house. The room where she felt at home, where she could be creative, and no one was there to stifle the process.

Her grandmother's old bedroom, where Raine mixed all her lotions and made her specialty soaps. This was the perfect place to work, since it was right next to the nursery, and she felt so much closer to her grandmother here. But as Raine pulled a few ingredients off the shelf, she thought of Max. At one time he'd consumed all of her thoughts, all of her heart and soul. And, damn him, he looked even better now than he had when she'd been totally in love with him.

Hollywood had put him on this pedestal, elevating him to superstar status in no time, and she'd been back home soaking it all in via media outlets talking up the hottest newbie on the scene.

And amid all that talk, flashing cameras and Max throwing that signature dimpled grin to the reporters, Raine had been back in Lenox, nursing a broken heart…and coming to grips with an unexpected pregnancy.

Max had never known he'd been a father. Had never known the grief, the anguish, she'd gone through in losing the baby. He'd been living the dream and loving life while she'd been burying the last bond of love they had.

But now Raine had a second chance, and she wasn't going to blow it just because Max was back in town. No matter how much her heart fluttered when she'd seen him, no matter how sexy and handsome he looked, no matter how heated his gaze was when he looked at her.

Raine had more important priorities now, like making sure this legal guardianship of her cousin's baby went through and keeping her grandmother's home from going into foreclosure. Since she wasn't exactly flush with cash, Raine had used the rest of her meager savings and had taken out a loan against the property in order to pay for the adoption.

However, none of that had felt like a sacrifice to her, because Jill had entrusted Raine with Abby…and Raine wasn't about to disappoint her. So there was no way in hell she'd go down without a fight…not after getting nearly everything she'd ever wanted. Where there was a will, there was a way, and Raine had more will than anything else.

* * *

Max helped his mother to her bedroom, which was now a guest room on the first floor. With her being a little lethargic at times, he'd made sure all of her things were on the first floor so she didn't have to climb steps.

Although she would say she was fine, he could see that she was tired and just being stubborn. He knew she'd be even more so when her radiation treatments started. So he'd let her keep her pride and just keep his mouth shut, but he would make her as comfortable as possible, which was why he'd made sure the nurse who had been here the past two days would stay on and come by for a few hours a day.

As he settled her into bed, he eased down to sit beside her.

"Care to tell me what Raine was doing here?" he asked.

His mother rested against her plush pillows. "She brought me a lovely gift bag."

Narrowing his eyes, Max gave her a skeptical look. "So she just stopped by, because she knew you'd had surgery, and now you two are all chummy?"

Elise laced her fingers together across her lap and smiled. "Actually, no. During the past several summers when I've been staying here, she's taken care of the landscaping, brought me fresh vegetables, fruits and eggs."

"Wait, back up." Max held up a hand, even more confused than he'd been seconds ago. "Raine does the landscaping?"

"During the summer months, she does a great deal of it. Just the flower beds, Max. You don't have to look so angry. We have another man do the grass cutting."

Raine worked for his mother? What the hell had happened to her dreams? To her trust fund? She shouldn't have to work odd landscaping jobs for his mother. The thought of those small, dainty hands marred with calluses bothered him.

Most of the shallow women he knew back in L.A. wouldn't dream of doing their own landscaping, let alone someone else's.

"Who else does she work for in the summer?"

Elise shrugged a delicate shoulder. "Several families around here. Not her own, of course. Her mother is mortified that Raine does so much manual labor."

"And what kind of manual labor does she do?" he asked.

"She's quite the gardener and farmer. She prides herself on growing her own organic plants to keep them as natural and healthy as possible. Her grandmother would be so pleased."

Max knew Raine had never felt a familial bond with anyone other than her cousin, Jill, and her grandmother. He'd seen firsthand how that elderly woman had catered to Raine, showed her all she would need to know about running a farm, raising animals and growing gardens. Raine's maternal grandmother was accepted in Lenox because she was sweet and elderly but when a twenty-something woman tries to follow in those footsteps…well, he assumed that bohemian lifestyle didn't go over so well in the posh, hoity-toity land of tea sippers and pearl wearers.

"I just saw her house," Max stated. "It needs quite a bit of work. I can't believe she'd let it get like that."

His mother shrugged. "None of my business. But if she doesn't take care of it, the Historical Society will come in and make her. That house is a landmark in Lenox, even with the barns. In fact those barns are kept up better than her house. That girl cares more about the animals and the people around her than she does her own comfort."

As much as Max wanted to know more about Raine, his mother looked tired as her eyelids were growing heavy. He would be here for a few months, so there was no doubt he'd find out all he wanted about Raine and her new life.

His life was always splashed all over the internet and

in the tabloids…or the life the media tended to fabricate. There was no doubt Raine knew more about his life over the years than he knew about hers. It wasn't like he'd find anything if he did a Google search on her name…at least nothing of use.

"Is there anything I can get you before I go?" he asked, turning his attention back to his mom.

His mother grabbed his hand and squeezed. "No, I'm just glad you're here."

"I wouldn't be anywhere else, Mom."

"Please, Max, don't make this about your father." Her eyes held his, a sad smile forming on her lips. "He's busy this time of year."

Max nodded, really not wanting to get into this argument again. "He's been busy his whole life, Mom. I'm not here to fight, but I also won't pretend that it's okay to put work before family, because it's not. I work across the country, and I'm here."

Her eyes misted. "All I've ever wanted is for the two of you to make peace. That's all."

Guilt weighed heavily on Max because he knew of his mother's wishes, but he and Thomas Ford would never get along, because they viewed life from opposite ends of the spectrum.

Max leaned forward, kissing his mother on the cheek. "Good night, Mom. See you in the morning."

He turned off the light on his way out of the room and pulled the door shut behind him. It was odd spending the night in his old home. The memories that filled these halls, these rooms, played through his mind like a movie. The glimpses he caught seemed like another lifetime, another person.

As he went back downstairs, he recalled the time he'd snuck Raine in after they'd first started dating. His parents had been out at some charity dinner and wouldn't be home for hours. He knew they wouldn't approve, and to be honest, that just made the clandestine encounter all the more appealing.

He'd never forget how it had felt kissing her in that dark foyer as soon as they'd stepped through the door. As he stood at the base of the steps now, he could still see that young couple, arms intertwined, lips locked. Max had waited weeks to get her alone to kiss her, and she'd been so worth the wait.

Max sighed, raking a hand over his face. Teenage love was so complicated at the time, but looking back, he realized that was the best experience of his life. He and Raine had had something special, something he'd convinced himself could stand the test of distance and time.

But no matter how many letters he had written, emails he had sent or calls he had made, she'd never acknowledged him after he left. And he refused to tell anyone how deeply her rejection had hurt. Then and now. Although years had passed since they'd last seen each other, they'd once been very much in love. So how could Raine be so cold and act like they'd shared nothing?

Max was still recovering from that heartache—and seeing her up close, knowing she had a baby, a life, only twisted that knife a little deeper into his already wounded heart.

Three

The snow wasn't letting up at all and neither was Abby. Raine had no clue how mothers had more than one child. And twins? Mercy, those women deserved a special place in heaven. She was having a hard enough time just focusing on this one kid, not to mention holding down a job, fixing dinners, showering, taking a bathroom break…

But Raine had always wanted to be a mother, and she would not trade a moment of the sleepless nights for anything. Especially since Jill had needed Raine, and there was no way Raine could turn her back on her cousin when she needed someone the most.

Being shut out of your family because of decisions you made was the common connection she and Jill shared. They'd always been close, but this baby truly secured that tight band around their love.

And regardless of genetics or DNA, Abby was 100 percent Raine's. From the moment the precious baby girl had tightened her chubby little hand around Raine's finger, she knew no greater bond could exist. Even those accidental gassy smiles were like another stamp on her heart, solidifying the fact that Raine couldn't love Abby any more even if Raine herself had given birth to Abby.

Hearing the growing cries, Raine shook the bottle on

her way back to the nursery. Early morning sunlight spilled through the window, and she picked up the fussy baby and prayed to God that, after this bottle, Abby would sleep for a couple hours. Because Raine truly didn't know how much longer she could go on little to no sleep.

Sweet dimpled hands came up to grip the sides of the bottle, and Raine sank into the cushy rocker in the corner of the room. Resting her head against the back of the cushion, she closed her eyes as Abby greedily sucked down the milk.

Thankfully they had nowhere to go today, seeing as how the snow kept coming down in big, thick flakes. And when she'd glanced out at the driveway, her car had been there. The tow service must've brought it after she'd gone to bed, and she had no doubt there would be a hefty bill on her credit card statement since she had to give them the account number when she had called.

From what she'd seen, only the headlight and the grille were damaged, but she hadn't waded through the snow to find out any more.

Raine opened her eyes and glanced down at Abby whose own eyes had drifted shut.

"Now you want to sleep," Raine said with a smile. "When I'm holding and feeding you, but when you're alone in your bed, you want to scream."

Raine knew the feeling of being alone, left out and neglected. But there was no way this baby would ever feel anything less than secure. Perhaps that's why Abby kept crying. She instinctively knew that Raine couldn't handle it and would hold her to calm her down. The truth was, Raine just hated the thought of the baby feeling scared or abandoned.

There was no worse feeling in the world.

"We have each other," she whispered to Abby. "And you'll always know what love is."

Finally when the bottle was depleted and Abby was

breathing peacefully, Raine swiped the milk from beneath Abby's soft, full lips and laid the baby back in the crib.

Raine slid the curtain from the hook and blocked out the bright sun. Tiptoeing as quietly as possible, Raine eased the door closed behind her.

Should she go finish making the rest of her lavender soaps, take a brief nap and then start in on filling the on-line orders, or throw a load of laundry in, and fold and put away the two baskets waiting on her?

Did the to-do list never end?

She'd just gone into her workroom when she glanced out the window and saw a full-sized black truck pull up her drive. In a mad dash, she ran down the stairs, because, if someone rang her doorbell, she'd not be greeting them with the most pleasant of smiles. She'd personally murder anyone who woke Abby from her long overdue nap.

Raine jerked open the door just as Marshall Wallace lifted his hand to the bell. She resisted the urge to ignore this unwanted visitor, not that she didn't like Marshall, but she knew why he was here, and she wasn't in the mood.

"Hey, Raine," the young, polished man said with a wide smile. "Your father wanted me to drive out here and check on you."

"Hi, Marshall." She curled her hands around the door. "As you can see, I'm fine. So go back and tell the mayor he did his civic duty."

God forbid her father trek out here in the elements to see how she and Abby were doing. The salt and snow would probably ruin his designer shoes.

And that was just another common thread she and Max had shared. Their fathers always put work ahead of family. Even though Max was one of the most recognized men in Hollywood, he'd dropped everything to be with his mother. Not that she needed a lot of care, but he was here for the love and support.

"Have you thought any more about my offer?" Marshall asked, shoving his hands into the pocket of his thick brown coat.

Raine sighed. Another reason why she always cringed when Marshall came to her house. The man was relentless in his quest to date her. He'd started pursuing her years ago after Max had left. He'd been so persistent and in her face, she'd let it slip that she was pregnant so he'd back off. Then she'd regretted her decision and had sworn him to secrecy.

She'd given into his advances once, though, and they'd gone out. The entire evening Raine felt like she was dating her brother…if she had had a brother, she figured that's what it would be like.

"Marshall, I'm just so busy right now with Abby, focusing on the adoption and working on my online orders. You wouldn't want to go out with me. You should look for someone with more time and freedom."

"I'd be more than happy to come here with dinner. We don't have to go out."

Oh, Lord. If he thought he'd come over, eat dinner and play house, he was sorely mistaken. Even she wasn't that desperate.

Raine dodged his less-than-subtle approach and returned his smile. "Tell my father I'm fine, and so is the baby, not that he ever asks about her. I appreciate you coming out, Marshall."

As she started to close the door, a big black boot stepped over the threshold and blocked her.

"I hope you'll at least consider my offer, Raine," he told her, easing his body just inside the door frame. "That time we went out, I felt a connection with you."

A connection? This was worse than she thought. Surely whatever he felt was just like…indigestion. There was no way that lame date sparked something romantic on his end.

Of course, he could just be horny, and that was a whole other matter she didn't want to get into with him.

"Marshall, I don't have time to date right now. I'm sure a busy man like you understands."

There, she'd appealed to his male ego and even stroked it a little. If he didn't back off, she'd just have to be blunt and tell him to get the hell off her property. But her mother *had* raised a lady, despite her mother's views to the contrary, so Raine would make every effort to be polite.

Marshall nodded. "I won't give up on us, Raine."

Before she could sputter a "There is no us," he'd turned and was heading back to his truck. Was this dude for real? She'd never once led him to believe there was hope. Even after their date when he'd gone to kiss her good-night, she'd done the swift head turn, and he'd caught her cheek.

Closing the door, Raine sagged against it and squeezed her eyes shut. Why did life hate her? Why, within the span of twenty-four hours, did she have to encounter the only man she'd ever loved and now was fighting off the one man who wouldn't take no for an answer? Apparently Cupid had struck Marshall, and now he was determined to make her his Valentine. No thank you.

Damn, Valentine's Day was two days away, and Marshall was probably looking for a date. That was a big hell no.

The only Valentine she wanted was asleep upstairs. Besides, Valentine's Day didn't mean much to her. She'd spent nearly all of them single, except when she had dated Max. He'd given her this little gold locket and had told her that she'd always have his heart.

She should've known an eighteen-year-old boy was only out for sex, but those pretty words had made her fall in love with him even more. And she'd die before she ever admitted she still had that locket. So what? She had kept quite a few things from high school. Just because that particular piece was in her jewelry box didn't mean anything.

God, she couldn't even lie to herself. She'd kept that locket because she'd wanted to hold on to that hope that one person truly loved her for her, for the quirky way she was.

But that love was not only naive, it was a fabrication.

The banging on the door jarred Raine's body, making her jump. Pressing a hand to her chest to try to control her rapid heartbeat, she turned back to the door. Marshall really didn't give up, did he?

She threw open the door, ready to be brutally honest with the man, but it wasn't Marshall standing before her. It was Max.

With the collar of his black coat up around his neck and his dark knit cap pulled low on his forehead, he looked mysterious…sultry even. And that sexy stubble along his jawline only made him look more ruggedly handsome. With those dark eyes staring back at her, Raine felt that gaze all through her body, infiltrating places she wished would stay dormant where this man was concerned.

"What are you doing here?" she asked, blocking him from seeing inside.

"Wanted to make sure you had your car back and to see if you needed anything. The roads are pretty bad, and they're calling for several inches per hour for the next day."

Raine didn't want her heart to melt at his worry. And she didn't know why the notion of Max checking up on her made her belly dance with nerves, when the visit from Marshall had simply annoyed her.

She didn't want the belly-dancing nerves. She wanted to stay angry with Max for the rest of her life, but seriously, she had to get over the teenage attitude. They now led different lives. It was over and way past time to move on.

"I'm good right now," she replied.

"How bad was the car?" he asked.

Raine peered out around him to assess the damage. "I haven't gone out to see up close, but it looks minimal. I'm sure I can still drive it."

"Not in this weather, you can't." He pointed to the four-wheel-drive truck he had. "I used the truck dad keeps in the garage, because there was no way my rental would've gotten me here."

Abby's screeching cry sounded through the house, and Raine resisted the urge to cry herself.

"I'm sorry," she said. "I need to get her."

She turned from the door and ran up the steps. Abby was clearly not happy, but the second her eyes landed on Raine, she calmed down.

"You really just want me here, don't you, sweet pea?" she cooed as she picked Abby up and laid her against her shoulder. "You need to learn to sleep without me coming in here all the time."

But how could Raine be upset? Even though she was in a zombielike state nearly every day, there was just no way she could be angry or even feel put out by this precious bundle.

"You're just tired yourself, aren't you?"

Reaching into the crib, Raine grabbed the yellow blanket and wrapped it around Abby. Maybe she would be entertained in her swing while Raine worked on the soaps. Perhaps Abby would fall asleep there and get some much needed rest.

As she turned from the crib, she froze when she saw Max standing in the doorway.

"I thought you left," she said, trying not to cringe over him being in her home. Her run-down home.

This man was used to Beverly Hills mansions, probably threw lavish patio parties where guests mingled over champagne and caviar. And here he was in her home, with its carpet tearing, linoleum peeling, ceilings chipping…the list went on and on.

"I wasn't done talking."

Raine snickered. "I wasn't under the impression we had anything more to discuss."

"Is she okay?" he asked, nodded toward Abby.

"She's fine. She doesn't like to be alone."

His eyes returned to hers. "Sounds like she takes after her mother."

Raine started to correct him, but technically Raine *was* Abby's mother. Just because she was adopted—or would hopefully be soon—didn't make the relationship any less real. And Max wasn't going to be sticking around anyway, so really anything she did or did not do was none of his business.

Shifting Abby to the other shoulder, Raine patted her bottom and swayed side to side. "What did you need to talk about that you braved this weather to come see me?"

He opened his mouth, but Abby started screaming right in Raine's ear, and Max straightened in the doorway. "What's wrong?"

Raine pulled Abby back and looked at her. Abby was rubbing her eyes, fussing and puckering that little lip. It was the pucker that always got her.

"She's just tired," Raine explained. "She fights sleep."

"Fights sleep?"

"Trust me. It sounds insane, but there's no other term for it."

Raine moved over to the rocker and started singing "You Are My Sunshine." Usually that song calmed Abby down. Raine had gone through the song twice before Abby relaxed against her. Max eased out into the hall, and Raine appreciated the privacy. It wasn't that she was uncomfortable with him here, but… Oh, who was she kidding? She was extremely uncomfortable. Here she was all frumpy in her fleece socks, paint-stained sweatpants and a hooded sweatshirt that read Meat Sucks in big, block letters.

Added to that, the house was a mess. She hadn't been able to really clean since Abby came, and the past week had been hell because there was no sleep happening in this house...for either of them.

And she wasn't even going to get into the repairs that needed to be done. Basically the house and everything and everyone in it needed an overhaul. Too bad none of that would be happening anytime soon.

"I need to rock her again," Raine hollered over the baby's cries, hoping Max would take the hint and let himself out.

He nodded. "I can wait in the living room. We need to talk."

Talk. One word. Four simple letters that sparked myriad emotions...fear being the number one contender.

What did he want to talk about? Okay, that was probably a stupid question, but did he really want to rehash the past, or did he have an ulterior motive?

Before she could question him, Max had turned and walked from the room. Raine attempted to shift her attention as she moved toward the rocker, swiping the pacifier off the changing table first. Maybe this would work. Raine wasn't a fan of the thing because she dreaded weaning Abby from it in the months to come, but something had to help this poor baby sleep, and if the pacifier worked, then, hey, Raine was all for it.

Abby instantly started sucking, her moist lids lowered over her eyes, and she sniffled a little, but for the most part calmed right down.

In no time she was asleep...again. Hopefully for a few hours this go-round. Raine couldn't keep coming into the nursery every time the baby cried, but she couldn't just stand outside the door and listen to it, either. Surely there was a happy medium.

Raine placed Abby back in the crib and eased out of the room. Now, if she could just get Max to leave, she'd be able to dodge this inevitably awkward chat. And not only would their talk be awkward, but her emotions were bound to make her more than uncomfortable. The man kept sparking things within her…she just couldn't let that flame rekindle.

When she passed the hall mirror, she caught a glimpse of herself and resisted the urge to straighten up the lopsided ponytail and all the tendrils that had spilled from it. Max had already seen her, and she wasn't out to impress him, anyway. It wasn't like she could even compare to the supermodels and A-list actresses that had clung to his arm through the years.

Besides that, she wasn't sorry for who she was. She was happy with her meager life, and she wouldn't feel ashamed simply because her high school sweetheart was in her living room.

At the top of the steps she straightened her shoulders and silently applauded herself for the mental pep talk. Now she had to face Max, figure out what he thought they needed to discuss and get him out of her house. Because she couldn't afford for those old feelings to come creeping back up again.

Four

Max glanced at the various photos spread across the mantel. Most were of Raine with her grandmother from years ago, but now newer ones had been placed in frames. Pictures of Raine with Abby, Abby sleeping, a black-and-white picture of Abby's hand holding onto what he presumed to be Raine's finger.

But he never saw a picture of the baby with a man…or Raine with a man for that matter. The fact she was alone with this baby shouldn't make him feel relieved, because in reality, that just made him a jerk, but he'd be lying if he didn't admit that he'd gotten a sick feeling in the pit of his stomach when he had thought of her creating a family with someone else.

When he'd decided to come home, he knew the chances of running into her were pretty good, and he'd dreaded the thought of seeing some lucky man standing at her side.

Max was supposed to be that man. Max had spent day after agonizing day trying to reach Raine once he'd hit L.A. He just couldn't figure out why she'd lied and said she'd be right behind him. Why not just cut ties before he left and spare him that misery?

But she'd strung him along, and her rejection had sent him into a downward spiral which eventually culminated in his near-fatal motorcycle accident. He'd cared for nothing, living recklessly and damning the world around him. But the wreck had really opened his eyes.

Max released a deep, slow breath. He had no idea what possessed him to drive out here today when the weather was so bad, but he'd seen her stranded in the snow, then socializing with his mother, as if there was no history between them, and couldn't get over the fact that so much had been left hanging between him and Raine. He knew they'd both moved on, but that didn't stop him from wanting closure.

He needed answers, and he wasn't leaving until he got them. Raine may have shut that chapter in her life, but he was about to reopen it.

As Raine descended the staircase, she held all the poise and glamour her mother had raised her to have, but he couldn't suppress a grin because of her bedhead, the verbiage on her T-shirt and the way she tried to be so regal when she looked like a hot mess.

But that's one of the things he'd always admired about her. She never cared what people thought of her image; her only worry was caring for others.

"You should go," she stated. "The weather isn't getting any better."

Max glanced over at one of the photos on the mantel. "I snapped this picture."

Her eyes drifted to the photo he was pointing to. A young Raine had her arms thrown around the neck of her grandmother, both women were laughing for the camera. Max could practically hear the laughter, and he was instantly transported back to that day.

"She always loved you," Raine murmured. "She thought for sure you were the one."

Max stared at the elderly woman in the photo and swallowed the lump in his throat. "Life happens. Plans change."

"What do you want from me, Max?" she asked softly.

Max turned his attention back to her and noted her defensive stance with her arms crossed over her chest, but he could also see how visibly tired she was. "I want closure."

"So bringing up the past will...what? Suddenly make things better?"

He shrugged. "Maybe I figured after all this time I deserved some answers."

Raine held his gaze a moment before she burst out laughing. "Did you come here to humiliate me?"

"What?"

She shook her head and moved farther into the room. "Max, we're living in two different worlds. Why on earth would you find it necessary to come all the way here just to discuss a period of our lives that really isn't relevant anymore?"

His cell vibrated in his pocket before he could utter a comeback. Not relevant? The absence of Raine in his life had nearly destroyed him. There wasn't a day that went by that he hadn't thought about her, wondered what she was doing. No way in hell was she not relevant in his life.

The number on his screen belonged to his mother, and a moment of panic set in when he answered. Sasha, the nurse, was there with her, so surely nothing was wrong.

"Honey," his mother began. "Have you left Raine's house yet?"

"No, why?"

From across the room, Raine studied him.

"Sasha just went out to get something from her car when a trooper pulled up, thinking she was leaving. We're under a level three advisory, and unless it's an emergency, no one's allowed on the roads."

Max shot his gaze to the wide window in the front of Raine's living room. "You're kidding?" he said, as he watched big fat flakes cling to the window.

"Afraid not."

"I can't leave you alone," he told her. "I'll head out right now and be there shortly."

"Don't risk getting fined or even hurt, Max. Sasha is here, we're safe and warm. There's nothing she can't provide for me. Besides, I'm fine. I'm tired, but nothing a nap can't fix."

Max knew all of this, but it was the fact he was going to be stuck here with Raine that was giving him fits. Trapped with Raine *and* a baby. What the hell, Fate?

"I know, but I came back home to help you, and I can't do that if I'm not there."

"I'm sure it will be fine later tonight or maybe tomorrow. We need it to stop snowing so the state workers can keep the roads clear."

He continued to watch the snow come down, showing no sign of letting up. The dark gray skies weren't looking too kind even though it was still early in the morning. Shouldn't the sun be out?

"I'll get back to you as soon as I can," he promised. "I'll call and check in, too."

Max hung up with his mother and eased the phone back into his pocket before turning back to Raine.

"Looks like I'm stuck here," he said.

Her eyes widened. "I'm sorry…*what?*"

"Seems the county is on a level three advisory, and no one is allowed out unless it's an emergency."

Raine jerked her attention to the window. Her shoulders slumped, and she released a heavy sigh. "Life sucks," she muttered.

Max shook his head. "I'm no happier about this than you are."

She focused her narrow gaze on him. "Don't even think of taking advantage of this situation."

"Excuse me?"

"The snowstorm, the stranded victim." She pointed a finger at him. "I hope you don't think we're going to bond or have some passionate reunion."

Max laughed. "You're still just as outspoken as you used to be."

Raine dropped her hand. "I'm nothing at all like I used to be," she groused. "That girl grew up when life smacked her in the face."

Max wanted to know more, wanted to know what had happened. God, did he ever want to know. Something made Raine hard now, and he hated that. He wanted to see that free spirit he'd fallen in love with, but at the same time, maybe it was better this way. Maybe having her hate him was for the best, because he certainly wasn't too thrilled with her, either.

"Go on with whatever it is you were doing," he said. "Pretend I'm not here."

"Not so eager to chat now?"

He shook his head. "Not when you're so upset. Besides, looks as if I'll be here for a while."

"No matter how long you're here, I won't want to discuss the past."

She turned on her heel and nearly stomped off. Max smirked. Now what the hell was he going to do? He had work he needed to do, but his laptop was back at his mother's house, and there was no way in hell he'd ask Raine for her computer.

He pulled out his phone and checked his emails. This movie deal he was working on could not be put on hold. He'd waited years to prove he was worthy of directing his own film, and, with the help of Bronson Dane, producer of every film worth any mention in Hollywood, Max knew this was the big break he'd been waiting for.

When Bronson had approached him with this project,

Max had nearly cried. Seriously, he'd never been so close to happy tears in his life.

And this snowstorm and being stranded with Raine for God knew how long would not put a damper on his work. He could communicate with his phone and her computer… if she let him use it. And when the snow cleared, he was getting the hell out of here.

Raine mixed a touch of aloe and a hint of jasmine, but her shaky hands tipped the bottle and made a mess over her scarred countertop. Resting her palms on the edge of the work space, she hung her head between her shoulders as the recent events took control of her emotions.

Why? Why did he have to come back just when she was really starting to turn her life around? The sales from her lotions and soaps were really promising, and next month the Farmer's Market would reopen, and she'd start pulling in even more money with the vegetables she'd been growing this winter. She already had several potted plants thriving in her meager indoor greenhouse, and it wouldn't be long before she was outside gardening again. Things were looking up.

And most important, she had Abby who had come into her life just before Christmas and she couldn't be more blessed.

So why did her ex-turned-Hollywood-hotshot have to show up at her house, looking like he'd just stepped off the ski slopes in Vail, and wreak havoc on her hormones?

Raine laughed. There, she'd admitted it to herself. She was as attracted to Max now as she had been years ago, but, just because he was still the sexiest man alive, it didn't mean she would act on her lustful feelings. She had no time, nor did she have the inclination, to travel down that path of heartache again.

Heavy footsteps sounded outside her door, and she froze.

When those steps moved into the room, she closed her eyes and willed him to go away.

"You okay?" he asked.

No, she wasn't okay, but the standard answer was "Fine," right?

She turned, leaned her butt against the edge of the counter and crossed her arms. "You need something?"

His eyes searched hers as if he was looking for answers only she could give. Yeah, she had nothing. No emotions, no feelings. Right now she felt as if she'd been wrung dry.

"I hate to bother you, but if I'm going to be stuck here, I need to get some work done. Do you have a laptop or computer I could use?"

He wanted to work? Great, that would keep him out of her hair for a while.

"I have a laptop in my bedroom," she said. "I'll go get it."

As she moved forward, he stepped in her path, stopping her with his wide, muscular body. His hands came up to gently grip her forearms.

Her eyes lifted to meet his, and that clench in her heart nearly brought her to her knees.

"Max," she whispered. "Don't make this any harder."

"I'm not doing anything," he said. "No matter what happened between us in the past, I can see you're wearing yourself thin. You look ready to fall over, Raine."

Yes, those were the words she wanted to hear. Nothing like a blow to the self-esteem to really perk up an already crappy day. She hesitated to tell him this was her everyday appearance, and he was just used to women who popped up in the morning with makeup in place and hair perfectly coiffed.

"I'm fine," she assured him. "I have a lot on my plate right now, and I hadn't anticipated being stuck with you. It's thrown me off a little."

"I'm not too thrilled about being stranded here, either.

My mother is recovering from major surgery, and I promised I'd help."

Raine pulled back the throttle on her own anger and self-pity. "I'm sorry about your mom, Max. The doctors got all the cancer out, and Elise told me after her radiation treatments, she'd be fine. But I'm sure you're still scared."

Max nodded, taking a step back and resting his hands on his hips. "When she first called me, I was in a meeting with a producer who was asking me to be part of his next film. He wants me for the director."

Raine listened about this other life Max had, a life she knew nothing about. Other than seeing him in movies, which was hard to watch at first, she'd not heard a word about any behind-the-scenes stuff.

"I've wanted to direct a movie for years, and the moment my big break was happening, my world back home fell apart," he went on. "Cancer. It's amazing how one word can make you rethink your entire life, every minute, every word you've said. I knew I had to get here, but she assured me that the nurse and my father would be with her through the surgery in Boston, and I could come here later, because she planned on undergoing radiation here in Lenox."

"You're here now," Raine told him softly. "I know she's happy to have you back."

Max's sultry blue eyes met hers. "What about you, Raine? Are you glad to have me back?"

Raine swallowed, looked him in the eyes and…couldn't come up with an answer. On one hand she loathed him for not fulfilling his promise to her, for hurting her at such a young age, but, on the other hand, how could she hold so tightly to the past? He hadn't tried to contact her in ten years…that was hard to let go.

But he was here now to care for his sick mother. Technically she didn't need him, but he'd come to show his love and support. How could she find any fault in that?

"It's okay," he said, taking a step closer and closing the narrow gap. "Under the circumstances, I'm not thrilled to be here, either."

She knew he referred to his mother's state, but a part of her wondered if he also meant her. Was he bitter toward her? All she was guilty of was falling in love, being naive and waiting for her Prince Charming to send for her.

And the baby they'd created.

Seeing him after all this time only brought back that rush of emotions associated with knowing she was carrying his baby, knowing he wasn't sending for her…and then the miscarriage. Those several months were the darkest of her life, and Max Ford held the key to the past she never wanted to revisit again.

"If we're going to be stuck together for who knows how long, I think it's best if we don't bring up the past," she said. "We're not the same people, and I just can't focus on something that happened so long ago. Not when I have Abby to care for. She's my future."

Max continued to stare at her, holding her with that piercing blue gaze. The room seemed to shrink, but in reality all she saw was him. Broad shoulders, tanned features beneath dark stubble, faint wrinkles around his eyes and mouth. He'd aged, but in the most handsome, beautiful way…damn him.

"Where's Abby's father?" he asked.

Raine jerked away from the shock of the sudden question. "That's none of your business."

"It is if he lives here."

"He doesn't."

"Is he part of your life?" Max asked.

"No."

His hand came up, cupping the side of her cheek. She barely resisted the urge to close her eyes, inhale his masculine scent, lean into his strong hold, but she could afford none of those things and honestly had no idea why he was touching her.

So Raine glared back at him, refusing to let him get past the wall of defense she'd built so long ago.

"You used to be so soft, so easy to read," he murmured. "What happened when I left?"

"Reality." She backed up until her spine hit the counter. "Reality was harsh, Max, and it woke me up to the life I was living, not the life I wanted."

God, it hurt to look at him. The longer he was here, in her home, in Lenox, the longer those memories from fifteen years ago would assault her. The loss of him, the loss of their baby.

"I'm going to go start lunch," she stated. "You're more than welcome to eat with me but no more dredging up the past again. Are we clear?"

He took a step forward, then two, placing a hand on either side of her body to trap her. Leaning in, his face came within inches of hers.

"We can't get past this tension between us until we discuss it. Maybe that makes me the naive one, Raine." His eyes darted to her lips. "Or maybe I'm a fool for still finding you just as attractive as I did then."

Raine couldn't breathe, all air had whooshed from her lungs the second he'd locked her between his sturdy arms. But just as soon as he leaned in, he pushed away.

"Don't worry. I know we're two different people," he stated as he neared the door. "And no matter what I feel now, whether it's old feelings or new hormones, I have my own set of worries."

He turned toward the door, then glanced over his shoulder. "And be warned. We will discuss our past before I leave Lenox."

Five

"Yes, Mother, Marshall was here."

Max stopped just outside the kitchen when he overheard Raine's exhausted tone. Seems some things hadn't changed. Apparently her mother could still bring out the frustration and weariness in Raine's voice.

After working for a couple hours on Raine's laptop, he set out to see what she was up to. Now that he knew, Max couldn't help but feel sorry for her.

"No, I didn't need him to stay. I'm a big girl, and I'm fine. Abby is fine, too, not that you asked."

Really? What grandmother wasn't doting over a grandchild? Was the relationship between Raine and her parents still so strained that Abby wasn't even a consideration in their lives?

Or maybe Raine didn't want them to be in the baby's life. Who knows? And to be honest, he couldn't focus on Raine's problems. If he did, he'd find himself deeper entrenched in her world, and he could not afford to get caught there again.

"I have to go," Raine said. "Abby's crying."

Max smiled at the silent house, the obviously sleeping baby.

"Please tell Dad not to send Marshall out here again.

The man is getting mixed signals, and they aren't coming from me."

Who the hell was Marshall? From the tone and Raine's plea, he had to guess someone her parents deemed suitable to be a boyfriend or the perfect spouse. Yeah, he had never fit that mold when he had wanted the title. Her parents had delusional thoughts of Raine marrying some suave and sophisticated political figure. Did Raine look like First Lady material?

Obviously her parents didn't know her at all, or they chose not to care what she wanted. He firmly believed the latter.

And that phone call answered the "man in her life" question. Apparently her mom and dad were relentless in trying to find the right "suitor," which made him laugh on the inside. Would her parents ever give up and see that Raine was a grown woman more than capable of making smart decisions?

Max eased into the room. Raine's back was to him, her eyes fixed on the falling snow outside the wide window that stretched above her sink. The paint on the interior of the windowpane had peeled away from the trim, and the faucet was dripping, whether to keep the pipes from freezing or because it was old, Max had no clue. But he couldn't get involved. He was just here to wait out this freak snowstorm.

The old yellow Formica countertops were the exact same as what he'd remembered, but now they were chipped along the edges. The old hardwood floors were scarred and in desperate need of refinishing.

What the hell had Raine done with all that trust fund money she was due to get when she turned twenty-five? She certainly didn't invest it back into her house.

"How long are you going to stand there?" she asked without turning around.

Max moved farther into the room, unable to hide his smile. "Just seeing if it's safe to come in."

She tossed him a glance over her shoulder. "I started making lunch, but my mother's call threw me off."

Max gripped the back of one of the mismatched chairs at the table. "You and your parents still don't have a good relationship? After all these years?"

Raine opened her refrigerator and pulled out asparagus.

"We've never quite seen eye to eye on things," she stated, rinsing the vegetable. "My mother is trying to turn me into some snobby pearl-wearing socialite, and my father is too busy worrying about his political standing in the town to worry about such nuisances as his child or grandchild… unless we're in public."

Max hated hearing this, hated that he wanted to hold a grudge against her, but he also couldn't believe how she was treated by her own family.

"So what are you doing that your parents dislike so much?" he asked, pulling out the chair, turning it around and straddling it. He rested his arms over the back.

Raine laid the stems on a baking sheet and placed them in the oven. "I'm not doting all over the movers and shakers of this town. I'm too different, meaning I grow my own vegetables, make my own soap and lotions, sell eggs, an occasional goat for milk, and in the summer I do some landscaping for a few families. Your parents' second home here is one of my jobs."

Max watched as she busied herself with this healthy organic lunch he'd rather pass on. But now that he was in here, he would probably stay.

"Mom mentioned you worked for her. She's impressed with you."

Still he was dying to know what had happened. In the years that he'd been gone and would visit his parents in Boston, Raine's name had only come up in the beginning.

His mother hadn't mentioned once that Raine had worked at the Lenox house in the summer.

She pulled out what he assumed to be tofu, and started packing it and placing it in the skillet on the old gas stove. "I rarely see your dad, but your mother comes to Lenox quite often. I assume to get away from the city life."

Max nodded. "That's why she wanted to recover from her surgery and take radiation in Lenox—because it's so quiet and peaceful. Since her oncologist expects her to make a full recovery, and has been in touch with the local hospital, he said she'll be fine to continue treatments here." As the skillet sizzled and aromas filled the spacious kitchen, Max kept his eyes on Raine as she turned to face him. Even in her sloppy clothes she looked adorable. But damn, he didn't want her to look adorable. He wanted her to be overweight and have a face covered in warts. An overbite? Thunder thighs? Anything?

Of course even if Raine had gained two hundred pounds and had a blemished face, he'd still see that young girl he'd fallen in love with. And a piece of his heart would always belong to her for that reason alone, no matter who they were today. Her beauty went so far beyond physical, nothing could ruin his image of her.

"I'm sorry you're trapped here with me," she said. "I'm sorry I was grouchy earlier, but I'm just…I'm not sure what to say to you. I mean, our past aside, you're Max Ford, Hollywood's hottest actor, and I'm…"

She glanced down at her boxy outfit and laughed. "You get the picture."

Max tilted his head. "No, I don't. Are you saying you're not worthy enough to be trapped with me? Why the hell not? Just because I'm famous? I'd much rather be trapped with you than any L.A. high-maintenance type."

Raine continued to laugh. "As you can see, I'm anything but high maintenance."

She turned back to her stove and flipped the…meat? No, tofu wasn't meat. Raine hated meat, and her shirt even advertised the fact.

"That's one of the things that drew me to you to begin with."

Her hands froze, her back rigid.

"I liked your simplicity," he went on. "I liked the fact you didn't care what others thought and that you were determined to be your own person. It was so refreshing to find someone else at the theater that day who was just like me."

Raine's mind flashed back to that day he spoke of, and she had no doubt his mind was replaying the same moment.

That day her parents had given her strict orders to go to the local Shakespearean Theater and try out for a role. Any role, just something that would make it look like the family was supporting the local arts and to get her out of the house to socialize.

But she'd seen Max with his mischievous smile and stunning baby-blue eyes, added with that chip on his shoulder, and she had felt like she'd found her new best friend…and for a time she had.

"Seems like a lifetime ago," he said.

Raine nodded, refusing to let this cooped-up ambience cloud her vision. They were kids with immature emotions. But when he'd left… God, it still pierced her heart. She hated admitting that, even to herself, but it hurt like hell being rejected by the one person she'd leaned on and loved so completely. And then discovering the pregnancy…

"Yeah," she agreed. "A lifetime."

Refocusing on lunch, she turned off the burner and slid the tofu burgers onto her grandmother's old floral plates. He had said he wasn't eating, but he had to have something, and she'd made plenty. Once she had all the food on the table, she had to laugh at Max's expression.

"You have something to say?" she asked when he continued to stare at the plate of food.

He burst out laughing, shaking his head. "Looks good."

Raine kept her smile in place. "You're such a liar."

"Yes," he agreed. "I'll have you know I have an Oscar award and several Golden Globe awards to prove that I'm awesome at lying."

"You hate everything on your plate," she said. "Even the best actor in Hollywood can't hide that."

Max picked up his fork, held it above his plate. "You think I'm the best actor?"

Great. Why didn't she just tell him she owned all of his movies and they were in her nightstand? God, that would make her extremely pathetic, and it would seem like she was clinging to a past that had left her vulnerable and shattered.

First the locket she kept, now this. Next she'd have a shrine in her basement like some stalker.

"You know you're good at what you do," she said, picking up her own fork and jabbing a piece of asparagus.

"I love the work I do. I think when you love what you're doing, it comes through, no matter the job."

Raine nodded, remembering that's how their bond had started years ago. They both had had dreams, aspirations that no amount of parental guilt could diminish.

"I suppose you don't have a frozen pizza in your freezer?"

Raine eyed him across the table and raised a brow. "You didn't just ask me that, did you?"

With a shrug, Max grinned. "Worth a shot. I'm not surprised you're still so…"

"Earthy?" she finished.

Max cut into his tofu and slid a bite into his mouth. His slow chew, the wrinkling of his nose and the quick drink of water had Raine sitting back in her seat, laughing.

"God, you're priceless," she said through fits of laughter. "I would've thought you had moved past this. Isn't everything in L.A. about being fit and thin? People wanting to be healthy?"

Max took another drink of water. "Yeah, but most people either use drugs, plastic surgeons or home gyms."

"Well, I prefer to go about staying healthy the old-fashioned way."

Several minutes passed as Max toyed with his food before he spoke again.

"So upstairs, you were making lotion?" he asked.

Popping her last bite of asparagus in her mouth, Raine nodded. "I make organic soaps and lotions. I usually sell gift baskets at the Farmer's Market during the spring and summer, so I'm working on the startup for that right now. I also have an online business that's growing."

"You took a gift bag to my mother."

At his soft words, Raine glanced across the scarred table to find his piercing blue eyes on her.

"Yes."

"Even though my parents never liked us together."

Raine nodded. "Your mother was caught in a rough spot, Max. She just wanted you and your father to make peace."

Max grunted and shoved his chair back. "My father and I never had peace before or after you were in my life."

"Even now?" she asked.

"Especially now," he confirmed.

Max came to his feet, picked up both plates and set them on the counter. He stared out the window which was quickly becoming covered with icy snow. He wasn't getting out of here anytime soon.

"Nothing I ever do will please that man," he said. "Which is why I do whatever the hell I want."

Raine came to her feet, not sure what to say, to do.

"I used to do things just to piss him off," Max went on.

"Dating you for example. I loved being with you, but parading you around him, knowing he disapproved, made me feel like I had the upper hand."

Raine knew all of that, or at least she'd always had that feeling, but she'd never heard him say the words aloud until now.

"I think we used each other," she told him. "I knew my parents frowned upon everything I did, so dating someone who had no aspirations of college or a political career really made me laugh. They were so angry, and I loved it."

He glanced over his shoulder and grinned. "Guess we didn't turn out too bad for rebellious teens."

Raine thought of her depleting bank account, the baby sleeping upstairs who wasn't technically hers until the judge said so and all the repairs her home needed. Spring couldn't get here soon enough, because she desperately needed to sell a couple of goats and get set up at the local market. That was her best source of income.

A loud pop came from the back utility room and Raine jumped.

"What the hell was that?" Max muttered, already moving in the direction of the noise.

Raine was afraid to find out, but she followed him. As soon as they opened the pocket door, she groaned at the sight of the hissing furnace that may date back to Moses's time.

"That's not good," he stated.

Raine leaned against the door. "God, I so don't have time for this."

Not to mention money. What the hell was she supposed to do now that her furnace gave out? Could things possibly get worse? "I thought the thermostat was going bad," she said. "I had no idea it was the entire unit."

Max squatted down looking at the furnace, jimmying around a few things, but to no avail. When he came to his feet, he turned to her and sighed. "There's no way anyone can come look at this as long as the roads are in this condition." Raine nodded, forcing herself not to cry. What would crying do? Would it keep the three of them warm? No, so she needed to take those frustrations and redirect her energy toward something productive.

"I have some wood in the barn and two fireplaces, one in the living room and one in my bedroom. But the one in the living room hasn't been cleaned out for some time, so I'd be afraid to use it. We'll have to use the one in my room."

Her bedroom. Where they'd all have to sleep tonight if the roads weren't any better. Raine nearly laughed in hysteria at all the crap life was throwing at her.

Oh, well. She'd always heard the saying "Don't pray for a lighter load, pray for a stronger back."

"Let me get my coat, and I'll go get the wood," Max offered.

"No." She held up a hand to stop him, but he ran into her, forcing her to feel those hard pecs beneath his thick wool sweater. "You've only got those fancy city shoes on, and my chickens are like dogs and will bombard you for affection. I'll do it."

"Chickens are like dogs?"

Raine laughed. "Yeah. They would've run up to you when you got here, but they're in the barn staying warm, and you got inside before they could get out of their little flap and onto the porch. You step in that barn, and I guarantee you'll be surrounded." She blew out a breath. "Then you'll trip, fall on your butt into a snow pile and will be of no use to me."

Something sparked in his eyes, and she realized perhaps that hadn't been the best choice of words. "I meant—"

"I know what you meant," Max said, cutting her off. "But I can't let you carry in all the wood that we'll need. You'd have to make numerous trips, and I'd rather do it.

Don't forget, I was a country boy before I lived in Hollywood. I'm not afraid of some chickens, Raine."

"You will be when they chase after you and knock you down."

He merely raised a brow as if he didn't believe her. She smiled in return, more than ready for the show to begin.

<u>Six</u>

Humiliation had long since settled in.

Max lay on his back, staring up at the sky. He'd barely taken a step inside the barn before he was…attacked by feathers. God, the feathers were everywhere.

Thankfully he'd donned his heavy coat and wool cap, but there was that sliver of flesh on the back of his neck that was exposed to the icy snow. Max shivered and sat up. No way in hell was he turning around to see Raine, because he knew she was plastered at the back door waiting for him to bring the wood back. He had no doubt she was also laughing her ass off when his feet flew in the air, and he landed face up in the mounting snow piles. The bucket had flown to who knows where, because he was just trying to stay upright and not get mauled by feathers and beaks.

Which totally took his mind off the fact that some very delicate areas were going to be bruised and sore. He doubted Raine would offer to rub him down.

Damn, she hadn't been kidding about these chickens. They were everywhere. Clucking, pecking, swarming. Weren't they just supposed to lay their eggs and sit on them?

Max came to his feet, shaking the snow off his back. He found the bucket had flown closer to the barn door, which was one thing in his favor. He moved to the wood pile,

which was located in the corner under a bright blue tarp…
right next to the small flap where the chickens obviously
came in and out of.

"'Scuse me." He waded through the stalking chickens,
feeling even more absurd for talking to them. "Just need
to get some wood."

He stocked the bucket with several pieces and carefully
moved back out of the barn. Thankfully those little hea-
thens wanted to stay warm, so between the house and the
barn he only had to tackle the snow mounds.

As Max stepped up to the back door, Raine swung it
open for him. One hand held the door, the other covered her
mouth. But the way those beautiful eyes were squinting, he
could tell she was dying to laugh and holding it in…barely.

"Go ahead," he muttered. "Get it out of your system."

Quickly she removed her hand and composed herself.
"I have no idea what you're talking about."

He sat the bucket down and picked up the empty one
before turning toward her. His face was mere inches from
hers, causing her to tilt her head back slightly.

"Now who's a terrible liar?" he asked.

Raine's eyes darted to his lips, and he was damn glad
he wasn't the only one having a problem controlling desire. But could he trust what he was feeling? Were these
merely past emotions or brand new ones brought on by her
spunky behavior that he found so refreshingly sexy? And
the way she stubbornly tried to keep that vulnerability of
hers hidden added yet another layer of irresistible appeal.

She'd been private and vulnerable before, but as a
mother, he found her to be even more so now. That protective nature of hers really had a part of him wanting to dig
deeper to unearth more Raine mysteries. But his realistic
side told him to back off.

"I'll unload this bucket," she said, evidently trying

to break the moment. "I think one more trip ought to be enough."

"Trying to get me out of here?" he asked gruffly.

Raine swallowed. "Trying to stay warm."

Max inched closer until her warm breath settled on his face. "There are a number of ways to stay warm, Raine. If I recall, you always loved hot showers."

Her lids fluttered down as she sighed. "Max…I can't… I just can't revisit the past."

"I'm not talking about the past," he murmured, easing his bucket to the ground and placing his hands on her narrow waist. "I'm talking about right here, right now, and the emotions we're both feeling."

"You don't know what I'm feeling," she whispered.

Teasing her by brushing his lips across hers for the briefest of moments, he said, "No, but I know what I'm feeling."

Max claimed her mouth, damning himself for allowing her to get under his skin so quickly. But she tasted so good, so intoxicating…and even after all these years, so familiar. Her delicate fingertips skimmed along his jawline as she cupped the side of his face.

There was no hesitation, Raine was all in, and she gave back as much as he was willing to take. He parted her lips with his tongue, drawing her body closer to his, as she met him thrust for thrust.

A shrill cry broke through the silence, killing any passion.

Raine jumped back, her eyes darting to the baby monitor on the counter. Immediately she brought her gaze back to him, her hand coming up to cover her mouth.

"Don't," he warned her. "Don't say you're sorry. Don't say it was a mistake."

She shook her head, crossing her arms over her chest. "Fine, but it won't and can't happen again."

Stepping around him, Raine left the room and rushed up

the stairs toward the nursery. From the monitor he heard her soft voice as she soothed Abby. Instantly the baby quieted.

And when Raine started to sing, he was taken back to when they'd first met, and she'd tried out for the only solo in the play. Her sweet, angelic voice had instantly blown away the cast and crew. All gazes were magnetically drawn to that shy girl on stage with her prissy little pleated skirt and staid sweater, more than likely chosen by her mother. He'd instinctively known that the prim-and-proper getup really had not suited Raine. She was much more of a jeans and T-shirt kind of gal. Even then.

Maybe she hadn't changed all that much. And if that was the case, he was in bigger trouble than he thought.

Max picked up his bucket and stormed back out into the freezing snow, hellacious chickens and all, because if he stuck around to listen to her much longer, he'd be pulled into a past that he'd barely come out of alive the last time. He couldn't afford to feel those emotions ever again.

Well, so much for the weather cooperating. It was nearly ten o'clock, the streets were dark and desolate, and the snow had shown no sign of slowing down.

Abby had just taken her bedtime bottle and hopefully would sleep a few hours.

Max had put up the Pack 'N' Play pen in the master bedroom, where they had a nice fire going. Thankfully the room was spacious, and Abby could sleep in the corner of the room.

Raine and Max were prisoners as well, considering the rest of the house was quickly becoming colder. Max had brought up plenty of wood to last through the night and into the morning.

So here they were. In the bedroom with a sleeping baby and a whole cluster of hormones and that damn kiss hovering in the air between them.

Oh, and a past that had never gotten proper closure. Great. Just great. Exactly what they didn't need. Why couldn't they both still be angry and bitter? Did passion really override all else here?

"I'm going to go change," she whispered to Max who was sitting on the bed, propped up against pillows and doing something on her laptop.

When Max glanced over, eyeing her from head to toe, all those points in between tingled as if he'd touched her with his bare hands. And she knew from personal experience what those hands felt like roaming up her torso.

Even though a lifetime had passed between then and now, a touch like Max's wasn't one she could easily forget. How could she? When his simple touches, his soft caresses, not only sent shivers racing all over her body, but they also left an imprint so deep, she knew she'd never truly erase it from her mind.

So, yeah, that tingling wasn't going to stop anytime soon if she didn't put a lid on those damn memories and stop letting him affect her now.

Raine turned to her dresser and grabbed the oldest, ugliest set of pajamas she owned. There was no need in putting on anything cute or seductive. That was the dead last thing they needed. Not that she had a great deal of "sexy" lingerie, but she'd better keep anything skimpy out of this room while he was in it…and circumstances all but begged them to get naked and horizontal.

With a soft click, she closed the bathroom door and started to change. She'd just undressed completely and pulled the PJ shirt over her head when the door opened. Raine quickly tried to tug the shirt below her panties, but it just wasn't long enough.

"What the hell are you doing?" she demanded, not speaking as loud as she wanted for fear of waking Abby.

Max's eyes raked over her bare legs, definitely not helping the tingling.

"We need to talk, and I didn't want to wake Abby," he said, closing the door with a soft click.

Raine rolled her eyes. "You couldn't have waited until I was dressed?"

Like a predator to its prey, he stepped forward, narrowing the distance between them. Apparently he didn't know the term "personal space."

"There's nothing here that I haven't seen," he said, his gaze locked onto hers. "Throw your pants on if that makes you feel better."

"Turn around."

That cocky grin spread across his face. "Are you really going to stand there and act like you're not turned on? That the fact we're stuck here together hasn't had you thinking, wondering?"

It was all the thinking and wondering that was driving her out of her mind. Hormones were evil. They reared their ugly heads when nothing could be done. Well, something could be done, but at what price? Because she sure as hell couldn't risk her heart again.

Not only that, she had to concentrate on the adoption. What would it look like if she were to delve into a torrid affair with Hollywood's hottest bachelor?

"Max, I realize that in L.A. you flash that grin and get what you want, *who* you want." She gripped her shirt tighter. "Yes, I'm attracted, but for all I know that's just old memories rising up."

He took one last step forward until they were toe to toe and brought his hands up to gently cup her face. "What if it's not just old memories?"

Raine sighed, because, if she were honest with herself, she wanted nothing more than to rip off his clothes and see if they were even better in bed than they used to be. And there wasn't a doubt in her mind they would be phenomenal.

"I live in the real world, Max," she said, pushing the erotic image of the two of them out of her head. "If we slept together, what happens next? I have a farm, a baby, here, and, in a few months, you'll be back in L.A., working on your next project, and you will totally forget about Lenox."

About me.

A flash of pain swept through his eyes, and his brows drew together. "My parents may have moved to Boston when I left for Hollywood, but I never forgot Lenox…or the people here."

The ache from his abandonment when she'd needed him the most years ago killed any desire she may have been feeling now. But at least, if she were stupid enough to get entangled with him again, she'd know upfront that he would leave without looking back.

And all she needed was the Family Court judge to get wind of the fact that Max Ford, Hollywood hotshot and rumored playboy, was snowbound in her home.

"Listen," she began, looking him dead in the eye. "We both chose our separate lives. It's ridiculous to act on any feelings we're having now, just because we're victims of the current circumstances."

"I prefer to call this fate."

Still holding the hem of her shirt so it didn't ride up and show off her goods, Raine stepped back, forcing his hands to fall away. No matter the cold she felt once his touch was gone, this was for the best. Distance now would spare her heartache later.

"So you want to…what? Have sex and then when the snow thaws just go back home and pretend nothing happened?"

Max scrubbed a hand over his face and groaned, looking up at the ceiling. "I don't know what the hell I want, Raine."

Before this got too far out of control, she wrestled into her pants while he obviously battled with himself over right and wrong.

He turned, leaning against the edge of the vanity and crossed his arms over his wide chest. "All I know is, since we kissed, I can't shake this feeling."

"What feeling?"

Max shifted, meeting her gaze. "That I want you."

Well, that was a change. She couldn't deny him, couldn't deny herself. Whatever happened in the past could live there. Raine wanted to live for the moment, but she also had to be realistic at the same time. "I want you, too." Unable to help herself, she reached out and rested a hand on his firm shoulder. "But I need more than sex. I want to find a man who will love me and Abby. Getting this sexual tension out of the way by sleeping together won't help either of us in the long run, no matter how tempted I am."

Because if she slept with him again, Raine knew she'd fall into that deep abyss of her past. She'd fall back into that mind-set that Max was the one.

"We may be stuck here for days," he murmured, reaching up to stroke her jawline. "You going to avoid the devil on your shoulder that long?"

Raine swallowed and answered honestly. "I'm going to try."

Seven

Raine had to admit she was quite proud of herself when morning rolled around, and she still had her clothes on. She'd spent the night with Max, in a bed, trapped in a freak snowstorm, and she'd held on to her dignity…not to mention her panties.

Max was not lying beside her in all his fully clothed glory. The only other person in the room was Abby, who had finally fallen back asleep at six after taking her third bottle of the night.

Raine held back a chuckle. She wouldn't be surprised if Max had decided to try to fix the stove downstairs in order to get some peaceful sleep. Abby hadn't had a bad night, actually. She'd only gotten up three times which was good, but in Max's world he wasn't used to being dead asleep one second and woken by a screaming kid the next.

And Raine was still shocked at Max's five a.m. gesture. On the third and final cry of hunger from Abby, Raine had thrown back her covers only to have Max's hand still her movements.

The man had not only gone down to the freezing first floor to retrieve the bottle from the fridge but he had returned and fed Abby. And if that wasn't enough to melt her heart, he'd also sat at the foot of the bed and gently rocked the baby back and forth.

And here she thought Max had been sleeping during the other feedings. Apparently he'd been watching her.

Easing out of bed, Raine tugged her pajama top down and attempted to smooth her hair away from her face. She padded into the bathroom and brushed her teeth, pulled her hair up into a ponytail and did her best not to cringe at the dark circles under her eyes. Yeah, she was quite the catch. If her sexy shoe collection of an old red pair of Crocs slip-ons and her very well-worn work boots didn't reel him in, surely this haggard housewife look would.

Not that she was trying to be a catch, mind you, but still…she should at least try not to look drab all the time. Working from home and raising an infant really did a number on your beauty regime. Not that she'd had much of one to begin with, but she should at least put forth a little effort.

Her mother would be totally mortified if she saw the lack of makeup in Raine's bathroom, the dollar-store shampoo in her shower and the one little bottle of lotion she used after a bath…her own concoction, of course.

Growing up, Raine remembered her mother having pots and bottles of various lotions to firm up this and de-wrinkle that. And the makeup. Good God, the makeup that woman owned could rival any beauty counter at the mall. Raine never wanted to be that high maintenance, that fake, to have to put all of that on just to step out and have lunch with "friends."

Still trying to remain quiet and not wake Abby, Raine left the warmth of her bedroom and went out into the frigid hall, taking the baby monitor with her.

As she hit the bottom of the steps, she shivered slightly but still didn't have a clue where Max went. Then she overheard him talking on the phone, his voice coming in from the kitchen.

Hand on the newel post, Raine froze, knowing she had no business eavesdropping, but she couldn't stop herself.

"My mother is doing great," he said. "I'm not with her because of this freak snowstorm…yeah, you saw that? I heard another six inches just today, too. It's hell on the East Coast, and I can hardly wait to get back to L.A. Between you and me, I'd trade palm trees for snow-covered evergreens any day."

Why that honest fact bothered her was silly. She knew Max was only here to care for his mother, and he had absolutely no qualms about playing house with her. He'd been here one day, and already she'd gotten comfortable. And after that near fatherly display from him earlier this morning, she was so much more attracted. Damn that man and his power over her hormones.

"I'm not at my mother's," he went on. "I stopped by to visit an old friend and got stuck here. But I'm using her laptop, so…yes, it's a she."

Max's masculine laughter sounded through her house, and she didn't even want to know what the person on the other end had said to garner such a response.

"I'm more than capable of working and playing when necessary," he said, still smiling. "She's an old friend…. Yes, I agree."

Raine decided now would be a good time to make her presence known before he said something she wasn't ready to hear. She moved to the doorway and leaned against the frame, arms crossed over her chest. She simply waited until Max fully turned around, but, instead of looking like he'd been caught, like most people would've, the man merely winked and continued smiling.

Even the way he oozed confidence was a turn on. Granted since he'd come back into town, she hadn't been turned off.

Raine tried her hardest to tune him out as she grabbed a

premade smoothie from the fridge and headed toward the stairs. She had her own work to do, and it didn't consist of watching Hollywood hottie Max Ford parade around her house wearing the same clothes from yesterday, with bed-head and day-old stubble.

Why did he have to be so damn sexy? Stomping up the stairs, because she was mature like that, she sighed. Had *she* been stuck somewhere overnight, she wouldn't have woken up looking sexier…not by a long shot. For some reason her looks deteriorated in the dark hours, because, when she woke, her hair was all lumped to one side in a matted mess, her eyes were bloodshot, and she was always a tad cranky.

Raine checked in on Abby once more before going into her workroom and setting the monitor on the counter. She had a small space heater she kept at her feet so she clicked it on high and closed the door to keep the warmth in.

Whatever Max wanted to do downstairs in the cold was his own business. They were safe and warm, so long as they stayed upstairs, and so far the electricity had held up which was surprising in a snowstorm that came on this fast.

Looking over her spreadsheet of items she wanted to make for the Farmer's Market in six weeks, Raine tried to block out the fact that her furnace had died. She simply couldn't think about that right now—although the blast of icy cold air when she'd gone downstairs had been a very real reality. The unit couldn't be fixed today even if she had the money, so her attention was best suited for work and Abby. Not the pathetic bank account, not the snowstorm and certainly not her handsome new roomie.

Downstairs the backdoor slammed. Raine smiled at the thought of Max going out. Obviously he hadn't learned his lesson the first time he had encountered her loving Or-pington chickens.

But he hadn't met Bess and Lulu yet—the equally loving

goats. They hadn't come out the other day, but it was only a matter of time before they realized a new person was here.

A giggle rose up in her, and, regardless of how cold it was on the first floor, she simply had to know how this all played out. Besides, she would have to feed her animals shortly anyway.

Grabbing the baby monitor, she padded down the hall, ran down the steps and stood just inside the kitchen door to watch Max.

Sure enough Bess and Lulu had gone through the rubber flap which gave them access in or out. The kindly goats encircled him, and, even with his jacket collar pulled up to his chin and his black knit cap pulled down over his ears and forehead, Raine saw the thread of fear and confusion in his blue eyes. Perhaps she should've warned him…

Nah, this was so much more entertaining.

She eased the back door open enough to yell out. "They're like dogs. They love people."

"What the hell does that mean? I've never owned a dog," he called back.

Raine shook her head. "Just pet them and keep walking. They'll go back in the barn when you come in."

She watched as he went into the barn closest to the house to gather more wood. Part of her wanted him to get tangled up in the chickens again, simply because the last episode had been so amusing, but another part of her was a little excited to see this city boy back in Lenox. Once upon a time he'd felt so at home here on her grandmother's farm. They'd ridden horseback, laughing excitedly as teens do, and had had a picnic out in the fields behind the property.

But that was long ago. Her grandmother was gone, the horses had been sold for the new roof, and all that was left were the bittersweet memories.

Tears clogged her throat. Turning back time wasn't an option, not that she would want to endure all of that heartache again, but she certainly missed being so happy, so loved.

By the time Max made it back to the house, she'd blinked away the tears, but the pang in her heart was just as fierce as when she'd first seen him nearly two days ago standing on the side of the icy road ready to assist.

Max brushed by her as she held the screen door open. He stomped his feet on the stoop before stepping inside. Raine took the bucket as Max pulled off his coat, boots and hat.

"It's still coming down," he said, hanging his coat on the peg by the door. "My tracks were covered by the time I came back out of the barn."

"I've given up listening to news reports. It will stop when it stops."

And the longer he was forced to stay here, the longer she had to fall deeper into memories, deeper into those emotions she couldn't afford.

Max turned to grab the bucket, but froze as his gaze held hers. "You okay?"

Raine nodded, pasting on a smile. "Of course."

"I've lived in L.A. a long time, Raine. We're professional liars, and you are holding something back."

Even if he hadn't been surrounded by "professional liars," he'd always known her so well. They hadn't changed that much.

"Seeing you out there brought back a flash of memories. That's all."

"Memories shouldn't make you sad," he said softly.

Raine eased the bucket down beside her, crossed her arms over her chest. "No, the memory was beautiful."

Running a hand through his sleep-mussed hair, Max stepped closer. "We may have gone our separate ways, Raine, but that doesn't mean I stopped caring for you. And even though we're stuck in this hellish snowstorm, I have to say I'm not sorry to be here."

"You're not?"

Shaking his head, he slid his hands up her arms. "Not at all. Maybe this is fate's way of making us talk, forcing us to settle this rocky area that's been between us for years."

Raine glanced down to their socked feet, so close together. Now he wanted to talk? What about when he'd left? What about sending for her and the promise of them starting their lives together? He hadn't been so keen on talking when he'd left her behind, pregnant and alone.

She looked back up, catching a sliver of pain in his eyes as he watched her. "We can't change anything about the past, Max. And you aren't staying in Lenox any longer than you have to. I heard you on the phone. I know you have a big deal waiting for you in L.A., and that's great… so opening up about what happened between us years ago won't solve anything. It won't bind us together, and it won't erase all the hurt."

"No," he agreed. "But it may make this tension between us easier to live with."

Raine laughed. "Tension? We have tension from so many different angles, Max."

Those strong hands curved around her shoulders, pulling her against his solid, hard chest. Raine had to tip her head to look up at him.

"There's a way to get rid of some of this tension," he whispered against her lips a second before claiming them.

She curled her fingers into his sweater, knowing that letting him sink further into her life was a vast mistake, but she couldn't help herself. Leaning against Max, being in his arms again, felt like no time had slid between them. No pain, no hurt.

He teased her lips as his hands slid down to the hem of the long-sleeved shirt she'd slept in. When his chilled fingers hit her bare skin, she sucked in a breath, but he continued to explore farther beneath her shirt.

His hands encompassed her rib cage. Max skimmed his thumbs along the underneath side of her breasts. She'd not bothered with a bra this morning, and she was so glad she hadn't. Not that her barely B cups needed confinement anyway, but, like a fool, she had wanted that extra connection with him. She wanted to feel his skin against hers.

And she'd known the second she'd seen him in her house yesterday that she wouldn't be able to resist him on any level.

Before Raine knew it, her shirt was up and over her head. Wrapping his arms around her waist, he lifted her and strode toward the stairs.

Raine tilted her head back as Max's mouth traveled from her lips, down the column of her throat and to her breast. She gripped the side of his head, trying to hold him there, silently begging for him to never stop.

He held her against the thick post at the base of the steps, pulled back slightly and released her. "Tell me to stop," he said, his voice raspy. "Tell me this is wrong, because I can't even think when I'm with you. All I know is I want you, here…now."

Raine palmed his cheek. "I want to tell you to stop. I know this is wrong, but right now, I want nothing more than to be with you."

In no time Max had shed his clothes and was jerking down her bottoms and panties.

"It's really cold down here," she muttered between kisses and sighs. "Let's go upstairs."

In a swift move, he lifted her and carried her up the steps and into her bedroom where Abby was sleeping soundly in the warmth of her Pack 'N' Play pen.

Max continued on into the bathroom and eased the door shut with his foot before carefully placing Raine back on her feet.

Light spilled through the small window on the far wall

and the sight of Max gloriously naked nearly sent her trembling knees buckling. Over the years he'd filled out in all the right places, but that scar stemming from his chest to his shoulder gave her pause.

She reached out, her fingertip lightly traveling over the faded red line. "Does it still hurt?" she whispered.

He grabbed he hand, kissed her fingertips. "That was long ago."

She knew when it was; she also appreciated the fact he wasn't about to let their past come into this room with them.

He kissed her deeply, wrapping his arms around her waist and arching her back. Raine had to clutch onto his shoulders and hold on for the ride.

As he gripped her tight, his lips left hers and continued their descent, making a path of goose bumps and trembling nerves down her throat and toward her breasts.

"Protection?" she panted.

He froze, rested his forehead against her chest. "I have nothing with me. I wasn't exactly planning on being stranded here."

"I've never been without protection," she said. "I know I'm clean, and I'm on the pill."

Lifting his head, his heavy-lidded eyes met hers. "I've always used protection, too, but it's your call, Raine."

In silent response, she tilted her hips into his and smiled.

Max lifted her, and she wrapped her legs around his waist. He turned and eased her down on the edge of the marble vanity. Raine couldn't wait another second. She maneuvered her body, pushed with her ankles and enveloped him. Then she stiffened. It had been so long since she'd been with someone. But this was Max…well, she wanted it to last. Silly and naive as that may sound, she never wanted their time together to end.

For this moment, Hollywood didn't exist, her problems

didn't exist. Right now all she knew was Max, and that was more than enough to satisfy her.

Max's hands slid up her sides, palmed her breasts, as her hips started moving, slowly at first and then faster as he kissed her, explored her.

Raine held on to his shoulders, using him for leverage as she pumped her hips.

"Raine," he rasped. "I…"

Whatever he was about to say died on his lips. Which was just as well, because right now all she needed was release. She wasn't doing this for sweet words, wasn't with him for the long-term. They both knew that.

Max grabbed the back of her head and slammed his mouth onto hers, his other hand reaching between them to touch her intimately.

Clever man that he was knew exactly what to do to her… he'd never forgotten.

Within seconds Raine's body shivered as wave after wave of ecstasy rolled through her. She tore her mouth from his, needing to somehow break that bond before she was pulled any deeper under his skin.

Max gripped her waist with both hands as he held her as far down as she would go when his own body stilled. For a second their gazes locked, but Raine had to look away. As his climax came to an end, she wondered what she'd seen in those baby blues, but, she knew if she delved too far into what had just happened, she'd be even more hurt when he left this time.

And she wasn't about to make the same mistake twice.

Eight

Well, hell. Awkward, party of two? Your bedroom is now available.

Raine pulled her robe from the back of the bathroom door and shoved her arms into the sleeves. Without a word, she opened the door to the bedroom and left. And Max watched her walk away without a word.

She'd done her best to distance herself during sex, she'd even avoided eye contact as much as possible, but he knew she'd felt something. And try as he might to deny it, he had, too.

Couldn't people just have a good time without feelings getting all jumbled into the mix? Ostensibly they couldn't. All that past between them, the current sexual tension and the fact he kept feeling this pull toward her. Maybe he felt the need to protect her because of her obvious vulnerability with the baby, the old house falling apart, her apparent financial crisis.

And what she'd done with tens of thousands of dollars from her trust fund was beyond him, but she clearly hadn't poured it into this place.

Max sank to the couch and slid his wool socks back on. At some point he would have to wash his clothes and take a shower…that shower probably would've been a good idea before the sex, but he hadn't been thinking. He hadn't been thinking of much other than Raine since he had stepped foot back in Lenox and came face-to-face with his past.

Obviously he had to go down to the freezing first floor to retrieve his clothes because he only had the ones he'd worn over here yesterday.

When he got downstairs, Raine was picking up her own clothes and trying to get into them without removing her robe. Okay, so she was plainly not comfortable with what just happened.

As if they needed another layer of tension.

Raine's cell chimed. He glanced around the room and saw it lighting up on the end table. She rushed toward it, pulling her shirt over her head and over that damn robe. Max shook his head and went to gather up his own clothes from around the room.

Scooping up the phone, she answered it. "Hello."

Max didn't make a move to leave the room once he had his things—if she wanted privacy, she could walk away. Yeah, he was in a mood and had no one to blame but himself. He'd been selfish. He'd wanted Raine, and he hadn't given a damn about the consequences or the fact that he'd have to stay here afterward and actually cohabitate until this damn storm passed.

"No, Marshall, I'm still fine."

Marshall? Who the hell was that? Max made no attempt to hide his curiosity as he pulled on his boxer briefs and jeans while staring across the room at her as she continued to talk. She kept shaking her head, glancing up to the ceiling, sighing…didn't take a genius to figure out she had no interest in talking to this Marshall person.

"My friend Max is here, and he's helping with anything I need."

Friend? After what they'd just done, he sure as hell felt

like more than a friend. But what would she tell the dude on the phone? My ex and current lover is here?

Max felt he was more than friend status, because, well... because he just was. Although his exact title was rather iffy, and he wasn't altogether certain he wanted to delve too deeply into that area.

So, okay, friend it was.

"Yes, he's a good friend," she continued. "No, we're not dating. We dated as teenagers... Yes, Marshall. It's Max Ford, the actor... Yes, I know how famous he is."

As she spoke, her gaze caught his, and then the smile that spread across his face. Raine merely raised a brow as if she dared him to say a word.

Max knew he was famous but hearing her discuss his celebrity status with another man only made him smile wider. Had Raine watched his movies? Had she seen when he'd won an Academy Award?

He found himself wanting to know more and wanting to share that aspect of his life with her.

Share his life? Yeah, sex muddled the brain.

"I don't really think that's any of your business," she said into the phone as she crossed the room and rested her shoulder on the windowsill. "I need to go, Marshall."

She barely got the words out before she hung up and clutched her phone in her hand. With her back to him, she sighed, and he could see her shoulders tense up. Max closed the distance between them.

"Problems with your boyfriend?" he murmured as he came to stand directly behind her.

Raine threw him a nasty look. "Marshall is not my boyfriend, no matter how much my mother and father want him to be because of his political aspirations. We went on one date, and I'm still trying to block it out."

Max slid his fingertip along the side of her neck, shifting her hair aside so he could taste her. He couldn't get

enough. Raine was one sexy woman, but, all fired up like
this, he was finding her irresistible.

"Sounds like he doesn't know what to do with a beautiful woman," Max muttered against her skin. "His loss."

Raine trembled beneath him, and Max grinned as he allowed his lips to gently roam over her neck. She tilted her
head to the side with a slight groan.

"What are you doing?" she asked on a sigh.

"Taking advantage of this situation."

Her head fell back on his shoulder as he slipped his
hands around her waist and pulled her against him.

"What just happened in my bathroom wasn't the smartest move we could've made," she said, but made no attempt
to free herself from his embrace.

"Maybe not, but it was inevitable."

A low cry came filtering through the house from the
strategically placed baby monitors.

"Does this mean playtime is over for the adults?" he
asked as Raine stepped around him and headed for the
steps.

She gripped the newel post and stared at him from across
the room. "I think maybe it shouldn't have started," she
whispered.

Max watched her ascend the steps to the second floor
and couldn't help but laugh. Her words held no emotion, and
he knew, in her mind, Raine was saying what she thought
the situation called for.

But he'd felt her come apart in his arms, when he'd held
her, kissed her, tasted her. She had allowed that wall of defense to come down, and she'd let herself feel.

Through the monitor he heard her consoling the baby.
She was such a wonderful mother. He wondered, if she'd
have come to L.A. when he'd tried to contact her, would
they have had a family of their own? Would their baby have

Raine's earthy nature and his creative side? Would he or she have Raine's soft green eyes or his bright blue ones?

Max wasn't one to get caught up in domestic bliss, but just being in her home one day and seeing this whole new side to her made him think. They'd shared the same dreams once, and she'd fulfilled the majority of hers—so had he for that matter, but at what cost?

Max glanced into the kitchen where bottles vertically sat in the drying rack, a can of formula beside that, a stroller folded up in the corner of the living room, a bouncy seat over by the window.

All of these obvious signs of a baby had him trying to picture his immaculate home in West Hollywood. Yeah, he didn't think all this brightly colored plastic would go with the black-and-chrome features his interior designer had meticulously chosen.

Raine came back down the steps cradling Abby against her chest. The sight of her fresh after intimacy and holding a sweet baby tugged at his heart, and there wasn't a damn thing he could do about it. He didn't want to play house with her; he didn't want to get swept into this crazy world of organic foods, overly friendly goats and diaper changes.

He wanted to get the hell out of Lenox once his mother's treatments were over, and he wanted to start working with Bronson Dane on this film that would launch his career to another level. But the pull he was feeling toward Raine was growing stronger and stronger by the minute.

"I'll put more wood in the fireplace in your room." Max went into the kitchen to retrieve the forgotten bucket of wood. "Mind if I grab a shower?"

He watched as Raine used one hand to jiggle the baby and one hand to mix a bottle. The woman truly was a natural mother. Another tug on his heart had him pausing.

Max's own biological mother had abandoned him, and the Fords had taken him in. Elise had been the best mother he could've asked for. She'd been patient, loving and so nurturing.

Max saw those same characteristics in Raine.

"Not at all," she told him. "Use my bathroom. If you want to leave your clothes on the bed, I'll wash them real quick for you. There's another robe in there hanging by the shower. It's big and thick, and shouldn't be too bad for you to wear for a couple hours."

"Um…okay. Thanks."

"I'm going to get a large space heater I have in the garage. We can see how well it does down here," she added. "It's not like we can keep staying up in the bedroom."

No, wouldn't want to tempt fate any more than necessary.

"When you're done, I'll grab a shower if you can watch Abby for a few minutes."

Babies didn't necessarily make him uncomfortable, but he wasn't quite ready to play nanny.

Although getting up to feed Abby had been…nice. Holding someone so precious and innocent had flooded him with a mix of emotions…namely love. Falling for Abby was not the smartest move.

Max shook off the impending feelings and concentrated on the here and now. This first floor was turning into an icebox. He needed to call someone about that furnace and have them look at the fireplace, as well. His mother surely knew enough people around this town that they could get a reputable name to come out as soon as the roads were clear.

"Sure," he said. "I'll be right back down."

After he showered, he'd call his mom and check in and get that name. Max knew his mother was in good hands, but he still wanted to keep touching base with her. The plow trucks should be coming through, and hopefully he wouldn't be stuck here much longer.

Because he had a sinking feeling that the longer he was here, the more he'd slide into that life that he and Raine had planned out. A life they were meant to have with kids and a house and him fulfilling his acting dreams.

Yes, they'd had their lives all perfectly drawn out like a blueprint. And they'd each gotten what they'd wanted out of life, but they were technically alone. So much time had passed that Max wouldn't know what to do if he were to be in a committed relationship. He had never made time for one, so he'd never really thought much about it.

For the past couple years his main goal had been career oriented, and getting that directing job with Bronson had been at the top of his priority list. But now, being with Raine really opened his eyes to his personal life…and the lack thereof.

So, yeah, getting the hell out of here would be the best thing for both of them.

"Not one word."

Raine had to literally bite her lips to keep from speaking, laughing, even cracking a smile. She totally failed on the latter.

"There was no thick robe hanging by the shower, and I didn't think to look to make sure it was there until I was out of the shower, at which point you'd already nabbed my clothes."

Across the room, Abby swung in her baby swing, and Raine was looking toward the doorway where Max stood with bare feet, bare legs and a silky, floral robe that barely came together in the middle. He was gripping the material together with both hands in an attempt to keep his goods hidden.

Like she hadn't just seen them. Not only that, this look was certainly not a turn on. It was, however, quite laughable.

"Maybe I put that robe away," she muttered, swallowing the laughter. "At least you have something to wear until your clothes are done."

His eyes narrowed. "You did this on purpose."

Now Raine did laugh. "Oh, I wish I'd thought that far ahead. I swear I thought I had a big white bathrobe on the back of the door. I can go find it for you."

She started to pass by him when he grabbed her arm. "What do I do if she cries?" he asked, his eyes darting to Abby.

Raine looked to the baby who was smiling up at the miniature spinning mobile of bears above the swing.

"She seems pretty happy," she said. "I'll only be a minute. It's probably in the other bathroom or in the laundry room. Besides, you were amazing with her in the middle of the night. I never thanked you."

Max shrugged. "You'd been up enough times and needed to rest. I figured if I did anything wrong, you'd intervene."

Raine smiled. "I was so glad to just lay there, I wouldn't have stopped you."

She moved away before he could stop her again. The image of Max Ford in her living room wearing a silky robe, watching a baby while waiting on a fluffier robe made her chuckle. If only his dad could see him now.

As much as Raine had despised Max's father, she knew, even to this day, Max wanted approval from the man. But no matter how many awards, how many movies or charities Max worked with, his father had never accepted Max was following a dream and loving what he did.

She recalled Max telling her one time that his dad had always wanted him to go into the family business. Since Max was adopted and an only child, there was no one else to inherit Tom Ford's dynasty.

But even before Max became famous, and a power broker in his own right, he'd had zero desire to be a restaurateur.

Within moments, Raine had found the robe and met him back in the living room. He hadn't moved an inch, and his eyes were locked on Abby.

"How long will she stay in that thing and be content?" he asked.

Raine shrugged. "She really is self-entertaining. She's just cranky through the night."

Max took the other robe, peered down at it, eyed the baby and then looked to her.

Laughing again, Raine rolled her eyes. "You can change. I swear Abby won't look."

Dropping the silky robe at his feet, Max displayed all his glorious muscles and potent male virility right in her living room. Keeping his blue-eyed stare locked on Raine the entire time, he grabbed the new robe and slid into it.

The man was gorgeous, and he knew it. Jerk.

"Looks like the snow is finally letting up," he stated, tying the belt as best he could around his waist. "You have plans for Valentine's Day?"

Raine crossed her arms and smirked. "Oh, yes. Abby and I plan on wining and dining on bottles of goat milk and decadent chocolates."

Max laughed. "I'm serious. You don't have any plans?"

"Do you really think I would've just had sex with you if I had plans to be with someone else in two days?"

Max nodded. "No, but I thought I should ask."

"It's after the fact now," she said.

He stepped forward, looking both ridiculous in that robe, yet sexy. "Maybe we could do something, since we both don't have plans."

Raine took a step back, holding up her hands before he could reach out and touch her. "Wait a minute, Max. I'm not looking for a Valentine or a date. What just happened between us was only you and me working off some tension and past memories. That's all."

"Old friends can't go out and enjoy the day?"

Go out? Sleeping together had been one thing—an amazing fantasy come true that she wouldn't soon forget—but to go out where people could see her on a date…

She couldn't afford *any* misstep in this adoption. And Max Ford was so recognizable that there's no way they'd go unnoticed.

"Old flames gallivanting around town where my father is mayor? Uh, no." She hated her father's status, except when she could use it to her advantage. "Besides, Valentine's Day doesn't mean much to me."

"Because you're single?"

Raine laughed. "Because it's just a day. I don't need a sentimental holiday to remind me of what I don't have."

She turned from him, not wanting him to read any more into what she said…or didn't say. She squatted down in front of Abby and flicked at the spinning bears. The baby smiled, eyes transfixed on the toys.

"Don't be embarrassed, Raine."

Her hand froze on the swing as she threw him a glance over her shoulder. "Excuse me?"

"That didn't come out right." He took a seat in the chair closest to the swing and rested his arms on his knees, leaning forward to look her in the eye. "We all had dreams. Some didn't come true, others did. I just don't want you to feel embarrassed that I asked about Valentine's Day. If you don't want to do anything with me, I understand. But the offer is there if you choose to."

Raine resisted the urge to snicker as she turned back to Abby. "I'll be fine."

Because his offer of a pity date was really topping her list for Valentine's Day. She'd much rather spend the day alone than be with someone who was only passing through and felt obligated to throw extra attention her way.

And the sex did not count. She'd been on board with that, and its sole purpose was to clear the tension between them.

Yes, that was the second time she'd thought that, but she wasn't trying to convince herself. Really. It had meant nothing. Just two people, taking advantage of the situation of being forced together.

Raine came to her feet. "I need to get this wood upstairs before I hop in the shower."

Max stood, placing a hand over her arm. "I'll get it."

She watched him walk away in that ridiculous robe and didn't know whether to laugh or cry…or take a picture and sell it to a gossip magazine.

"I'll go check on your clothes," she called after him.

Raine stopped the swing and lifted Abby out. "You're so lucky you have no clue what's going on. Word of advice? Stay a kid."

Because adulthood truly sucked sometimes. Sexual tension, worry over making a wrong decision, anxiety over making family happy…at one time she'd wanted to please her parents, but, as Raine got older, she quickly learned pleasing her mother was an impossible feat.

That was one thing Raine swore on her life that she would never let Abby worry about. Raine would be her baby's number one supporter and Abby would never have to wonder where she stood.

Nine

Max resisted the urge to groan as his mother rambled on about how this prime opportunity would be perfect for him and would help the community as well. It was a win-win… or so she kept telling him.

"The timing is perfect," she informed him.

Day two was coming to a close, and the snow had stopped, but the streets were covered, and cars were still parked in their little snow mounds.

"Mom, you know I love theater, but this is such short notice." He gripped the phone and turned from the bedroom window. When Raine had finished her shower, he'd come up here for privacy when he'd called his mother, and he'd also wanted to check the fire. Plus he felt putting some distance between him and Raine was best for now. After they'd had sex earlier, his libido had decided to join the party late, and he wanted her even more now.

And seeing her with dewy skin and silky wet hair hadn't helped. He'd had to get out of her presence quickly, but now that he was up in her room, the steam from the bathroom billowed out as did her fresh jasmine scent, probably from some exotic lotion or soap she made.

"Honey," his mother went on. "This is what you do. The play won't open until the first of April. You have almost two months to prepare, and since it's only a week long, you'll finish just in time to get back to L.A."

She had a point, several in fact, and they were all valid. And he really did love the Shakespearian Theater in Lenox. That's where he'd gotten his start. And where he'd met Raine.

Her soft voice filtered up from the first floor. She was singing again, as she did most of the time when she thought he wasn't around.

When they'd been teens and she'd sang on stage, he'd fallen so hard, so fast. Returning to the same stage suddenly didn't sound so bad.

"I'll do it," he conceded. "Can you have someone email me the script? I'd like to know a little more about what I'm getting into here."

His mother squealed with delight. "I knew we could count on you, Max! This will really raise a lot of money for the theater. It needs renovations that only a good chunk of funding can repair. You don't know how proud I am of you."

Max chatted a bit longer, making sure Elise was doing okay and feeling good. She assured him that she was fine but worried about him being alone with Raine. He blew that off because there was no way in hell he would discuss his out-of-control emotions where his ex was concerned.

And he would not analyze the fact he felt it his civic duty to help fix up the place where he had first fallen in love with Raine. So he wanted the theater to be back to its perfected state…so what? That didn't mean anything more than it was. When Max hung up, he glanced at the clock and realized it was Abby's bedtime. He turned off the overhead light and clicked on the bedside lamp to get the room ready for her. Not that he was growing cozy with this baby routine; he was just trying to help, that's all.

By the time he started toward the steps, Raine was coming up, clutching Abby to her chest and a bottle in the other hand.

"Sorry," he said as they met on the landing. "I didn't mean to be in the way."

"Oh, it's fine. I was working on some seed packets downstairs, so we're good."

When she started to move on up, Max touched her shoulder. "Can you come back down and talk, once she's asleep?"

Raine's gaze held his, and he didn't know if she was worried or scared of why he was asking her for more time alone.

"Just to talk," he added. "I'd like to talk to a friend right now."

Her eyes softened, shoulders relaxed and a sweet smile spread across her face. "I'll be right back down. I think that heater is doing a good job in the living room. I'll meet you there."

Somewhere along the way, tripping over chickens, getting felt up by goats and having sex on her bathroom vanity, Max felt as if they'd forged this new bond, something deeper than they'd ever had before. That could be the sex talking, but he truly didn't think so.

In any event, that didn't stop him from wanting to know more about the past—about what the hell had actually happened.

Max headed down to the kitchen to check the fridge, but when he glanced in and only saw goat cheese and some other questionable items, he decided it may just be best to avoid a snack. If he stayed here any length of time, he'd lose weight.

He was used to caviar, steak, fine cuisine. God, at this point he'd settle for a hot dog as opposed to asparagus, but Raine would probably kick him out in the snow if he mentioned the mystery meat.

After several minutes, Raine came back down, empty bottle in hand. As she rinsed it out in the sink, she eyed him.

"So, what's up?"

Leaning against the counter next to her, he shrugged. "Just spoke with my mother. She asked me to do some theater work while I'm in town."

Raine held his gaze for a moment before turning back to her task, shaking the bottle and resting it vertically in the strainer. She dried her hands and Max waited. Surely she'd have some input, some reaction.

But she said nothing as she walked over to the back door and checked the locks, flipping the back light off.

"It's cold in here," she stated, then walked into the living room.

"She said it's for some charity to benefit the arts and that the theater needed some major renovations," he went on as he followed her into the comfy room. "I know it's short notice, but I'm warming up to the idea. Might be nice to go back to the place where I got my start."

"I wouldn't know," she muttered as she strode toward the couch.

Max stood in the wide arched doorway watching as she picked up a few toys and a pink blanket from the floor. She stacked everything up into a neat pile in the corner and turned back to him.

"What?" she asked.

Resting his hands on his hips, Max shrugged. "You tell me. You don't think I should help out?"

"Not my business to say one way or another."

"Really? Then what did you mean a minute ago by you wouldn't know?"

Raine raked a hand through her messy hair and sighed. "It's been a long day, Max, and I kind of need to sleep when Abby does, because, in case you didn't notice last night, she's not the best sleeper."

"Why do you do that?" he asked, stepping farther into the spacious room.

"Do what?"

"Run. When things are uncomfortable, you run to avoid them."

Her glare searched his for a second before she laughed. "You're kidding right?"

"Not at all."

He stood directly in front of her, ready to battle it out if need be, but she wasn't going anywhere. Not this time.

"I thought we weren't going to rehash this," she said. "If you want to talk about running, then maybe you should turn that judgmental finger away from me and point it at yourself."

"I never ran, Raine. I wasn't the one who got scared."

In a split second her palm connected with his cheek, shocking the hell out of him.

"Scared?" she repeated. "You have no idea how scared I was when you left. You have absolutely no clue what I went through, so don't you dare tell me about running and being scared."

Max rubbed his stinging skin and took in her tear-filled eyes. "What happened, Raine? What terrified you so much all those years ago that it would resurrect such strong emotions?"

She blinked back tears and looked away, shaking her head. "Dredging up the past won't change a thing, and trying to do so is just making this time between us now uglier. There's no reason we can't be civil."

He grabbed her shoulders. "We were a hell of a lot more than civil earlier. Don't you dare even think of denying the fact we were good together."

"You don't get it, do you?" she asked, jerking free of his grasp. "You are here by chance, Max. I have a life here, a baby who depends on me. As much as I wanted what happened between us to be simple and not get to me, it has." She released a deep, shuddering breath. "It made me remember, made me think of things I have no business reminiscing about. And when you mentioned the theater, that was the last straw, and I was taken right back to that time we met."

Max listened, his heart clutching, as her voice cracked on the last word. Right now he hated himself. Hated how he'd upset her, hated that he'd left—even though he had done everything to get her to follow—and he hated that fate had slammed him back into her life so suddenly that neither of them knew how the hell to handle all these emotions. Shaking his head, he sighed. There was so much between them—anger, resentment, betrayal.

"Listen," he said softly, meeting her watery gaze. "I didn't bring that up to make you remember or to hurt you. I just wanted a friend to talk to, and you understand me. Despite all the time that's passed, Raine, I'm still the same man."

"The same man as what?" she whispered. "Because the man I fell in love with shared the same dream as me. The man I adored and felt safe with would've never hurt me."

"Hurt *you?*" he asked. "You think I wasn't hurt? You ignored me, Raine. I worked damn hard to get a place ready for us. I had a small apartment with a little balcony, and I couldn't wait to show you."

Raine jerked back. "What? But…I waited to hear from you."

Max's heart thudded in his chest as he absorbed her shocking words. "I called." He wanted so bad to reach out and touch her, but not yet. Not when emotions were so raw. "I called every day. Your mother told me that you weren't home or that you were sick. Finally she told me that you couldn't bring yourself to call me because you'd changed your mind, and you were dating someone else."

Tears slid down Raine's pale cheeks. "She lied."

Max watched as confusion and doubt washed over her,

and that pit in the bottom of his stomach deepened. All this time he'd thought she'd purposely given him the brush-off, but, now, seeing her shock, he knew they were both victims here.

"You didn't have a clue, did you?" he whispered, his own shock spearing his heart, causing the ache to settle in all over again.

He didn't know what was more agonizing—Raine ignoring his plea or someone else sabotaging their dreams.

"No." She opened her tear-glistened eyes. "You wanted me?"

Max stepped forward, closing the distance between them. "I couldn't wait to get you out of here, Raine. I hated leaving you behind, knowing you wouldn't be appreciated and loved like you were with me."

"Your career took off so fast," she said. "I kept seeing you with women in the tabloids, and, when I didn't hear from you, I just…"

Max closed his eyes, unable to see the hurt he'd involuntarily caused. He was a coward. Knowing he'd caused even a moment of anguish for Raine put a vise grip on his heart.

Why did he take her mother's word for it? Why didn't he fight harder? Hindsight was layering guilt upon his shattered heart, and he deserved every bit of angst. He'd brought this upon himself for not going after what was most important in his life.

"When I couldn't get in touch with you, I worried I'd made a mistake in leaving. I thought about coming back." His voice was thick with emotion. "Instead, I turned reckless when your mother said you'd moved on. I didn't care what happened to me."

"The motorcycle wreck you were in not long after you left." She spoke aloud as if talking to herself. "That's where that scar on your shoulder is from?"

He nodded. "I was so angry at you for shutting me out,

and all that time you had no clue how much I wanted to be with you. My God, can you forgive me?"

Raine smiled through her tears. "We were victims, Max. There's nothing to forgive. We both know who's at fault here."

Anger bubbled up in Max. Fury and bitterness soon followed.

"Did your parents despise us together that much?"

Raine swiped at her damp cheeks. "My mother offered me my trust fund early if I would stop seeing you and date this boy who planned to go to law school and had aspirations of running for State Senate further down the road. Needless to say, I refused."

This was news to Max, which just proved how strong and loyal Raine was. Too bad her parents never saw what a treasure she truly was.

"What are we going to do?" she asked.

He focused his attention back on her, on the glimmer of light at the end of this long, dark tunnel. "You need to confront your parents."

Raine nodded. "You want to join me?"

"If I come along, things could get ugly. How about I watch Abby while you go pay them a visit?"

Raine stood stock-still. "You'll watch Abby? Alone?"

Max shrugged. "I think I've got the hang of it. Feed her, change her and let her sleep. Does that cover it?"

Raine's sweet laughter filled the room. "That covers it for the amount of time I'll be gone."

She reached for him, wrapping her arms around his waist and resting her head against his chest. "I have no idea what to say. I know they'll defend their actions, but they stole everything from me. You were my life, Max."

How could they get over this massive hurdle that seemed to constantly be placed in front of them? Could they move past this revelation? So much time had elapsed, but his feelings were stronger now than they were when he and Raine had been eighteen.

Emotionally, if they could move on, where would they move *to*? He had a life in L.A., and she had a life here with her work, her baby.

Abby. He couldn't let Abby or Raine out of his life, but how the hell did he make this work? Had they missed their opportunity?

"After I talk to my parents, where does that leave us?" Raine asked, searching his eyes for answers he wasn't sure he had.

"It leaves us with a lot to discuss." He reached out, stroked her rosy cheeks. "And to decide if we think this will work again."

Her lids fluttered down as she brought her hands up to clasp his wrists. "The stakes are too high."

"Does that mean you won't try?"

"It means I'm scared," she murmured, raising her gaze to his.

Max slid his lips across hers. "Me, too."

Coaxing her lips apart, he wrapped his arms around her waist, pulling her body flush with his. He wanted to take away her pain, make her forget all the bad between them. He worried she'd push him away, but, when her hands traveled to his shoulders and around his neck, he knew they were meeting in the middle.

With a patience he'd never known before, Max lifted the edge of her shirt until she helped to rid herself of it. He fused their mouths together once more, taking her bra straps and sliding them down her arms.

Raine arched her back, allowing him perfect access to her neck, her chest. All that smooth, silky skin waiting to be explored. He took his time, making each stroke of his tongue, each simple kiss, count.

They may have screwed up in the past, and he could

very well be making a colossal mistake now, but damned if he could stop himself.

He pivoted her until they hit the wall. Sudden, frantic movements had them shedding the rest of their clothes. Garments lay all around them in random piles.

Max took his fingertips and traveled over her bare hips, into the dip at her waist and up to her breasts. Her body trembled beneath his gentle touch. Goose bumps sprung up all over her skin.

"What are you doing to me?" she whispered, searching his face. "The things I want with you…"

"I want them, too, Raine."

He only prayed to God they were talking about the same things, because, even though he'd be leaving Lenox in a few months, he wanted to spend time with her. He wanted to get to know her all over again. And when the time came for him to leave…well, they'd deal with that bridge when it was time to cross it.

Ten

Whoever was pounding on the door would be very sorry.

Didn't people in this town know she had a finicky baby who didn't sleep too well? No? Well, they should. This was the second time someone had pounded on her door, and she was about to put up a Do Not Disturb sign.

Springing from the bed, Raine grabbed her robe and tiptoed from the bedroom, careful not to disturb Max or Abby.

She nearly twisted an ankle racing down the steps, because, if whoever was at the door decided to reach for the doorbell, that would surely wake Abby. And Raine wasn't *about* to let that happen.

Making sure the robe was tied and everything was tucked in, she yanked open the door.

"Marshall," she said, jerking back. "What are you doing here?"

His eyes raked over her body, and Raine so wished she'd grabbed the thick terry cloth robe because the blast of cold air was doing nothing to hide the fact she was completely naked underneath.

"I wanted to check in on you, and let you know that the roads have been downgraded from a level three to a level two. Which means you can go out, but only if necessary..."

Behind her, Raine heard the steps creak. She didn't have

to turn to know who was there, but she glanced over her shoulder and nearly swallowed her tongue.

If she had thought Max Ford was sexy as hell before... well, now she needed some water. The man had on only his jeans—unbuttoned—and was cuddling Abby against his bare chest. Yeah, he may not want this family life, but he looked damn good wearing it. If Abby had woken up fussy, she surely wasn't now. She was nestled against Max's warm, broad chest.

A sliver of sorrow slid through her. This could've been their life...but their baby had died along with her dreams.

And even though she and Max had uncovered a major secret last night, she hadn't been able to confess that she'd been pregnant. Max had already been dealt a blow and was beating himself up. There was no way she was going to drop another life-altering bombshell.

They had enough issues to sort through as it was.

Marshall lifted a brow. "I see you weren't alone during the snowstorm," he stated.

Max came to stand directly behind Raine and she turned her attention back to Marshall. "Thanks for letting us know about the roads."

Marshall didn't take his eyes off Max. "I'll be sure to let your father know you're okay, Raine."

With that he turned and marched off the snow-covered steps.

Raine closed the door, flicked the lock and spun around to lean against it. "Well, that was awkward."

Max held Abby out toward her. "Awkward is not knowing what to do when she wakes crying and smells like... well, you know what she smells like."

Raine laughed and took the baby. "Don't be afraid of a dirty diaper, Max."

"I'm not afraid of the diaper," he said defensively as he followed her back up the steps. "I'm more afraid of the baby in the diaper. What if I did something wrong and hurt her or got crap all over the place?"

Heading back into the nice toasty-warm master bedroom, Raine laid Abby on the bed and grabbed a fresh diaper from the dresser.

"First, you can't hurt her by changing her diaper." Raine unzipped the footed pajamas. "Second, the wipes are here for a reason, and, believe me, I've gone through my share."

Raine quickly changed the diaper and picked Abby back up, patting her back. When she turned to Max, he had his arms crossed over that wide chest sprinkled with dark hair. He stole her breath.

"You're a wonderful mother."

Needing to lighten the tension, she shrugged. "Being a good mother has nothing to do with changing diapers."

"No, but I've see how loving you are with her, how patient and gentle. I'm a nervous wreck."

Raine smiled. "I was a nervous wreck too when I brought her home for the first time. But I learned quickly, and I'm still learning. I'll screw up at some point, and all I can do is hope she loves me through my faults."

And she prayed Abby would love her when she learned she wasn't her biological mother. No matter the genes, Raine loved this baby more than anything in the world. And she'd do everything in her power to give her a life full of choices and opportunities...not demands and expectations.

"So you think Marshall has run back to your dad, yet?" Max asked.

Raine cringed. "I have no doubt he was on his cell the second he got back into his truck. But who cares? My parents don't control me."

Moving around Max, she took Abby and laid her back down in the Pack 'N' Play pen with her favorite stuffed cat. She turned back to Max and sighed.

Now that the damage was done, Raine could only hope

the news of Hollywood's hottest bachelor playing house with her wouldn't hurt this drawn-out adoption process.

"My parents have never been happy with my decisions," she went on. "Finding both of us half naked is nothing that will disappoint them. I'm almost positive I'm at the bottom of the list for Daughter of the Year, anyway."

Max eased down on the edge of the bed and stared at her. "I know your father barely mentions her, but, surely they love having a grandchild."

Raine shrugged. "I'm sure they do in their own way, but they've already asked if I've put her on the waiting list for the private schools because so many of them are years to get into. They can't believe that I've considered home-schooling."

Max rested his elbows on his knees and continued to study her. "So they want to control her?"

"The way they couldn't control me," she confirmed, rubbing her arms. "I won't let it happen. Abby will make her own path in life, with my guidance, not my demands."

"You really are a single mother," he murmured. "You have no one to help you."

Raine lifted her chin. "I don't need any help. I sure as hell don't want help in the form of control."

"Good for you," he stated. He reached out, took her hands and pulled her toward him. "But that has to be hard on you…being alone, doing it all. Is Abby's dad nowhere in the picture? Surely he could give financial support."

Raine shook her head. There was no need to get into the whole backstory of Abby's life. If she and Max could work through their past problems—and that was a big *if*—then she would come clean about everything. And that meant both babies.

"It's just me," she reiterated. "But we're making it work. And as soon as I get back to a heavier volume of work in the spring and summer, things will really look up."

The way he studied her made her nervous. She didn't want him to dig deeper into her life, into her closet of skeletons. He would only end up more hurt, and she couldn't do that to the man she loved.

And she'd never blamed him for deserting her when she was pregnant...because he had had no clue. But she *had* blamed him for killing their dreams. Now she knew the truth, and the guilt consumed her for hating him all these years.

"I'll pay to have your furnace replaced."

Raine jerked her hands from his. "Like hell you will! I'll pay for it. We're okay right now as long as my firewood holds out. These old stoves heat really fast. I should have enough wood for another month anyway. Plus that space heater downstairs didn't do too badly."

"So what will you do when the wood runs out if the weather is still cold? You know the East Coast is finicky."

Raine shrugged. "I'll figure out something. I always do in a pinch."

"Why not just let me help?" he asked.

Raine glanced over at Abby who was waving her little arms and sucking on a stuffed cat's furry tail. "Because you're here for a short time." She turned back to him and offered a smile. "And I won't always have someone to come riding to my rescue."

"Because you won't let them or because you are alone?"

Why did he have to put things into perspective so simply?

"Both," she replied honestly. "I'd rather do things on my own than pretend to be someone I'm not just to have the help and support of my family."

"What happened to all the money you got when you turned twenty-five?" he asked, then shook his head. "I'm sorry...I shouldn't have asked that. I'm just surprised that you're struggling when I know you had a good chunk of change coming your way."

Raine backed away from him and moved to the dresser, pulling out a pair of black yoga pants and a sweatshirt.

She didn't care that he watched; she wanted to get dressed so she could start her day, and then he could be on his way since the roads were clear. They both needed time to think about the past…and the future.

"My parents had that little rule changed when I rebelled and decided that the money could be mine, provided that I adhered to their 'simple' guidelines."

Max's brows drew together. "They kept the money from you? That's…archaic. Why did they do that?"

She pulled out a pair of heavy socks and yanked them on, as well. "Because I loved you, because I planned on leaving and because I ran into some…trouble when you left."

"What kind of trouble?"

Oh, no. There was no way she could get into that conversation. Not after they'd succumbed to passion so many times over the past two days, and not when her heart was starting to gravitate toward him again. She had to steel herself. There was already way too much hurt hovering between them.

"We'll save that for another time," she promised.

Max looked as if he wanted to say more, but he merely nodded.

"I need to get some wood, feed the chickens and the goats." She grabbed a ponytail holder from the top of the dresser and pulled her hair into a top knot. "You care to watch Abby for a minute?"

He glanced over and nodded. "She seems harmless, but, if I smell something, I'll let you know."

Raine laughed, grateful he didn't push the issue. "Thanks. I'll hurry."

"Watch that one goat," he called after her. "He likes to get all up in your business."

Raine laughed and headed out of the room. Max was starting to enjoy it here. He hadn't said so, but she could tell. After only two days of living in her crazy farm-girl world, Hollywood icon Max Ford was comfortable, content and liking it. He smiled, he opened up, and he even let down his guard.

If the paparazzi got wind he was here, they'd be all over him. Raine giggled as she went to the back door and shoved her feet into her rain boots. The paparazzi at her house would seriously tick off her parents, and, if she was a teen again, she'd so be calling the media, but she was a mother and an adult. Pettiness had no place in her life.

And there was no need in starting any more fights than necessary, though she knew her mother or father would be calling shortly to confirm that Max had indeed been stuck here.

As she stepped off the back step, Bess and Lulu came through the weatherproof rubber flap and ran out to her, the chickens following behind. She nearly tripped but caught herself. She loved her life, loved raising a garden, loved her chickens and goats, loved her home that needed more repairs than she knew what to do with, and she loved being a mother.

The adoption progression was beyond frustrating, but her attorney had assured her everything was fine, and sometimes the process took longer than others.

So, now Raine played the waiting game…and tried to figure out just what to do with her heart and Max Ford.

Eleven

Abby started fussing; and Max tried shaking her stuffed cat, holding up another toy that had tag things all over it and even a silky blanket. Nothing was making her happy. And she wasn't in full-fledged-crying mode with the red face and snot, but he seriously wanted to avoid that type of confrontation.

So he bent down into the Pack 'N' Play pen—he thought that's what Raine had called it—and picked Abby up. Instantly she stopped fussing.

"Are you kidding me?" he asked her.

Drool gathered just below her bottom lip and slid down her chin, and Max wasn't repulsed. She was so damn cute he wanted to squeeze her. He refrained, but held her against his chest, inhaling the sweet scent.

He'd worked with babies on a couple of films, but his actual interaction with them was slim because the mother was always nearby, and once the scenes were shot, the baby would leave.

Max took a seat in the chair closest to the fireplace. He'd be kidding himself if he didn't admit that seeing Raine as a mother clenched his heart. They'd had the perfect life planned for themselves, and kids were a huge part of it.

As he looked at Abby, he realized her features were

nothing like Raine's. Where Raine had soft green eyes, Abby's were dark brown. Raine had pale skin and Abby's was a bit darker.

Apparently she took after her dad. And Max hated the man...a man he didn't even know. But how could Max resent a man for making a child with Raine? Raine was a victim just like Max. They'd both moved on as best they could once their lives together had been ripped apart.

Abby squirmed a bit on his lap, so he sat her on the edge of his knee and bounced her. "I'm not sure if I'm doing this right, but if you start screaming, I guess I'll know you don't like it."

Raine's cell chimed from the dresser, and Max nearly laughed. He had no doubt that was either Raine's mother or father calling to confirm that their daughter had a sleepover.

Who the hell took away money rightfully due to their child? Not only that, who kept it when there was a baby in the mix?

Max had no idea really what to do with Abby, so he came to his feet and starting walking through the house.

And there was no way he could let this furnace situation go. He'd already asked his mother who to contact, and she'd done some calling of her own to cash in on some favors. Raine could hardly argue once the furnace was paid for and installed.

"Your mama is stubborn," he told Abby as they paced through the hall.

He stopped at the room where Raine had been making lotions and smiled. She'd been fiddling with things like that when they'd dated. She was always trying out some new homemade soap or making candles. She didn't care that she wasn't popular or that her mother's high-society friends thumbed their noses at Raine. And that was one of the main things Max had found so attractive about her.

He wondered when she'd be making that visit to have a

come-to-Jesus meeting with her parents. But he wouldn't push. She needed to approach this in her own way, on her own time.

And he would be there to support her.

Figuring she'd be back in soon, he headed downstairs toward the kitchen. Abby started fussing a bit more, and he assumed she was probably hungry. Raine had given her a bottle somewhere around five this morning, but then Abby had gone back to sleep. How often did babies eat?

This parenting thing was beyond scary, but Raine seemed to know exactly what to do and when to do it. Were there books? An instruction manual?

Abby started to squirm and cry. This was going to get ugly real fast if he didn't do something. He prayed to God Raine already had bottles made up, because he'd only seen her make a few, and he had no idea how to do one himself. Sometimes she used goat's milk; sometimes she used a powder and water mix.

He sincerely hoped there was goat's milk in the fridge, because he had no clue the ratio for the powder and water, and there was no way in hell he'd be milking any farm animal. He'd risk the roads and hit the nearest grocery store first.

Max opened the fridge, saw two premade bottles, thanked God above for small mercies and grabbed one. Holding onto Abby, he pried the top off and quickly stuck the bottle in her mouth like plugging up a dam.

Blessed peace. He only hoped he was doing the right thing. He cradled her in his arm and propped the bottle up with the other hand. He paced around the room and from the wide window over the sink, he saw Raine go from the barn with the chickens, into the goat barn. She moved slowly over the mounds of snow, but she looked so comfortable in her daily chores. He couldn't even imagine her trying to do all of this on her own, but she was managing somehow.

As he continued to feed Abby and pace, he walked by a small built-in desk area in the corner. Papers lay strewn across the top, but it was the paper tacked on the wall beside the desk that brought him up short. It was a court date regarding…custody?

Was she in some sort of custody battle? He glanced closer at the paper and noticed another name. Jill Sands.

Max drew back. Jill…as in Raine's younger cousin? What the hell was going on?

He glanced down at the baby who had closed her eyes and continued to suck the milk.

Max knew whatever was going on in Raine's life wasn't his concern, but why hadn't she said anything? Obviously Abby wasn't biologically Raine's, yet she hadn't said a word.

The stomping of her boots on the stoop outside the back door had him moving away from the desk. Even though he felt a bit hurt at not knowing, he couldn't exactly expect her to open up to him after all these years apart.

The back door opened, letting in a cold blast of air. Raine slid out of her snow-covered boots and stepped onto the linoleum before shrugging out of her coat and hanging it on a peg. She shoved her gloves into the pockets and hung up her small red cap.

When she turned around, she froze, then smiled.

"Well, I certainly didn't expect you to be feeding her."

Max smiled back as he glanced down at a very content baby. "She was quite vocal, so I assumed that's what she wanted. Hope I didn't mess up."

Raine's eyes roamed over his chest and up to his face. "You're doing just fine."

"You better stop looking at me like that," he said with a

slight grin. "The roads are clear, and I should probably get back home to check on my mom."

The passionate scrutiny that had been visible seconds ago vanished from her eyes. She nodded and reached for Abby.

"Let me take her." With ease she took the baby, bottle and all, and cradled her. "I wasn't thinking."

She'd erected a wall. Just like that she'd taken the baby, stepped back and wouldn't look him in the eyes. Oh, no. This was not going to end this way…hell, this didn't have to end. Did it?

"Raine." He waited until she looked back at him. "Don't do this. Don't shut me out just because our forced proximity is over. We are working toward something here."

"I'm not shutting you out, Max. I'm just scared."

"There's nothing to be afraid of."

He seemed so confident. But that was Max. He'd always had more confidence than her.

"I expect to see you again soon," he said, easing closer and running a hand up her arm. "Will you be coming to my mother's for anything?"

"She hasn't placed any new orders, but I may stop by to check on her. And I need to discuss a couple of things about her gardening, since I'll be placing more seed orders soon."

Max nodded. "What can I do before I go?"

She glanced to Abby and shook her head. "We're good. Thanks for everything, though."

"I didn't really do anything," he said.

Her eyes held his. "You did. More than you know."

"I want to see you," he stated. "Outside the house. Just because I'm leaving now doesn't mean I don't want to see where this goes."

Raine nodded. "I want that. And as we discussed, I'm going to confront my parents soon."

"Let me know when. I'm here for you and Abby."

Raine stepped closer, easing the baby to the side and rising up on her toes to place a soft kiss on his cheek.

"My door is always open for you, Max."

The door to her heart was also wide open, but she couldn't tell him that, couldn't risk him leaving for good again. He would leave, she had no doubt. But would he fight for them?

"Glad to hear it," he said.

"You don't know how much I appreciate you being here, helping with Abby and gathering wood." Raine glanced down to Abby and back to Max. "It's hard being a single mom. I try not to complain, but sometimes I worry if all these balls I have in the air are just going to come crashing down on me."

Max laid a hand on her shoulder, another on Abby's tiny arm. "As long as I'm in the picture, I won't let anything crash down on you again."

Her heart throbbed. Now she could only hope and pray Max wanted to stay in that picture.

Raine didn't want to jump up and down, but when she saw the tiny little green sprouts popping up from the rich soil, she nearly did. Not everyone could grow vegetables in the winter. Well, they could, but she doubted they'd go to all the pains she did to ensure organic seeds and chemical-free soil.

The warm light was perfect and so was the rotation schedule of moving the pots around in the light. Raine was so excited about the little bean sprouts and kale. And her clients would be happy too that they were getting a jump start on their crops. When the weather broke and the risk of frost was gone, she could transplant these vegetables into the ground for her clients, and they could have their fresh produce before most other people.

And the stash she'd be able to take to the Farmer's Market would be larger than last year. Thankfully each year her business grew. She had no less hopes for this spring.

Her cell vibrated against the worktable, and Raine smiled at the number on the screen.

"Hi, Jill," she answered.

"Hey," her cousin replied. "I haven't called for a while but got a break from classes and wanted to check in. I heard you all got a crazy amount of snow. Everyone okay?"

Raine leaned back against her counter and crossed her arms. "Yeah, we're all good now. The furnace went out, but I have enough wood to last until the warmer weather gets here."

She hoped.

"Oh, Raine, I'm sorry. I swear, you really do always look on the bright side of life. I wish I could be more like you."

Raine smiled. "You're more like me than you know."

"How's Abby? I loved the picture you sent me last week of her in that cute little crocheted hat with a pink bow. She's getting so big."

"She's doing great. Still a bit cranky at night, but much better than she used to be with bedtimes."

Jill sighed. "Sometimes I wonder if I burdened you."

"Never," Raine said, coming to stand fully upright. "That beautiful baby has never been, nor will ever be, a burden to me. I love you, and I love her."

"You're the best thing that's ever happened to me...and to Abby," Jill replied with a sniff. "I know I made the right decision in letting you adopt her. She's getting more love and care than I ever could've provided."

Raine's heart clenched because, for a very brief moment, Jill had considered an abortion.

"I've always wanted a family," Raine told her cousin. "And Abby is such a huge part of my life now. I can't recall what it was like without her."

"I'd like to come visit over summer break," Jill said. "If that's okay with you."

"That's more than okay with me," Raine said. "I'm really proud of you for putting your baby's needs ahead of your own."

"I know I made the right decision. There's no way I could've taken care of a child and continued my schooling…and I couldn't abort her. The thought now makes me sick. So adoption was the only other choice."

Raine teared up. She couldn't wait for that official piece of paper.

"I need to get to my next class," Jill said. "But I wanted to make sure you all were okay. I love and miss you, Raine."

"Love and miss you, too. See you soon."

Raine hung up, clutched her phone to her chest and closed her eyes. Jill was doing what she should be, with no help from her parents. Jill's mother and Raine's mother were sisters. They were certainly cut from the same snotty, holier-than-thou cloth, as well.

When Jill had become pregnant, it was like déjà vu for Raine all over again. Things happen…Raine hated to tell her mother that they were all human, and not everyone was perfect.

Raine may not have been in the best financial position to adopt, but she was much better off than Jill, and Raine's business was continuing to grow.

There was no way Raine would've sat back during Jill's struggle. Jill needed support like Raine never had, and when Abby was old enough to understand, Raine and Jill would sit down and tell her the truth.

But for now, Abby was hers and Raine would love her as her very own.

Twelve

Max made sure his mom was comfortable in her favorite chair in the patio before he went to get her lunch. The nurse had left, and Max was doing what he'd originally come here to do.

While he was beyond thankful for the time he'd spent with Raine, he was needed here. He also wanted a break from Raine and her sultry curves, her snappy comebacks and the maternal love he saw in her eyes each time she looked at Abby.

If he was going to fight for them, Max had some serious thinking to do. While he would not give up this movie opportunity with Bronson Dane, he also could not walk away from Raine again without seeing if they could make things work.

There had to be a way. Fate wouldn't be that cruel to throw them together just to rip them apart once more.

But now that he was home again, he figured his mother would be a good source of information. Plus, knowing her, she'd want to hear about his three days snowbound with his first love.

As Max brought his mother a tray of sandwiches and fruits, she smiled up at him.

"Thank you, sweetheart." She picked up the glass of

water and took a sip before looking back at him. "How are Abby and Raine doing?"

Wow...that didn't take long.

"They're great," he said, taking a seat in the floral wing-back chair. "So just ask what you want to know, and let's skip the chitchat."

Elise laughed, reaching for a grape. "I'm a mother, Max. It's my job to put my nose in your business."

"Well, that guy you called about the furnace phoned me, and I gave him the go-ahead to replace the unit and repair her stove, so she could be warm sooner rather than later."

His mother's eyes widened. "She agreed to let you do that?"

"Oh, no, but I'm doing it anyway."

"Good for you," she murmured. "She needs someone to help her. God knows that snooty mother of hers won't. And don't get me started on her father."

"Yeah, when did he become ruler over Lenox?"

"Not long after we moved." Elise waved a hand in the air and reached for another piece of fruit. "That man can't control his family, so he tries to control the city."

Max could see that. Raine's father had been an arrogant jerk when Max and Raine had dated as teens. Little did he know it was Raine's mother who was so underhanded.

"I think Raine is a lovely girl, and I'm just sorry I didn't see it years ago," his mother finally said, her eyes seeking his.

Max jerked his attention to her and eased forward in his seat. "She's no different now than she was when we were teens. What changed your mind?"

"I never truly had a problem before," she admitted. "But I wanted peace in my house. You and your father already had so much tension between you...I didn't want a girl to drive that wedge deeper."

"I loved her."

"I see that now," she said. "My own shortsightedness had a hand in keeping you two apart."

Max shook his head. He wasn't getting into the real reason he and Raine had parted ways.

"Raine is the hardest worker I've ever seen," Elise continued. "She goes out of her way to make sure her clients are well informed of exactly what they're getting with their plants and seeds. She's very concerned about chemicals and unnatural gardening. The fact that she does all this research in order to have the best is really remarkable."

"How many clients does she have in town?"

His mother shrugged. "I'd say around thirty or so. She's quite busy in the summer. I don't know how she'll juggle the business with Abby when the time comes. Of course, I'll still be here, so it would be no hardship to let the little princess come inside while her mother works."

Max had so many questions. Too many and he almost felt guilty gossiping about Raine with his mother. God, he'd resorted to being one of the busybodies in town. Now all he needed was a teacup and matching saucer.

"Her mother has tried to get the ladies not to hire Raine, and some of them have listened," she said. "I personally need someone here when I'm not around in the summer, and, since Raine started several years ago, she's been nothing but a blessing to me."

Max stared at his mother. Was this the same woman who had tried to convince him as a teen that Raine wasn't right for him and he should move on?

His mother smiled softly and eased back in her seat, ignoring her lunch. "I know what you're thinking. I know what I said in the past, and I believed what I said at the time was what was best for that point in our lives, Max."

"You told me not to see her anymore," he reminded her. "You said she wasn't good for our family."

"And at the time she wasn't," Elise insisted. "Max, your

father didn't think she was good for you. And no matter what I thought, I couldn't stand to see our family torn apart by teenage hormones. You were two rebellious teens, and you fed off each other's defiant ways."

"I loved her, Mom," he repeated. And he still cared deeply for her. "I would've married her had she come to L.A. when I tried to get her there."

"I know you would've," she said softly. "I know how much you cared for her, but at the time I just couldn't have my family ripped apart. You two weren't ready to be together, to be that far away on your own. You had stars in your eyes. Your father used to have that same look."

For the first time when discussing his father, Max really looked at his mother. Her eyes had darted down, her mouth no longer smiling. Max loathed his father. The man was nothing but a careermonger who did anything and everything to get to the top, to be the best. He had sacrificed his family, his personal life and ultimately the relationship with his son. There was no way Max was like his father. He wouldn't sacrifice his family...at least not intentionally.

But he was so far past caring what his father thought. He did, however, care about how his mother was being treated.

"When will Dad be here to visit?" he asked, already figuring the answer.

"He's so busy, Max. You know how he is..."

Max nodded. "I know. I just assumed he would take some time off."

He didn't push. No need in stating the obvious and making his mother feel worse about a marriage that was obviously one-sided. Did his father see what all he was missing in life? Was a chain of five-star restaurants that important when your wife was recovering from breast cancer surgery?

Max stewed in silence as his mother ate, but a few more questions kept gnawing at him. Did his mother know about the adoption or guardianship or whatever the hell was going on with Raine? Surely she did, because Raine hadn't been pregnant, and his mother would've known. Hell, the whole town more than likely knew about this, so why wouldn't she tell him the truth?

Didn't she think he'd understand? He was adopted himself for pity's sake. Perhaps that was another reason he'd fallen so hard, so fast, for little Abby.

But he wasn't done with Raine. They were just getting started. He'd get her to open up, he'd break down that wall of fear, and then he'd figure out just how the hell they could make this work.

As Raine assembled her last basket for the morning, her doorbell rang. She glanced over at Abby, who was pleased as punch in her Pack 'N' Play pen, and left her to head downstairs to see who her unexpected visitor was.

She frowned when she peered out the window alongside the door and saw a man in a blue work uniform standing on her front step. Cautiously easing open the door only a couple inches, she kept her hand on the knob. "Yes?" she asked.

The man held out a clipboard with what appeared to be an order form. "Good morning, ma'am. I'm here to install your new furnace. I was informed the old one has not been removed, so I'll need to do that first."

Raine stared down at the order, then back up at the man. "Excuse me? New furnace?"

Then it hit her. Max. Damn it. Most women got flowers and got all weepy. She got a new furnace and tears pricked her eyes. She was so not normal.

"Um...no. No, the old one hasn't been removed." She allowed the furnace man to enter. "It's right back here."

As much as she wanted to protest, she knew this worker didn't want to get caught in the middle of a feud, and she also knew when to just let someone help. And that was a totally new concept for her, since Raine didn't get reinforcements from anyone. Yet, stubbornness aside, how could she deny that Max had been there for her more in the past several days than her parents had been most of her adult life?

When Raine showed the man where the furnace was, he went back out to his truck and another man came in as well to assist. Raine wasn't too comfortable being alone in her house with two strange men, but that was life. She was a single woman, and this was just how it worked.

Once she realized they didn't need her standing around staring at them, she went back upstairs, grabbed her cell from her work area and then picked up Abby.

She quickly dialed Elise's house and wasn't surprised when Max answered.

"You seriously paid for a furnace?" she asked, not beating around the bush.

"I seriously did," he said with a chuckle. "Did you try to kick out the workers yet?"

Raine smiled and shifted Abby's weight. "I thought about it, but then realized I would only be hurting myself and Abby if I didn't accept your very generous and much appreciated gift."

"Wow. The old Raine would've fought me tooth and nail over this."

Her smile spread across her face as she started to head back downstairs. "Yeah, well, I'm not the same Raine, and I'm not an idiot. I need a furnace and you want to gift it to me. I'll take it."

Max laughed again. "I'm very impressed with the new Raine. Would the new Raine happen to have any plans for Valentine's Day?"

Was he flirting with her? She hadn't flirted since…way too far back to remember.

"Sorry. The new Raine has a baby and no sitter."

"I'd like to have both of you for my date," he stated. "I'm kind of greedy."

"What about your mother? Will a nurse be watching her that night?"

Abby's little arms were waving about and nearly knocked the cell from between Raine's shoulder and ear. Raine eased her head the other direction to ward off slobbery fingers.

"Well, Mom claims my father is coming to town to spend the day with her."

Raine stepped into the living room, settled Abby into her swing and turned it on. "You don't sound convinced."

"I believe he wants to come, but work always gets in the way."

Raine watched Abby as she swung back and forth. The men in the other room were making quite the racket, and Raine couldn't believe she was contemplating a date with Max. Seriously? And if they went on a date, where would that lead? Back to bed?

Marshall had already seen Max at her house, so that secret was no longer well kept. Perhaps if that became an issue with the adoption, this "date" would go a long way in proving Max wasn't just a fling. Even though she couldn't necessarily define what they were at the moment, they'd definitely gone beyond just sex.

But was she ready to take that next step and go on a real date?

"I'm not sure," she said.

"I don't want you to be uncomfortable, but I know we have a good time together. What do you say?"

"Can I think about it?"

Max chuckled. "You can, but you have a day to do it."

"If I did agree, what would we do?" she asked.

"I have plans in place if you say yes. That's all you need to know."

Shivers coursed through Raine. How could she refuse

a man when he'd already given her and their time together so much thought and consideration?

He was right in the sense that they did enjoy each other's company, and she didn't have anything else to do.

Oh, who was she kidding? She wanted this date like she wanted her next breath.

"If you're sure you can handle me and Abby, then I guess we're available."

"Perfect," he said. "I'll be at your house tomorrow at five. Does that work?"

Giddiness swept through Raine, and she spun in a little circle. Max couldn't see her, and, even if he could, she didn't care.

"Where will we go?" she asked.

"All you need to worry about is being yourself. Don't get all fussed up. I just want to see the natural Raine I spent three days with in the snowstorm."

Raine wrinkled her nose. "You're serious? Because natural Raine isn't worthy of public places."

"You'll be fine," he assured her with a laugh. "Promise."

By the time she hung up, Raine was intrigued as to what he had planned. Max being back in town had already turned into something she'd never expected. How could she not fall for him again? Especially when she ached for him with all her heart and soul.

Although she knew she should probably keep her distance, deep down she knew there was no way she could stay detached from him. Her emotions were too profound, their bond too strong. And since they'd been intimate and had begun to confront their past issues, that bond had only grown.

He was extending this olive branch to her. She had no doubt he wanted to see where this newfound relationship led. She did, too.

But as much as she wanted to savor this time together, she knew they both needed to proceed with caution.

Because neither of them could afford another emotional landslide.

Thirteen

When Max took his first step over the threshold of the Shakespearian Theater, he had to stop and take it all in. The large red-velvet curtains draped from the stage at the far end. The slanted rows of seats and the tiered balconies on either side were completely empty, but in a few short weeks would be overflowing with an eager audience...he hoped.

This play was for charity, and they needed to raise an insane amount of money for the theater's renovations. Of course he'd donate a large sum as well, perhaps double the amount brought in from the play.

And since he'd just been faxed the script yesterday morning, he'd barely had time to look it over, but he did know he was playing a Roman soldier. Just what he wanted to do—sport a sheet, a metal chest plate and wield a sword. But for the sake of the arts and as a favor to his mother, he'd do it. God knows he'd played worse characters over the course of his career.

As he made his way down the aisle, that thrill shot through him of doing live theater again. There was nothing like that immediate feedback, the cheers, the standing ovations...and the ego boost that inevitably followed. The vanity of acting was just part of the process, and he'd learned long ago to face it head-on, but not let it consume his life. Too many talented actors had fallen, because their ego had gotten in the way of their dreams.

Max made his way to the back of the stage where he'd told the director he'd meet him.

An elderly man was bent over in the corner mumbling something about cords and wiring. Max smiled and cleared his throat to get the man's attention.

"Oh, oh. I didn't know you were here." He came to his feet, extending his hand. "It's an honor to meet you in person, Mr. Ford."

"Call me Max," he replied, pumping the other man's hand.

"I'm Joe. I'm the director here. I can't tell you how thrilled we were when your mother said you'd take on this part. We had a local man scheduled to play the role, but he had to bow out at the last minute."

"I'm happy I can help."

Joe slid his hands into his pockets and rocked back on his heels. "How is your mother doing? Hated to hear about her illness."

"She's on the mend and doing remarkably well," he told the older gentleman. "We're really lucky they caught the tumor in time. The doctor expects a full recovery and no chemo, so she's happy."

"That's fantastic news," Joe said with a smile. "We all just love her around here. She's always been such an advocate of the arts and it's nice to have someone like her in our corner."

Max nodded toward the wires. "Having some problems over there?"

The director sighed, shaking his head. "I can't get this mess figured out. We need to have the lighting updated, and I'm trying to get through this one last play before having it replaced."

"Is it the time or the money that's the hold up?" Max asked.

"A little of both." Joe laughed, moving over the squat down again. "I really need to get an electrician in here before we do this production at the end of the month…"

"Call someone and I'll cover all costs. See how fast they can get it done."

Joe's head whipped around. "You're serious?"

Max nodded, squatting down beside Joe. "Absolutely. I can do some things, but this may be out of my element."

Joe grinned. "Yeah, I heard rumors there may be collaboration between you and Bronson Dane. Any truth to that?"

Shrugging, Max smiled. "We'll see." Coming to his feet, he rested his hands on his hips. "Now, why did you need to meet me today? Don't tell me you're spending Valentine's Day working."

Joe laughed. "My wife would kill me. I wanted to talk to you in person before any other actors arrived. Now that you've seen the script, are you comfortable with it? Do you want any changes?"

"I thought the script was great. I'm really looking forward to doing live theater again."

"Wonderful. That's such a relief."

Max studied the man and noticed he was much more relaxed now. "Did you think I'd come in, throw my weight around and try to take over your production?"

Joe raised his brows. "We've had that happen before. Not with you, of course. Last summer we had a certain A-list actor who wanted some things changed before he'd commit."

Max knew who Joe referred to. Even though L.A. was on the other side of the country, the acting industry really was small, and word traveled fast…especially when other performers were all too eager to slip into some diva's shoes.

"Well, I assure you," Max went on, "I'm thrilled to be

helping out with the charity and to get back to my roots. Are we starting rehearsals Monday?"

"Yes. Since we're pushing the envelope with the lead role change, you'll be coming in at the start of dress rehearsal, so I'm afraid there's not much time to get acquainted with the cast."

"I'm flexible." Max walked around behind the stage, checking out the lighting, looking at the various exits. "This place hasn't changed since I started here fifteen years ago."

"Not too much has. I've been here for almost ten years, and we've replaced the sound system and done some minor updating, but that's about it."

Max glanced to the small dressing area in the corner for the quick changes that were sometimes needed between sets when there wasn't time to change in a dressing room.

As if he were watching it happen, he saw a younger version of Raine and himself sneaking into that room and closing the door. They'd fooled around for hours on end in there. They'd arrive early for rehearsal and while the director and sound manager were busy talking, he and Raine would make out. Pathetic, but they were in the throes of a teenage love that consumed their every waking moment.

"If that's okay with you…"

Snapping out of his reverie, Max turned back to the elderly man. "I'm sorry, what?"

"I said I was going to have you and Patricia come in earlier on Monday. Since you're the leads, I thought you'd want to go over some key scenes without the rest of the cast here."

Max nodded. "That should be fine. If my mother is feeling up to it, I may bring her to a few of the rehearsals just to get her out of the house."

"We'd love to have her."

Max shook the man's hand again and walked around the

theater, taking in all the familiar surroundings, letting the nostalgia seep through him.

After several minutes of strolling down memory lane, Max knew he needed to get ready for his date with Raine. He was pretty anxious for their time together. Granted being around Abby made him a little uneasy, but he was starting to get more comfortable with her. It was just…she was so tiny he seriously feared he'd hurt her.

The snow was still stark white, except for the black slush that lined the side of the streets, but, for the most part, it remained beautiful and crisp.

As Max maneuvered his way back home, he realized how much he'd missed this weather. He hated to admit it, even to himself, but he'd once loved the winters here. When he'd been a kid, they'd had so many snowstorms. Canceled school, sleigh rides and sneaking off with Raine had been the major highlights from his youth.

He may not know what the hell he was doing with her, but he knew for sure that, when he was with her, he had that same feeling he had always had when they'd been together in the past…*perfection*. There was simply no other way to describe it.

L.A. would be waiting for him when he returned in two months. But for right now, he wanted Raine. He wanted to spend more time with her, with Abby, and, when it came time to leave again, who knows, maybe she'd come this time.

Raine didn't have much in the way of going-out clothes, but she settled for her nice jeans, black knee boots and a pink top that rested just off her shoulders. A bit sexy, but not obvious and trampy.

She nearly snorted. She was so not the poster child for seduction. She'd had to scrounge to find some makeup so she at least looked a little feminine.

And Max had called earlier, upset and frustrated because his father's plans to come visit had fallen through so they would either have to cancel their plans or spend Valentine's Day with his mother.

So did this really constitute a date since his mother and her baby would be there? Um…no. Apparently fate had intervened and taken the romance out of the most romantic night of the year. She nearly laughed. This whole *spending the evening with his mother* bit felt a little like working backward. Shouldn't they have done this *before* falling back in bed together?

Raine left her bathroom and picked up Abby from the Pack 'N' Play pen. Abby looked absolutely adorable with her red leggings, black-and-red shirt with hearts and black furry booties. There was a matching black hat with a red bow on it, but Raine wasn't so sure Abby would keep it on. Raine would at least try.

She had just descended the last step when the doorbell rang. Nerves settled low in her belly. This was nothing major. Just because it was Valentine's Day and just because Max had invited her and Abby to spend it at his house didn't mean anything. They were old friends. Okay, so they were old lovers. No, wait, they were new lovers.

Biting back a groan, Raine headed to the door. She honestly didn't know what they were right now. They'd slept together, argued, rehashed a very rocky point from their past and now they were having dinner. If she didn't know better, she'd think they'd slipped right back into their old pattern…except now she had a baby in the mix.

She jerked open the door, and Max stood there with a potted…basil plant?

Raine laughed. "You never were predictable."

"Why should I be? I always prided myself on standing out in a crowd."

"Basil, Max?"

He shrugged, stepping into the foyer. "You like to grow your own things so I thought you'd like an herb."

Unable to resist, she went up on her tiptoes and kissed Max on the cheek. "You're very sweet." Raine didn't want to think about how handsome he looked in his perfectly pressed dress pants and cobalt blue shirt, matching his eyes. Nor did she want to think about the lengths Max had gone to in order to get this plant at this time of year. The fact he didn't do the traditional roses on Valentine's Day warmed her heart and touched her in places his niceties had no place touching. He was leaving in less than two months, and she refused to let her heart go with him this time. Spending time with Max was going to happen, she refused to deny herself. But she was older and wiser now, and she had to be realistic.

"Are you two ready to go?" he asked, holding his arm out waiting for her to take it.

"I need to get the car seat from my vehicle first."

Max shook his head. "I bought one and put it in already. Well, the store manager had to install it because I was afraid to screw it up, but it's in and ready to go."

Oh, God. That was it. Her heart tumbled and fell into a puddle at his feet. Damn this man. How could she even consider handing him her heart again when it had been shattered in so many pieces last time? For heaven's sake, she was still recovering, if she were completely honest with herself.

"Everything okay?" Max asked, searching her eyes.

Raine offered a smile and shifted Abby in her arms. "We're good. All ready to go."

He slid a hand over her cheek, brushing her hair aside. "You look stunning, Raine. Too bad we can't stay in."

"Perhaps it's for the best."

"You don't believe that."

She stared up into his crisp blue eyes and held his stare.

"I do. As much as I love being together, we both know you'll be leaving soon. So let's just enjoy the time we have and worry about everything else later."

He captured her lips softly, then eased back. "I couldn't agree more."

Raine followed him out, angry at herself for the pity party she waged deep inside. There was that sliver of heartache in her that wanted him to stay. Wanted him to deny that he'd leave.

And didn't that make her naive?

Did she honestly think that they'd make love a few times, set up house with Abby, and he'd be all ready to throw his life in L.A. away and play daddy? She wasn't that gullible as a teen, so why now?

Because she wanted what she'd never had. Because she wanted to have that family, and, dammit, she wanted it with Max.

Once they were settled in his SUV, she forced herself to calm down. Wishing and wanting things that would never come to fruition was an absolute waste of time. She had other worries in her life, other people who loved and depended on her.

Like Abby. Each day that passed without a word from the courts made Raine more irritable and nervous.

Hopefully spending the evening with Max and Elise would provide the perfect distraction.

Fourteen

"She is just precious."

Max watched as his mother's eyes lit up while she held Abby. The baby kept trying to suck on the side of his mother's cheek, and Raine went to the diaper bag.

"She's getting hungry," she explained, mixing formula into the bottle. "Here, I can take her."

His mother looked up at Raine and smiled. "Would you mind if I fed her?"

"Not at all."

Raine shook the bottle and handed it over, along with a burp cloth. Max watched as his mother nestled Abby into the crook of her arm, and instantly Abby took to that bottle, holding onto his mother's hand.

Max couldn't stop the smile from spreading across his face. Just this alone was worth spending Valentine's Day with the women in his life.

"Why don't you two go for a walk or something," his mother suggested, looking across the sitting room to him. "I'm fine with this little angel, and I'm sure the last thing either of you want to do is babysit me."

Max laughed. "I'm not babysitting, and this is no hardship to spend my evening with three of the most beautiful ladies I know."

"Cut the charm, Romeo," Raine chimed in. "We already agreed to be your dates for the night."

His mother laughed. "Go on, you two. I've taken care of a baby in my time. Abby and I will be just fine."

Max really hated his father right now. Absolutely hated the man for always putting his work ahead of his family. Granted Max's mother wasn't sick at the moment, but she was just coming off of major surgery, and it was Valentine's Day, for pity's sake. What the hell could possibly be more important than your own wife?

He wasn't even married to Raine and still wouldn't have thought to spend today with anyone else. He wanted to have a good time with her while he was here. He wanted to make memories…and that revelation scared him. They'd already made memories in the short time he'd been here, but part of him wanted more. A lot more.

Max glanced over at Raine. "I have the greatest idea. Grab your coat."

Raine quirked a brow at him, and he shrugged, waiting for her to argue. But, surprisingly, she grabbed her coat, hat, scarf and gloves and bundled up as he did the same.

Max whispered his plan to his mother before he left the room, and she smiled up at him, indicating he should take his time and not to worry about Abby.

He grabbed Raine's hand and led her from the room, through the kitchen and into the attached garage off the utility room.

"What are we doing?" she asked as he flicked a switch, flooding the spacious three-car garage with lights.

"You'll see."

He went to the far wall where two sleds were hanging. More than likely these old things hadn't been used since before he left for L.A., but he knew his parents never got rid of anything and kept everything in an orderly fashion.

"Are you serious?" Raine asked when he held the sleds up.

"Very serious. This California transplant can't let all this good snow go to waste."

Raine glanced back toward the inside of the house, then back to him. "But your mother…"

"Is fine," he finished. "She knows we'll be a little bit. Let's have fun. Mom is loving this baby time, and I haven't been sledding in years."

He saw the battle she waged with herself, and then a wide grin spread across her face. "Oh, all right."

They headed out the back of the house where there was a good-size slope leading down to a large pond out in the distance. Max had loved this house as a kid. Sleigh riding in the winter, fishing in the summer. Of course his dad had always been too busy for either activity, so Max usually had a buddy over.

He took his boot and cleared a pile of snow out of the way before tossing down his sled. "Let's go slow a couple times to get this packed some, then we can race."

"You're on."

By the time they'd climbed back up the hill the third time, they were both out of breath.

"Apparently I'm not in as good of shape as I thought," he said, panting.

"Well, I'm blaming the heavy meal in my belly and carrying this sled. It's not me."

Max laughed. "We'll go with that. You ready, hotshot?"

She sat the sled atop the snow and settled onto it. "Let's see what you've got."

"On three." He sat down, placing his hands beside him in the snow to push off. "One…two…three!"

They shot down the hill, her sled turned at the last minute, slamming into his and knocking them both from the sleds and into a pile of snow. Even though snow slid into the top of his coat and made his neck cold and wet, he couldn't deny he was having a blast. And Raine's sweet laughter resounded through the night, wringing his heart and making him wonder again "What if?"

With her body half on his and half in the snow, he rolled over to his back and pulled her fully onto him.

Her wide eyes stared back at him, her smile still in place.

"You're the most beautiful woman I know," he whispered. "I love to hear you laugh, to know I'm the one who brought a bit of happiness into your life."

"I'm really glad you came home. Not for the circumstances, but because I needed this." Her eyes dropped to his mouth. "I needed you."

Because anything he said at this point would be too heavy and emotional, he made better use of his mouth and slid his lips against hers. She returned his kiss softly, gently, then eased back.

"Your mom is looking better and better. I'm so glad we came tonight."

"Me, too."

"She really loves Abby."

Just as he was about to bring up Abby and the court documents he'd seen, cold, wet snow went up his shirt… thanks in part to Raine and the snowball she just shoved beneath his coat.

"Raine," he yelled, laughing as she came to her feet and started running away. "Payback's coming, sweetheart. You better run."

He quickly rolled and fisted a huge ball of snow and launched it at her back as she retreated. On cue, she squealed and returned a ball of her own. Max chased her around the flat part of the yard, volleying one ball after another until he'd had his fill, and then he charged after her and caught her around the waist. His arm wrapped around her from behind as he lifted her up. Her laughter filled the night, and Max didn't know when he'd felt this alive, this free, this in—

No. Love didn't come into play. He was just getting caught up in nostalgia. They'd been apart too long. How could he trust that he'd truly fallen back in love?

When she wiggled, Max eased her down to her feet and turned her around to face him. He smoothed the hair back from her face that had escaped her knit hat.

Raine's eyes searched his, and he knew she wanted more. He knew she wanted everything they'd dreamed of years ago. He knew it, and part of him even still ached for that. But going slow was the only option, because, if this was going to work, they had to nurture the relationship and protect it at all costs.

"You're so special, Raine," he said huskily. "You'd really like L.A. If you ever wanted to visit, I'd love to show you around."

"I'm pretty happy here."

"I am, too," he admitted. "More than I thought."

Raine gasped, and, before she could ask questions or he could say more asinine things without thinking, he captured her lips and pulled her tighter against him.

When he pulled back, she fluttered her lashes up at him, and he knew those questions hadn't left her mind, but he still wasn't ready to answer them.

"What do you say we go inside and get some hot chocolate?" he suggested. "We can relieve Mom of baby duty."

Raine nodded. "You know we aren't done here, right?"

He knew exactly what she referred to. "I know, but let's just enjoy this for now. I'm in a territory I had no idea I was heading toward, and I need to think."

"Neither of us planned this, Max. We were both blindsided, but I have to consider Abby first."

"I wouldn't expect any less from you."

She continued to hold his gaze. "And I can't afford to

let my heart get wrapped up in you again if I'm going to get hurt."

A band slid around Max's chest, squeezing tight. The ache of hearing her talk about heartbreak meshed with his own.

"I won't let you get hurt," he professed, hoping he could keep that promise. "I care for you, Raine. I care for you in a different way than I did the first time…and I have no idea what the hell to do about it."

She reached up with her gloved hand and cupped his jaw. Such delicate hands, such a strong woman.

"We'll figure this out together," she told him. "But right now I can barely feel my toes, and I need that hot chocolate you promised."

Max kissed her on her icy-cold nose and led her back into the house. He truly had no idea what he would do about these feelings he had for Raine. He only hoped to hell that, by the time he left Lenox, he had some answers, because right now all he knew was that he had the film of a lifetime waiting on him, he had a mother he was tending to, and he had an ex-girlfriend who was starting to work her way into his heart.

A heart she'd already broken once before. They had both been ripped open again upon discovering the truth. Could they risk so much for another chance?

Fifteen

Raine stopped in her tracks as she adjusted the carrier in one hand and the diaper bag in the other. She'd run out to deliver a few of her new lotions and soaps to some clients, and to leave some samples at area businesses.

After a long morning of running errands, all she wanted to do was relax and lay Abby down for a nap. But there was a note on her door, and as Raine grew closer, her smile grew wider.

Surprise waiting for you inside. Had to use spare key.
You need to find a new hiding spot.
M

In the past three weeks since Max had been in Lenox, he'd spent a good portion of his time caring for his mother, but Raine and Abby were oftentimes over there, as well. Their alone time was limited, which meant this newfound love she had for him was not based on sex.

Max Ford was still the one for her. He was the one now, just like he was the one then.

Raine slid her key into the lock and went inside. Eager to see this infamous surprise, she set her stuff down and uncovered Abby from the blanket shielding the cold air from her in the carrier.

Taking the baby, Raine started to walk through the house. She tried to focus on the anticipation, instead of her mother's phone call earlier in which Raine was scolded for spending more time with Max's mother than her.

Raine had simply stated that Elise accepted her for who she was. Granted that hadn't always been the case, but Raine loved Max's mother. She was sweet, loving and not judgmental.

Her mother had been damn lucky Raine hadn't gone off on her about Max's shocking revelation. But that conversation was not to be held over the phone. Oh, no. That would be a face-to-face meeting. Soon.

Shoving aside the hurt, Raine searched the living room, kitchen and entryway. Nothing.

Climbing the steps, she wondered if it was something big and obvious or something small, and she'd already walked right by it.

She glanced in her work space area, in the nursery, but, when she hit the doorway to her bedroom, Raine froze. There draped across the bed was a beautiful long blue gown. Another note lay atop the gown.

I've lined up a sitter. Don't worry, she's trustworthy. Be ready at five, and I'll pick you up. Tonight is all about you. Not Abby, not my mother and not work... for either of us.
M

She read the note again. Tonight was the opening of the play at the theater. Was he taking her? What about his mother? Wasn't she going to attend? Who had he lined up for a sitter?

While she was beyond thrilled with the idea of going

to the show tonight, and, even more thrilled that Max had gone to so much trouble to get this exquisite dress for her, her mind was whirling with questions.

Her cell vibrated in her pocket. Raine sat Abby in the Pack 'N' Play pen in the corner of the room and pulled her phone out, smiling at the caller ID.

"You are determined to get me to the theater again, aren't you?"

"I'm relentless when I want something," Max stated. "And since I know your mind is going a mile a minute, I'm letting you know that my mother's nurse will be watching Abby. You know Sasha from school, and she's very trust-worthy."

Okay, Raine was relieved that the sitter was someone she knew.

"Where did this dress come from?" she asked, eyeing the narrow waist and hoping the thing fit.

"That's not for you to worry about. The bathroom should have a bag with shoes, jewelry and new makeup in it. I had a lot of help from some friends, but I want you to be pampered tonight, and I want you in the front row...just like you used to be."

Tears pricked Raine's eyes, and she swallowed hard. "I can't believe you did this."

"I've been planning it for some time," he confessed. "And I knew you wouldn't accept the gifts and theater ticket if I offered, so I made sure everything was in place."

"You're sneaky." She headed to the en suite bath and nearly keeled over at the designer labels on the makeup he'd bought. "Max, I can't even imagine what you spent on this stuff. You're insane."

"No, I just want you to have nice things, and if I want to pamper you one night, I will. Now, rest up because I plan on giving you an amazing night and showing you that some-times you need to put yourself ahead of others."

"I put myself ahead of others," she insisted.

Max's rich laughter filtered through the phone. "When? From what I've seen, if it's not Abby, it's your clients. And everyone I've talked to has said what a hard worker you are and how you are always running around town delivering plants, lotions, soaps, giving advice on healthier lifestyles."

Raine shrugged even though he couldn't see. "I do what I can for my clients. It's how I make my living and am able to stay home with Abby."

"All the more reason for you to get out of the house tonight."

Raine smiled. "All right. I'll be ready at five."

"Wonderful. Sasha will be there just before, and you can go over Abby's feeding and bed schedule. I plan on keeping you out very late."

Oh, the promise in that declaration sent shivers racing through her body.

"I'll be ready."

After they said goodbye, Raine gathered up the bags of shoes and jewelry, and nearly floated back into the bedroom to look at the dress one more time. Blue was her favorite color; he hadn't forgotten. She knew this wasn't a coincidence. Max Ford hadn't forgotten one single thing about her in all the time he'd been gone.

Thrumming with anticipation, Raine set the jewelry on top of her vanity and gingerly opened the black velvet boxes. Her eyes traveled appreciatively over the expensive sparkling jewels, but she knew exactly what piece she should wear tonight.

The locket.

"Loraine."

Raine cringed as she stood from her front row seat after the final curtain call. There were only two people on this earth who called her Loraine and she knew at least one of them was standing right behind her.

As she turned, she pasted on a smile and came face to face with her parents. Yes, they all lived in the same town, but she still tried to avoid them at all costs.

"Mother, Father." She eyed her mother in her perfectly coiffed hair and her simple strand of pearls around her neck. "I didn't expect to see you here."

"Anything to help raise money for the arts," her father piped up, his voice rising to make sure all surrounding spectators heard him.

Raine nearly rolled her eyes. What he meant to say was *anything to look good for the upcoming mayoral election later in the year.* She had no doubt whatever monies her parents had donated, they were all too willing to share the amount and take all the accolades for their generosity.

"Are you alone?" her mother asked, glancing around.

"I'm here to see Max."

"Is that so?" her father asked. "I suppose you two are… friends? Marshall mentioned seeing him at your house the other day."

And Raine had no doubt if they hadn't been in public her father would've gone into greater detail, because there was no way Marshall mentioned the Max sighting in such a casual way.

Just looking at these two made her ill…a terrible thing to think about her parents, but they'd robbed her of her dreams, her life and her only love with no remorse whatsoever.

Raine slid her small clutch beneath her arm and sighed. "What I have going on in my life is none of your business. You made sure of that when you cut me off financially after deciding I was an embarrassment to you."

Her mother's eyes darted around. "Let's not get into this here, Loraine."

"Don't want to air your dirty laundry, Mother?" She laughed bitterly. "I'm pretty sure everyone already knows something happened between us. Besides, no one cares. That was years ago, and if you're still letting this rift consume you, then maybe that's the guilt talking."

Raine's father stepped forward and held up a hand. "Listen, Loraine. Let's not do this. Why don't you bring Abby over to the house this weekend?"

Raine tilted her head. "You know, I don't think so. I'm happy with my life. I don't need pity, and I don't need your money. What I always wanted from you was acceptance and love, but that will never be. And if we weren't in public promoting Max's play, I'd jump right into just how despicable you two are for your actions. Now, if you'll excuse me, I'm going backstage."

As Raine turned, her mother's words stopped her cold. "He was wrong for you years ago, and he still is, but for different reasons. He's a player, Loraine. Don't make a fool of us by chasing after Max Ford."

Oh, there were so many comebacks, but Raine chose the one that would annoy her mother the most.

Raine glanced over her shoulder, offered her sweetest smile and said, "I'm not chasing after Max. I'm just having sex with him."

Shaking and bubbling with anger, Raine gracefully walked away with a class that her mother would normally appreciate…under other circumstances. Raine had to smile as she made her way backstage. She'd never truly spoken her mind with her parents, never sassed or back talked as an adult, because, no matter how cruel her parents had been in recent years, they were still her parents.

But damn it felt good to see her mother's reaction to that proclamation. The woman deserved so much more anger spewed her way, but they were in public, and this was Max's night. Besides, she couldn't risk causing a scandal when she was still in limbo with this adoption.

Max was in his dressing room, a slew of roses in various colors sat on the vanity. He turned toward the door when she entered.

"A packed house and a standing ovation," she said. "From the whistles and roses being tossed your way, I'd say opening night was a success."

Max crossed the small room and enveloped her in his arms. "And having you in the front row was the greatest moment of the entire night."

When he eased back, his eyes darted down to her necklace. "Raine…you kept it? After all this time?"

He brought his gaze back up to hers, and she couldn't help but smile. "It meant too much. Even after you left, I couldn't get rid of it."

Max lifted the locket, popped it open and studied the picture inside. A picture of the two of them smiling for the camera on a warm, sunny day in the park. The picture was too small to capture anything but their faces, but Raine had that moment in time embedded into her mind.

"We were so young," he murmured.

Reaching up, Raine cupped the sides of his face and kissed him. "Don't go back there. Let's focus on now."

He nodded, closing the locket. "This is so much better than the jewelry I'd chosen."

"I was hoping you wouldn't mind," she said.

"Not at all." He brushed his lips ever-so-softly against hers. "You're stunning tonight."

"And you look nice with eyeliner," she teased.

His eyes gleamed mischievously. "I bet you say that to all the guys," he said.

Raine slid her hands up his bare arms. "I think you look sexy as a gladiator. Maybe you could wear this getup sometime for me."

Max nipped at her neck. "I'm wearing it now."

Swatting away his advances, she laughed. "We're in your dressing room, there are hordes of people running around outside this door, and the press is casing the place for glimpses of you when you leave."

Max snorted. "First of all, the press got enough pictures of me when I came in. Second, the door has a lock. And third, you look so damn hot in this dress, I can't wait until we get home."

"Whose home?" she asked, grinning.

"Well, my mother is at my house, and the sitter is at yours." His hand went to the zipper at the back of her glimmering blue gown and slowly unzipped until the top sagged just at her breasts. "Looks like this is it. Ever made love in a dressing room?"

Made love. The fact those two words slipped through his lips had her hoping for more.

"I have," she informed him, sliding her arms out of the fitted sleeves. "I believe it was about fifteen years ago. With you."

"Then I'd say we're past due for an encore."

Raine took a step back and allowed her dress to shimmy down her torso and puddle at her feet. Max's eyes raked down her body, giving her a visual sampling and sending shivers racing through her.

Closing the small gap between them, Max spanned her waist with his strong hands and tugged her against his chest. And, as if the dam broke, he assaulted her mouth. His hands were all over—roaming up her back, combing through her hair, pulling at her panties.

Raine ran her hands over his thick white costume and had no clue how to get him out of it. Finally, he released her long enough to extricate himself from the thing. He shucked his white boxer briefs and was on her again, this time lifting her up against him until she wrapped her legs around his waist.

Her back pressed against the wall as he pulled aside the cups to her strapless bra. Raine arched into him, allowing him all the access he wanted and more.

When he gripped her panties and literally tore them off, Raine laughed. "You really are in a hurry."

He slid into her in one swift, quick thrust. "You have no idea," he murmured against her mouth. "I've barely held it together with wanting you."

Did he mean just tonight...or for longer?

Raine tilted her hips, not wanting to worry about anything beyond right now and how amazing it felt to be with Max. He gripped her waist and slanted his lips across hers as he continued to make love to her.

In no time Raine's body shook as waves of pleasure coursed through her. Molding herself against his bare chest, she wrapped her arms around his neck and held on as he started pumping faster. His body stilled against hers, his warm breath fanning out across her shoulder and neck, sending even more chills all over her bare skin.

In an ironic sort of way, they'd come full circle. This theater held such a special place in her heart, since this is where she'd met and fallen in love with him.

Max leaned his head back, looked down at her and grinned. "I have another surprise in store for you."

Raine laughed. "I'm not quite ready again."

"Not that," he said with a slight grin. "I've arranged a dinner for us."

"Where?"

"Here."

Raine tilted her head. "Here? At the theater?"

That cocky grin spread across his face. "I wanted tonight to be special. And before you worry about the sitter, she was well paid to stay as late as we need."

Warmth spread through Raine. Max had taken care of everything, and he was all about pleasing her, meeting her needs.

But it was time they opened up about their feelings, now and years ago. Where were they headed here? Because this certainly felt like more than just a pass through. Yes, he was leaving, but would he return? Would he want to see where this long-distance relationship could lead?

And Max still didn't know the truth about the baby she'd lost. His baby. Their baby.

This evening may not be the perfect time to address it, but hadn't the past been buried long enough? There would be no ideal time, and her nerves wouldn't get any calmer. He needed to know about this adoption she was facing—fighting—as well, because, if he was truly ready to get involved with her, this adoption would affect him, too.

Looking into Max's eyes, she knew tonight would change their lives, one way or another, forever.

Sixteen

Something was off with Raine. They'd made love, though it was frantic and hurried, and a deeper bond had formed between them back in his dressing room.

But he couldn't chalk up her tension to all of that, because, when she'd stepped into the room, she'd already been wound up pretty tight. He didn't know what had happened between her arrival at the play and when it finished, but something—or someone—had upset her. If he had to wager a guess, he'd lay money on her parents.

With his hand on the small of her back, Max led her up the back stairs to the stage area.

"All of this is going to spoil me," she murmured, throwing a smile over her shoulder. "A beautiful dress, a play and now dinner on stage?"

He laughed. "Don't forget the dressing room."

"I'll never forget the dressing room."

He led her closer to the table that had been set up amid the coliseum decor. With the crisp white tablecloth, a tapered candle flickering, fine china and a single red rose across her plate, Max hadn't left out one single romantic detail.

"You went to a lot of trouble for me tonight."

"No trouble," he replied as he pulled out her cloth-covered chair. "I called McCormick's in town, asked if they could deliver a few things, and then I paid one of the guys on the crew here to set this up. I really did nothing but make a few calls."

Before sitting in her seat, Raine turned, placed her hands on his shoulders and leaned in to kiss his cheek. "You've done so much more, Max. This time that you've been here… it's been amazing. I can't thank you enough for making me take a break and have fun again."

Before she could turn and take a seat, he gripped her shoulders and slid his lips over hers. "You deserve breaks, Raine. You deserve fun. You just needed someone to show you."

Her gaze held his, and he lost himself in their beautiful emerald-green depths. This was not what he'd planned on. Nothing prepared him for all the emotions, all the feelings, he'd be forced to face. He'd pretty much been resigned to the fact he'd see Raine during his lengthy visit and had even assumed he'd be swept back into the past.

But he hadn't planned on looking at her and seeing a future.

"I ran into my parents before I saw you," she confided. "I need to talk to them about what happened."

"It won't be easy, but they need to be held accountable for ruining our lives."

Raine wound her arms around his waist and rested her head against his chest. "I have no idea what to say. I know they'll defend their actions, but they stole everything from me."

Leaning down, Max kissed her gently on the forehead. "We won't let them win."

She gazed up at him with her heart in her eyes, and Max felt a surge of emotion. So much time had passed, but his feelings were even stronger now than they were when he and Raine had been eighteen. However, their future still seemed so uncertain, and he had no clue where they went from here.

Exhaling slowly, he took her hand and helped her into her seat before taking his own. He'd made sure to have her favorites here tonight. Already they'd created memories, but he didn't want the night to end.

When he glanced across the table, he froze. Raine stared down at her plate, not moving or attempting to eat.

"You don't like the menu?" he asked.

Shaking her head, she lifted her gaze. "The menu is fine. But I think we've hit a point where I need to tell you about Abby."

He waited, not letting on that he already knew. She was opening up, and he wanted to take full advantage of this important step she was taking in their relationship.

"You've asked a couple times about Abby's father." Easing forward, Raine rested her elbows on the table. "He's not in the picture…and I'm not her biological mother. Jill is."

Max reached across the small round table and took her hands in his. "You're adopting Jill's baby?"

Raine nodded. "She's just not at a point in her life where she can care for a baby. At first she mentioned abortion, but, once we talked through everything, she realized that wasn't the best decision. I may not be financially sound, but I had to try to make this work. You know I've always wanted a family."

"I know," he whispered. "And you're Abby's mom in every way that counts, Raine. Just like Elise is mine."

A smile spread across her face. "I knew you'd get it. I hesitated on telling you, because I had to wait and see where we were going with this. At first you were just stuck at my house, but now there's so much more."

"You don't need to explain," he said gruffly. "Adopting Abby is remarkable, Raine."

"Actually, she's not legally mine, yet."

Max stroked his thumbs along the back of her hands. "When will everything be finalized?"

Blowing out a breath, Raine shrugged. "I wish I knew. My attorney can't figure out what the holdup is, either. I've been approved through Social Services with my home visits, background check and everything. All my attorney can figure is that sometimes this process takes longer than others."

That threw Max for a loop. If everything was complete, what was the problem? He would look into that, because there was no way this adoption shouldn't go through.

"I'm glad you told me," Max said. "I'm glad you're getting this dream of motherhood because you're amazing at it, Raine."

A flash of hurt flickered in her eyes, but she offered a quick smile. "There are days I question if I'm doing it right, but I just have to keep moving forward doing the best I can."

He raised his wine glass. "Then let's celebrate us, Abby and the newfound life we've discovered. We may not know what's going to happen, but for now we are happy, and I want you to remember this night forever."

Raine picked up her own glass and clinked it to his. "I'll never forget any of the time you've been back in Lenox, Max. It's been the best few weeks of my life."

Max took a long, hard drink of the wine, wishing for something stronger. Hollywood was waiting for him, but the future he'd originally planned sat directly within reach.

No matter how they decided to approach the future, he had a feeling someone would inevitably get hurt. He only prayed to God they survived this time.

Seventeen

Raine had been up all night playing over and over in her head the scenario that would greet her today when finally confronting her parents. She expected denial, defense and even derision, but she would stand her ground and not leave until she had adequate answers. She was owed that much.

Max had been much more understanding, much more supportive than she would've been if the roles had been reversed. The thought that her parents had sabotaged her life, her every dream, made her so mad she could hardly control the trembling.

Without knocking, she marched straight through the front door of her childhood home…or, more accurately, museum. The cold, sterile environment was no place to raise a child. As her rubber-soled work boots thunked through the marble foyer, Raine winced inwardly. She was just grateful that Abby had never been forced to spend much time in this place. Approaching her father's home office, she overheard another familiar male voice. Great. Just who she was *not* in the mood for.

Raine stepped into the spacious room with the back wall of floor-to-ceiling windows and took in the bright, sunshiny day. This day was about to get very dark, very fast.

"I need to talk to you," she said, interrupting whatever her father was saying.

She hadn't heard the specifics of the conversation. She was too overwrought to focus on anything but her past right now.

Marshall turned in the leather club chair he sat in. "Raine," he said, raising a brow. "You're looking…natural today."

Raine laughed, knowing full well he was referring to her farm-girl attire. "I look like this every day, Marshall. I need to speak to my father. You're excused."

"Loraine," her father exclaimed, coming to his feet. The force of his actions sent his office chair rolling back and slamming into the window. "You surely can wait until our meeting is over."

Raine crossed her arms over her chest. "Oh, it's over. I need Mother in here, as well."

Her father shook his head. "I'm sorry, Marshall. I don't know what's gotten into her. I'll call you this afternoon."

Marshall came to his feet and approached Raine. "I hope everything is okay. Would you like to call me later and talk?"

"Marshall," she told him, placing a hand on his arm. "I've been nice about this, but I'm just not interested in you in that way. We went out once, but that was it for me."

Marshall's cheeks reddened. "Can't blame a guy for trying."

More like can't blame a guy for trying to kiss the ass of her father the mayor, but whatever. She didn't have time to think or worry about Marshall's feelings right now.

Raine waited for her father to get off the house intercom. Marshall left, and moments later Raine's mother swept into the room. The woman always felt the need to make a grand entrance…pearls and all.

"What a lovely surprise…" Her mother's words trailed

off as she raked her eyes over Raine's wardrobe. "Heaven's sake, Loraine. Couldn't you have freshened up before coming out in public?"

"I showered, and my underwear is clean. That's as fresh as I get," she defended with a smile. "But I'm not here for you to look down your nose at me and throw insults my way, because you think you're on another level."

"Loraine, that's enough," her father bellowed from behind his desk. "Whatever foul mood you're in, we don't deserve this."

Raine snickered, moved around the spacious office and flopped down on the oversized leather sofa in the corner. Propping her dirty work boots upon the cushion, she glared back at her father.

"Is that so? Do you really want to get into what the two of you deserve? Because I don't think you'll like what I believe is proper punishment for your actions."

Her mother let out her signature dramatic sigh. "For heaven's sake, Loraine, I don't have time for whatever game you're playing. If you have something to say, just say it. I have a luncheon to get ready for."

"Oh, yes. We wouldn't want family to come before your precious tea and cucumber sandwiches."

Her father rounded his desk, opened his mouth, but Raine held up her hand. "No. For once you two will be quiet, and I'll do the talking. And you may want to sit because this could be a while."

Her parents exchanged worried looks and came to sit in the matching wingback chairs opposite the sofa Raine sat on.

"It's apparent you're upset," her father stated. "I've never seen you like this."

Rage bubbled in her, and she clasped her hands in her lap to control the trembling. "Ironically, I've never felt like this."

In all the scenarios in her mind she'd created over the past few days, nothing truly prepared her for this moment of confronting them about the past. She needed to keep the anger in the forefront because if she allowed that sharp, piercing hurt to come into play, she'd break down and cry.

"I'll give you guys one chance to tell me the truth about what happened when Max left for L.A. And after all this time, I believe one chance is quite generous on my part."

When both of them widened their eyes in response, she felt that sickening feeling in the pit of her stomach. A little thread of generosity within her had hoped that her parents hadn't been that cruel, that they hadn't purposely altered her future, decimating her dreams.

But the silence in the room was deafening…and heart wrenching.

"We did what we thought was best," her mother stated, straightening her shoulders. "You were too young to be that serious."

"Was I now?" Raine eased forward on the couch and glared across the space between them. "How many times did he call, Mother? How soon after he left did he try to send for me?"

Her mother shrugged. "I don't recall, Loraine. It was so long ago, I'd nearly forgotten the matter."

Tears burned her throat, but Raine willed herself to remain strong. "So let me get this straight. You'd forgotten the matter like it was a trip to the grocery store? This was my *life* you destroyed. Do you not care? Did you even care when I was crying myself to sleep night after night—or when I discovered I was pregnant? Did it ever dawn on you to tell me the truth?"

"No."

Her father's quick answer had Raine gasping. Who were these people? She'd known that they'd never been supportive but to be this heartless and cruel? The thought of *ever* treating Abby in such a manner was purely sickening.

Raine came to her feet. "I just want to know why. Not that it matters, but why would you purposely do this to me?"

"Because Max was chasing a dream, and the odds were against him of making anything of himself," his father said. "We wanted more for our little girl. Don't you understand?"

Raine laughed, though she was on the verge of tears. "What I understand is you two thought you could run my life. You thought taking away my money would make me see your way. Well, I hate to tell you, I couldn't care less about your precious money or your idiotic expectations for my life."

"You'll understand better when Abby gets older," her mother insisted. "You'll want what's best for her, too."

"Yes, I will," Raine agreed. "But even though I'll try to shelter her, I will let her make her own mistakes—and I won't stand in the way of her dreams. Maybe if you two had an ounce of what I felt for Max, you would've been pleased to see your child so happy and in love."

"You weren't in love, Raine," her father chimed in. "You two were in lust. You liked each other because you felt a connection and got a kick out of being rebellious together. And you thought fleeing to the other side of the country would secure your little fantasy."

"No, we *understood* each other," she countered. "We confided in each other because we knew how important the other's dreams were, and we didn't stifle each other."

"He left you pregnant, Loraine." Her mother came to her feet, crossing her arms over her chest. "He was off living that dream, while you were here degrading yourself."

"How dare you?" Raine asked, her voice menacingly low. "Max had no clue my condition, or I assure you, he would've been here."

Now her father rose, sighing and shaking his head. "You

think Max Ford would've given up his dream of living in L.A. and becoming an actor to stay here and play house?"

Raine leveled her gaze with him and gritted her teeth. "I know he would've. He loved me. And he more than anyone knows the consequences of coming from a broken and unloving home."

"You're still naive if you believe he's back for you," her mother said. "He's only here for his mother, and then he's gone again. Don't set yourself up for more heartache, Loraine. You have Abby to think about now."

"I know how to raise my daughter."

"She's not yours, honey," her mother said softly, as if that would ease the hurt of the words.

"She *is* mine. I am legally adopting her. She's mine in every sense of the word as soon as the judge signs off."

Anger still high and tension mounting heavily between them, Raine knew this conversation was going nowhere. She wasn't sure what she'd expected when she'd come in here. Denial and defensiveness, of course. Perhaps some antagonism, too. But a part of her had really hoped for an apology. Not that it would've changed matters, but Raine wanted to think that her parents cared.

Now she knew for sure they only cared about their image. God forbid she taint their social standing by being unwed, pregnant, with no boyfriend in sight.

But there was still a little girl inside her that had held on to that slender thread of hope that they would accept her for who she was, and not how her actions or aspirations could drive their social standings.

"Now that I know the truth, I doubt you'll be seeing much of me," she told them.

"You're just angry because it's fresh." Her father started toward her with his hands extended. "Don't say things you don't mean now."

Raine stepped back, silently refusing his gesture. "I'll

still be angry years from now, and I mean every word I've said. I will not be coming around, and, as for the trust fund you've dangled over my head for years, keep it. You've tried your damnedest to get me to see your way, but I'll never be like either of you." She released a ragged breath. "I care about helping people and making my little part of the world a better place. And I couldn't care less what others can do for me, and how far in life I will advance by lying and being deceitful."

Raine brushed past her parents and headed toward the door before she turned over her shoulder. "Oh, and stop sending Marshall to my house. In fact, consider this our last contact unless you decide you can love me for me and not for how I make you look to your friends."

Max wanted to feel sorry for himself, considering he was covered in spit up and smelled like baby powder after that very questionable diaper change. How many wipes were too many to use? And more to the point, would a hazmat suit be overkill? Because the stuff that had been in that diaper surely had to be toxic.

As Max laid Abby in her crib for a nap, he thought about Raine and wondered how her talk with her parents was going. But before he could dwell too much on that, Abby let out a wail, and Max had no clue what it meant.

He peered over the edge of the crib, and she looked up at him, her chin quivering, her face red.

"All right, little one," he said, picking her up again. "You know I'm the newbie here, and you think you can sucker me into holding you the whole time your mommy is gone, right?"

When she instantly stopped fussing, Max laughed and patted her back as she laid her head against his chest and let out a deep sigh.

Being wrapped around her little fingers was just fine with him.

Max couldn't stand the thought of her being upset. Yes, she was a baby; yes, they cried. But that special place in his heart, for that family of his own, was starting to be filled with this little bundle of sweetness.

He moved to the rocking chair in the corner of the room next to the window. Early morning sunlight streamed in, and Max cradled Abby in the crook of his arm as he rocked her. She closed her eyes, sucked on her chubby little fist and quickly fell asleep, trusting in him to keep her safe.

Max loved her. Right this moment, knowing he'd made her stop crying simply by his touch warmed a place in him that he had no idea existed. This is what he wanted…what he'd wanted years ago with Raine.

A family had never entered his mind until he'd met and fallen for Raine. Growing up, he'd known he'd been adopted, and he had also known how much his mother had loved him, but his father…well, if that man cared about Max, he had a very odd way of showing it. Max had always sworn, if he ever became a father, he would tell his child every day how much he was loved. Max studied Abby's sweet face, her long lashes sweeping over the top of her full pink cheeks, her perfectly shaped mouth, her wisps of black curly hair. Everything about her was precious, and Max found himself being pulled deeper into her innocent world. First Raine and now Abby. As if resisting one woman wasn't enough.

"You have more love than you'll ever know," he whispered to Abby as she slept peacefully. "Your mama will make sure of it."

When his cell vibrated in his pocket, he carefully shifted to the side to get it out. Checking the screen, he saw Bronson Dane's number. He couldn't take the call. Not right now. Not when he was so confused about what the hell was going on in his mind…in his heart.

And if anybody had told him months ago that he would ignore a call from Hollywood hotshot Bronson Dane, Max would've called them insane. But Bronson would leave a message, and Max would call him back when he was ready. There was so much that hinged on his decision for the future.

He could no longer deny the fact he was totally in love with Raine. More than likely those feelings had never gone away; they were just buried beneath years of hurt. But he also loved Abby, loved being back in Lenox and loved performing at the theater like he used to. Granted he'd only performed the first night, and there were several performances left, but that one live crowd was enough.

There was no way he should've fallen in love with his hometown. He'd never been one for nostalgia or getting enveloped by old memories and letting them consume him. But here he was, wondering how he could make everything work—have a family and keep his career at the status level it was.

On the flip side, there was the movie waiting for him when he returned in a few weeks. And even though his mother was really doing fine and didn't need his assistance, he wanted to stay and support her for as long as possible.

But there was no way he could be in two places at once, and Raine's heart was here in Lenox. Here in her grandmother's old home with these insane people-loving chickens, goats that goosed your rear end when you walked out and a host of renovations that required doing. Yet Raine had never needed the perfect, polished lifestyle that so many around her did. And he was just as guilty of looking for happiness in a lifestyle instead of being content with the blessings he had.

Looking back, he'd truly had it all when he'd been eighteen. Money didn't mean much because he'd been miserable, if he were honest with himself, for the past fifteen years.

And now that he'd been staying in Lenox, mostly in his childhood home, but some of the time in a house that was so much less than what he was used to, he found himself free and happy.

But he was torn between following his heart and staying true to those dreams. The major question now was, which dream did he follow?

Eighteen

Max was ready to put Abby down again when the doorbell rang.

"Who in the world is that?" he muttered, walking from the nursery toward the staircase.

He held Abby against his chest as he opened the door without looking through the side window to see who the visitor was.

And the second he opened the door, he wished he would've looked first.

"Maxwell," his father greeted.

He glared at his father as Thomas Ford eyed the baby, then brought his gaze back to Max's.

"Dad. I'm surprised to see you here." He shifted a restless Abby in his arms. "Is there a reason you came?"

His father stepped forward, causing Max to step back. "I stopped by the house to see you and your mother. When she said you were here, I decided to come see you."

"Because you think your wife doesn't need your attention?"

Max turned, disgusted with his father. Years of unresolved anger bubbled within him. He strode into the living room, leaving his father to follow or go away. He didn't really care.

"I haven't seen you in over a year," Thomas said, following Max into the living room. "I'd think you'd be more excited to see me."

Max placed Abby in her swing and turned it on low before turning back to his father. "And I'd think you'd have been here for Mom during her recovery, but I see even this health scare did nothing to alter your priorities."

Thomas took a seat on the floral sofa and crossed his ankle over his knee. "I didn't come here to argue. I just wanted to see my son, and your mother didn't know how long you'd be gone."

Max didn't offer to take his dad's coat because he didn't intend on his father staying long, so he remained standing and rested his hands on his hips. "I'll be here until Raine gets back."

"Hmm, I had no idea you two were this…involved." After a tense silence, Thomas cleared his throat. "Well, I came by because—"

Abby started fussing, and Max ignored whatever his father was about to say. He turned off the swing and eased Abby's pudgy little legs from the seat and carried her into the kitchen. Thankfully Raine had premade bottles in the fridge. She claimed Abby was okay to take them cold, and it didn't need to be warmed up in the bottle warmer.

Juggling Abby in one arm, Max pulled out a bottle and popped off the lid, letting it bounce onto the scarred countertops.

He lay Abby down in the crook of his arm and placed the bottle between her little pink lips. She greedily sucked away, and Max turned to see his father standing in the doorway.

"You're looking pretty comfortable here," Thomas claimed. "Your mother wonders if you're planning on staying."

"I'm not," he answered. "I'm here for Mom, and I'm

helping Raine, too. I have a movie to start filming at the end of next month. I can't do that from here."

"I was hoping I could talk to you about the future and your plans."

For the first time Max really studied his father. The deep creases around his eyes, his heavy lids. The man was aging, and all he had to show for it was a chain of prosperous restaurants along the East Coast. More memories were made with his work than with his family. And this fact made Max feel sorry for his father. The man's last moment on earth would be at work.

"What about my plans?" Max asked.

"I know you have no desire in taking over the restaurants," his father stated. "And I'm not asking you to give up your life. But I was hoping I could get you to consider assuming the ownership in name only. I have a very well-staffed set of managers at all locations, and I don't plan on retiring just yet, but I do need to slow down."

Max was shocked. Never in his life would he have guessed his father would cut back on work.

"Why now?" Max asked, patting Abby's bottom as she started to drift off to sleep.

"When your mother was diagnosed with cancer, I started rethinking my life. I haven't been the best husband, certainly not the best father." Thomas shook his head and sighed. "I can't go back and change what I did or didn't do, but I can make better decisions from here on out. And that's why I want to set the wheels in motion so I can concentrate on your mother...and maybe even spend more time with you, if you'd like that."

Max had to lean back against the counter, because his father's heartfelt words really rattled Max. The man had come here, seeking Max out, to have this discussion. As much as Max wanted to ignore his father's request, he couldn't. The man may have had an epiphany late in life about what was important, but he was extending that olive branch and only a total jerk would knock it away.

"This is a surprise," Max admitted to his father. "Is this something I can think about for a few days, or do you need to know now?"

"If you're willing to think about it, take your time." For the first time in longer than Max could remember, his father smiled. "I just want us to be able to be the family we should've been. And I want that no matter what you decide about the business."

Abby's lips fell away from the bottle, and milk ran down her rounded cheek as she slept. Max set the bottle on the counter and used the pad of his thumb to wipe the moisture away.

With his heart in his throat, he knew if his father was opening up about his emotions, then Max needed to, as well. He had questions, and there was only one person who could answer them.

"Why did you adopt me?" he asked, leveling his father's gaze from across the room. "I know Mom couldn't have children, but you were always so distant."

Thomas crossed the room, pulling out a chair from the mismatched set around the kitchen table. He took a seat, raked a hand over his silver hair and faced Max.

"I never really wanted children. I wasn't sure I'd make a good father. I was so intent on making a name for myself, making a nice income for Elise, because she never had a lot growing up. I was determined to provide more for her than her family had."

Something tugged at Max's heart. He'd been wanting to provide more for Raine than her family had…stability and—dare he say—love.

"I knew she wanted a child, and I was gone so much," his father went on. "I guess I thought a baby would fill the void of my absence. Hindsight is so much clearer."

Max eased Abby onto his shoulder and gently patted her back. Raine had told him if she didn't burp she could get reflux. There were so many rules for babies, but, surprisingly, Max felt he was catching on…and enjoying this little slice of parenting.

The front door opened and closed. He straightened and met Raine's eyes as she rounded the doorway into the kitchen. Her gaze went from Max to his father.

"Um…sorry, I didn't know you would be here," she said, slowly crossing the room. "Let me just take Abby and lay her down. I'll stay out of your way."

Thomas came to his feet. "No need to rush out. I need to get back to Elise."

Max met Raine's questioning look and offered a smile. "I'll be home in a little while."

Thomas nodded and glanced to Raine. "Good to see you again, Loraine. You have a beautiful baby there."

Raine smiled. "Thank you. I hope I didn't interrupt anything. I hate for you to rush off…"

Thomas grinned. "I think I'm done here, and I'll see Maxwell at home later. You two enjoy your day."

Max watched his father stroll out of the room and waited until the front door shut, leaving just him and Raine and a sleeping Abby.

"What just happened?" she asked, holding the baby to her chest.

"My dad wants to be my dad."

Raine's brows lifted. "That's…great. Why aren't you smiling?"

"Because I'm torn, and he threw a big decision at me. One I need to seriously consider."

"Want to talk about it?"

Max shook his head. "Not right now. I'd rather hear how things went with your parents."

Raine sighed. "Let me put her down."

Max followed Raine upstairs and waited outside the nursery while she lay the baby down. Once she came out and gently pulled the door closed behind her, she motioned for him to follow her into the bedroom.

"They didn't deny it," she told him, crossing her arms over her chest. "They tried to defend themselves by saying I would do the same thing for Abby to protect her from making wrong decisions."

Max felt his blood pressure soar. "How can they justify something so heartless and cold?"

Raine shook her head. "I have no idea. I just want to move on. I can't keep dwelling on the past, and I can't keep getting disappointed by them over and over again."

Max closed the space between them and enveloped her into his arms. "I'm so sorry, Raine. I want to go back in time and change things, but I know that's impossible. The truth is out now, and you can do what you want with it."

"I want to pretend my parents aren't so deceitful, but when they didn't even apologize, I knew they only were thinking of themselves and their social status."

Her arms came around his waist as her head settled perfectly beneath his chin. He honestly had no clue what he was going to do. He had so much waiting for him in L.A., yet all he could think of was what was in his arms right now.

How could he have both? Years ago they'd been ready to try, but now? Would Raine give up her life here? Would she take Abby and follow him, let go of this farm that means the world to her?

He didn't want to add to her angst, but he couldn't ignore the fact he was leaving in a few weeks.

"You mean so much to me, Raine," he whispered.

She eased back, her eyes locked onto his. "You don't sound happy about that."

"I just didn't expect to fall back into your life so easily," he admitted. "I didn't expect to get so attached to Abby."

"Why are you upset about it?"

"Because I can't stay," he said. "As much as I've loved being here, as much as I've loved every minute with you, I have a life back in L.A. and professional responsibilities."

Raine shifted out of his arms and emptiness settled in just as fast as that wall of defense erected around her when she wrapped her arms around her waist.

"I knew you'd leave," she said, her tone low, her voice sad. "I'd hoped you wouldn't, but Lenox isn't for you."

"Last night, seeing you in the front row brought back a flood of emotions for me, Raine. I wanted to turn back time when you used to sit right there and watch my performances. Back then, and now, you love this farm, and I wouldn't ask you to give it up for me. But we're different people now."

Tears slid down her cheeks.

"I know," she choked out, raising her face to meet his eyes. "How can I be upset when we've had such a wonderful time together?"

"Raine—"

She held up a hand. "No. Don't apologize for being who you are. You're Max Ford. You live in L.A., make amazing movies and live your dream. You're getting ready to take that dream to another level. If I asked you to stay, that would be selfish, and you'd resent me later."

Max ran a hand down his face, the day-old stubble scratching his palm. "I wish more than anything things could be the same."

Raine smiled as another tear escaped her bright green eyes. "I know.... Me, too. But I want you to be happy, and I know you want that for me."

"More than anything." He swiped the moisture away from her cheeks with the pads of his thumbs and kissed her lips. "Let me make love to you, Raine. Let's make the most of the time we still have together."

She melted into Max's embrace, knowing their time was limited, knowing when he left this time, she would be even more crushed than the first.

Nineteen

"That's really great, Noah," Max said as he drove through the dirty, snow-lined streets. "I'm so happy for you and Callie."

"You promise you'll be here for the wedding?"

Noah Foster's voice resounded through the speakers in Max's rental car. His best friend had finally set a date for his wedding. No way would Max miss such a special time, especially considering all that Noah and Callie had been through.

"I swear I'll be there," Max promised. "I talked with Bronson earlier today, and they were hoping to start production earlier."

"Aren't you staying with your mother until the end of April?"

Max turned onto another two-lane road, heading toward Raine's parents' house. "My mother is doing remarkably well, and actually my father has taken some time off to take her to her treatments."

"Whoa, that's shocking."

"Seems Thomas Ford had a change of heart where family is concerned." Max still wasn't sure what to think, but he was pretty excited his father had done an about-face. "He would've been here to help sooner, but he was trying to tie up loose ends at one of the restaurants before he took off."

"Sounds like this ordeal with your mom really scared some sense into him," Noah stated. "It's a shame it took that, but at least he's come around."

"He's even coming to the performance tonight to see me."

Max wasn't going to lie. The fact that his father was stepping up and showing support, after all the years of ignoring the fact that Max was an actor and a damn good one, made his heart swell.

"That's really great, Max." Noah was silent for a moment before he said, "You haven't mentioned Raine yet. Everything okay?"

Max and Noah had been friends for a long time, and Noah knew everything, including all about Raine...the early years.

"That's a botched-up mess," Max muttered, gripping his steering wheel. "I'll have to fill you in when I get home. Long story short, our relationship was sabotaged when I left here. I'm on my way to talk to her parents right now."

"Tell me you're not," Noah said. "I don't know what you found out, but doing anything when you're upset is a bad idea."

"I disagree. I think this is the perfect time for me to talk to them."

"Does Raine know what you're up to?"

Max made his final turn, the house in question sitting straight ahead atop a small hill surrounded by white, pristine snow.

"No, she doesn't," Max told his friend. "I can't leave here and not have my say with them. They hurt her, Noah. She's totally devastated, and I won't tolerate them thinking their actions were acceptable."

"You're in love with her," Noah stated simply. "And don't

even bother trying to deny it, because I can hear it in your voice. This woman has always been the one."

Max clenched his jaw because any words at this point would damn him. Noah was right. Raine had always been the one. But at this point in their lives, when they were both settled into what they loved doing, how could he uproot her? She'd promised to follow him once; he didn't think she'd offer again.

And she hadn't made any overtures to indicate otherwise. In fact, when they'd made love yesterday afternoon, it was almost as if she was starting to say goodbye. It was just best this way. Sometimes people weren't meant to be together, and there was only so much love could do.

Which meant he couldn't tell her that he loved her. If he did, he'd surely beg her to come with him. He'd offer to pay off her farm, sell it, do anything she wanted if she'd follow him to L.A. And in time she would resent him for keeping his dreams alive and well, while she relinquished everything she knew and loved.

"You still with me?" Noah asked.

Max pulled into the wide, circular drive and killed the engine. "I'm still here, but I need to go. I just pulled into the drive."

Noah sighed. "Just don't do anything too rash. If this is the woman you love, these people could be your in-laws one day."

Max snorted. "There's no chance of that."

He disconnected the call and sighed. At one time these people would've been his in-laws, but they'd destroyed any chance of that when they had decided to take fate into their own hands and ruin not only his life but Raine's. And for that alone he was going to have a serious meeting with them.

Yes, Raine would probably not like the fact that he was at her parents' house, but someone had to stand up for her.

Someone had to show her just how much support she had. She'd been fighting her battles alone for far too long, so he had to do this for her sake.

He stepped from the car and ignored the biting wind that swept right through his heavy coat. Damn, L.A. weather was so much friendlier.

After ringing the doorbell, Max stepped back and waited. So many thoughts swirled through his mind on what he wanted to say. He truly had no idea how to even begin, but something told him he'd know once he got in there, all those years of pent-up anger and hurt emotions rushing to the surface. A younger lady answered the door, dressed head to toe in black. A maid? Her eyes widened as recognition of who he was set in. That wasn't his ego talking, he was very aware that people knew who he was. But he wasn't about to throw his celebrity status around. This had nothing to do with him and everything to do with the woman he cared about.

"Hello," he said with what he hoped was a charming smile. "I need to speak with Mr. and Mrs. Monroe, please."

"Of course." She stepped back and opened the door wider. "Please, come in. They are upstairs in the study. I can go—"

"I know where the study is," he said, cutting her off. "Thank you."

Dismissing her, he walked past the young woman and made his way up the wide, curved staircase. Fury bubbled within him at the fact these people lived like this, while Raine's house was falling apart.

Selfish snobs.

As he moved down the hall, he stopped when he recognized Marshall's voice.

"I've done all I can to stop the adoption from going through, but there's nothing else I can do to hold it off,"

Marshall said. "Raine passed all inspections and home visits from social services."

Max waited in the hall, just outside the door, and he had a feeling his temper was going to go from bad to worse very, very soon.

"You have a law degree," Raine's father barked. "How can you not find a loophole to halt this adoption? She's a single mother for crying out loud."

Max fisted his hands at his sides but remained quiet.

"And she has no money," her mother chimed in. "This is ridiculous. Why does she insist on being so stubborn?"

"One reason the courts are moving ahead is because this is the home where Jill wants the baby. Hard to argue with the mother's wishes, especially when the guardian is the mayor's daughter."

"And being the mayor you'd think my assistant could pull some strings," her father complained.

"She's going to be even more difficult since she learned what happened years ago." Her mother's tone softened. "Maybe we should've let her go. Maybe she would've learned her lesson and come back home eventually—"

"No, had she gone when Max left, he would've married her," Marshall argued. "If for no other reason than for the baby."

Max froze. *Baby? What the hell?*

"That was a blessing she lost that child," her mother said. "My God, it was nearly impossible to keep that a secret."

The wide hallway suddenly became narrower, as Max's world slowly closed in on him. Raine had been pregnant when he'd left? Why hadn't she told him?

An image of Raine pregnant with his child nearly brought him to his knees.

Max swallowed, raked a hand over his face and planned his next move. First, he needed to talk with those three hypocrites in the room behind him. Then, he'd go have a very long talk with Raine.

Dear Lord. He'd been a father?

Between that crushing blow and the fact these people—who supposedly cared about Raine—were trying to prevent her adoption, Max needed to clear his head and fast. He had come here for a reason, but his motives had just changed.

Stepping around the door frame, Max met the eyes of Marshall and Raine's father. Then her mother turned, her mouth dropping open as she gasped.

"Not expecting company, I see," Max said easily as he crossed the room to stand with the three people he loathed most in the world. "I was able to hear enough of your little powwow to know that Raine's life is still being manipulated by the people who are supposed to love and care for her the most."

"This is really none of your concern." Her mother lifted her chin, then crossed her arms over her chest. "And it is extremely rude to just barge in here."

Max glared at her. "You really want to lecture me on manners? I don't think you want to go there."

"What do you need, Max?" Raine's father asked.

With a shrug, Max met the man's gaze. "I'm just here to stand up for Raine. To let you all know that I'll be leaving soon, but I know enough now to realize that I need to make a few things clear before I go."

Marshall laughed. "You have no business here, no matter who you are."

In a flash, Max reached out and had Marshall by the collar, eliciting another gasp from Raine's mother. "Don't even think of running your mouth to me. What kind of a man would purposely try to keep a child away from a loving mother? You're a lowlife, spineless jerk, and you belong with these two."

He shoved the man away and looked back to Raine's father.

"Get out, Max."

"I will," he agreed. "But first let me tell you, if this adoption doesn't go through, I will raise all kinds of hell in this town. I never use my status to get what I want, but I will do that, and more, if Raine doesn't keep Abby. You remember that the next time you all try to play God with Raine's life."

"She could have a much better life," her mother pleaded. "If she'd just listen to her father and me. She could have her money and find someone worthy to settle down with."

"First of all, Raine doesn't care about the money. She cares about people, though I have no idea where she learned that fact of life from." Max shoved his hands in his jean pockets, rocked back on his heels. "Second of all, you don't get to decide who is worthy for her. Raine is happy with her life, and, when she wants to settle down, she will."

And it would kill him. Knowing she'd fallen in love and made a life with another man would absolutely crush him.

"You altered our lives years ago," he went on. "Now stay away from her if you're not going to be supportive."

"Supportive?" Marshall piped up. "You left when she was pregnant."

Waves of fury coursed through him. "If you don't shut the hell up, I'm going to punch you in the face. I think we all know why I wasn't around for the baby."

His eyes found Raine's parents as he forced himself to remain calm and not go all Alpha male and start throwing things.

"You won't tell Raine—"

Max laughed at her mother's final plea. "About you trying to sabotage her future again? You bet I will. I don't lie to those I care about."

He turned to walk out the door and glanced back over his shoulder. "Oh, and, Mayor? I wouldn't worry about running for reelection. I have a feeling things wouldn't work out for you."

"Did you just threaten me?"

Max smiled. "Not at all. Just letting you know how it feels to have your dreams and future altered."

He all but ran down the stairs and out the door. He needed air. He needed to think.

He needed to get to Raine.

A baby? They'd been so ready to start their future, and she'd been pregnant. Had she known when he'd left? Why hadn't she said anything…then or now? How could she keep something so vital from him?

Nausea welled up, and he had to remember to take deep breaths as he slid behind the wheel of the car. Gripping the steering wheel, he closed his eyes and prayed for strength… because, God help him, if Raine knew about that baby before he left, he wouldn't be able to look her in the eye again.

Twenty

Raine carefully sprinkled two little seeds into each of the small pots lined up along her workstation on the enclosed patio. The small heater kept the space warm enough for the plants to thrive in the winter months and warm enough for Abby to enjoy her little bouncy seat while Raine worked.

The side door to her home opened and closed. Raine eased her head around the patio door to see in through the kitchen. Max stomped the snow off his boots and shrugged out of his coat, laying it over the back of a kitchen chair. He never failed to make her heart skip, make her stomach get all tied in wonderful knots. He was beautiful, all tall and broad.

"I'm out here," she called before taking bits of rich soil and covering each of the seeds. He hadn't mentioned coming by today, but she was glad he had. With his evenings taken up with the performances, she treasured their time together during the day.

"Hey," she said with a smile as he stepped down onto the patio. "What's up?"

"I just came from your parents."

Raine's hands froze in the dirt. "What?"

"I wanted to have a talk with them before I go back to L.A."

Dread settled into her stomach. "But you're not leaving for another month."

He rested a shoulder against the wall beside her workbench. "Bronson called this morning, and he wants to start filming as soon as possible. With my father taking a break from work, and my mother doing so well with her radiation, I've decided to head back at the end of the week when the play wraps up."

She knew this moment was coming; she just hadn't planned on it being so soon. They were supposed to have more time.

Tears pricked her eyes as she tried to focus back on planting. "What did you need to see my parents about?"

"I wanted them to quit making your life miserable," he told her. "But when I arrived, Marshall was there, and I got some bombshells of my own."

Covering the last seed in soil, Raine slid off her gloves and turned to face him. "What's that?"

"Your parents were trying to stop this adoption, and Marshall was helping them."

"What?" she gasped. "They wouldn't do that to me."

Max quirked a brow. But didn't offer a response.

Raine's eyes darted to Abby who had fallen fast asleep in the bouncy seat. Fear clutched Raine, squeezing the breath right out of her lungs.

"Why?" she whispered.

"Because they still want to control you, and you're not the daughter they wanted you to be. You have a mind of your own, and they don't like it."

Raine rubbed her forehead, feeling a headache coming on. How could her parents be so cruel? At what point would they stop trying to ruin her life?

"I learned something else while I was there," he said, his voice low.

She met his gaze, and a muscle ticked in his jaw. The

way he looked at her with heavy lids, flared nostrils…
something was wrong.

"What is it?" she asked.

"We had a baby."

He knew. Her parents had taken one last stab at killing
anything she and Max may have shared. Raine gripped the
edge of her workbench and willed her knees not to buckle.

"Yes, I was pregnant." Her eyes met his and held. "We
had a little boy."

Max's shoulders sagged, and he exhaled as if he'd been
holding it, waiting to hear the truth from her.

"I'm sorry, Max. I'm so sorry."

Raine couldn't stop the tears. Couldn't stop from thinking of that dark time when she'd wanted that baby and this
man in her life. And she'd ended up losing both.

"When would you have told me?" he asked. "Ever?"

Raine swallowed, trying to get her emotions in check,
because this conversation was happening whether she was
ready or not.

"Someday," she said honestly. "I couldn't yet. We were
still so emotionally damaged from everything in our past.
I just couldn't pile on more hurt. And I was scared."

"Of what?"

Her eyes held his. "That you'd hate me."

Max wiped a hand down his face and pushed off the
wall. Closing the space between them, he gripped her shoulders and forced her to look at him.

"Did you know before I left?" he asked.

She stared up at him and shook her head. "No," she
whispered. "I found out after you left. We'd made love that
night before. That's when I got pregnant."

Tears glistened in his blue eyes, and Raine wrapped her
arms around him, as if she could absorb some of the hurt.

"I wanted to tell you, Max. But I waited to hear from
you and…well, you know how that panned out."

"I hate them," he rasped. "I hate them for destroying something we had. Just tell me, what happened to our son?"

"I went into labor at twenty-eight weeks. He wasn't developed enough, and they couldn't save him." Raine forced herself to keep talking through the pain. "He was so tiny, and to me he was perfect. I planned a funeral out of town for him a few days later, but I had to stay away because my parents would only agree to pay for it if I still kept the secret. Heaven forbid people in the town know.

"Ironically, my parents didn't even come to the graveside service. It was pretty much me, Jill, my grandmother and the pastor."

He studied her face and swiped away her tears. "You must hate me for not being here. I can't even imagine what you went through, because right now my heart is breaking."

"It was the worst moment of my life," she admitted. "That's why keeping Abby is so important to me. I can't lose her."

"You won't. I've made sure of that."

His hardened tone told her that he had indeed done something to make sure this adoption would go through. She didn't need to know what, just knowing this man was in her corner was enough to have her heart swelling.

Silence enveloped them before Max eased back, dropped his hands, forcing her to drop hers. "Why not tell me about the pregnancy when I came back?" he asked.

Raine shrugged. "I really didn't know how to tell you. It was so long ago, yet the emotions are still just as raw. Seeing you, it brought all of that back again, and I wanted to get a better grasp on it before I opened up to you."

"I deserved to know, Raine."

She hitched in a breath. "Yes, you did. But I know how much I still hurt over the loss, and I couldn't stand the thought of hurting you that way. Not when I'd fallen in love with you again."

Max shook his head. "Don't. Please don't tell me you love me, Raine. I can't stay here, and I don't want to leave you hurting again."

Too late.

"I can't keep my feelings inside, Max. I know you're leaving, but you have to know how I feel."

"I can't give you what you want, what you deserve," he said. "It's not fair for you to give your love to me again, when I'm not going to be here."

Raine wanted to know; she had to know.

"Do you love me?" she asked. "Honestly?"

Those magnificent blue eyes held hers. "More than I thought I could."

God, was it worse knowing? She choked back a sob.

"I knew you did," she whispered. "I knew it by your actions, but hearing you say it…"

As much as she hated it, she started to cry. Her hands came up to shield her face as Max's warm, strong arms enveloped her. She sobbed into his chest for the love they shared, for the love that couldn't be bridged through the distance. All the years apart had driven an impossible wedge through them.

Raine stepped back, wiped her face. "I'm sorry. I just… I hate this. It's like we were given a glimpse at a second chance, but I knew it wouldn't work."

Max swiped at his eyes, too macho to have a sniveling crying fit like she'd done. "I can't ask you to leave here, Raine. And I can't stay."

Obviously love did have its boundaries, because, if he'd asked her to come with him, she would. Maybe he wasn't ready for the family life; maybe he was too set in his ways in L.A.; maybe he enjoyed living freely without being tied down to one woman and a baby.

Glancing down at Abby, Raine knew there was no

way she'd give up this baby. But giving up this house, the farm—she'd sacrifice all that for Max.

"I need to get to the theater since tonight's performance starts earlier," he said. "My mom and dad are coming. Maybe you'd like to see if Sasha could watch Abby and come sit in the front row one last time?"

As much as she wanted to, she couldn't. Nothing would compare to the other night when they'd made love in his dressing room, had dinner on the stage. She wanted that memory to be the last one in the theater, because she doubted she'd ever step foot in there again.

"I can't," she told him. "It's better this way."

Max nodded. "So, this is it? Are we saying goodbye here?"

Too choked up with emotion to speak, Raine bit her quivering lip and nodded.

Max placed his hands on either side of her face and forced her to look him in the eye. "I do love you, Raine. Never doubt that. And if you ever need me, just call."

She needed him now. She needed him to stay, to be her rock and her partner. But it wasn't fair to ask him to give up his life in L.A. for Lenox.

"I want…" Max stopped, shook his head and dropped his hands. "Will you call me? Keep me updated on Abby and how you're doing?"

"Sure." *God, this was lame.* "I'll let you know when the adoption goes through."

He stared at her another minute, then he turned, squatted down to a sleeping Abby and kissed her forehead. "Take care of your mommy for me, little one."

Raine nearly threw her arms around him and begged him to stay, but she held herself in place as Max spared her one last glance over his shoulder.

"Goodbye, Raine."

"Bye, Max."

And he was gone.

Raine couldn't hold herself together another second. The dam burst, and she buried her head in her hands, resting her elbows on the wooden bench.

How could a heart be ripped apart so many times in one life and still keep beating?

She would get past this; she knew she was strong…and that she had so much to live for. After all, she still had Abby. She'd wanted a baby for years, and here she was a mother. So she had to look to the blessings she had and find a reason to smile again.

And she would…eventually. But right now, she wanted to throw a self-pity party and feel sorry for all she'd lost.

How would she ever be able to look at pictures of Max in the media or see a movie starring him and not remember how those hands had felt on her body? How he'd gone to her parents and taken up for her—and Abby? How he'd looked with tears in his eyes as he had told her goodbye—

When a large hand brushed across her arm, Raine jumped and turned to see Max. His coat was covered with snow, as was his hair.

"What are you doing?" she sniffed, embarrassed he'd caught her having a breakdown.

"I fell," he said with a smile. "Literally. Bess and Lulu came running out and tripped me. Then the chickens joined in."

Raine smiled at the mental image, then reached up to touch his face. "Are you hurt?" she asked.

Max gripped her hands and held them between his icy ones. "Yes. I'm miserable. I said goodbye two minutes ago, and I can't handle it, Raine. How will I live across the country knowing my heart is here?"

Hope spread through her. *Please, please, please, let him be saying he wants more.*

"I don't care where we live," he said. "If I have to live

on the farm and fly to L.A. when necessary, then I will. Or if you want to sell and move, we'll do that. I just can't leave, Raine. I can't leave you."

She threw her arms around him, not caring about the snow wetting her long-sleeved T-shirt. She squeezed him, never wanting to let him go.

"What made you change your mind?" she asked as she eased back.

"When your crazy goats tripped me, I laughed. I mean, how could I leave here? I love everything about it. I want to make a home with you and Abby, if you'll let me. I know that may take more time in the courts for me to be her adoptive father, but—"

"You're serious?" Raine asked. "You want to be her father?"

Max bent down and captured Raine's lips in a soul-searing kiss. "And your husband."

Raine squealed, waking Abby. "Oops," she said, laughing.

"Let me get her," Max offered.

He lifted her from the bouncy seat and rested her against his dry shoulder. "I have the two most beautiful girls in the world," he said, wrapping his wet arm around Raine. "Nothing is more important than this right here."

"But what about the film you're going to start shooting?" she asked.

"You can come with me for a bit until you need to be back for your Farmer's Market."

"You're not embarrassed that I like to make and sell my own things? I mean, you can purchase whatever you want, and I'm scraping by here."

"You have a career you enjoy, Raine. I would never take that from you."

Raine smiled up at him. "I love you."

Max kissed her forehead. "I love you, too. Now, we

need to add some livestock to this farm and get this house fixed up."

"To sell?" she asked.

"Sell? Hell, no, we're not selling. We can keep a place on each coast. I have a feeling we'll be traveling a lot, because I'm going to spend as much time with you as humanly possible. I'm also going to want more babies."

Raine laughed. "You really want it all. Amazing you got all of that from Bess and Lulu tripping you."

"I fell for you long ago, Raine. I know when I have a good thing, and I don't plan on ever letting go." Max slid his arm around her, pulling her in tight against his chest. "I plan on holding both of my girls forever."

* * * * *

"Are you all right?"

Elena cupped Nick's jaw and tried for a confident smile. "I'm fine."

One long finger stroked down her cheek, sending a raw shimmer through her. "Then why do I get the feeling that you're not quite comfortable with this?"

"Probably because I haven't done *this* in a while."

Something flared in his gaze. "How long?"

"Uh—around six years, I guess."

He said something soft beneath his breath. "Six years ago you slept with me."

The breath caught in her throat. "I'm surprised you remember."

"I'm not likely to forget," he said quietly, "since you were a virgin."

For a split second she was afraid he might abandon the whole idea of making love, so she took a deep breath and boldly trailed a hand down his chest. "I'm not a virgin now."

He trapped her hand beneath his, then used it to pull her close so that she found herself half-sprawled across his chest. "Good."

* * *

Just One More Night
is part of The Pearl House series: Business
and passion collide when two dynasties forge
ties bound by love

JUST ONE
MORE NIGHT

BY
FIONA BRAND

MILLS &
BOON®

Published in Great Britain 2014
by Mills & Boon, an imprint of Harlequin (UK) Limited,
Eton House, 18-24 Paradise Road, Richmond, Surrey, TW9 1SR

© 2014 Fiona Gillibrand

ISBN: 978 0 263 91457 3

51-0214

Fiona Brand lives in the sunny Bay of Islands, New Zealand. Now that both her sons are grown, she continues to love writing books and gardening. After a life-changing time in which she met Christ, she has undertaken study for a bachelor of theology and has become a member of The Order of St Luke, Christ's healing ministry.

To the Lord, whose "word is a lamp unto my feet, and a light unto my path."
—*Psalms* 119

For God so loved the world that he gave his one and only Son, that whoever believes in him shall not perish but have eternal life.
—*John* 3:16

Many thanks to Stacy Boyd, Allison Carroll and all of the editorial staff who work so hard to help shape and polish each book, and always do a fabulous job.

One

Elena Lyon would never get a man in her life until she surgically removed every last reminder of Nick Messena from hers!

Number one on her purge list was getting rid of the beach villa located in Dolphin Bay, New Zealand, in which she had spent one disastrous, passionate night with Messena.

As she strolled down one of Auckland's busiest streets, eyes peeled for the real estate agency she had chosen to handle the sale, a large sign emblazoned with the name Messena Construction shimmered into view, seeming to float in the brassy summer heat.

Automatic tension hummed, even though the likelihood that Nick, who spent most of his time overseas, was at the busy construction site was small.

Although, the sudden conviction that he was there, and watching her, was strong enough to stop her in her tracks.

Taking a deep breath, she dismissed the overreaction which was completely at odds with her usual calm precision and girded herself to walk past the brash, noisy work site. Gaze averted from a trio of bare-chested construction workers, Elena decided she couldn't wait to sell the beach villa. Every time she visited, it seemed to hold whispering echoes of the intense emotions that, six years ago, had been her downfall.

Emotions that hadn't appeared to affect the dark and dangerously unreliable CEO of Messena Construction in the slightest.

The rich, heady notes of a tango emanating from her handbag distracted Elena from an embarrassingly loud series of whistles and catcalls.

A breeze whipped glossy, dark tendrils loose from her neat French pleat as she retrieved the phone. Pushing her glasses a little higher on the delicate bridge of her nose, she peered at the number glowing on her screen.

Nick Messena.

Her heart slammed once, hard. The sticky heat and background hum of Friday afternoon traffic dissolved and she was abruptly transported back six years....

To the dim heat of what had then been her aunt Katherine's beach villa, tropical rain pounding on the roof. Nick Messena's muscular, tanned body sprawled heavily across hers—

Cheeks suddenly overwarm, she checked the phone, which had stopped ringing. A message flashed on the screen. She had voice mail.

Her jaw locked. It had to be a coincidence that Nick had rung this afternoon when she was planning one of her infrequent trips back to Dolphin Bay.

Her fingers tightened on the utilitarian black cell, the perfect no-nonsense match for her handbag. Out of the blue, Nick had started ringing her a week ago at her apartment in Sydney. Unfortunately, she had been off guard enough to actually pick up the first call, then mesmerized enough by the sexy timbre of his voice that she'd been incapable of slamming the phone down.

To make matters worse, somehow, she had ended up agreeing to meet him for dinner, as if the searing hours she'd spent locked in his arms all those years ago had never happened.

Of course, she hadn't gone, and she hadn't canceled, either. She had stood him up.

Behaving in such a way, without manners or consideration, had gone against the grain. But the jab of guilt had been swamped by a warming satisfaction that finally, six years on, Messena had gotten a tiny taste of the disappointment she had felt.

The screen continued to flash its message.

Don't listen. Just delete the message.

The internal directives came a split second too late. Her thumb had already stabbed the button that activated her voice mail.

Nick's deep, curt voice filled her ear, shooting a hot tingle down her spine and making her stomach clench.

This message was simple, his number and the same arrogant demand he'd left on her answerphone a number of times since their initial conversation: *Call me.*

For a split second the busy street and the brassy glare of the sun glittering off cars dissolved in a red mist.

After six years? During which time he had utterly ignored her existence and the fact that he had ditched her after just one night.

Like that was going to happen.

Annoyed with herself for being weak enough to listen to the message, she dropped the phone back into her purse and stepped off the curb. No matter how much she had once wanted Nick to call, she had never fallen into the trap of chasing after a man she knew was not interested in her personally.

To her certain knowledge Nick Messena had only ever wanted two things from her. Lately, it was the recovery of a missing ring that Nick had mistakenly decided his father had gifted to her aunt. A scenario that resurrected the scandalous lie that her aunt Katherine—the Messena family's housekeeper—had been engaged in a steamy affair with Stefano Messena, Nick's father.

Six years ago, Nick's needs had been a whole lot simpler: he had wanted sex.

The blast of a car horn jerked her attention back to the busy street. Adrenaline rocketing through her veins, Elena hurried out of the path of a bus and stepped into the air-conditioned coolness of an exclusive mall.

She couldn't believe how stupid she had been to walk across a busy street without taking careful note of the traffic. Almost as stupid as she'd been six years ago on her birthday when she'd been lonely enough to break every personal rule she'd had and agree to a blind date.

The date, organized by so-called friends, had turned out to be with Messena, the man she'd had a hopeless crush on for most of her teenage years.

At age twenty-two, with a double degree in business and psychology, she should have been wary of such an improbable situation. Messena had been hot and in demand. With her long dark hair and creamy skin, and her legs—her best feature—she had been passable. But with her propensity to be just a little plump, she hadn't been in Messena's league.

Despite knowing that, her normal common sense had let her down. She had made the fatal mistake of believing in the heated gleam in Nick's gaze and the off-the-register passion. She had thought that Messena, once branded a master of seduction by one notorious tabloid, was sincere.

Heart still pumping too fast, she strolled through the rich, soothing interior of the mall, which, as luck would have it, was the one that contained the premises for Coastal Realty.

The receptionist—a lean, elegant redhead—showed her into Evan Cutler's office.

Cutler, who specialized in waterfront developments and central city apartments, shot to his feet as she stepped through the door. Shadow and light flickered over an expanse of dove-gray carpet, alerting Elena to the fact that Cutler wasn't the sole occupant of the room.

A second man, large enough to block the sunlight that would otherwise have flooded through a window, turned, his black jacket stretched taut across broad shoulders, his tousled dark hair shot through with lighter streaks that gleamed like hot gold.

A second shot of adrenaline zinged through her veins. *"You."*

Nick Messena. Six feet two inches of sleekly muscled male, with a firm jaw and the kind of clean, chiseled cheekbones that still made her mouth water.

He wasn't male-model perfect. Despite the fact that he was a wealthy businessman, somewhere along the way he had gotten a broken nose and a couple of nicks on one cheekbone. The battered, faintly dangerous look, combined with a dark five-o'clock shadow—and that wicked body—and there was no doubting he was potent. A dry, low-key charm and a reputation with women that scorched, and Nick was officially hot.

Her stomach sank when she noticed the phone in his hand.

Eyes a light, piercing shade of green, clashed with hers. "And you didn't pick up my call, because…?"

The low, faintly gravelly rasp of his voice, as if he had just rolled out of a tangled, rumpled bed, made her stomach tighten. "I was busy."

"I noticed. You should check the street before you cross."

Fiery irritation canceled out her embarrassment and other more disturbing sensations that had coiled in the pit of her stomach. Positioned at the window, Nick would have had a clear view of her walking down the street as he had phoned. "Since when have you been so concerned about my welfare?"

He slipped the phone into his jacket pocket. "Why wouldn't I be? I've known you and your family most of my life."

The easy comment, as if their families were on friendly terms and there hadn't been a scandal, as if he hadn't slept with her, made her bristle. "I guess if anything happened to me, you might not get what you want."

The second the words were out Elena felt ashamed. As ruffled and annoyed as she was by Nick, she didn't for a moment think he was that cold and calculating. If the assertion that her aunt and Stefano Messena had been having an affair when they were killed in a car accident, *the same night she and Nick had made love,* had hurt the Lyon family, it went without saying it had hurt the Messenas.

Her jaw tightened at Nick's lightning perusal of her olive-green dress and black cotton jacket, and the way his attention lingered on her one and only vice, her shoes. The clothes were designer labels and expensive, but she was suddenly intensely aware that the dark colors in the middle of summer looked dull and boring. Unlike the shoes, which were strappy and outrageously feminine, the crisp tailoring and straight lines were more about hiding curves than displaying them.

Nick's gaze rested briefly on her mouth. "And what is it, exactly, that you think I want?"

A question that shouldn't be loaded, but suddenly was, made her breath hitch in her throat. Although the thought that Nick could possibly have any personal interest in her now was ridiculous.

And she was absolutely not interested in him. Despite the hot looks, *GQ* style and killer charm, he had a blunt, masculine toughness that had always set her subtly on edge.

Although she could never allow herself to forget that, through some weird alchemy, that same quality had once cut through her defenses like a hot knife through butter. "I already told you I have no idea where your lost jewelry is."

"But you are on your way back to Dolphin Bay."

"I have better reasons for going there than looking for your mythical lost ring." She lifted her chin, abruptly certain that Nick's search for the ring, something that the female members of his family could have done, was a ploy and that he had another, shadowy, agenda. Although what that agenda could be, she had no clue. "More to the point, how did you find out I would be here?"

"You haven't been returning my calls, so I rang Zane."

Her annoyance level increased another notch that Nick had intruded even further into her life by calling his cousin, and her boss, Zane Atraeus. "Zane is in Florida."

Nick's expression didn't alter. "Like I said, you haven't returned my calls, and you didn't turn up for our…appointment in Sydney. You left me no choice."

Elena's cheeks warmed at his blunt reference to the

fact that she had failed to meet him for what had sounded more like a date than a business meeting at one of Sydney's most expensive restaurants.

She had never in her life missed an appointment, or even been late for one, but the idea that Nick's father had paid her aunt off with jewelry, *the standard currency for a mistress,* had been deeply insulting. "I told you over the phone, I don't believe your father gave Aunt Katherine anything. Why would he?"

His expression was oddly neutral. "They were having an affair."

She made an effort to control the automatic fury that gripped her at Nick's stubborn belief that her aunt had conducted a sneaky, underhanded affair with her employer.

Quite apart from the fact that her aunt had considered Nick's mother, Luisa Messena, to be her friend, she had been a woman of strong morals. And there was one powerful, abiding reason her aunt would never have gotten involved with Stefano, or any man.

Thirty years ago Katherine Lyon had fallen in love, completely, irrevocably, and he had *died.*

In the Lyon family the legend of Katherine's unrequited love was well respected. Lyons were not known for being either passionate or tempestuous. They were more the steady-as-you-go type of people who tended to choose solid careers and marry sensibly. In days gone by they had been admirable servants and thrifty farmers. Unrequited love, or love lost in any form was a novelty.

Elena didn't know who Aunt Katherine's lover had been because her aunt had point-blank refused to talk about him. All she knew was that her aunt, an exceptionally beautiful woman, had remained determinedly single and had stated she would never love again.

Elena's fingers tightened on the strap of her handbag. "No. They were not having an affair. Lyon women are not, and never have been, the playthings of wealthy men."

Cutler cleared his throat. "I see you two have met."

Elena turned her gaze on the real estate agent, who was a small, balding man with a precise manner. There were no confusing shades with Cutler, which was why she had chosen him. He was factual and efficient, attributes she could relate to in her own career as a personal assistant.

Although, it seemed the instant she had any contact with Nick Messena, her usual calm, methodical process evaporated and she found herself plunged into the kind of passionate emotional excess that was distinctly un-Lyon-like. "We're acquainted."

Nick's brows jerked together. "I seem to remember it was a little more than that."

Elena gave up the attempt to avoid the confrontation Nick was angling for and glared back. "If you were a gentleman, you wouldn't mention the past."

"As I recall from a previous conversation, I'm no gentleman."

Elena blushed at his reference to the accusation she had flung at him during a chance meeting in Dolphin Bay, a couple of months after their one night together. That he was arrogant and ruthless and emotionally incapable of sustaining a relationship. "I don't see why I should help drag the Lyon name through the mud one more time just because you want to get your hands on some clunky old piece of jewelry you've managed to lose."

His brows jerked together. "I didn't lose anything, and you already know that the missing piece of jewelry is a diamond ring."

And knowing the Messena family and their extreme wealth, the diamond would be large, breathtakingly expensive and probably old. "Aunt Katherine would have zero interest in a diamond ring. In case you didn't notice, she was something of a feminist and she almost never wore jewelry. Besides, if she was having a *secret* affair with your father, what possible interest would she have in wearing an expensive ring that proclaimed that fact?"

Nick's gaze cooled perceptibly. "Granted. Nevertheless, the ring is gone."

Cutler cleared his throat and gestured that she take a seat. "Mr. Messena has expressed interest in the villa you've inherited in Dolphin Bay. He proposed a swap with one of his new waterfront apartments here in Auckland, which is why I invited him to this meeting."

Elena suppressed her knee-jerk desire to say that, as keen as she was to sell, there was no way she would part with the villa to a Messena. "That's very interesting," she said smoothly. "But at the moment I'm keeping my options open."

Still terminally on edge at Nick's brooding presence, Elena debated stalking out of the office in protest at the way her meeting with Cutler had been hijacked.

In the end, feeling a little sorry for Cutler, she sat in one of the comfortable leather seats he had indicated. She soothed herself with the thought that if Nick Messena, the quintessential entrepreneur and businessman, wanted to make her an offer, then she should hear it, even if only for the pleasure of saying no.

Instead of sitting in the other available chair, Nick propped himself on the edge of Cutler's desk. The casual lounging position had the effect of making him look even larger and more muscular as he loomed over her.

"It's a good deal. The apartments are in the Viaduct and they're selling fast."

The Viaduct was the waterfront area just off the central heart of the city, which overlooked the marina. It was both picturesque and filled with wonderful restaurants and cafés. As an area, it was at the top of her wish list because it would be so easy to rent out the apartment. A trade would eliminate the need to take out a mortgage to afford a waterfront apartment, something the money from selling the villa wouldn't cover completely.

Nick's gaze skimmed her hair, making her aware that, during her dash across the road, silky wisps had escaped to trail and cling to her cheeks and neck. "I'll consider a straight swap."

Elena stiffened and wondered if Nick was reading her mind. A swap would mean she wouldn't have to go into debt, which was tempting. "The villa has four bedrooms. I'd want at least two in an apartment."

He shrugged. "I'll throw in a third bedroom, a dedicated parking space, and access to the pool and fitness center."

Three bedrooms. Elena blinked as a rosy future without the encumbrance of a mortgage opened up. She caught the calculating gleam in Nick's eye and realized the deal was too good. There could be only one reason for that. It had strings.

He was deliberately dangling the property because he wanted her to help him find the missing ring, which he no doubt thought, since she didn't personally have it, must still be in the old villa somewhere.

Over her dead body.

Elena swallowed the desire to grasp at what was an exceptionally good real estate deal.

She couldn't do it if it involved selling out in any way

to a Messena. Maybe it was a subtle point, but after the damage done to her aunt's reputation, even if it was years in the past, *and after her own seduction,* she was determined to make a stand.

Lyon property was not for sale to a Messena, just like Lyon women were not for sale. She met Nick's gaze squarely. "No."

Cutler's disbelief was not mirrored on Nick's face. His gaze was riveted on her, as if in that moment he found her completely, utterly fascinating.

Another small heated tingle shot down her spine and lodged in her stomach.

As if, in some perverse way, he had liked it that she had said no.

Two

Elena dragged her gaze from the magnetic power of Nick's and fought the crazy urge to stay and continue sparring with him.

Pushing to her feet, she bid Cutler good day, picked up her handbag and stepped out the door. Nick was close enough behind her that the sudden overpowering sense that she was being pursued sent another hot, forbidden thrill zinging through her.

The door snapped closed. Nick's firm tread confirmed that he was in pursuit and the faint, heady whiff of his cologne made her stomach clench. Clamping down on the wimpy feeling that she was prey and Nick was a large, disgruntled predator, Elena lengthened her stride and walked briskly past the receptionist out into the mall.

She had just stepped out of air-conditioned coolness into the humid heat of the street when a large tanned hand curled briefly around her upper arm. "What I don't get is why you're still so angry."

Elena spun and faced Nick, although that was a mistake because she was suddenly close enough that she could see a pulse jumping along the line of his jaw.

She tilted her chin to meet his gaze, unbearably aware that while she was quite tall at five foot eight, Nick was several inches taller and broad enough that he actually made her feel feminine and fragile. "You shouldn't have crashed my meeting with Cutler or tried to pressure me when you knew ahead of time how I felt."

There was an odd, vibrating pause. "I'm sorry if I hurt you six years ago, but after what happened that night it couldn't be any other way."

His words, the fact that he obviously thought she had fallen for him six years ago, dropped into a pool of silence that seemed to expand and spread around them, blotting out the street noise. She dragged her gaze from the taut planes of his cheekbones, the inky crescents of his lashes. "Are you referring to the accident, or the fact that you were already involved with someone else called *Tiffany?*" A girlfriend he'd apparently had stashed away in Dubai.

Nick frowned. "The relationship with Tiffany was already ending."

Elena found herself staring at the V of bronzed flesh bared by the pale peach T-shirt Nick was wearing beneath his black jacket. Peach. It was a feminine color, but on Nick the color looked sexy and hot, emphasizing the tough, stubbled line of his jaw and the cool gleam of his eyes. "I read about Tiffany in an article that was published a whole month later."

She would never forget because the statement that Nick Messena and his gorgeous model girlfriend were in love had finally convinced her that a relationship with him had never been viable.

"You shouldn't believe anything printed in a tabloid. We broke up as soon as I got back to Dubai."

Elena ruthlessly suppressed the sudden, wild, improbable notion that Nick had ended his relationship with Tiffany because of her.

That was the kind of flawed thinking that had seen her climbing into bed with him in the first place. "That still didn't make it all right to sleep with me when you had no intention of ever following up."

A hint of color rimmed Nick's cheekbones. "No, it didn't. If you'll recall, I did apologize."

Her jaw tightened. As if it had all been a gigantic mistake. "So why, exactly, did you finish with Tiffany?"

She shouldn't have the slightest interest. Nick Messena meant nothing to her—absolutely nothing—but suddenly she desperately needed to know.

He dragged long, tanned fingers through his hair, his expression just a little bad-tempered and terminally, broodingly sexy. "How would I know why?" he growled. "Men don't know that stuff. It ended, like it always does."

She blinked at his statement that his relationships always ended. For reasons she didn't want to go into, there was something profoundly depressing in that thought.

She stared at his wide mouth and the fuller bottom lip, which was decorated with a small, jagged scar. She couldn't remember the scar being there six years ago. It suggested he had since been involved in a fight.

Probably a brawl on one of his construction sites.

Against all good sense, the heady tension she had so far failed to defuse tightened another notch. Feeling, as she was, unsettled by memories of the past, distinctly vulnerable and on edge from the blast of Nick's potent sexuality, it was not a good idea to imagine Nick Messena in warrior mode.

She dragged her gaze from his mouth and the vivid memory of what it had felt like to be kissed by Nick. "Maybe you go about things in the wrong way?"

He stared at her, transfixed. "How, exactly, should I 'go about' things?"

She took a deep breath and tried to ignore the piercing power of his gaze. "Conversation is not a bad starter." That had been something that had been distinctly lacking in their night together.

"I talk."

The gravelly irritation in his voice, the way his gaze lingered on her mouth, made her suddenly intensely aware that he, too, was remembering *that* night.

She could feel her cheeks warming all over again that she had actually offered Nick advice about improving his relationships. Advice had so far failed to be her forte, despite the psychology classes she had passed.

The heat that rose off the sidewalk and floated in the air seemed to increase in intensity, opening up every pore. Perspiration trickled down the groove of her spine and between her breasts. She longed to shrug out of the overlarge jacket, but she would rather die of heatstroke than take off one item of clothing in Nick's presence. "Women need more than sex. They need to be appreciated and…liked."

They needed to be loved.

He glanced down the street as if he was looking for someone. "I like women."

A muscular black four-wheel-drive vehicle braked to a halt in a restricted parking zone a few steps away; a horn blared. Nick lifted a hand at the driver. "That's my Jeep. If you want, I can give you a ride."

The words, the unconscious innuendo, sent another small, sensual dart through her. Climb into a vehicle with tinted windows with Nick Messena? *Never again.* "I don't need a ride."

His mouth quirked. "Just like you don't need my apartment or, I'm guessing, anything else I've got to offer."

Reaching out a finger, he gently relocated her glasses, which had once again slipped, back onto the bridge of her nose. "Why do you wear these things?"

She blinked at the small, intimate gesture. "You know I'm shortsighted."

"You should get contacts."

"Why?" But the moment she asked the question she realized what had prompted the suggestion. Fiery outrage poured through her. "So I can get a man?"

He frowned. "That wasn't what I meant, but last I heard there's nothing wrong with that…yet."

Her chin jerked up another notch. "I'm curious, what else should I change? My clothes? My shoes? How about my hair?"

"Don't change the shoes," he said on a soft growl. "Your hair is fine. It's gorgeous." He touched a loose strand with one finger. "I just don't like whatever it is you do with it."

Elena tried not to respond to the ripple of sensation that flowed out from that small touch, or to love it that he thought her hair was gorgeous. It would take more than a bit of judicious flattery to change the fact that she was hurt—and now more than a little bit mad. "It's called a French pleat." She drew a swift breath. "What else is wrong?"

He muttered something short and indistinct that she didn't quite catch. "There's no point asking me this stuff. I'm not exactly an expert."

"Meaning that I need expert help."

He pinched the bridge of his nose. "How did we get onto this? It's starting to remind me of a conversation with my sisters. And before you say it, no, I can categorically say I have never thought of you as a sister."

His gaze, as it once again dropped to her mouth, carried the same fascinated gleam she had noticed in Cutler's office. Her breath stopped in her throat at the heart-pounding thought that he was actually considering kissing her. *Despite all of her deficiencies.*

A horn blast from a delivery vehicle that wanted the restricted parking place jerked her attention away from the tough line of Nick's jaw.

A split second later the passenger door of the Jeep popped open. Nick ignored the waiting vehicle. "Damn, I did hurt you," he said softly.

Elena tried to suppress a small stab of panic that, after six years of stoically burying the past, she had clearly lost control to the point that she had revealed her vulnerability to Nick.

Pinning a bright smile on her face, she attempted to smooth out the moment by checking her watch, as if she was in a hurry. "It was a blind date. Everyone knows they never turn out."

"It wasn't a blind date for me."

The flat tone of Nick's voice jerked her gaze back to his.

Nick's expression was oddly taut. "Six years ago I happened to overhear that a friend of yours had organized a blind date for you with Geoffrey Smale. I told Smale to get lost and took his place. I knew you were the girl I was taking out, and I slept with you for one reason—because I liked you."

* * *

Broodingly, Nick climbed into the passenger-side seat of the Jeep. He shot an apologetic glance at his younger brother, Kyle, as he fastened his seat belt.

Kyle, who had a military background and a wholly unexpected genius for financial investment, accelerated away from the curb. "She looked familiar. New girl?"

"No." *Yes.*

Nick frowned at the surge of desire that that thought initiated. The kind of edgy tension he hadn't felt in a very long time—six long years to be exact. "That's Elena Lyon, from Dolphin Bay. She works for the Atraeus Group."

Kyle's expression cleared as he stopped for a set of lights. "Elena. That explains it. Zane's PA. And Katherine's niece." He sent Nick an assessing look. "Didn't think she would be your type."

Nick found himself frowning at the blunt message. Kyle knew he was the one who had found their father's car, which had slid off the road in bad weather, then rolled.

His stomach tightened on a raft of memories. Memories that had faded with time, but that were still edged with grief and guilt.

If he hadn't been in bed with Elena, captivated by the same irresistible obsession that had been at the heart of his father's supposed betrayal, *with another Lyon woman,* he might have reached the crash site in time to make a difference.

The coroner's report had claimed that both his father and Katherine had survived the impact for a time. If he had left Elena at her door that night and driven home, there was a slim possibility he might have saved them.

Nick stared broodingly at the line of traffic backed up

for a set of lights. Kyle was right. He shouldn't be thinking about Elena.

The trouble was, lately, after the discovery of a diary and the stunning possibility that his father had not been having an affair with Katherine, he hadn't been able to stop thinking about Elena. "So...what is my type?"

Kyle looked wary. "Uh—they're usually blonde."

With long legs and confidence to burn. The exact opposite of Elena, with her dark eyes, her vulnerability and enticing, sultry curves.

Feeling in need of air, Nick activated the electric window. "I don't always date blondes."

"Hey, I won't judge you."

Although, for a while, it had been blondes or nothing, because dating dark-haired girls had cut too close to the bone. For a couple of years the memory of his night with Elena had been too viscerally tied into his grief and the gnawing guilt that he had failed to save his father.

Kyle sent him the kind of neutral, male look that said he'd noted Nick's interest in Elena, but wasn't going to probe any further. It was the kind of unspoken acceptance that short-circuited the need for a conversation, and which suited Nick.

His feelings for Elena were clear-cut enough. He wanted her back in his bed, but he wasn't prepared to think beyond that point.

Kyle turned into the underground parking building of the Messena building. "Any success locating the ring?"

Nick unfastened his seat belt as Kyle pulled into a space. "I've been asked that question a lot lately."

By his mother, his older brother, Gabriel and a selection of great-aunts and -uncles who were concerned about the loss of an important heirloom piece. Last but not least, the insurance assessor who, while engaged in a revaluing exercise, had discovered the ring was missing.

Climbing out of the Jeep, Nick slammed the door. "I'm beginning to feel like Frodo Baggins."

Kyle extracted his briefcase, locked the vehicle and tossed him the keys. "If that's the little guy off *Lord of the Rings,* he had prettier eyes."

"He also had friends who helped him."

Kyle grinned good-naturedly. "Cool. Just don't expect me to be one of them. My detective skills are zero. "

Nick tapped in the security PIN to access the elevator. "Anyone ever tell you you're irritating?"

"My last blonde girlfriend."

Nick hit the floor number that would take them to Gabriel's suite of offices and a discussion about diversifying his business interests. "I don't recall your last girlfriend."

Of all the Messena clan, Kyle was the quietest and the hardest to read. Maybe because of his time in Special Forces, or the fact that he had lost his wife and child to the horror of a terror attack, he had grown to be perceptibly different to them all.

"That was because I was on an overseas posting."

"She was foreign?"

"No. A military brat."

"What happened?"

He shrugged, his expression cagey. "We both moved on."

Nick studied Kyle's clean profile. With his obdurate jaw and the short, crisp cut of his hair, even in a sleek business suit he still managed to look dangerous. "So it wasn't serious."

"No."

Kyle's clear-cut indifference about his last casual relationship struck an odd chord with Nick. Kyle had cared about his wife and child, to the point that he hadn't cared about anyone since.

Nick hadn't lost a wife and child, not even close, but it was also true that for years, ever since their father had died, *and the night with Elena,* he had not been able to form a relationship.

The elevator doors slid open. Moving on automatic pilot, Nick strolled with Kyle through the familiar, hushed and expensive interior of the bank.

Normally, his social life was neatly compartmentalized and didn't impinge on the long hours he worked. But lately his social life had ground to a halt.

Dispassionately he examined the intensity of his focus on Elena, which, according to his PA, had made him irritable and terminally bad-tempered. He had considered dating, but every time he picked up the phone he found himself replacing it without making the call.

The blunt fact was that finding out that the past was not set in stone had been like opening up a Pandora's box. In that moment a raft of thoughts and emotions had hit him like a kick in the chest. Among them the stubborn, visceral need to reclaim Elena.

He couldn't fathom the need, and despite every effort, he hadn't been able to reason it away. It was just there.

The thought of making love with Elena made every muscle in his body tighten. The response, in itself, was singular. Usually when he finished a relationship it was over, his approach to dating and sex as cut-and-dried as his approach to contracting and completing a business deal.

But for some reason those few hours with Elena had stuck in his mind. Maybe the explanation was simply that what they'd shared had been over almost before it had begun. There hadn't been a cooling-off period when the usual frustrations over his commitment to his business kicked in.

But as much as he wanted Elena, bed would have to wait. His first priority had to be to obtain answers and closure. Although every time he got close to Elena the concept of closure crashed and burned.

Despite the buttoned-down clothing and schoolmarm hair, there had always been something irresistibly, tantalizingly sensual about Elena. She had probably noticed he'd been having trouble keeping his hands off her.

It was no wonder she had practically run from him in Cutler's office.

Nick had *liked* her.

A surge of delighted warmth shimmered through Elena as she strolled through a small park.

Six years ago Nick had cared enough to step in and protect her from a date that would have been uncomfortable, at best. More probably it would have ended in an embarrassing struggle, because Geoffrey Smale had a reputation for not taking no for an answer.

Feeling distinctly unsettled and on edge at this new view of the past, Elena made a beeline for the nearest park bench and sat down.

For six years she had been mad at Nick. Now she didn't know quite what to feel, except that, lurking beneath all of the confusion, being discarded by him all those years ago still hurt.

The problem was that as a teenager she'd had a thing for him. Summers spent in Dolphin Bay, visiting her aunt and watching a bronzed, muscular Nick surfing, had definitely contributed to the fascination.

Walking away from the night they'd spent together would have been easier if he had been a complete stranger, but he hadn't been. Because of her summers with her aunt at the original Lyon homestead on the beach, and because of Katherine's work for his family as a housekeeper, Elena had felt connected to Nick.

Too restless to sit, she checked her watch and strolled back in the direction of the Atraeus Hotel, where she was staying.

As she approached a set of exclusive boutiques a glass door swung open, and a sleek woman wearing a kingfisher-blue dress that showed off her perfect golden tan stepped out onto the street.

The door closed on a waft of some gorgeous perfume, and in the process Elena's reflection—that of a slightly overweight woman dressed in a plain dress and jacket, and wearing glasses—flashed back at her.

Even her handbag looked heavy and just a little boring. The only things that looked right were her shoes, which were pretty but didn't really go with the rest of her outfit.

Not just a victim, a *fashion* victim.

Nick's words came back to haunt her.

He didn't like her glasses or the way she did her hair. He hadn't mentioned her clothes, but she was seeing them through his eyes, and she was ready to admit that they were just as clunky, just as boring as the glasses and her hair.

As much as she resented his opinion, he was right. Something had to change. *She* had to change.

She could no longer immerse herself in work and avoid the fact that another birthday had just flown by. She was twenty-eight. Two more years and she would be thirty.

If she wasn't careful she would be thirty and alone.

Or she could change her life so that she would be thirty and immersed in a passionate love relationship.

Feeling electrified, as if she was standing on the edge

of a precipice, about to take a perilous leap into the unknown, she studied the elegant writing on the glass frontage of the store. A tingling sense of fate taking a hand gripped her.

It wasn't a store, exactly. It was a very exclusive and expensive health and beauty spa. The kind of place she was routinely around because her employer, the Atraeus Group, numbered a few very high-quality spa facilities among its resort properties. Of course, she had never personally utilized any of those spa facilities.

But that was the old Elena.

Her jaw firmed. She had made a decision to change. By the time she was finished, she would be, if not as pretty, at least as sleek and stylish and confident as the woman in the blue dress.

The idea gained momentum. She would no longer allow herself to feel inadequate and excluded, which would mean inner as well as outward change.

She could walk in those doors now if she wanted. She had the money. After years of saving her very good salary, she had more than enough to pay for a makeover.

Feeling a little dizzy at the notion that she didn't have to stay as she was, that she had the power to change herself, she stepped up to the exquisite white-and-gold portal. Taking a deep breath, she pushed the door wide and stepped inside.

After an initial hour-long consultation with a stylist called Giorgio, during which he had casually ticked almost every box on the interview form he had used, Elena signed on for every treatment recommended.

First up was weight loss and detox, which included a week in a secluded health spa. That was followed by a comprehensive fitness program and an introduction to her new personal trainer. A series of beauty and pamper treatments, and a comprehensive hair, makeup and wardrobe makeover completed her program.

The initial week at their spa facility would cost a staggering amount, but she was desperate.

According to Giorgio she wasn't desperate; she was worth it.

Elena wasn't about to split hairs. As long as the spa could carry out its promise and transform her, she was happy to pay.

Her heart sped up at the changes she was about to make. Hope flooded her.

The next time she saw Nick Messena, things would be different. *She* would be different.

Three

One month later, Nick Messena watched, green gaze cool, as Elena Lyon walked with measured elegance down the aisle toward him, every step precisely, perfectly timed with the beat of the Wedding March.

Mellow afternoon sunlight poured through stained glass windows, illuminating the startling changes she had made, from her long, stylishly cut, midnight-dark hair to the tips of her outrageously sexy pink high heels. Her bridesmaid's dress, a sophisticated confection of pink lace and silk that he privately thought was just a little too revealing, clung to lush, gentle curves and a mouthwateringly tiny waist.

As the bride reached the altar, Elena's gaze rested briefly on Kyle who was Gabriel's groomsman, then locked with his. With grim satisfaction, he noted that she hadn't realized he had changed roles with Kyle and taken over as Gabriel's best man. If she had, he was certain she would have very quickly and efficiently organized someone else to take her place as maid of honor.

Dragging her gaze free, Elena briskly took charge of the flower girl, Gabriel and Gemma's daughter Sanchia, who had just finished tossing rose petals. Nick's brows jerked together as he took stock of some of the changes he had barely had time to register at the prewedding dinner the previous evening. For the first time he noticed a tiny, discreet sparkle to one side of Elena's delicate nose. A piercing.

Every muscle in his body tightened at the small, exotic touch. His elusive ex-lover had lost weight, cut her hair and ditched the dull, shapeless clothing she had worn like a uniform. In the space of a few weeks, Elena had morphed from softly curved, bespectacled and repressively buttoned-down, into an exotically hot and sensuous swan.

Jaw clamped, Nick transferred his attention to the bride, Gemma O'Neill, as she stood beside his brother.

As the ceremony proceeded, Elena kept her attention fixed on the priest. Fascinated by her intention to utterly ignore him, Nick took the opportunity to study the newly sculpted contours of Elena's cheekbones, her shell-like lobes decorated with pink pearls and tiny pink jewels.

The sexily ruffled haircut seemed to sum up the changes Elena had made: less, but a whole lot more.

As Nick handed the ring to Gabriel, Elena's dark gaze clashed with his for a pulse-pounding moment. The starry, romantic softness he glimpsed died an instant death, replaced by the familiar professional blandness that made his jaw tighten.

The cool neutrality was distinctly at odds with the way Elena had used to look at him. It was light-years away from the ingenuous passion that had burned him from the inside out when they had made love.

A delicate, sophisticated perfume wafted around him. The tantalizing scent, like Elena's designer wardrobe, her new, sleek body shape and the ultramodern haircut—all clearly the product of a ruthless makeover artist—set him even more sensually on edge.

Gabriel turned to take the hand of the woman he had pledged to marry.

A flash of Elena's pink dress, as she bent down to whisper something to Sanchia, drew Nick's gaze, along with another tempting flash of cleavage.

With a brisk elegance that underlined the fact that the old Elena was long gone, she repositioned Sanchia next to Gemma. Nick clamped down on his impatience as the ceremony proceeded at a snail's pace.

Elena had been avoiding him for the past twenty-four hours, ever since she had arrived in Dolphin Bay. The one time he had managed to get her alone—last night to discuss meeting at the beach villa—she had successfully stonewalled him. Now his temper was on a slow burn. Whether she liked it or not, they would conclude their business this weekend.

Distantly, he registered that Gabriel was kissing his new bride. With grim patience, Nick waited out the signing of the register in the small, adjacent vestry.

As Gabriel swung his small daughter up into his arms, Elena's gaze, unexpectedly misty and soft, connected with his again, long enough for him to register two salient facts. The contact lenses with which she had replaced her trademark glasses were not the regular, transparent type. They were a dark chocolate brown that completely obliterated the usual, cheerful golden brown of her irises.

More importantly, despite her cool control and her

efforts to pretend that he didn't exist, he was aware in that moment that for Elena, he very palpably *did* exist.

Every muscle in his body tightened at the knowledge that despite her refusals to meet with him, despite the fact that every time they did meet they ended up arguing, Elena still wanted him.

With an effort of will, Nick kept his expression neutral as he signed as a witness to the ceremony. In a few minutes he would walk down the aisle with Elena on his arm. It was the window of opportunity he had planned for when he had arranged to change places with Kyle.

Negotiation was not his best talent; that was Gabriel's forte. Nick was more suited to the blunt, laconic cadences of construction sites. A world of black and white, where "yes" meant *yes* and "no" meant *no* and not some murky, frustrating shade in between.

As the music swelled and Elena looped her arm through his, the issue of retrieving an heirloom ring and unraveling the mystery of his father's link with Elena's aunt faded.

With Elena's delicately enticing perfume filling his nostrils again, Nick acknowledged that the only "yes" he really wanted from Elena was the one she had given him six years ago.

Elena steeled herself against the tiny electrical charge that coursed through her as she settled her palm lightly on Nick's arm.

Nick sent her another assessing glance. Despite her intention to be cool and distant and, as she'd done the previous evening, pretend that she didn't look a whole lot different than she had a month ago, Elena's pulse rate accelerated. Even though she knew she looked her very best, thanks to the efforts of the beauty spa, she was still adjusting to the changes. Having Nick Messena put her new look under a microscope, *and wondering if he liked what he saw,* was unexpectedly nerve-racking.

Nick bent his head close enough that she caught an intriguing whiff of his cologne. "Is that a tattoo on your shoulder?"

Elena stiffened at the blunt question and the hint of disapproval that went with it. "It's a transfer. I'm *thinking* about a tattoo."

There was a small tense silence. "You don't need it."

The flat statement made her bristle. "*I* think I need it and Giorgio thought it looked very good."

"Damn," he said softly. "Who is Giorgio?"

A small thrill went through her at the sudden, blinding thought that Nick was jealous, although she refused to allow herself to buy into that fantasy.

From what she knew personally and had read in magazines and tabloids, Nick Messena didn't have a jealous bone in his body. Most of his liaisons were so brief there was no time for an emotion as deep and powerful as jealousy to form. "Giorgio is...a friend."

She caught the barest hint of annoyance in his expression, and a small but satisfying surge of feminine power coursed through her at the decision not to disclose her true relationship with Giorgio. It was absolutely none of Nick's business that Giorgio was her personal beauty consultant.

In that moment she remembered Robert Corrado, another very new friend who had the potential to be much more. After just a couple of dates, it was too early to tell if Robert was poised to be the love of her life, but right now he was a touchstone she desperately needed.

Taking a deep breath, she tried to recall exactly what

Robert looked like as they followed Gabriel, Gemma and Sanchia down the aisle. ·

She felt Nick's gaze once again on her profile. "You've lost weight."

Her jaw clenched at the excruciating conversation opener. It was not the response she had envisaged, but all the same, a small renegade part of her was happy that he had noticed.

Her new hourglass shape constantly surprised her. The diet, combined with a rigorous exercise regime had produced a totally unexpected body. She still had curves, albeit more streamlined than they used to be, and they were now combined with a tiny waist.

She was still amazed that the loss of such a small amount of weight had made such a difference. If she had realized how little had stood between her and a totally new body, she would have opted for diet and exercise years ago. "Can't you come up with a better conversational opener than that?"

"Maybe I'm out of touch. What am I supposed to say?"

"According to a gossip columnist you're not in the least out of touch. If you want to make conversation, you could try concentrating on positives."

"I thought that was a positive." Nick frowned. "Which columnist?"

Elena drew a swift breath. After her unscheduled meeting with Nick in Auckland she had, by pure chance, read that he had dated a gorgeous model that same night. She said the name.

His expression cleared. "The story about Melanie."

"Melanie. Rhymes with Tiffany."

Nick's gaze sliced back to hers. "She's a friend of my sister, and it was a family dinner. There was no date. Have you managed to sell the villa yet?"

"Not yet, but I've received an offer, which I'm considering."

The muscles beneath her fingers tensed. She caught his flash of annoyance. "Whatever you've been offered, I'll top it by ten percent."

Elena stared ahead, keeping her gaze glued to the tulle of Gemma's veil. "I don't understand why you want the villa."

"It's beachfront. It's an investment I won't lose on, plus it seems to be the only way I can get you to agree to help me search for the ring."

"I've looked. It's not there."

"Did you check the attic?"

"I'm working my way through it. I haven't found anything yet, and I've searched through almost everything."

Her aunt had been a collector of all sorts of memorabilia. Elena had sorted through all the recent boxes, everything else she had opened lately was going back progressively in time.

There was a small, grim silence. "If you won't consider my purchase offer, will you let me have a look through before you sell?"

Her jaw set. "I can't see Aunt Katherine putting a valuable piece of jewelry in an attic."

"My father noted in a diary that he had given the ring to Katherine. You haven't found it anywhere else, which means it's entirely probable that it's in the house, somewhere."

Elena loosened her grip on the small bouquet she was holding. Nick's frustration that he wasn't getting what he wanted was palpable. Against all the odds, she had to fight a knee-jerk impulse to cave and offer to help him.

Determinedly, she crushed the old overgenerous Elena: *the doormat.*

According to Giorgio her fatal weakness was that she liked to please men. The reason she had rushed around and done so much for her Atraeus bosses was that it satisfied her need to be needed. She was substituting pleasing powerful men for a genuine love relationship in which she was entitled to receive care and nurturing.

The discovery had been life altering. On the strength of it, she intended to quit her job as a PA, because she figured that the temptation to revert to her old habit of rushing to please would be so ingrained it would be hard to resist. Instead, she planned to branch out in a new, more creative direction. Now that she'd come this far, she couldn't go back to being the old, downtrodden Elena.

Aware that Nick was waiting for an answer she crushed the impulse to say an outright yes. "I don't think you'll find anything, but since you're so insistent, I'm willing for you to come and have a look through the house for yourself."

"When? I'm flying out early tomorrow morning and I won't be back for a month."

In which time, if she accepted the offer she was considering, the villa could be sold. She frowned at the way Nick had neatly cornered her. "I suppose I could spare a couple of hours tonight. If I help you sort through the final trunks, one hour should do it."

"Done." Nick lifted a hand in brief acknowledgment of an elderly man Elena recognized as Mario Atraeus. Seated next to him was a gorgeous brunette, Eva Atraeus, Mario's adopted daughter.

Elena's hand tightened on Nick's arm in a weird, instant reflex. Nick's gaze clashed with hers. "What's wrong?"

"Nothing." She had just remembered a photograph she stumbled across a couple of months ago in a glossy women's magazine of Nick partnering Eva at a charity function. They had looked perfect together. Nick with his strong masculine good looks, Eva, with her olive skin and tawny hair, looking like an exotic flower by his side.

The music swelled to a crescendo as Gabriel and Gemma, with Sanchia in tow, stopped to greet an elderly matriarch of the Messena clan instead of leaving the church.

Pressed forward by people behind, Elena found herself impelled onto the front steps of the church, into a shower of confetti and rice.

A dark-haired young man wearing a checked shirt loomed out of the waiting crowd. He lifted a large camera and began snapping them as if they were the married couple. Embarrassment clutched at Elena. It wasn't the official photographer, which meant he was probably a journalist. "He's making a mistake."

Another wave of confetti had Nick tucking her in closer against his side. "A reporter making a mistake? It won't be the first time."

"Aren't you worried?"

"Not particularly."

A cluster of guests exiting the church jostled Elena, so that she found herself plastered against Nick's chest.

"I said I wasn't going to do this," he muttered.

A split second later his head dipped and his mouth came down on hers.

Four

Instead of pulling away as she should have, Elena froze, an odd feminine delight flowing through her at the softness of his mouth, the faint abrasion of his jaw. Nick's hands settled at her waist, steadying her against him as he angled his jaw and deepened the kiss.

She registered that Nick was aroused. For a dizzying moment time seemed to slow, stop, then an eruption of applause, a raft of excited comments and the motorized click of the reporter's camera brought her back to her senses.

Nick lifted his head. "We need to move."

His arm closed around her waist, urging her off the steps. At that moment Gemma and Gabriel appeared in the doors of the church, and the attention of the reporter and the guests shifted.

Someone clapped Nick on the shoulder. "For a minute there I thought I was attending the wrong wedding, but as soon as I recognized you I knew you couldn't be the groom."

Relieved by the distraction, Elena freed herself from Nick's hold and the haze of unscripted passion.

Nick half turned to shake hands with a large, tanned man wearing a sleek suit teamed with an Akubra hat, the Australian equivalent of a cowboy. "You know me, Nate. Married to the job."

Elena noticed that the young guy in the checked shirt who had been snapping photos had sidled close and seemed to be listening. Before she could decide whether he was lingering with deliberate intent or if it was sheer coincidence, Nick introduced her to Nate Cavendish.

As soon as Elena heard the name she recognized Cavendish as an Australian cattleman with a legendary reputation as one of the richest and most elusive bachelors in Australia.

Feeling flustered and unsettled, her mind still locked on Nick's statement that he was married to the job, she shook Nate's hand.

Nate gave her a curious look as if he found her familiar but couldn't quite place her. Not surprising, since she had bumped into him at Atraeus parties a couple of times in the past when she had been the "old" Elena. "You must be Nick's new girl."

"No," she said blandly. "I'm not that interested. Too busy shopping around."

Nick's gaze touched on hers, promising retribution. "It's what you might call an interesting arrangement."

Nate shook his head. "Sounds like she's got you on your knees."

Nick shrugged, his expression cooling as he noticed the journalist. "Another one bites the dust."

"That's for sure." Nate tipped his hat at Elena and

walked toward the guests clustered around Gabriel and Gemma.

Nick's gaze was glacially cold as he watched the reporter jog toward a car and drive away at speed.

Elena's stomach sank. After working years for the Atraeus family, she had an instinct about the press. The only reason the reporter was leaving was because he had a story.

Nick's palm landed in the small of her back. He moved her out of the way of the crowd as Gemma and Gabriel strolled toward their waiting limousine. But the effect that one small touch had on Elena was far from casual, zapping her straight back to the unsettling heat of the kiss.

Nick's brows jerked together as she instantly moved away from his touch. A split second later a vibrating sound distracted him.

Sliding his phone out of his pocket, he stepped a couple of paces away to answer the call.

While he conducted a discussion about closing some deal on a resort purchase, Elena struggled to compose herself as she watched the bridal car leave.

A second limousine slid into place. The one that would transport her, Nick and Kyle to the Dolphin Bay Resort for the wedding photographs.

Her stomach churned at the thought. There was no quick exit today. She would have to share the intimate space of the limousine with Nick then, sit with him at the reception.

Too late to wish she hadn't allowed that kiss or the conversation that had followed. Before today she would have said she didn't have a flirtatious bone in her body. But sometime between the altar and the church gate she had learned to flirt.

Because she was still fatally attracted to Nick.

Elena drew a breath and let it out slowly.

She should never have allowed Nick to kiss her.

Her only excuse was that she had been so distracted by Gemma finally getting her happy-ever-after ending that she had dropped her guard.

But Nick had just reminded her of exactly why she couldn't afford him in her life.

Nick Messena, like Nate Cavendish, was not husband material for one simple reason: no woman could ever compete with the excitement and challenge of his business.

Nick terminated his conversation and turned back to her, his gaze settling on her, narrowed and intent. "Looks like our ride is here."

Elena's heart thumped once, hard, as Nick's words spun her back to their conversation on the sidewalk in Auckland. The breath locked in her throat as she finally allowed the knowledge that Nick was genuinely attracted to her to sink in. More, that he had been attracted to her six years ago, *before* she had changed her appearance.

The knowledge that he had wanted her even when she had been a little overweight and frumpy was difficult to process. She was absolutely not like the normal run of his girlfriends. It meant that *he liked her for herself.*

The sudden blinding thought that, if she wanted, she could end the empty years of fruitless and boring dating and make love with Nick sent heat flooding through her.

Nick was making no bones about the fact that he wanted her—

"Are you good to go?"

Elena drew a deep breath and tried to slide back into her professional PA mode. But with Nick looming over her, a smudge of lipstick at the corner of his mouth, it was difficult to focus. "I am, but you're not."

Extracting a handkerchief from a small, secret pocket at the waist of her dress, she handed it to him. "You have lipstick on your mouth."

Taking the handkerchief, he wiped his mouth. "An occupational hazard at weddings."

When he attempted to give the handkerchief back, she forced a smile. "Keep it. I don't want it back."

The last thing she needed was a keepsake to remind her that she had been on the verge of making a second mistake.

Slipping the handkerchief into his trousers' pocket, he jerked his head in the direction of the limousine. "If you're ready, looks like the official photo shoot is about to begin." He sent her a quick, rueful grin. "Don't know about you, but it's not exactly my favorite pastime."

Elena dragged her gaze from Nick's and the killer charm that she absolutely did not want to be ensnared by. "I have no problem with having my photo taken."

Not since she had taken one of the intensive courses offered at the health spa. She had been styled and made up by professionals and taught how to angle her face and smile. After two intimidating hours beneath glaring lights, a camera pointed at her face, she had finally conquered her fear of the lens.

A good thirty minutes later, after posing for endless photographs while the guests sipped champagne and circulated in the grounds of the Dolphin Bay Resort, Elena found herself seated next to Nick at the reception.

Held in a large room, which had been festooned with white roses, glossy dark green foliage and trailing, fragrant jasmine, the wedding was the culmination of a romantic dream.

A further hour of speeches, champagne and exquisite food later, the orchestra struck a chord. Growing more tense by the second, Elena watched as Gabriel and Gemma took the floor. According to tradition she and Nick were up next.

Nick held out one large, tanned and scarred hand. "I think that's our cue."

Elena took his hand, tensing at the tingling heat of his touch, the faint abrasion of calluses gained on construction sites and while indulging his other passion: sailing.

One hand settled at her waist, drawing her in close at the first sweeping step of a waltz. Elena's breath hitched in her throat as her breasts brushed his chest. Stiffening slightly, she pulled back, although it was hard to enjoy dancing, which she loved, when maintaining a rigid distance.

Nick sent her a neutral glance. "You should relax."

Another couple who had just joined the general surge onto the floor danced too close and jostled her.

Nick frowned. "And that's why." With easy strength he pulled her closer.

Feeling a little breathless, Elena stared at the tough line of Nick's jaw and decided to stay there.

"That's better."

As Nick twirled her past Gabriel and Gemma, Elena tried to relax. Another hour and she could leave. Tension hit her again at that thought because she would be leaving with Nick, a scenario that ran a little too close to what had taken place six years ago. The music switched to a slower, steamier waltz.

Instead of releasing her, Nick continued to dance, keeping her close. "How long have you known Gemma?"

Heart pounding with the curious, humming excitement of being so close to Nick, Elena forced herself to concentrate on answering his question. "Since I started coming to Dolphin Bay for my vacations when I was seventeen."

"I remember seeing you on the beach."

Elena could feel her cheeks warming at the memory of just how much time she used to spend watching Nick on his surfboard or messing around on boats. "I used to read on the beach a lot."

"But not anymore?"

She steeled herself against the curiosity of his gaze, his sudden unnerving focus. "These days, I have other things to occupy my time."

He lifted a brow. "Let me guess—a gym membership."

"Fitness is important."

"So, what's behind the sudden transformation?"

Elena stiffened against the urge to blurt out that he had been the trigger. "I simply wanted to make the best of myself."

They danced beneath a huge, central chandelier, the light flowing across the strong planes and angles of Nick's face, highlighting the various nicks and scars.

He tucked her in a little closer for a turn. "I liked the color your eyes used to be. They were a pretty sherry brown, you shouldn't have changed that."

Elena blinked at the complete unexpectedness of his comment. "I didn't think you'd noticed."

No one else had, including herself. A little breathlessly she made a mental note to go back to clear contacts.

"And what about these?" he growled. His thumb brushed over one lobe then swept upward, tracing the curve of her ear, initiating a white-hot shimmer of heat.

He hooked coiling strands of hair behind one ear to further investigate, his breath washing over the curve of her neck, disarming her even further. "How many piercings?"

Despite her intense concentration on staying in step, Elena wobbled. When she corrected, she was close enough to Nick that she was now pressed lightly against his chest and his thighs brushed hers with every step. "One didn't seem to be enough, so I got three. On my lobes, that is."

His gaze sharpened. "There are piercings...elsewhere?"

Her heart thumped at the sudden intensity of his expression, the melting heat in his eyes. She swallowed, her mouth suddenly dry. "Just one. A navel piercing."

He was silent for a long, drawn-out moment, in which time the air seemed to thicken as the music took on a slower, slumberous rhythm. A tango.

Nick's hand tightened on her waist, drawing her infinitesimally closer. "Anything else I should know?"

She drew a quick, shallow breath as the heat from his big body closed around her. The passionate music, which she loved, throbbed, heightening her senses. Her nostrils seemed filled with his scent. The heat from his hand at her waist, his palm locked against hers, burned as if they were locked into some kind of electrical current.

She squashed the insane urge to sway a little closer. Wrong man, wrong place and a totally wrong time to road test this new direction in her life.

The whole point was to change her life, not repeat her old mistake.

Although, the heady thought that she could repeat it, if she wanted, made her mouth go dry. She hadn't missed the heat in Nick's gaze, or when he'd pulled her close, that he was semiaroused. "Only if you were my lover, which you're not."

"You've got a guy."

She frowned at the flat statement, the slight tightening of his hold. As if in some small way Nick considered that she belonged to him, which was ridiculous. "I date." Her chin came up. "I'm seeing someone at the moment."

His gaze narrowed with a mixture of disbelief and displeasure. "Who?"

A small startled thrill shot through her at the sudden notion that Nick didn't like it one little bit that there was a man in her life, even if the dating was still on a superficial level.

A little drunk on the rush of power that, in a room teeming with beautiful women, *she* was the center of his attention, she touched her tongue to her top lip. It was a gesture she became aware was an unconscious tease as his focus switched to her mouth.

Abruptly embarrassed, she closed her mouth and stared over Nick's shoulder at another pair of dancers whirling past. "You won't know him."

"Let me guess," he muttered. "Giorgio."

Elena blushed at the mistaken conclusion. A conclusion Nick had arrived at because she had deliberately failed to clarify who, exactly, Giorgio was. "Uh—actually, his name is Robert. Robert Corrado."

There was a stark silence. "You have *two* guys?"

She wasn't sure if the two tentative pecks on the mouth she had allowed, and which had been devoid of anything like the electrifying pleasure she had experienced when Nick kissed her, qualified Robert to be her *guy*. "Just the one."

Nick's gaze bored into hers, narrowed and glittering. "So Giorgio's past history?"

Elena tried to dampen down the addictive little charge of excitement that went through her at Nick's obvious displeasure. "Giorgio's my beauty consultant."

Nick muttered something short and succinct under his

breath. Another slow, gliding turn and they were outside on a shadowy patio with the light of the setting sun glowing through palm fronds and gleaming off a limpid pool.

Nick relinquished his hold, his jaw set, his gaze brooding and distinctly irritable. "Is Corrado the one you got the piercings for?"

The question, as if he had every right to expect an answer, made her world tilt again.

She had speculated before, but now she *knew.*

Nick was jealous.

Five

Elena dragged her gaze from Nick's and looked out past the pool and the palms to the ocean. Anything to stop the crazy pull of attraction and the dangerous knowledge that Nick really did want her.

The fact that he had been attracted to her before she had lost weight—that he actually liked her simply for who she was—was bad enough. But his brooding temper, as if the one night they had shared had somehow given him rights, was an undertow she wasn't sure she could resist. "Not that it's any of your business, but Robert doesn't care for piercings."

He definitely didn't know about the one she had gotten in her navel, or the pretty jeweled studs she had bought to go with her new selection of bikinis.

"So you didn't get the piercings for him."

The under note of satisfaction in Nick's voice, as if she had gotten the piercings for him, ruffled her even further. "I didn't get the piercings for *anyone*."

But even as she said the words, her heart plummeted. She had tried to convince herself that the piercings were just a part of the process of change, a signpost that declared that she wasn't thirty—yet. But the stark reality was that she had gotten them because they were pretty and sexy and practically screamed that she was available. She had gotten them for Nick.

"You haven't slept with Corrado."

Annoyed at the way Nick had dismissed Robert, Elena stepped farther out onto the patio, neatly evading his gaze. "That's none of your business. Robert's a nice man." He was safe and controllable, as different from Nick as a tame tabby from a prowling tiger. "He's definitely not fixated on piercings."

"Ouch. That puts me in my place." Nick dragged at his tie. Strolling to the wrought iron railing that enclosed part of the patio, he pulled the tie off altogether, folded it and shoved it into his pocket.

Drawn to join him, even though she knew it was a mistake, Elena averted her gaze from the slice of brown flesh revealed by the buttons he had unfastened.

The balmy evening seemed to get hotter as she became aware that Nick was studying the studs in her ear and the tiny glimpse of the butterfly transfer. "I'm guessing from the pink earring that there's a pink jewel in your navel?"

The accuracy of his guess made her stiffen. The old adage "give him an inch and he'll take a mile" came back to haunt her. "You shouldn't flirt with me."

"Why not? It makes a change from arguing, and after tonight we may never see each other again."

Elena froze. The attraction that shimmered through her, keeping her breathless and on edge, winked out. She stared at the strong line of his jaw, the sexy hollows of his cheekbones, aware that, somehow, she had been silly enough, vulnerable enough, to allow Nick to slide through her defenses. To start buying into the notion that just because he found her attractive it meant *he* had changed.

The day Nick Messena changed his stripes she would grow wings and fly.

Lifting her chin, she met his gaze squarely. "*If* you find the ring." The instant the words were out, she wished she could recall them. They had sounded needy, as if she was looking for a way to hang on to him.

Nick glanced out over the pool, the sun turning the tawny streaks in his dark hair molten. "You make it sound like a quest. I'm not that romantic."

No, his focus was always relentlessly practical, which was what made him so successful in business.

Swallowing a sudden ache in her throat, Elena did what she should have done in the first place: she turned on her heel and walked back to the reception. As she strolled, Nick's presence behind her made her tense. By the time she reached her table he was close enough that he held her chair as she sat down.

He dropped into the seat beside her and poured ice water into her glass before filling his own.

Elena picked up the glass. The nice manners, which would have been soothing in another man, unsettled her even further. "If Aunt Katherine did receive the ring, then I guess all the gossip was true."

Nick sat back in his seat. "I don't want it to be true, either," he said quietly.

For a split second she was caught and held by the somberness of his expression.

A set of memories from her summers on the beach at Dolphin Bay flickered, of Nick yachting with his father.

It had usually been just the two of them, sailing, making repairs and cleaning the boat after a day out.

One thing had always been very obvious: that Nick had loved his father. Suddenly, his real agenda was very clear to Elena. He wasn't just searching for a valuable heirloom. He was doing something much more important: he was trying to make sense of the past. "You don't want to find the ring, do you?"

"Not if it meant an affair."

"You think they weren't having an affair?"

"I'm hoping there's another reason they spent time together."

Her stomach tightened at the knowledge that Nick was trying to clear his father, a process that would also clear her aunt. That despite his reputation there were depths to Nick that were honorable and true and *likable*.

That she and Nick shared something in common.

Elena watched as Nick drank, the muscles of his throat working smoothly. At that moment Gemma signaled to her.

Relieved at the interruption, Elena rose from her seat. She felt unsettled, electrified. Every time she thought she had Nick figured out, something changed, the ground shifting under her feet.

After a quick hug, Gemma stepped back. Almost instantly, she tossed the bouquet. Surprised, Elena caught the fragrant, trailing bunch of white roses, orchids and orange blossom.

Feeling embattled, she dipped her head and inhaled the delicious fragrance. Her throat closed up. After years of brisk practicality as a PA, she was on the verge of losing control and crying on the spot because she realized just how much she wanted what Gemma had: a happy ending with a man who truly, honorably loved her. "You should have given it to someone else."

Gemma frowned. "No way. You're my best friend and, just look at you, you're gorgeous. Men will be falling all over you." She gave her another hug. "I won't be happy until you're married. Who's that guy you're seeing in Sydney?"

Elena carefully avoided Gemma's gaze on the pretext that she was examining the faintly crushed flowers. "Robert."

Gemma grinned and hooked her arm through Gabriel's, snuggling into his side. "Then marry him. But only if you're in love."

Elena forced a smile. "Great idea. First he has to propose."

Elena walked back to her seat, clutching the bouquet. She was acutely aware that Nick, who was standing talking with a group of friends, had watched the exchange.

Gray-haired Marge Hamilton, an old character in Dolphin Bay, with a legendary reputation for gossip in a town that abounded with it, made a beeline for her. "Caught the bouquet I see. Clever girl."

"Actually, it was given to me—"

Marge's gaze narrowed, but there was a pleased glint in the speculation. "You'll be next down the aisle and, I must say, it's about time."

Elena's discomfort escalated. Nick was close enough that he could hear every word. But as embarrassing as the conversation was, she would never forget that, despite Marge's love of gossip, she had been fiercely supportive of her aunt when the scandal had erupted.

Elena dredged up a smile. "As a matter of fact, I'm working on it."

Marge's gaze swiveled to her left hand. A small frown

formed when she noted the third finger was bare. "Sounds like you have someone in mind. What's his name, dear?"

Elena's fingers tightened on the bouquet as she tried to make herself say Robert's name, but somehow she just couldn't seem to get it out. Something snapped at the base of the bouquet. There was a small clunk as a small plastic horseshoe, included for luck, dropped to the floor. "He's...from Sydney."

"Not that hot young Atraeus boy?" Marge sent a disapproving glance at Zane, who had flown in from Florida and happened to be leaning on the bar, a beer in his hand.

"*Zane?* He's my boss. No, his name is—"

Marge frowned. "At one point we thought you actually might snaffle one of those Atraeus boys. Although, any one of them is a wild handful."

Elena could feel herself stiffening at the idea that she was hunting for a husband in her workplace and, worse, the suggestion that the whole of Dolphin Bay was speculating on whether or not she could actually succeed. "I *work* for the Atraeus Group. It would be highly unprofessional to mix business—"

Nick's arm curved around her waist as casually as if they were a couple. His breath feathered her cheek, sending heat flooding through her.

"Were you about to say 'with pleasure'?"

Marge blinked as if she couldn't quite believe what she was witnessing. "I can see why you didn't want to say his name, dear. A little premature to announce it at a family wedding."

With surprising nimbleness she extracted a gleaming smartphone from her evening bag and snapped a picture. Beaming, she hurried off.

Elena disengaged herself from Nick's hold. "I was

about to say that it would be unprofessional to mix business with a *personal relationship*."

"Last I heard, personal relationships should be about pleasure."

"Commitment would be the quality I'd be looking for."

She noted Marge sharing the photo with one of her cronies. "The story will be all over town before the sun sets."

"That fast?"

"You better believe it. And, unfortunately, she has the picture to prove it."

"I must admit I didn't expect her to have a phone with a camera." Nick looked abashed.

Infuriatingly, it only made him look sexier. Elena had to steel herself against the almost irresistible impulse to smile back and forgive him, and forget that he hadn't responded to her probe about commitment. "Never underestimate a woman with a lilac rinse and a double string of pearls."

"Damn. Sorry, babe, it'll be a five-minute wonder—"

"Approximately the length of time your relationships last?" But, despite her knee-jerk attempt to freeze him out, Elena melted inside at the casual way Nick had called her "babe," as if they were intimately attached. As if she really were his girl.

Taking a deep breath, she forced herself to recall every magazine article or gossip columnist's piece she had ever read about Nick. And every one of the gorgeous girls with whom he'd been photographed.

Nick's expression sobered. "Okay, I guess I deserved that."

Elena set the gorgeous bouquet down on the table. "So, why did you do it?"

Nick's gaze was laced with impatience. "You should

ignore the gossips. They've had me married off a dozen times. I'm still single."

Elena pulled out her chair and sat down. She couldn't quite dredge up a light smile or a quip for the simple reason that a small, tender part of her didn't want there to be *any* gossip about her and Nick. The night she had spent with Nick, as disastrous as it was, had been an intensely private experience.

She didn't know if she would ever feel anything like it again. In six years she hadn't had so much as a glimmer of the searing, shimmering heat that had gripped her while she'd been in Nick's arms.

If people gossiped about them now, assuming they were sleeping together, that night would be sullied.

Nick frowned. "Is this about Robert?"

Elena almost made the mistake of saying *who?* "Robert isn't possessive." He hadn't had time to be, yet.

"A New Age guy."

She tried to focus on couples slow dancing to another dreamy waltz as Nick took the chair beside her. "What's so wrong with that?"

"Nothing, I guess, just so long as that's what you really want."

Elena's chest squeezed tight at the wording, which seemed to suggest that she had some kind of choice, between Robert and Nick.

Somehow, within the space of a few short hours the situation between them had gotten out of hand. She didn't think she could afford to be around Nick much longer. They needed to resolve the issue of the ring, and whatever else it was he was looking for, tonight.

She pushed to her feet again, so fast that her chair threatened to tip over.

Nick said something curt beneath his breath as he rose

to his feet and caught the chair in one smooth movement. In the process, her shoulder bumped his chest and the top of her head brushed his jaw.

He reached out to steady her, his fingers leaving an imprint of heat on her upper arm. Elena stiffened at her response to his touch, light as it was. She instantly moved away, disengaging.

Blinking a little at the strobing lights on the dance floor, and because her new contacts were starting to make her eyes feel dry and itchy, she collected the pink, beaded purse that went with her dress. "If you want to look for the ring, I'm ready now. The sooner we get this over and done with the better."

She was still clearly vulnerable when it came to Nick, but that just meant she had to work harder at being immune.

As she strolled with Nick out of the lavish resort, she tried to fill her mind with all of the positive, romantic things she could plan to do with Robert.

Intimate, candlelit dinners, walks on the beach, romantic nights spent together in the large bed she had recently installed in her Sydney apartment.

Unfortunately, every time she tried to picture Robert in her bed, tangled in her very expensive silk sheets, his features changed, becoming a little more hawkish and battered, his jaw solid, his gaze piercing.

Annoyed with the heated tension that reverberated through her at the thought of Nick naked and sprawled in her bed, she banished the disruptive image.

Six

Tension coursed through Nick as he walked through the resort foyer and down the front steps. Outside the sun had set, leaving a golden glow in the west. The air was still and balmy, the cool of evening infusing the air with a soft dampness.

"My car's this way." He indicated the resort's staff parking lot.

Elena paused beside his Jeep, which was parked in the manager's space. "No towing service in Dolphin Bay?"

"Not for a Messena."

She waited while he unlocked the Jeep. "I keep forgetting you're related to the Atraeus family. Nothing like a bit of nepotism."

He controlled the automatic desire to flirt back and held the door while Elena climbed in. As she did so, the flimsy skirt of her dress shimmied back, revealing elegant, shapely legs and the ultra-sexy high heels.

He found himself relaxing for the first time since Elena's pronouncement that she had a boyfriend. Although the hot pulse of jealousy that Elena had not only been ignoring his calls, but that sometime in the past few weeks she had started dating someone else, was still on a slow burn.

Robert Corrado. Grimly, he noted the name.

It was familiar, which meant he probably moved in business circles. Given that Elena was Zane's PA, she had probably met him in conjunction with her work for the Atraeus Group.

The thought that Corrado could be a businessman, and very likely wealthy, didn't please Nick. He would call his personnel manager and get him to run a check on Corrado first thing in the morning.

Jaw taut, he swung into the cab. The door closed with a thunk, and Elena's delicate, tantalizing perfume scented the air, making the enclosed space seem even smaller and more intimate.

The drive to the villa, with its steep bush-clad gullies and winding road, took a good fifteen minutes despite the fact that the property was literally next door to the resort, tucked into a small private curve of Dolphin Bay.

Security lights flicked on as he turned into the cypress-lined gravel drive. He checked out the for-sale sign and noted that it didn't have a Sold sticker across it yet.

Satisfaction eased some of his tension. He didn't need another property, and with its links to his father's past he shouldn't want this one. His offer to Elena had been a tactic, pure and simple, a sweetener to give him the opening he needed to research the past.

Although, once he had decided to make the purchase, the desire to own the property had taken on a life of its own.

On thinking it through, he had decided that his motives were impractical and self-centered. In buying the villa he hoped to somehow soothe over the past and cement a link with Elena.

Whichever way he looked at it, the whole concept was flawed. It presupposed that he wanted a relationship.

The second he brought the Jeep to a halt, Elena sent him a bright professional smile and unfastened her seat belt. "Let's get this over and done with."

With crisp movements, she opened her door and stepped out onto the drive.

Jaw tightening at the unsubtle hint that, far from being irresistibly attracted, Elena couldn't wait to get rid of him, Nick locked the Jeep.

He padded behind Elena, studying the smooth walls glowing a soft, inviting honey, the palms and lush plantings.

Elena was being difficult about the property, but he was certain he could bring her around. With the deal he was negotiating to buy a majority share in the Dolphin Bay Resort, in partnership with the Atraeus Group, it made sense to add the property to the resort's portfolio.

As Elena unlocked the front door, the sense of stepping back in time was so powerful that he almost reached out to pull her close. It was a blunt reminder that almost everything about a liaison with Elena had been wrong from the beginning, and six years on, nothing had changed.

The tabloids exaggerated his love life. Mostly he just dated because he liked female company and he liked to relax. If he wanted to take things further, it was a considered move with nothing left to chance, including the possibility that he might be drawn into any kind of commitment.

With Elena the situation had always been frustratingly

different; *she* was different. For a start, she had never set out to attract him.

Six years ago he had muscled in on her blind date because he had overheard a conversation in a café and gotten annoyed that her friend had set her up with a guy who could quite possibly be dangerous.

But, if he was honest, that had only been an excuse. Elena had been on the periphery of his life for years. She was obviously naive and tantalizingly sweet, and the idea that some other guy could date Elena and maybe make love to her had quite simply ticked him off.

She had been a virgin.

The moment he had logged that fact was still burned indelibly into his mind.

The maelstrom of emotions that had hit him had been fierce, but tempered by caution. At that point he'd had no room in his life for a relationship. His business had come first—he had been traveling constantly and working crazy hours. Elena had needed love, commitment, *marriage,* and he hadn't been in a position to offer her any of those things.

The accident and his father's death had slammed the lid on any further contact, but years later the pull of the attraction was just as powerful, just as frustrating.

Despite applying his usual logic—that no matter how hot the sex, a committed relationship didn't fit with his life—he still wanted Elena.

The fact that Elena wanted him despite all of the barriers she kept throwing up made every muscle in his body tighten. They were going to make love. He knew it, and he was certain, at some underlying level, so did she.

And now he was beginning to wonder if one night was going to be enough.

* * *

Elena stepped inside the villa and flicked on the hall light. Nick, tall and broad-shouldered behind her, instantly made the airy hall seem claustrophobic and cramped, triggering a vivid set of memories.

Nick closing the door six years ago and pulling her into his arms. The long passionate kiss, as if he couldn't get enough of her….

Elena's stomach tightened at the vivid replay. With one brisk step she reached the next series of light switches and flicked every one of them.

They didn't require that much light, since the boxes they needed to search were in the attic. She didn't care. With tension zinging through her, and Nick making no bones about the fact that he wouldn't be averse to repeating their one night together, she wasn't taking any risks.

The blazing lights illuminated the small sunroom to the left, the larger sitting room to the right and the stairs directly ahead.

Sending Nick a smile she was aware was overbright and strained, she started up the stairs. "Help yourself to a drink in the kitchen. I'll change and be right back."

There were four bedrooms upstairs. The doors to each were open, allowing air to circulate. Elena stepped inside the master bedroom she had claimed as her own. A room her aunt had refused to use and which was, incidentally, the same room she and Nick had shared six years ago.

With white walls and dramatic, midnight-dark floor-boards, the bedroom was decorated in the typical Medinian style, with a four-poster dominating. Once a starkly romantic but empty testament to her aunt's lost love, Elena had worked hard to inject a little warmth.

Now, with its lush, piled cushions and rich pomegranate-red coverlet picked out in gold, the bed glowed like a warm, exotic nest. A lavish slice of paradise in an otherwise very simply furnished house.

Closing the door behind her, she began working on the line of silk-covered buttons that fastened the pink dress, her fingers fumbling in their haste.

As she hung the lavish cascade of silk and lace in her closet, her reflection, captured by an antique oval mirror on a stand, distracted her. In pink lingerie and high heels, her hair falling in soft waves around her face, jewels gleaming at her lobes and her navel, she looked like nothing so much as a high-priced courtesan.

Not a good thought to have when she was committed to spending the next two hours with Nick.

Dragging her gaze from an image she was still struggling to adjust to, she pulled on a summer dress in a rich shade of red.

Unfortunately the thin straps revealed the butterfly transfer on her shoulder. Maybe it was ridiculous, but she didn't want Nick to see the full extent of the fake tattoo. With all of the changes she had made, the addition of a tattoo now seemed like overkill and just a little desperate.

Unfastening the gorgeous pink heels, she slipped on a pair of comfortable red sandals that made the best of her spray-on tan, shrugged into a thin, black cardigan and walked downstairs.

When she entered the sitting room, she saw Nick's jacket tossed over the back of a chair. The French doors that led out to the garden were open, warm light spilling out onto a small patio.

As she flicked on another lamp, Nick stepped in out of the darkness, the scents of salt and sea flowing in with him. He half turned, locking the door behind him, and the simple, intimate motion of closing out the night made her heart squeeze tight.

With his jaw dark and stubbled, his shirt open at the throat, he looked rumpled and sexy and heartbreakingly like the young man she had used to daydream about on the beach.

Although the instant his cool, green gaze connected with hers that impression evaporated. "Are you ready?"

"Absolutely. This way." She started back up the stairs, her heart thumping faster as she registered Nick's tread behind her.

As she passed her bedroom, she noted that in her rush to get downstairs she had forgotten to close the door. The full weight of her decision to invite the *only* man she had a passionate past with to the scene of her seduction, hit home.

If she had been thinking straight she would have asked someone to come with them. A third person would have canceled out the tension and the angst.

Relieved when Nick didn't appear to notice her room or the exotic makeover she'd given the bed, she ascended another small flight of stairs. Pushing the door open into a small, airless attic, she switched on the light. Nick ducked underneath the low lintel and stepped inside.

He stared at the conglomeration of old furniture, trunks and boxes. "Did Katherine ever throw anything away?"

"Not that I've noticed. I suppose that if the ring is anywhere on the property, it'll be here."

As always when she thought of her aunt, Elena felt a sentimental softness and warmth. She knew Katherine had adored all of her nieces and nephews, but she and Elena had shared a special bond. She had often thought that had been because Katherine hadn't had children of her own.

Feeling stifled by the stale air and oppressive heat,

Elena walked to one end of the room to open a window. The sound of a corresponding click and a cooling flow of air told her that Nick had opened the window at the other end.

"Where do we start?" Nick picked up an ancient book, a dusty tome on Medinian history.

"Everything on that side of the room has been searched and sorted." She indicated a stack of trunks. "This is where we need to start."

"Cool. Sea trunks." Nick bent down to study one of the old leather trunks with their distinctive Medinian labeling. "When did these come out?"

"Probably in 1944. That's when the Lyon family immigrated to New Zealand."

"During the war, about the same time my family landed. I wonder if they traveled on the same ship."

"It's possible," Elena muttered. "Although, since your family owned the ships it was unlikely they would have socialized."

Nick flipped a trunk open. Another wave of dust rose in the air. "Let me get this right. My grandparents would have traveled first-class so they wouldn't have spoken to your relatives?"

Still feeling overheated, Elena ignored her longing to discard her cardigan. "The Lyons were market gardeners and domestic servants. They would have been on the lower decks."

With a muffled imprecation, Nick shrugged out of his tightly fitted waistcoat. Tossing it over the back of a chair, he unfastened another button on his shirt, revealing more brown, tanned skin.

Dragging her gaze from the way the shirt clung across his chest, Elena concentrated on her trunk, which was filled with yellowed, fragile magazines and newspapers.

Nick, by some painful coincidence, had opened a trunk filled with ancient women's foundation garments. He held up a pair of king-size knickers in heavy, serviceable cotton. "And the fact that some of them settled here in Dolphin Bay was just a coincidence, right?"

The tension sawing at her nerves morphed into annoyance. She had never paid any particular attention to her family's history of settlement, especially since her parents lived in Auckland. But now that Nick was pointing it out, the link seemed obvious. "Okay, so maybe they did meet."

Nick extracted a corset that appeared to rely on a network of small steel girders to control the hefty curves of one of her ancestors. "It was a little more than that. Pretty sure Katherine's grandparents worked for mine."

Elena vowed to burn the trunk, contents and all, at the earliest possible moment. "I suppose they could have been offered jobs."

He closed the lid on the evidence that past Lyon women had been sturdy, buxom specimens and pulled the lid off a tea chest. "So, maybe the Messena family aren't all monsters."

Feeling increasingly overheated and smothered by the cardigan, Elena discreetly undid the buttons and let it flap open. The neckline of her dress was scooped, revealing a hint of cleavage, but she would have to live with that. "I didn't say you were. Aunt Katherine liked working for your family."

The echoing silence that greeted her quiet comment, was a reminder of the cold rift that still existed between their families—the abyss that separated their lifestyles—and made her mood plummet.

Although she was fiercely glad she had ruined the camaraderie that had been building. Stuck in the confined space with Nick, the past linking them at every turn, she had needed the reminder.

Elena opened the trunk nearest her. A cloud of dust made her nose itch and her eyes feel even more irritated. She blinked to ease the burning sensation.

Too late to wish she'd taken the time to remove her colored contacts before she'd rejoined Nick.

Nick dumped an ancient bedpan, which looked like it had come out of the ark, on the floor. When she glanced at him, he caught her eye and lifted a brow, and the cool tension evaporated.

Suddenly irrationally happy, Elena tried to concentrate on her trunk, which appeared to be filled with items that might be found in a torturer's toolbox. She held up a pair of shackles that looked like restraints of some kind.

"Know what you're thinking." Nick grinned as he straightened, ducking his head to avoid the sloping ceiling. "They're not bondage." He closed the box of books he'd finished sorting through. "They're a piece of Medinian kitchen equipment, designed to hang hams in the pantry. We've got a set at home."

Elena replaced the shackles and tried not to melt at Nick's easy grin. She couldn't afford to slip back into the old addictive attraction. With just minutes to go before he was out of her life, now was not the time to soften.

She glanced at her watch, although her eyes were now watering enough that she had difficulty reading the dial.

"Are those contacts bothering you?"

"They're driving me nuts. I'll take them out when I go downstairs."

Once Nick was gone.

Nick closed the lid on the box with a snap that echoed through the night.

There was a moment of heavy silence in which the

tension that coiled between them pulled almost suffocatingly tight.

"Damn," he said softly. "Why are you so intent on resisting me?"

Seven

The words seemed to reverberate through the room.

Elena glared at Nick. "What I don't get is *why* you want me?"

"I've wanted you for six years."

"I've barely seen you in six years."

Nick frowned as a gust of wind hit the side of the house. "I've been busy."

Building up a fortune and dating a long line of beautiful girls who never seemed to hold his interest for long... and avoiding her like the plague because she would have reminded him of *that* night.

And in that moment Elena acknowledged a truth she had been avoiding for weeks.

Now, just when she was on the point of getting free and clear, and at absolutely the wrong time—while they were alone together—it dawned on her that Nick was just as fatally attracted as she.

Outside it had started to rain, large droplets exploding on the roof.

Elena rubbed at her eyes, which was exactly the wrong thing to do, as one of the contacts dropped out. Muttering beneath her breath, she began to search, although with the dim lighting and with both eyes stinging, she didn't expect to find it.

Sound exploded as the rain turned tropically heavy. Moist air swirled through the open window.

She was suddenly aware that Nick was close beside her.

"Sit down, before the other one drops out."

"No. I need to find the lens, although it's probably lost forever." Added to that, her eyes were still watering, which meant her mascara was running.

Swiping at the damp skin beneath her eyes, Elena continued to search the dusty floorboards.

Something glittered, but when she reached for it, it turned out to be a loose bead. At that moment the wind gusted, flinging the window wide. Jumping to her feet, she grabbed at the latch and jammed it closed.

A corresponding bang informed her that Nick had closed the other window. As she double-checked the latch, Nick loomed behind her, reflected in the glass.

"Don't you ever listen?" The low, impatient timbre of his voice cut through the heavy drumming on the roof. His hands closed around her arms, burning through the thin, damp cotton of her cardigan. "You need to sit down."

Obediently, Elena sat on an ancient chair. Nick crouched in front of her, but even so he loomed large, his shoulders broad, his bronzed skin gleaming through the transparent dampness of his shirt. The piercing lightness of his eyes pinned her. "Hold still while I get the other lens out for you."

Elena inhaled, her nostrils filling with his heat and scent. Her stomach clenched on the now-familiar jolt of sensual tension. "I don't need help. All I need is a few minutes in the bathroom—"

Cupping her jaw with one large hand, he peered into her eyes. "And some drops."

Nick was close enough that she could study the translucence of his irises, the intriguing scar on his nose to her heart's content. "How would you know?" But she was suddenly close enough to see.

"I've worn contacts for years. Hold still."

As Nick bent close, his breath mingled with hers. She swallowed and tried not to remember the softness and heat of the kiss they'd shared on the steps of the church.

With a deft movement he secured the second contact on the tip of his forefinger.

Reaching into his pocket, he pulled out a small container of eyedrops and a tiny lens case. Setting the drops on the top of a nearby trunk he placed the lens gently in the case and snapped it closed.

Before he could bulldoze her into letting him put the drops in, Elena picked up the small plastic bottle and inserted a droplet of the cooling solution in each eye. The relief was instant. Blinking, she waited for her vision to clear.

Nick pressed the folded handkerchief she had given him earlier in the day into her hand. "It's almost clean."

"Thank you." Elena dabbed in the corners and beneath both eyes, then, feeling self-conscious, peeled out of the damp cardigan. "What else have you got in those pockets?"

"Don't ask."

Acutely aware that if Nick had another item in his pockets, it was probably a condom, Elena peered into a dusty mirror propped against the wall.

For a disorienting moment she was surprised by the way she looked, the tousled hair and exotic curve of her cheekbones, the pale lushness of her mouth.

She had definitely made outward changes, but inside she wasn't nearly as confident as that image would suggest.

Although according to Giorgio, that would change once she resurrected her sex life.

The thought that she could resume her sex life, here, now, if she wanted, made her heart pound and put her even more on edge.

An hour later, they emptied the final trunk. "That's it." Relief filled Elena as she closed the lid. "If the ring isn't here, then Katherine didn't receive it. I've already been through everything else."

"You searched all of the desks and bureaus downstairs?"

Elena wiped her hands off on a cloth. "Every cupboard and drawer."

Absently, she picked up a photo album, which she'd decided to take downstairs.

Picking up the cloth, she wiped the cover of the album. Glancing at the first page of photos, her interest was piqued. Unusually, many of the photos were of the Messena family.

She was aware of Nick's gaze fixing on the album. Somewhere in the recesses of her mind disparate pieces of information fused into a conclusion she should have arrived at a long time ago. Nick had taken a special interest in any photo album he had come across.

As she tucked the album under her arm and bent to retrieve her damp cardigan, a small bundle of letters dropped out from between the pages. Bending, she picked them up. The envelopes were plain, although of very good parchment, a rich cream that seemed to glow in the stark light. They were tied together with a white satin ribbon that shimmered with a pearlized sheen.

Her throat closed up. Love letters.

The top envelope was addressed to her aunt. Heart beating just a little faster, because she knew without doubt that she had found a remnant of the relationship her aunt had kept secret until she died, Elena turned the small bundle over.

The name Carlos Messena leaped out at her, and the final piece in the puzzle of just why her aunt and Stefano Messena had been personally linked fell into place. "Mystery solved," she said softly.

Nick tossed the cloth he'd used to wipe his hands with over the back of a broken chair. Stepping over a pile of old newspapers that were destined for the fire, he took the letters.

"Uncle Carlos," he said quietly, satisfaction edging his voice. "My father was the first son, he was the second. Carlos died on active duty overseas around thirty years ago. So that's why Dad gave Katherine the ring. It was traditionally given to the brides of the second son in the family. If Katherine and Carlos had married, it would have been hers."

With careful movements, he untied the faded ribbon and fanned the letters out on the top of a trunk, checking the dates on each letter.

Holding her breath, because to read the personal exchanges, even now, seemed an invasion of privacy, Elena picked up the first letter. It was written in a strong, slanting hand, and she was instantly drawn into the clear narrative of a love affair that had ended almost before it had begun, after just one night together.

Empathy held her in thrall as she was drawn into the brief affair that had ended abruptly when Carlos, a naval officer, had shipped out.

Elena refolded the letter and replaced it back in its envelope. Nick passed her the contents of the envelope he had just opened. On plainer, cheaper paper, it was written in a different hand. There was no love letter, but in some ways the content was even more personal: a short note, a black-and-white snapshot of a toddler, a birth certificate and adoption papers for a baby named Michael Carlos.

The mystery of Stefano's relationship with Katherine was finally solved: he had been helping her find the child she had adopted out. A Messena child.

Nick studied the address on the final envelope. "Emilia Ambrosi." He shook his head. "She's a distant cousin of the Pearl House Ambrosis. I could be wrong, but as far as I know she still lives on Medinos." He let out a breath. "Medinos was the one place we didn't look."

Elena dragged her attention from the sparse details of the Messena child. "You knew Aunt Katherine had had a baby?"

"It seemed possible, but we had no proof."

Feeling stunned at the secret her aunt had kept, she handed Nick the note, the snapshot and the birth certificate.

Gathering up the letters, she tied them together with the ribbon and braced herself for the fact that Nick would be gone in a matter of minutes.

She should be happy they had solved the mystery and found closure. Her aunt had tragically lost Carlos, but she had at least experienced the heights—she had been *loved.* They hadn't found the ring but, at a guess, Katherine had sent it to her son, who was probably a resident on Medinos.

Elena made her way downstairs to the second level. Placing the album and the sadly rumpled cardigan on a side dresser in the hall, she washed her hands and face, then waited out in the hall while Nick did the same.

Curious to see if Aunt Katherine had included any further shots of her small son in the album, she flipped to the first page. Unexpectedly, it was dotted with snapshots of the Messena children when they had been babies.

Nick's gaze touched on hers as he exited the bathroom, and the awareness that had vibrated between them in the attic sprang to life again.

She closed the album with a faint snap. "You must have suspected all along that a Medinian engagement ring, a family heirloom, was a strange gift for a mistress."

With his waistcoat hanging open, his shirt unfastened partway down his chest, the sleeves rolled up over muscular forearms, Nick looked tough and masculine and faintly dissolute in the narrow confines of the hall. "It wouldn't be my choice."

The thought that Nick obviously gave gifts to women he loved and appreciated ignited a familiar coal of old hurt and anger. After their night together she hadn't rated so much as a phone call.

"What would you choose? Roses? Dinner? A tropical holiday?"

She seemed to remember reading an exposé from a former PA of Nick's and her claims that she had organized a number of tropical holidays for some of his shorter, more fiery flings.

His expression turned wary. "I don't normally send gifts. Not when—"

"Great strategy." She smiled brightly. "Why encourage the current woman when there's always another one queuing up?"

There was a moment of heavy silence during which the humid, overwarm night seemed to close in, isolating them in the dimly lit hall.

Nick frowned. "Last I heard there is no queue."

Probably because he was never in one place long enough for the queue to form. Nick was more a girl-in-every-port kind of guy.

Elena found herself blurting out a piece of advice he probably didn't want to hear. "Maybe if you slowed down and stayed in one place for long enough there would be."

And suddenly Nick was so close she could feel the heat radiating off him, smell the clean scents of soap and aftershave, and an electrifying whiff of fresh sweat generated by the stuffy, overheated attic.

She stared at a pulse beating along the strong column of his throat. Sweat shouldn't be sexy, she thought a little desperately, but it suddenly, very palpably, was.

Nick's hand landed on the wall beside her head, subtly fencing her in. "With my schedule, commitment has never been viable."

"Then maybe you should take control of your schedule. Not," she amended hastily, "that I have any interest in a committed relationship with you. I have—Robert."

She didn't, not really, and the small lie made her go hot all over. But suddenly it seemed very important that she should have someone, that she shouldn't look like a total loser in the relationship stakes.

Nick's brows jerked together. "I'm glad we're clear on that point."

"Totally. Crystal clear." But her heart pounded at the edge in Nick's voice, as if he hadn't been entirely happy at her mention of Robert. Or that she had nixed the whole idea of a relationship with him.

Nick cupped her jaw, the heat of his fingers warm and slightly rough against her skin. "So this is just friendship?"

He dipped his head, slowly enough that she could avoid the kiss if she wanted.

A shaft of heat burned through her as he touched his mouth to hers. She could move away. One step and she could end the dizzying delight that was sweeping through her that maybe, just maybe, they had turned some kind of corner when they had uncovered the reason behind his father's relationship with her aunt.

That now that the past was resolved, a relationship between them wasn't so impossible.

Heart pounding as the kiss deepened, she lifted up on her toes, one hand curving over Nick's broad shoulder as she hung on. The tingling heat that flooded her, the notion that they could have a future, were all achingly addictive. She couldn't remember feeling so alive.

Except, maybe, six years ago.

That thought should have stopped her in her tracks. But the gap of time, the emotional desert she'd trudged through, *after Nick,* had taught her a salutary lesson.

She needed to be loved, and she absolutely did not want to remain alone. So far the search for a husband had proved anticlimactic. Good character and an appealing outward appearance just didn't seem to generate the "in love" part of the equation. Bluntly put, so far there had been no chemistry.

On the other hand, while Nick failed every sensible requirement, with him there was nothing *but* chemistry.

If she could have the chemistry and the committed relationship with Nick, she would be...happy.

His mouth lifted. He released her jaw as if he was reluctant to do so, as if he hadn't wanted the kiss to end, either.

Drawing a shaky breath, Elena relinquished her grip on Nick's shoulder.

A relationship with Nick? Maybe even with a view to marriage?

It was a major shift in her thinking. She didn't know if Nick could be anything to her beyond a fatal attraction. All she knew was that with his gaze fixed on hers and the unsettling awareness sizzling between them, the possibility seemed to float in the air.

That, and the knowledge that she was about to lose him in approximately two minutes.

She drew a swift breath. If she wanted Nick, she would have to take a risk. She would have to fight for him.

The fingers of her free hand curled into one of the lapels of his waistcoat where it hung open, her thumb automatically sweeping over the small button.

Surprise at the small possessive gesture flared in his gaze and was quickly replaced by a heat that took her breath. "I have to leave early in the morning."

She did her best to conceal her shock at how quickly he had cut to the chase and assumed that they would spend the night together, and the instant stab of hurt evoked by his blunt pronouncement that he had to leave. She had already known he was flying out on business. "Yes."

"You don't mind?"

She did, like crazy, but she wasn't about to let him know that. She had decided to take the risk of trying for a relationship with Nick. That meant she had to toughen up because a measure of hurt would naturally be involved.

She forced a smile. "I'm only here for a few days myself, then I need to be back in Sydney."

He wound a finger in her hair, the touch featherlight, and she tried not to love it too much. "For the record, my dating is usually on a casual basis. Most of it happens around yachting events when I'm racing."

That wasn't news to Elena. Her current Atraeus boss was a sailor, which meant there were quite often yachting magazines lying around in the office. Nick's name occasionally leaped out from the pages. "Which is quite often."

His breath wafted against her cheek, damp and warm and faintly scented with the champagne they'd drunk at the wedding. "Granted."

She inhaled and tried to drag her gaze from the slice of brown flesh and sprinkling of dark hair visible in the opening of his shirt. "But there have been a lot of women."

The album, which had been tucked under her arm, slipped and fell to the floor, as if to punctuate her statement.

His hands closed on the bare skin of her arms, his palms warm and faintly abrasive, sending darting rivulets of fire shimmering through her. "According to the tabloids. But we both know how reliable they are as a source of information."

Nick bent his head, bringing his mouth closer to hers. "If you don't want me to stay the night, just say so, and I'll leave you alone."

As he drew her close, she gripped the lapels of his shirt, preserving a small distance. Despite committing to a night with him, caution was kicking in. She needed more. "*Why* me?"

"For the same reason it's always been. I'm attracted to you. I like you."

A month ago, on a street in Auckland, he had said he

liked her. It wasn't enough, but coupled with the chemistry that vibrated between them and the fact that the rift between their families would now be healed, a relationship suddenly seemed viable.

Cupping Nick's stubbled jaw, she lifted up on her toes and kissed him. A split second later she found herself in his arms. With a heady sense of inevitability, she looped her arms around his neck, heat clenching low in her belly as she fitted herself even more closely against the hard angles and planes of his body.

After all the years of being calmly, methodically organized, of never losing her cool, there was something exhilarating about abandoning herself to a passionate interlude with Nick.

"That's better." He smiled, a glimpse of the uncomplicated charm that had always entrapped her, the kind of charm that made little kids flock around him and old ladies sit and chat. Except this time it was all for her and enticingly softer.

As Nick's mouth settled on hers, the reason he was so successful with women hit her. Despite the hard muscle and the wickedly hot exterior, he possessed a bedrock niceness that made women melt.

It was there in the way he noticed small things, like the color of her eyes and the fact that she was wearing contacts, the way he had rescued her from the blind date six years ago when he didn't have to get involved.

Her feet lost contact with the floor; the light of the hall faded to dim shadows as they stepped into a bedroom.

With a sense of inevitability, Elena noted the wide soft bed, with its lush piled cushions and rich red coverlet.

A lavish, traditional Medinian marriage bed, arrayed for a wedding. The room she had whimsically decorated.

The same room in which Nick had made love to her the last time.

Eight

Fitful moonlight shafted through a thick bridal veil of gauze festooning a tall sash window as Elena was set down on marble-smooth floorboards.

Nick shrugged out of his shirt, revealing sleekly powerful shoulders, a broad chest and washboard abs.

His mouth captured hers as he locked her against the furnace heat of his body. The hot shock of skin on skin momentarily made her head swim, but for all that, the kiss and the muscled hardness of his chest felt, oddly, like coming home.

Lifting up on her toes, she wound her arms around his neck and kissed him back. She felt the zipper of her dress glide down, the sudden looseness. Seconds later, she shrugged out of the straps and let the flimsy cotton float to the floor. Another long, drugging kiss and her bra was gone.

Bending, Nick took one breast into his mouth and for

long aching minutes the night seemed to slow, stop, as heat and sensation coiled tight.

She heard his rapid intake of breath. A split second later she found herself deposited on the silken-soft bed.

Feeling a little self-conscious and exposed, Elena slipped beneath the red coverlet, unexpected emotion catching in her throat as she watched Nick peel out of his trousers. She was used to seeing him in a modern setting as masculine, muscled and hot, but cloaked in moonlight and shadows, his bronzed skin gleaming in the glow of light from the hall, he was unexpectedly, fiercely beautiful, reminding her of paintings of Medinian warriors of old.

Dimly, she registered a rustling sound, like paper or foil. The bed depressed as Nick pulled the coverlet aside and came down beside her. The heat of his body sent a raw quiver through her as he pulled her close.

His gaze locked with hers, the softness she had noted in the hall giving her the reassurance she suddenly desperately needed.

He propped himself on one elbow, a frown creasing his brow. "Are you all right?"

She cupped his jaw and tried for a confident smile. "I'm fine."

One long finger stroked down her cheek. "Then why do I get the feeling that you're not quite comfortable with this?"

"Probably because I haven't done *this* in a while."

Something flared in his gaze. "How long?"

"Uh—around six years, I guess."

He said something soft beneath his breath. "Six years ago you slept with me."

The breath caught in her throat. "I guess, given what happened that night, you're not likely to forget."

"If the accident hadn't happened, I would still have remembered," he said quietly, "since you were a virgin."

For a split second she felt his indecision, the streak of masculine honor that had once been ingrained in Medinian culture. Abruptly afraid that he might abandon the whole idea of making love, that she might lose this chance to get him back in her life, she took a deep breath and boldly trailed a hand down his chest. "I'm not a virgin now."

He inhaled sharply and trapped her hand beneath his, then used it to pull her close so that she found herself half sprawled across his chest. "Good."

He rolled, taking her with him so that he was on top, his heavy weight pressing her down into the feather-soft mattress. Dipping his head, he kissed her mouth, her throat, and finally took one breast in his mouth.

Elena tensed, palms sliding across his shoulders, the sleek muscles of his back, as rivulets of fire seemed to spread out from that one point, culminating in a restless, aching throb.

He shifted his attention to her other breast, and in that moment heat and pleasure coiled and condensed, exploding into aching, shimmering pleasure as the night spun away.

Nick muttered something short and flat. Moments later his weight pressed her more deeply into the bed. She felt him between her legs, and relief flowed through her as slowly, achingly, he entered her.

The faint drag of what could only be a condom made her eyes fly open. The sound she had registered earlier suddenly made sense. Nick had sheathed himself, which meant he'd had the condom in his pocket.

The realization was like a cold dash of water. She shouldn't think about the condom. She shouldn't allow it to matter, but it did, because it meant he had been prepared to have sex with *someone,* not necessarily her.

Nick was oddly still, his expression taut as if he had gauged every one of the emotions that had just flitted across her face. "Something's wrong. Do you want me to stop?" A muscle pulsed along the side of his jaw. *"Yes, or no?"*

The words were quietly delivered, without any trace of frustration or need—just a simple question. Although she could see the effort it was costing him in the corded muscles of neck and shoulders.

The blunt, male way he had presented her with the choice brought her back to her original reason for making love: because she wanted another chance with him.

At the thought of losing him, contrarily, she wanted him with a fierce, no-holds-barred need that rocked her.

For every reason that shouldn't matter—because he was too elusive, too spoiled by the women he had dated and way too dangerous for her heart—he was the last man she could afford in her life.

And yet he was the only man to whom she had ever been truly, passionately attracted.

There was no logic to what she felt, no reason why he should smell and taste and *feel* right when no one else had ever come close.

Unless somehow, despite the frustration and anger and sheer loneliness of the past few years, she had somehow fallen for him, and he was *The One.*

She clamped down on the moment of shocked awareness. This was where she had gone wrong the first time with Nick—she had wanted too much, expected too much.

Every feminine instinct she had informed her that applying any form of pressure at this point would scare

Nick off, and she couldn't afford that. Framing his face with her hands, she drew his mouth to hers, distracting him from discovering that she might have done the one thing that seemed to scare men the most and fallen for him. "The answer is no, I don't want you to stop."

She promised herself she wouldn't cry as relief registered in his gaze and gently, slowly, he began to move.

There was a moment of utter stillness when he was fully sheathed and they were finally, truly one, and then he undid her completely by softly kissing her mouth.

His thumb brushed away a trickle of moisture that had somehow escaped one eye, then he pulled her closer still, holding her with exquisite care and tenderness as if he truly did love her. A heated, stirring pleasure that was still shatteringly familiar despite the passage of years, gripped her as they began to move.

Locked together in the deep well of the night, the angst and hurt of the past dissolved. Nothing mattered but the way Nick held her, the way he made her feel, as the coiling, burning intensity finally peaked and the night spun away.

In the early hours of the morning, Elena woke, curled in against the furnace heat of Nick's body. His arm was curved around her waist, keeping her close, as if even in sleep he couldn't bear to be parted from her.

A surge of pure joy went through her. She had taken the risk, and it was working. Nick had been tender and sweet, and the passion had, if anything, been even hotter, even more intense.

She was convinced that this time they really had a chance.

The false start six years ago had muddied the waters,

but the hurts of the past shrank to insignificance com-
pared with the happiness and pleasure ahead.

She smiled as she sank back into sleep. All was for-
given. She couldn't let the past matter when they were
on the verge of discovering the once-in-a-lifetime love
she was certain was their destiny.

A chiming sound pulled Elena out of a deep, dreamless sleep. She rolled, automatically reaching for Nick.
The pillow where his head had lain was still indented
and warm, but that side of the large, voluminous bed
was empty.

Moonlight flowed through the window, illuminating
the fact that Nick was pulling on clothes with the kind of
quick efficiency that denoted he was in a hurry. Silvery
light gleamed over one cheekbone and the strong line of
his jaw as he glanced at his watch.

The bronzed gleam of broad shoulders and the strong
line of his back disappeared as he shrugged into his shirt.

His gaze touched on hers as he buttoned the shirt with
quick efficiency. "I have to leave now, otherwise I'll miss
my flight out."

Elena jackknifed, dragging the sheet with her and
wrapping it around her breasts. The memory of Nick
explaining his schedule the previous evening flooded
back. "The flight to Sydney."

The side of the bed depressed as he pulled on socks
and shoes. "I have a series of business meetings I can't
cancel. They're important."

"Of course." More important than exploring the passion they had found together, or the spellbinding sense
that they were on the verge of discovering something
special.

She drew an impeded breath and killed the idea of suggesting that, since she lived in Sydney and was due back soon, maybe she could go with him. It was too soon to put that kind of pressure on their relationship.

She needed to remember one of the rules Giorgio had given her about dating: that men liked to feel as if they were the hunter, even if that wasn't strictly the case.

She forced one of her professional smiles. "Of course. I understand completely."

His gaze was oddly neutral as he collected his phone from the bedside table and shoved it into his pocket. A trickle of unease made her stomach tighten.

As if he had already distanced himself from what they had done.

Bending, he picked something up from the floor. When he straightened, she recognized the packet of love letters. "I'll return these."

"No problem. I'm sure your mother will be relieved to know that Stefano was helping Katherine find her adopted child."

Another lightning glance at his watch, then Nick leaned across the bed and kissed her, the caress perfunctory. "Thanks. It was…special."

Elena froze. The awkwardness of the moment expanded when she failed to respond, but she had quite suddenly reached the end of her resources.

She recognized this part. Nick had gotten what he wanted: closure for the scandal that had hurt his family and another night of convenient passion. Now he was trying to step away from any suggestion of a relationship by leaving as quickly as possible.

Her fingers tightened on the beautiful sheets as Nick strode from the room. She heard his step on the stairs, then the sound of the front door quietly closing. A few seconds later, the rumble of the Jeep's engine broke the stillness of early morning.

She blinked back the burning heat behind her eyes and resolved not to cry. She could see why Nick's relationships ended so easily. He had concluded a night of passion in the same way he conducted his business affairs: briefly and with his gaze fixed on the next goal.

The full folly of returning to the scene of her last mistake and sleeping with Nick again settled in. Dragging the silk sheet with her, she wrapped it around herself and walked to the freestanding oval mirror. The moonlight was incredibly flattering. She was actually, finally, attractive in the way she had longed to be.

Although that hadn't seemed to matter to Nick. It hadn't tipped the balance and made him fall for her.

Which, she realized, was exactly what she had secretly hoped when she had started on the whole process of improving her appearance.

Admitting that pleasing Nick had been her motivation to change was painful, but if she wanted to move on she had to be honest.

She had been stuck in relationship limbo for years. Just when she was on the verge of forming a positive, rewarding romantic friendship with a nice man, she had thrown herself at Nick again.

Hitching the sheet up, she walked to the window and dragged the thick drape of white gauze back. A pale glow in the east indicated that the sun would soon be up. She needed to shower, get dressed and make a plan.

She had made the mistake of allowing Nick to get to her, again.

But the fledgling love affair that had dogged her for six years was finally finished. There would be no replays.

She was finally over Nick Messena.

Nick grimly suppressed a yawn as he sipped an espresso during his flight to Sydney.

Kyle, who was with him to represent the bank's interests in the partnership deal he was negotiating with the Atraeus Group, turned a page of his newspaper. "Did you find the ring?"

Nick took another sip of coffee and waited for the caffeine to kick in. "Not yet."

Briefly he filled Kyle in on the love letters and the adoption papers they had found, and that he had stopped by and spoken to their mother before he had left Dolphin Bay.

That had been a priority. The stark relief on Luisa Messena's face had told him just how much she had been holding out for the information.

There was a small vibrating silence, which finally broke through the grim flatness that had gripped Nick ever since he had driven away from Dolphin Bay.

Kyle put his newspaper down. "You and Elena looked like you were getting on. Last I heard, she wasn't returning your calls—"

"We found some common ground."

"Something's happened." Kyle's gaze had taken on the spooky, penetrating look that was a legacy of his time in the SAS, New Zealand's Special Forces. Something about Kyle's calm neutrality inspired respect and actual fear in the high-powered financial magicians he dealt with on a daily basis. When he turned up with the scary eyes the deal usually got done in minutes.

Kyle shook his head. "You slept with her again."

Nick's fingers tightened on his coffee cup. "I shouldn't have confided in you six years ago."

Kyle shrugged. "Dad had just died. You were understandably emotional."

Nick finished his coffee and set his cup down on the seat tray with a click. "According to the family, I have the emotions of a block of stone."

"Whatever. You've slept with Elena Lyon twice. That's…complicated."

Wrong word, Nick thought. There had been nothing complicated about what they had done or how he had felt.

He had been caught up in the same visceral hit of attraction that had captured him the night his father had died. An attraction that had become inextricably bound up with loss and grief, and what he had believed was his father's betrayal.

With the knowledge that his father and Katherine had not been involved, he should have been able to view Elena in the same way he viewed other past lovers. As an attractive, smart woman who was in his life for a period of time.

But the realization that Elena hadn't ever slept with anyone but him had sounded the kind of warning bells he couldn't ignore.

His reaction had been knee-jerk. As addictive as those hours with Elena had been, after years of carefully avoiding emotional entanglements and commitment, he'd found he couldn't do a sudden, convenient U-turn.

As much as he had wanted to spend more time with her or, even more crazily, take her with him, the whole idea of being that close to someone again had made him break out in a cold sweat.

Kyle signaled to a flight attendant that he wanted a

refill for his coffee. "If you don't want to talk about it, that's cool, but you might need to take a look at this."

Nick took the tabloid newspaper Kyle had been reading and stared at the piece written about Gabriel and Gemma's wedding. The details of the ceremony were correct, but it wasn't his brother and his new bride in the grainy black-and-white wedding photos.

Someone had made a mistake and inserted a photo of himself and Elena kissing on the steps of the church. It was flanked by a shot of him helping Elena into the limousine when they were on their way to have the official photos taken. A third snap as they had left the reception together rounded out the article. Apparently they were now on their way to a secret honeymoon destination.

A trolley halted beside his seat. A pretty flight attendant offered to take his cup. Absently, Nick handed it to her, barely noticing her smile or the fact that she was blonde, leggy and gorgeous.

According to the tabloids, *according to Elena,* the flight attendant was his type.

Although not anymore.

Now, it seemed, he had a thing for brunettes. Fiery brunettes with hourglass figures and issues.

Just as the flight attendant was about to move on, she glanced at the newspaper and sent him a brilliant smile. "I thought I recognized you. Congratulations on your marriage."

"Uh—I'm not actually married."

She looked confused. "That's not you?"

"It's him," Kyle supplied unhelpfully. "They've split up already."

There was a moment of shocked silence. The flight attendant dredged up a brilliant, professional smile that was cold enough to freeze water. "Would you like me to get you anything more, sir?"

The words, *like marriage guidance or an actual heart,* hung in the air.

"He's happy," Kyle supplied, along with the killer smile that usually made women go weak at the knees. "We have everything we need."

The attendant gave Kyle a stunned look, then walked quickly off, her trolley rattling.

Nick folded the newspaper and gave it back to Kyle. "Thanks for making her think that I ditched my wife of just a few hours because I decided to turn gay."

Kyle disappeared behind his paper again. "Look on the bright side. At least now she thinks *I'm* the villain."

Broodingly, Nick returned to thinking about the second night he had spent with Elena. Another passion-filled encounter that was proving to be just as frustratingly memorable and addictive as the first.

He hadn't been able to resist her and the result was that Elena had gotten hurt.

Nick retrieved an envelope from his briefcase and stared at the faded copy of the birth certificate and the photograph of the toddler he had brought with him.

He had found the reason his father had been in the car with Katherine the night they had both died. Not because Stefano Messena had been having an affair, but for a reason that fitted with his character. His father had been helping Katherine locate her baby.

The reason he had passed the ring to Katherine was because it, and a sizable chunk of the Messena fortune, belonged to his long-lost cousin. His birth year was the same as Nick's, which would mean Michael Ambrosi would be his age: twenty-nine.

An image of his father the last time he had seen him

alive flashed through Nick's mind. His chest went tight at the vivid picture of Stefano Messena tying down a sail on his yacht, his expression relaxed as he enjoyed the methodical process. It was the picture of a man who liked to do everything right.

For the first time he examined the fact that he hadn't been able to let anyone close since his father had died.

Intellectually, he knew what his real problem was, or *had been.* He had known it the moment he saw the love letters and birth certificate hidden in Katherine Lyon's photo album.

Because he and his father had been so close, no matter how hard he'd tried he hadn't been able to disconnect and move on. He'd stayed locked in a stubborn mind-set of grief and denial. The last thing he had wanted was to immerse himself in another relationship.

His mother and his sisters had probed and poked at his inability to "open up." The words *dysfunction* and *avoidance* had figured largely in those conversations.

Nick had stepped around the whole issue. Maybe it was a male thing, but he figured that when he felt like becoming involved in a relationship, he would.

But something had changed in him in the instant he had discovered the possibility that Stefano Messena hadn't cheated on or betrayed anyone.

Emotion had grabbed at his stomach, his chest, powerful enough that for long seconds he hadn't been able to breathe.

His fingers tightened on the birth certificate.

Grimly he allowed himself to remember that night. The time spent waiting for the ambulance, even though he'd known it had been too late. The hurt and anger that had gripped him at the way his father had died.

He knew now that his father had just been unlucky.

The heavy rain had made the road slippery. He'd probably been driving so late because he wanted to get home.

Home to the wife and family he loved.

He slipped the birth certificate and the photograph
back into the briefcase. The moment felt oddly symbolic.

Nick didn't personally care about the ring, which, in
any case, rightfully belonged to Michael Ambrosi. He
had what he wanted: he had his father back.

When they landed in Sydney the press was waiting in
the arrivals lounge.

Nick groaned and put on his game face.

Kyle grinned. "Want me to take point?"

"Just promise not to speak."

"Name, rank and serial number only. Scout's honor."

"That would have meant more about an hour ago on
the flight."

The questions, all centered on Elena, were predictable. Nick's reactions were not.

Instead of staying doggedly neutral, cold anger
gripped him every time a journalist directed another intrusive or smutty question at him.

By the time he reached the taxi rank he was close to
decking a couple of the tabloid hacks.

When they reached the Atraeus offices thirty minutes later, his normally nonexistent temper had cooled.
But his lack of control pointed up a change in himself
he hadn't expected.

Usually when he walked away from a liaison he felt
detached, his focus firmly on his next work project.

Right at that moment, he was having trouble concentrating on anything but Elena.

What she was doing and how she was feeling *about
him* was coming close to obsessing him.

The thought that she might actually get a tattoo or, worse, go back to the mysterious Robert, suddenly seemed a far more riveting issue than the resort package that would take his business portfolio to a new level.

As they stepped into an elevator, Nick took out his cell and put through a call to his PA, instigating a security check on Corrado. And, more importantly, requesting a full rundown on all of Corrado's business interests and a photo.

He hung up as the elevator doors opened up on the floor occupied by the Atraeus offices.

Constantine Atraeus, who was dealing with the negotiation himself, walked out and shook hands.

Constantine was both family and a friend. In his early thirties, he was incredibly wealthy, with a reputation for getting what he wanted. Although the powerful business persona was offset by a gorgeous, fascinatingly opinionated wife, Sienna, and now a cute young daughter.

Minutes later, with the deal on the table, Nick should have been over the moon. Instead, he found it difficult to focus. Kyle kept sending him questioning glances because it was taking him so long to read the paperwork.

A slim brunette with silky dark hair strolled into the room. Constantine's new legal brief. Apparently the last one had bitten the dust because he had tried to put a prenup on Sienna Atraeus. Sienna had seen him to the door, personally.

Nick forced himself to finish the clause he was reading, even though he knew he was going to have to go over it again because he hadn't understood a word.

The problem, he realized, was the legal brief. For a searing moment he had thought she was Elena, even though a second glance confirmed that she didn't look like Elena at all.

His gaze narrowed as he tracked her departure. His pulse was racing, his heart pounding as his inability to concentrate became clear.

He wanted Elena.

He wanted her back, in his arms and in his bed, which was a problem given that he had walked out on her that morning for the second time. If she ever spoke to him again, that in itself would be a miracle.

It had been difficult enough getting her to trust him the last time. The process had been slow and laborious. From the first phone call, it had taken weeks.

She had stood him up, refused his calls and done everything in her power to avoid him. He had managed to get close to her only through the good luck that his brother had gotten married to Elena's best friend.

If he wanted Elena back, he was going to have to engineer a situation that would give him the time he needed to convince her to give him another chance.

Two of his Atraeus cousins had employed kidnapping as a method of securing that quality time, although Nick didn't seriously think a kidnap situation would repair the rift with Elena. Both Constantine and Lucas had had long-standing relationships with their chosen brides, with the added bonus that love had been a powerful factor in each relationship.

It was a factor Nick could not rely on. He was certain that after a second one-night stand, Elena would no longer view him as a relationship prospect.

For a split second disorientation gripped him. He could kick himself for the mistake he'd made. He'd had Elena back in his arms, and then let her go.

He had further complicated the situation by leaving the field clear for Corrado.

If he wanted Elena back he was going to have to move

fast. Normal dating strategies wouldn't work; he was going to have to use the kind of logic he employed with business strategies.

With this new deal they would have a vital link in common: the Atraeus Group. He wouldn't exactly be her boss, but it would bring her into his orbit.

He'd had two chances with Elena and had blown them both.

He didn't know if he could create a third, but he had an edge he could exploit.

Try as she might, Elena couldn't hide the fact that she couldn't resist him.

Nine

Master of Seduction Meets His Match.

Elena stared in horror at the tabloid coverage of the wedding. She hadn't read many of the words; it was the image of the bride and groom that riveted her attention.

Someone had made a terrible mistake. A photo of her and Nick on the steps had been used instead of one of Gemma and Gabriel. The black-and-white print made her bridesmaid's dress look pale enough to be a bridal gown, and Nick looked the part with his morning suit. The shower of confetti and rice added the final touch.

There was nothing either scandalous or libelous about the brief article. If the photograph had been the correct one, it would have been perfectly nice, if boring, coverage of a high-end society wedding.

Acute embarrassment gripped her as she imagined the moment Nick saw the article and the photo, which portrayed the exact opposite of what he had wanted.

As wonderful as the night had been, something had gone wrong. They had been finished the moment Nick had walked out of the bedroom without a backward look.

She hadn't tried to cling to him, but that didn't alter the fact that watching Nick walk away a second time had hurt.

Or that in a single night she had been willing to sacrifice almost every part of her life to be with him, if only he had truly wanted her.

Elena snapped the paper closed. She could not be a victim again. She had changed her external appearance and now she needed to work hard at changing her actual life.

First up, she would take the new corporate position Constantine Atraeus had suggested she consider. With her executive PA skills, the psychology papers she had done at university and her recent experience of health and beauty spas, she was uniquely suited to reinvigorate the Atraeus spas.

She would be an executive, which suited her.

She was tired of catering to the whims of the megawealthy Atraeus bosses, who had appreciated her skills but who never really noticed her as a person.

A hum of excited possibility gave the future a rosy glow. She would probably need her own personal assistant, although that was a leap.

Two brief calls later, and her life was officially transformed.

Zane wasn't happy, since he had just gotten used to her taking care of every possible detail of his working day and travel arrangements. However, he was pragmatic. Since Elena had lost weight, his fiancée, Lilah, hadn't been entirely happy with her as a PA, much as she liked Elena. It was nothing personal, it was just that Lilah had a protective streak when it came to Zane.

"She might relax more after the wedding," Zane explained.

Elena hung up, a little dazed. She would never have believed it, but apparently she was now too pretty to be a PA.

She walked across to her hotel mirror and stared at her reflection. She looked pale and washed-out, but if Zane Atraeus said she was too pretty, then she was too pretty.

Nick had said she was beautiful.

She could feel herself melting inside at the memory of the way he had said those words, the deep timbre of his voice.

Jaw firming, she banished a memory that could only be termed needy and self-destructive.

Instead of going weak at the knees at any little hint of male appreciation from Nick, she needed to form an action plan. She needed rules.

Rule number one had to be: Do *not* get sucked back into Nick Messena's bed.

Rule number two was a repeat of the first.

She would make the rest up as she went along.

Critically, she studied the suit she was wearing. It was pink. She was over pink. The suit was also too feminine, too *pretty*.

She needed to edit her wardrobe and get rid of the ruffles and lace, anything that might possibly hint that she had once been a pushover.

From now on, red was going to be her favorite color.

She would also make a note to encourage Robert a little more. If she was in a proper relationship, it stood to reason that she would not be so vulnerable to a wolf like Nick Messena.

One month later, Elena opened her eyes as pads soaked in some delicately perfumed, astringent solution were removed from her now-refreshed eyes.

Yasmin, the head beauty therapist at the Atraeus Spa she had spent the past three weeks overhauling, smiled at her. "You can sit up now, and I'll start your nails. Can't have you looking anything less than perfectly groomed for your date. What was his name again?"

"Robert."

There was a small, polite silence. "Sounds like a ball of fire."

"He's steady and reliable. He's an accountant."

Yasmin wrinkled her pretty nose. "I've never dated one of those."

Elena reflected on the string of very pleasant dates she'd had with Robert. "He has a nice sense of humor."

Yasmin gave her a soothing smile as she selected a bottle of orchid-red nail polish and held it up. "That's important."

Elena nodded her approval of a color that normally she wouldn't have gone near. But with her transformation, suddenly reds and scarlets seemed to be her colors. Idly, she wondered what Nick would think of the nail polish.

She frowned and banished the thought.

Yasmin picked up one of Elena's hands and set to work on her cuticles. "So, tell me, what does Robert look like?"

Elena shifted her mind away from its stubborn propensity to dwell on Nick, and forced herself to concentrate on Robert. "He has green eyes and dark blond hair—"

Yasmin set one hand down and picked the other up. "Sounds a little like Nick Messena."

Except that Robert didn't have quite that piercing shade of green to his eyes, or the hot gold streaks in his hair. "Superficially."

"Well, if he looks anything like Nick Messena, he's got to be sexy."

"I wouldn't say Robert was sexy…exactly."

"What then?"

Elena watched as Yasmin perfectly and precisely painted a nail. "He's…nice. Clean-cut and extremely well-groomed. Medium build. He's definitely not pushy or ruthless."

Every attribute was the exact opposite of Nick's casual, hunky, killer charm. She had checked weeks ago before she had made the decision for a first date with Robert. After all, what was the point of repeating her mistake? She wanted a man who would be good for her. A man who would commit.

Yasmin painted another nail. "He sounds close to perfect."

"If there was a textbook definition for the perfect date, Robert would be it."

"Talking about perfect men, I saw a photo of Nick Messena in a magazine the other day." She shook her head. "I can't believe how *hot* he is. That broken nose… It shouldn't look good, but it is to *die* for."

Elena's jaw tightened against a fierce surge of jealousy. Swallowing, she tried to put a lid on the kind of primitive, unreasoning emotion that made her want to find the magazine Yasmin had been mooning over and confiscate it.

Jealousy meant she hadn't quite gotten Messena out of her system. It meant she still cared. "Why is it that a broken nose makes a guy more attractive?"

"Because he fights. Perfect men look like they're fresh out of the wrapper. Untried under pressure." She grinned. "I must admit, I like a guy who doesn't mind getting sweaty."

Elena blinked at the sudden image of Nick years ago when she'd walked past a construction site and glimpsed him with his shirt off, covered in dust and grease smears, a hard hat on his head. "I think we should talk about something else."

"Sure." Yasmin sent her a patient you're-the-client look.

The following day, after another pleasant date with Robert during which she had partnered him to one of his company dinners, Elena was packed and ready to fly back to New Zealand. She would spend a couple of days in Auckland, then travel on to Dolphin Bay where she was poised to add a new level of service to the resort business: a pamper weekend that included a relationship seminar she had designed herself.

Her stomach tightened a little as the taxi driver put her luggage into the trunk. Just because she was on her way back to Dolphin Bay didn't mean she would run into Nick. Chances were, he wouldn't even be in the country.

And even if he was, she had successfully avoided him for years. She could avoid him again.

He would get Elena back; it was just a matter of time.

Despite the fact that she had hung up on him again.

Broodingly, Nick placed his phone on the gleaming mahogany surface of his desk.

Not a good sign.

A familiar surge of frustration tightened every muscle in his body as he rose from his office chair, ignoring the cup of coffee steaming gently on his desk. Prowling to the French doors, he looked out over Dolphin Bay.

A heat haze hung on the horizon, melding sea and sky. Closer in, a small number of expensive yachts and launches floated on moorings, including his own yacht, *Saraband*.

Stepping out on the patio, he looked down over his new domain. He now owned a 51-percent share of the resort chain. It was a new turn in his business plan, but one that made sense with his close ties to the Atraeus family and their meshing interests.

Gripping the gleaming chrome rail, he surveyed the terraced levels of the resort complex. His eye was naturally drawn to gleaming turquoise pools below dotted with swimmers and fringed with cooling palms. Though it was the peaked roof of the villa in the adjacent curve of the bay that held his attention.

A hot flash of the night he'd spent with Elena blotted out the lavish tropical scene. The heat of the memory was followed by a replay of the hollow sensation that had gripped him when he had walked out of the villa just before sunrise.

His mother and his two sisters had read him the riot act about his dating regime a number of times.

He now no longer had the excuse of his father's so-called betrayal. As one of his sisters had pointed out, he was out of excuses. It was time he confronted his own reluctance to surrender to a relationship.

A tap on his office door jerked him out of his reverie. The door popped opened. Jenna, his new ultra-efficient PA, waved the file he had requested and placed it on his desk.

As he stepped back into the office, she sent him one of the bright, professional smiles that had begun to put his teeth on edge.

She paused at the door, her expression open and confident. "A group of us are going into town for lunch. You're welcome to join us if you'd like."

Nick dragged his gaze from the lure of the file, which he'd been waiting on. Absently he turned down the offer. Jenna was five-ten, slim and curvy in all the right places. He would have to be stone-cold dead not to notice that she was gorgeous in a quirky, cute way that would obsess a lot of men.

Although not him.

He should find her attractive. A couple of months ago, he would have. The red-haired receptionist in the lobby was also pretty, and a couple of the waitresses in the resort restaurant were stunning. The place was overrun with beautiful, available women, if only he was interested.

Opening the file, he began to skim read. Zane had given him a heads-up that a pamper weekend the Dolphin Bay Resort was scheduled to run in the next few days was Elena's pet project.

He was aware that she had quit her job as a PA and was now heading up a new department, developing the lucrative spa side of the resort business. The pamper weekend and seminar, designed for burned-out career women, was a pilot program she had designed and was entitled What Women Really Want: How to Get the Best Out of Your Life and Relationships.

His door opened again, but this time it was his twin sisters, Sophie and Francesca, who were home for a week's holiday.

They were identical twins, both gorgeous and outgoing with dark hair and dark eyes. Sophie tended to be calm and deceptively slow-moving with a legendary obsession with shoes, while Francesca was more flamboyant with a definite edge to her character.

Sophie, sleek in white jeans and a white tank, smiled. "We've come to take you out to lunch."

Francesca, looking exotic in a dress that was a rich shade of turquoise, made a beeline for his desk and perched on the edge, swinging one elegantly clad foot. "Mom's worried about you." She leaned over and filched his coffee. "Apparently you've gone cold turkey on dating for three months, and you're not sailing, either. She thinks you're sickening for something."

With the ease of long practice, he retrieved his coffee. "You'll have to try another tack. First of all, Mom isn't likely to worry when I'm doing exactly what she wants by not dating. And I've gone without dating for longer periods than three months before."

Sophie circled his desk and dropped into his chair. "When you were building your business and didn't have time for the fairer sex."

"News flash," Nick growled. "I'm still building the business."

Sophie picked up the file he'd dropped on the desk when he'd rescued his coffee and idly perused it. "But you have slowed down. Haven't you got some hotshot executive shark cutting deals and intimidating all of your subcontractors?"

Nick controlled the urge to remove the file from Sophie's grasp. "I've got a team of sharks. Ben Sabin is one of them."

Sophie looked arrested. "But you knew who I was talking about."

Nick frowned at Sophie's response to Ben Sabin, who had a reputation for being as tough on relationships as he was troubleshooting his jobs. He made a mental note to have a word with Sabin and make sure that he understood that Nick's sisters, both of them, were off-limits.

Francesca pushed off the edge of the desk, the movement impatient but graceful. "So what's up? Mom thinks you've fallen for someone and it isn't working out."

Nick dragged at his tie, suddenly feeling harassed and on edge. He should be used to the inquisition. His family was large and gregarious. They poked and pried into each other's lives, not because they were curious but because they genuinely cared.

As prying as his mother and his sisters could be, in an odd way he usually loved that they hassled him. He knew that if he ever got seriously messed with by a woman, they would be as territorial as a pack of wolves protecting their young.

Sophie frowned at the file. "Elena Lyon? Didn't you used to date her?"

Francesca's gaze sharpened. She strolled around the desk and peered at the file. "It was a blind date, only Nick wasn't blind. He set it up."

Nick frowned. "How do you *know* this stuff?"

Francesca looked surprised. "I used to study with Tara Smith who waited tables at the Dolphin Bay Coffee Shop. She overheard you telling Smale to find someone else to date and that if you ever heard he was trying to date Elena Lyon again, the next conversation would be outside, on the sidewalk." Francesca smiled. "Pretty sure that's verbatim. Tara's now a qualified accountant—she doesn't make mistakes."

Nick felt like pounding his head on the solid mahogany door of his office, but that would be a sign of weakness—something he couldn't afford around his sisters.

A small frown pleated Sophie's brow. "Elena was Gemma's bridesmaid, the girl in the picture when the tabloids mistakenly put the wrong photo in the paper."

Francesca went oddly still. "That would be the series of photos that fooled everyone into thinking Nick had gotten married."

There was a heavy silence as if a conclusion that only women could achieve had just been reached.

Sophie's expression morphed back to calm and serene. Nick groaned inside. He didn't know how they had connected the dots, but both of his twin sisters now knew exactly how interested he was in Elena Lyon.

Nick controlled another powerful urge to retrieve the file. If he did that, the inquisition would worsen.

Sophie turned another page, brow pleated, reminding him of nothing so much as a very glamorous, earnest female version of Sherlock Holmes. "Elena was the maid of honor at Gabriel's wedding." There was a significant pause. "Now she's coming back to Dolphin Bay for a weekend."

Francesca's gaze snapped to his. "Did she plan this?"

Nick's brows jerked together at the implication that Elena was scheming to trap him, when as of ten minutes ago she was still refusing to take his calls. "There is nothing planned about it. She doesn't know I'm here."

That was a mistake.

Nick pinched the bridge of his nose and tried to think, but something about the twin's double act interfered with normal brain function.

Francesca's look of horror sealed his fate. Five minutes ago he had been an object of careful examination and pity, but now he was a predator. It was strange how the conversations usually went that way.

Francesca fixed him with a fiery gaze. "If you're letting her come here and she doesn't know you own the hotel, well, that's…predatory."

Sophie ignored Francesca's outrage as she placed the file back on the desk and eyed him with the trademark calm authority that thirty years from now would probably be scaring grandkids. "Do you want her?"

In the quiet of the room the bald question was oddly shocking.

Nick's jaw clenched. As family inquisitions went, this one was over. "There is no relationship. Elena works for the Atraeus Group. She's coming to Dolphin Bay to work."

As far as he was concerned, technically, the relationship he was angling for would begin *after* Elena arrived.

An hour later, after a fraught lunch spent sidestepping further questions and a raft of romantic advice, Nick made it back to his desk.

Opening the file he'd been attempting to read earlier, he studied the letter that had come with the pamper weekend program. He would recognize Elena's elegant slanting signature anywhere.

Unfastening the pale pink sheet from the file fastener, he lifted it to his nostrils. The faint exotic scent of lilies assailed him, laced with a musky under note that set him sensually on edge.

Loosening his tie, he sat back in his seat and studied Elena's pamper weekend package. Though designed for women, men were welcome to attend.

He flicked through the pages until he arrived at a quiz. Gaze sharpening, he studied a sheet of multiple-choice questions entitled The Love Test.

The stated object of the quiz, one of the few elements of the package aimed at men, was to find out if the man in a woman's life knew how to really and truly love and appreciate her.

He flicked through the pages, twenty questions in all that ignored the more commonly perceived signs of a good relationship, such as flowers, gifts and dating. Instead the quiz wound through a psychological minefield, dealing with issues such as emotional honesty, the ability to understand a woman's needs, and with commitment.

As far as Nick could make out, the quiz didn't focus on what a man could aspire to romantically so much as highlight the age-old masculine traits that would make him stumble.

The question on when a relationship should be consummated was a case in point. For most men the answer to that question was simple. Sex was a priority, because in a man's mind until he had made a woman his completely, there was an element of uncertainty that didn't sit well with the male psyche.

Setting the test sheets down, he turned to the answers, frowning as he read through. The questions he had taken a guess at were all wrong.

As far as he could make out, no ordinary man could hope to score well. It would take an intellectual studying psychology or some kind of New Age paragon.

Like Robert Corrado.

His jaw tightened. From the few comments Elena had made, if Robert took the test, he would pass with flying colors. From the research Nick had done on Corrado, he was inclined to agree.

His fingers tightened on the page, crumpling it. As highly as he was certain Robert would score, he didn't think he was the kind of man to make a woman like Elena happy. She would be bored with him in a matter of months. Elena needed a man who wouldn't be intimidated by her formidable strength of character, her passionate intensity.

Nick was that man.

The moment was defining.

He straightened out the page of answers and reattached it to the file. Over the years, commitment had not been a part of any of his relationships.

But now, with the expansion of his business, and several highly paid executives taking the lion's share of the work, he didn't have quite so much to do.

He had time on his hands. And, as luck or fate would have it, once again Elena Lyon was in his equation.

And he was on the brink of losing her to another man.

In that moment, an internal tension he hadn't known existed relaxed, and the focused, masculine drive to attain and hold on to the woman he wanted, that had been missing for so many years, settled smoothly into place.

Six years had passed. Years in which Elena had been single and free, prey to any male who cared to claim her.

But not anymore.

Elena was his. He had hurt her—twice—but there was no way he was going to tamely stand aside and give Corrado a chance at her.

His resolve firmly in place, he checked the answer sheets to find the highest-scoring answers for each question. His frown increased as he read. Out of a possible score of sixty, with a couple of lucky guesses thrown in, he might have made five points. If that wasn't bad enough, the grading system, at odds with the smooth New Age language, was punitive. Thirty points, a pass in any man's language, was considered to be "indifferent." Ten points was "extremely poor." At five points he balanced on the cusp of "disastrous" and "a relationship mistake of catastrophic proportions."

Irritation coursed through him. There was no possibility that any red-blooded male could score well. But information was power and if he wasn't mistaken, he had just been given the key to getting Elena back.

The pamper weekend and the seminar provided the window of opportunity he needed.

Setting the sheet of answers back on top of the file, he walked through to the next office. He offered Alex Ridley, the hotel manager, a well-earned few days off, during which time he would manage the resort. An hour later, he had cleared his schedule for those three days.

Elena wouldn't be happy when she arrived and found him in residence, but he would cope with that hurdle when they got to it.

After the way he had messed up, he was well aware that negotiation wouldn't work. With the skills Elena had honed during her years as a personal assistant to his Atraeus cousins, she would ruthlessly cut him off. Desperate measures were required.

Picking up the quiz, he broodingly read through the questions again.

He didn't know if he would ever be in a position to do the quiz, but at this juncture he needed to be prepared for any eventuality. Picking up a pen, he systematically ticked the correct answer for each question. The 100-percent score entitled him to encircle the grade that assured him he was A Perfect Relationship Partner.

It was cheating.

But as far as he was concerned, when it came to getting Elena back, all was fair in love and war.

Ten

Elena crossed Dolphin Bay's county line just minutes short of midnight. The Dolphin Bay sign was briefly illuminated in the wash of headlights as she changed down for a curve and braked. The familiar arching entrance to the Messena Estate loomed, and her heart beat a brief, unwelcome tattoo in her chest.

She had to stop thinking about Nick. By now he would be thousands of miles away, probably on some sand-blasted site in Dubai and doing what was closest to his heart: making millions.

A tight corner loomed. She slowed even further as she drove through a bush reserve, the road slick with recent rain and the moonlight blocked by large, dripping ponga ferns arching over the road.

The massive plastered gateposts of the resort glowed softly ahead. Relieved, she turned onto the smoothly sealed resort road and accelerated, climbing steadily.

The lush rainforest gave way to reveal a breathtaking expanse of moonlit sea. Nestled amidst bush-clad hills and framed by the shimmering backdrop of the Pacific Ocean, the resort glittered, patently luxurious and very, very private.

Minutes later, she drew up outside a security gate.

The resort boasted a conference center, a world-class private golf course, a marina and a helipad. They catered to the luxury end of the market and were open for business 24/7, but for security reasons—mostly centered around the extremely wealthy clientele who stayed there and their privacy needs—the gates were locked from midnight until six in the morning.

Guest were issued key cards in advance, but weirdly, her key card envelope, which had been couriered to her, had been empty. Since she didn't yet have a card, on arrival she had to ring the reception desk so they could dispatch someone to unlock the gate and let her in. It all seemed unacceptably low-tech to Elena. She had already sent a very short email to the manager informing him that he needed to lift his game in this respect.

Once she checked in, apparently she would be issued a key card and could come and go as she pleased.

Jaw locked, she pushed the door open, climbed out into the balmy night and took a moment to stretch the kinks out. Just a few yards away, water lapped on honey-colored sand, the soothing rhythm underpinned by an onshore breeze flowing through the pohutukawa trees that overhung parts of the beach. During daylight hours, the stunning red blooms would provide a brilliant contrast to the intense blue of sea and sky.

She examined the fortresslike wrought iron gates, searching for the intercom. A small red light winked off to one side. Seconds later a receptionist with a smooth, warm voice answered her and assured her that someone would unlock the gate for her shortly.

Tiredness washed through Elena as she strolled across the short patch of perfectly mown grass that separated the driveway from the beach. Peeling out of her strappy red high heels, she stepped down onto the sand.

It was close on high tide. Letting her shoes dangle from her fingers, she walked a few steps until she was ankle deep in the creamy wash of the waves, drawn by the sheer romantic beauty of the moon suspended over the water.

The throaty rumble of an engine broke the soothing moment. Reluctantly, she retraced her steps. Powerful headlights speared the murky darkness, pinning her. The SUV, which was black and glossy with expensive, chunky lines, came to a smooth halt behind the wrought iron gates, the engine idling.

The driver didn't immediately climb out. Frustrated, she attempted to identify who it was behind the wheel, but the glaring halogen headlights had killed her night vision. A peculiar sense of premonition tightened low in her belly.

The door swung open. A broad-shouldered figure swung smoothly out from behind the wheel and the premonition coalesced into knowledge.

Despite the fact that she was braced for the reaction, her stomach plunged. Dressed in faded jeans and designer trainers, a soft muscle T-shirt molding the contours of his chest and leaving tanned biceps bare, Nick looked as tall, dark and dangerous as the last time she had seen him, *naked and in her bed*.

She went hot, then cold, then hot again. A weird pastiche of emotions seized her: embarrassment, dismay, a familiar sharp awareness, a jolt of old fury.

He gave her a lightning-fast once-over, making her aware of the messy strands of hair blowing around her cheeks and her sand-covered feet. Despite the fact that she was dressed for work in a tailored gray suit, she suddenly felt underdressed.

"Nick." She reached for the smooth professionalism that went with the suit, the elegant shoes and her new executive status. "This is a surprise."

And his presence threw some light on the resort's failure to supply her with a key card. Obviously, for some reason of his own, Nick had wanted another conversation.

His gaze, between the bars, was considering. "Not my fault. You didn't return my calls."

Two phone calls, four weeks and two days out? After she had been dumped—*for the second time*—by a man who had a reputation for running through women?

She held on to her temper with difficulty. "Sorry. I've been a little busy lately."

"You've cut your hair."

"It was time for a change."

A whole lot of changes. The feathery, pixie cut went well with her new executive job. Plus, the new, sharper style made her feel that she was moving on emotionally.

His gaze was distant as he depressed a remote for the gate and she wondered if she'd imagined the initial flash of masculine interest.

With careful precision, she deposited the red shoes on the passenger seat of her car. "What are you doing here?"

The weird sense of premonition that had gripped her was back. In none of her contacts with the Dolphin Bay Resort had Nick's name been mentioned. He wasn't listed on the website or in any of the correspondence she'd received from the resort when she had set up the seminar. "Tell me you're a guest."

Although, he couldn't be a guest. His family's enormous luxury house was just up the road and guests didn't open gates.

His gaze connected with hers, sending chills zinging down her spine again, and the brief fantasy that this was just as much of a surprise to Nick as it was to her evaporated. He had been expecting her.

"I'm not a guest. Haven't you heard? As of two days ago, I'm a part owner of the Dolphin Bay Resort."

Elena parked her car outside the reception area. She was now officially in shock.

Although maybe she should have seen this coming. She knew Nick had been working on some deal at Gabriel and Gemma's wedding. She just hadn't put it together with the news that the Atraeus family were shifting shares around within the family.

She had assumed that an Atraeus would take over the New Zealand side of the resort business. She had forgotten that Nick Messena was an Atraeus on his mother's side.

Nick insisted on helping her with her bags, then waited while she checked in at the reception desk. The owner of the smooth voice was a tall redhead with a spectacular figure and a pleasant manner. Once Elena had signed the register and obtained a site map of the resort, she looped the strap of her handbag over her shoulder, picked up her briefcase and reached for her overnight suitcase. Nick beat her to it.

"I'll show you to your cottage."

"I have a map. I can find my own way."

"It's no problem. All part of the service."

Briefly, she considered trying to wrestle the case back then, gave up on the notion and reluctantly followed Nick as he stepped back out into the night. The resort wasn't a high-rise complex—it comprised a number of layers of apartments and cottages, each set in their own lushly landscaped areas to preserve privacy. Her cottage was located in sector C. According to the map, it couldn't be more than one hundred yards away.

As she strolled, she kept an eye on the curving path, which had narrowed, meaning that she had to move closer to Nick.

In her eagerness to keep distance between them, one of her heels slipped off the edge and sank into a thick layer of shells. His hand landed in the small of her back, steadying her. She stiffened, moving away from the heat of his palm, careful not to stumble again.

He indicated a branching pathway and an attractive hardwood building nestled among palms. A tinkling fountain was positioned to one side.

Seconds later, relieved, she slid her key card into the lock and opened her door. Soft light automatically filled the small, inviting hallway. She set her handbag and her briefcase down on the exquisite hardwood floors and turned to collect her case.

Moonlight glinted on the tough line of Nick's jaw. "Now that you're here,' he said with a smooth confidence that set her teeth on edge, "we can finally talk."

"It's late. And this conversation was over a long time ago." If memory served her correctly, it had involved three words and the last one had been "special."

His jaw tightened, the first kink in his composure

she'd seen so far, and suddenly the ball was back in her part of the court.

He set the case down. "I know I behaved badly last month, but I was hoping we could—"

"What, Nick?" She checked her watch, anything to take her mind off the riveting notion that Nick was working up to doing the one thing she had wanted when she had woken up after their night together. He was on the verge of suggesting they spend some time together.

The luminous dial indicated it was almost one in the morning.

He stepped a little closer. The wash of golden light from the porch of her cottage gleamed off his mouthwatering cheekbones. "Since you're here for the weekend I was hoping we could spend some time together." Startled that he had actually said the words, she dragged her gaze from the odd diffidence of his. It occurred to her that he seemed sorry that he had hurt her. As if he really did want—

She forced herself to edit that line of thought. This was Nick. She would not be fooled again.

Taking a deep breath, she dismissed the old, automatic desire to soften, to do exactly what *he* wanted. "I can't think why."

"Because I want another chance with you."

The words were flatly stated, and they sent an electrifying thrill through her. For a split second she was riveted to the spot, quite frankly stunned, then she pulled herself up short. "When did you decide this?"

"A month ago."

She blinked. "I don't believe you."

He shrugged. "It's the truth."

His gaze dropped to her mouth.

Did he actually want to kiss her?

She should be furious, but for the first time in years, armed by hurt, she felt in control of her emotions and entirely capable of resisting him.

Heart pounding, high on an addictive, giddy sense of victory, she held her ground. "I don't understand why."

"This is why." He stepped closer, filling the doorway, his gaze fastened on hers and, like a switch flicking on, her whole body was suddenly alive and humming.

Nick's breath wafted against her cheek, warm and laced with the faintest hint of coffee. After a month of misery and platonic dating, the thought of kissing Nick Messena should leave her utterly cold. Unfortunately, it didn't.

"Thanks for carrying my bag." With a deliberate motion, Elena took a half step back into the hall, closed the door and leaned back on it. Her heart was pounding out of control. She felt weird and slightly feverish, and there it was. Her problem.

Nick Messena, unfortunately, still qualified as a fatal attraction. Close to irresistible and very, very bad for her.

Just like the last time, he was making no bones about the fact that he wanted her, and that in itself was very seductive.

But touching Nick Messena, kissing him—doing anything at all with him—was crazy. He was the boyfriend no self-respecting woman should allow herself to have... except in her fantasies.

She touched her lips, which felt sensitive and tender, even though she hadn't been kissed.

So, okay...Nick Messena still affected her, but she was almost certain that for him there was little or no emotion involved.

He was all about the chase. Commitment was not his middle name.

But after what had happened the last time they had met, it was definitely hers.

Nick's pulse settled into a steady beat as he walked to his own cottage, which was situated next door to Elena's.

The encounter hadn't gone well, but he had been braced for that.

He'd made love to her and left her—twice. He was going to have a tough time reclaiming her trust.

His pulse picked up a notch as he glimpsed Elena, just visible through the wide glass doors in her sitting room, easing slim, delicately arched feet out of her shoes.

With the addition of the red shoes, the gray suit, which could have been dull and businesslike, was cutting-edge and outrageously sexy.

He watched as she walked into the kitchenette, her stride measured, her spine straight, before she finally disappeared from view. It was an award-winning act, but no amount of control could completely repress the sleek, feminine sway to her hips or the fire he knew was stored behind those guarded eyes.

The red shoes said it all. The passion was still there.

He had made a mistake in leaving her. He should have kept her with him, but it was too late to turn the clock back now.

On the plus side, he finally had her back in his territory. He had three days, and the clock was ticking.

Unlocking his door, he stepped inside and walked through to his shower. Now all he had to do was convince her that the chemistry that exploded between them was worth another try. She hadn't let him kiss her, but it had been close.

Satisfaction eased some of his tension as he peeled out of his clothing and stepped beneath twin jets of cool water.

The night hadn't been a complete washout.

Despite the fact that she had closed the door in his face, he was certain that Elena Lyon still wanted him.

Eleven

The next morning, Elena dressed with care for the official part of the program: the What Women Really Want seminar.

Keeping her mind firmly off the fact that, despite everything, she was still attracted to Nick, she studied the filmy pink-and-orange halter top and white resort-style pants. The hot, tropical colors of the top revealed her smooth golden tan and a hint of cleavage. The pants clung to her hips and floated around her ankles, making the most of her new figure.

The outfit was perfect for a luxury resort, but even so she was tempted to retreat behind the business persona that had been her protective armor for years. Picking up pretty pink-and-gold earrings, she determinedly fitted them to her lobes.

The sound of a door closing in the cottage next door distracted her. A glimpse of Nick, dressed in narrow dark

pants and a dark polo, strolling in the direction of the resort, made her heart slam against the wall of her chest.

The path he was using was the same one that led to her
cottage and one other. Since she had heard a door close
and then had seen Nick strolling *away* from the cottages,
there was no way he could be just casually strolling before breakfast. He was living in the cottage next door.

Last night, after Nick had left, she hadn't given any
thought to where he was staying. She had been too relieved that she had managed to say "no," and too busy
going over every nuance of the exchange.

But the fact that Nick had stooped to the tactic with
the key card and put her in a cottage next door to his
underlined that he was serious about wanting her back.

She took a deep breath and let it out slowly. Just because Nick was next door didn't change anything. When
he realized that she meant what she had said, he would
soon switch his attention to one of the many gorgeous
women she was sure would be at the resort.

After spraying herself with an ultrafeminine floral
perfume, she picked up her folder of workshop notes and
the quiz and strolled out of the cottage.

The restaurant was buzzing with guests enjoying
breakfast and sitting on the terrace looking out over the
stunning views. Relieved to see that Nick was not among
the diners, Elena chose a secluded table, and ordered
items that were listed on her diet maintenance plan.

Half an hour later, fortified by fresh fruit, yogurt and
green tea, Elena strolled into the conference center and
froze.

In a sea of femininity, Nick, dressed in black, his
shoulders broad, biceps tanned, was a shady counterpart
to the preponderance of white cotton, expensive jewelry
and flashes of bright resort wear.

His head turned and her heart jolted as his gaze locked with hers.

Jaw firming against the instant heightened awareness and a too-vivid flashback of the previous night, Elena quickly walked to the podium and made an effort to ignore him.

Setting her folder and her laptop down on the table next to the lectern, she booted up the laptop and connected with the large state-of-the-art computerized screen. Briskly, she opened the file and checked that there were no glitches with the software. With the first slide displayed, she was good to go.

A wave of excited feminine laughter attracted her attention. A group of half a dozen of the youngest, prettiest women was clustered around Nick. *Like bees to a honeypot.*

The knowledge that, just as she'd thought, Nick was in the process of hooking up with one of the very pretty women in her seminar made her freeze in place.

She sloshed water from a jug into the tumbler beside it, barely noticing when some spilled onto the table. Setting the jug down with a sharp crack, she looked for a napkin to wipe up the spill. It shouldn't matter that Nick was making conquests, setting up his next romantic episode.

She couldn't find a napkin. Irritation morphing into annoyance, she found a notepad, which she dropped on top of the small puddle.

A sexy rumble of masculine laughter punctuated by a husky feminine voice calling to Nick jerked her head up. She was in time to see a tawny-haired woman with the kind of sultry beauty and lean, curvaceous figure that graced lingerie billboards, fling herself at Nick.

Nick's arms closed around the goddesslike creature, pulling her into a loose clinch.

In that moment, Elena registered two salient facts. Firstly, that the woman Nick was now hugging casually against his side was Nick's cousin, although only by adoption, Eva Atraeus. Secondly, that Eva *was* the kind of woman who graced underwear billboards.

Once a very successful model and now the owner of her own wedding-planning business, Eva was the feminine equivalent of a black sheep in the Atraeus family. Single and determinedly strong-willed, she had side-stepped her adoptive father's efforts to maneuver her into an advantageous marriage. Instead, she had become notorious for serially dating a number of tabloid bad boys.

Elena's stomach tightened as she watched the casual but intimate exchange. It was clear that Nick and Eva knew each other very well.

Who Nick hugged shouldn't matter. Nick Messena didn't belong to her, and he was not husband material.

He'd had his chance, *twice*.

Scrunching up the sopping wet little pad, she tossed it into a nearby trash can. Grimly, she concentrated on stacking her notes neatly on the podium and remembering her last date with Robert. Frustratingly, she couldn't recall the name of the restaurant or what she had eaten. Her one abiding memory was that she had learned just a little too much about Australian tax law.

She checked her watch. She had given herself plenty of time to set up, and consequently had a good fifteen minutes left until the official start time to mingle with her clients.

Extracting her name tag from her handbag, she fastened it on to the left shoulder of her top then walked down onto the floor of the conference room to circulate.

Nick cut her off just as she reached a table set up with coffee, green tea, a selection of wheatgrass and vegetable juices, and platters of fresh fruit. "Looks like a good turnout. Congratulations."

Elena pointedly checked her wristwatch. "We start in just a few minutes."

"I'm aware of the start time. I'm sitting in on the seminar."

Elena reached for a teacup, her careful calm already threatening to evaporate. "You can't stay."

Nick's expression was oddly neutral. "It's my resort. I'm entitled to make sure that what you're doing works for the level of service and luxury we provide."

Elena tensed at the thought of Nick sitting in on her seminar. Jaw tight, she poured herself a cup of green tea. "Constantine approved the program—"

"In the same week he handed over control to me."

With calm precision, Elena set the cup on its saucer, added a slice of lemon and tried to control an irrational spurt of panic. If Nick wanted to crash the seminar she couldn't stop him.

Last night, before she had gone to bed, she had used her priority clearance to check the Atraeus computer files for the details of the resort deal. Nick owned 51 percent. It was a reality she couldn't fight. Not only was he the majority shareholder, it would appear he was also now the current manager.

Technically, he was also her employer for the entire New Zealand group of resorts.

She held the steaming green tea in front of her like a shield. The thin, astringent scent, which she was still trying to accustom herself to, wafted to her nostrils, making her long for the richness of coffee, although she quickly quashed the thought. She was intent on cutting anything bad out of her life. Like Nick Messena, coffee was banned. "The seminar is of no possible interest to you. It's designed for women—"

"There are other men here."

Two men, both booked in by their wives. She had already checked both of them out and couldn't help noticing that they were oddly similar in appearance. Both were medium height and trim as if they ate sensibly and exercised regularly. They were also well dressed and extremely well-groomed. *Like Robert.*

With an effort of will, Elena called up Robert's image again. Right now, with Nick looming over her looking muscular and tanned, as relaxed as a big hunting cat, Robert was a touchstone she desperately needed.

Although, distressingly, she was having trouble remembering exactly what he looked like. Whenever she tried to concentrate on Robert's face, Nick Messena's strong, slightly battered features swam into view.

She kept her expression pleasant as she sipped the bitter tea and tried not to watch longingly as Nick helped himself to black coffee, adding cream and two sugars.

A clear indication that he was settling in for the duration.

She took a sip of tea and couldn't quite control her grimace. "I decided to throw the seminar open to men who were interested in improving their relationships."

"And I'm not?"

She met his gaze squarely. "You said it, not me."

"The question was rhetorical. As it happens, now that the nature of my business is changing, I'm going to have a lot more time on my hands to dedicate to…relationships."

Elena almost choked on another mouthful of tea. She glanced at Eva who had just helped herself to coffee. Unbidden, her mind made an instant wild leap. As an Atraeus employee she had heard the rumor that Eva's father, Mario, who was terminally ill, had been trying to force a match between Eva and Gabriel Messena.

The rumor had been confirmed by Gabriel's new wife, Gemma. Since Gabriel had just married, that meant Mario would be looking for another bridegroom for his headstrong daughter. Of course Nick, as the second Messena son, would be Mario's natural choice.

"No way," Nick said flatly.

Startled, Elena carefully set her tea down before she had another spill. "No way, what?"

"Eva and I are just good friends."

Elena could feel her careful control shattering, the veneer of politeness zapped by a hot burn of emotion she had no hope of controlling. "Then why is she here?"

Somewhere in the recesses of her brain she registered that she must have taken a half step toward Nick, because suddenly she was close enough that she could feel the heat from his body, smell the clean scents of soap and masculine cologne.

Nick's gaze narrowed. "You're jealous."

Elena stared at the taut line of Nick's jaw and a small scar that was almost as fascinating as the nick across the bridge of his nose. "That would be when hell freezes over."

"You don't have to worry. I'm not interested in Eva. After last night you have to know that I want you back."

A tingling thrill shot through her, cutting through the annoyance that he knew she was jealous.

He still wanted her.

A surge of delight mixed with an odd little rush of feminine power put a flush on her cheeks and jerked her chin up a little higher.

But a familiar dash of panic doused the surge of excitement. The last thing she needed to know now was that, after everything that had gone wrong, there was a chance for them after all.

He had left her twice. She should be over him, but clearly she wasn't because the dangerous, electrifying attraction was still there.

Six years. The time that had passed since they had first slept together was a dose of reality she badly needed.

Those years had been lonely and more than a little depressing because she had been unable to settle into another relationship. Like any other woman her age, she had wanted to be loved and connected to somebody special. She had wanted all the trappings of marriage, the warmth and commitment, the family home, the babies.

She hadn't come close, because in her heart of hearts she hadn't been able to move on. She had still been in love with Nick.

She went still inside, the hubbub of conversation receding as she examined the extremity of her emotions, the single-minded way she had clung to the one man who had never really wanted her.

Could she possibly still be in love with Nick?

The thought settled in with a searing, depressing finality. If so, she had loved him through her teens and for all of her adult life, eleven years and counting, with almost no encouragement at all. The chances that she could walk away from him now and get over him didn't look good.

She knew her nature. As controlled and methodical as she was in her daily life, she was also aware of a lurking streak of passionate extremity that seemed to be a part of her emotional make up. Like her aunt Katherine, she obviously had a deep need for a lasting, true love. The kind of love that was neither light nor casual, and which possessed the terrible propensity for things to go wrong.

Nick set his coffee down, untouched. "Eva's a wedding planner. This resort is one of her most requested wedding venues."

Unbidden relief made her knees feel suddenly as weak as water. "If all you want is to gauge the effectiveness of the seminar, you don't need to attend. The head therapist of the spa facility is sitting in."

Nick crossed his arms over his chest. "I'm not leaving, babe."

A secret little thrill shot down her spine at Nick's casual use of "babe," a term that carried the heady subtext that they were a couple and he was stubbornly bent on proving that fact.

A little desperately she skimmed the room and tried to restore her perspective. "I am not your *babe.*"

Ignoring the steady way he watched her, she checked her watch, set her tea back down on the table and walked back to the podium.

Once the first session started it was easier to focus. Nick, true to his word, hadn't left but was occupying a seat near the back of the room. She would have to tolerate his presence until he got tired of material he could have absolutely no interest in and left. The other two men, Harold and Irvine, obviously keen to learn, were seated in the front row.

After introducing the other speakers who were there for the day, Elena surrendered the podium to a beauty therapist who wanted to talk about the latest skin-care technology. While that was going on Elena handed out her quiz.

When she reached Nick's row, which was occupied by Eva and a couple of the more elderly women, she bypassed him without handing out a quiz sheet.

A lean hand briefly curled around her wrist, stopping

her in her tracks. "Whatever that is you're handing out, I'd like to see it."

Reluctantly she handed him the quiz. "It's not something you'd be interested in."

He studied the sheet. "As it happens, I'm pretty sure I do know what women really want."

Her temper snapped at a sudden visual of Nick with dozens of women marching through his bedroom. "Sex doesn't count."

He went still. "Maybe I'm not all about sex. You think I'll score low?"

"I think your score will be catastrophic. Most men can't get above thirty percent."

"What would you say if I believe I can score at least eighty?"

"I'd say that was impossible."

"Then you wouldn't mind a wager on that?"

She drew a swift breath. "Name it."

"You in my bed, for one more night."

She blinked at the sudden flash of heat evoked by that image.

Although, he would never get past 10 percent. She had tried the test on her male hairdresser who was used to dealing with women all day. He had aced it at 55 percent. Nick definitely didn't have a chance. "What do I get when you lose?"

"A free rein to make whatever changes you want to our spa services. And I'll leave you alone."

She met his gaze. "Done."

There was a small smattering of applause.

Embarrassed, Elena swung around to find that the entire seminar group had stopped to listen, including the beauty therapist.

The elderly lady sitting next to Nick said, "When can he do the test?"

"Now would be a good time," Elena muttered grimly.

Twenty minutes later, Elena studied Nick's test with disbelief. She had checked through on her answer sheet, a sheet that only she had access to, twice. He had scored 85 percent, and she was almost certain that he had fluffed one of the easy questions to show off.

She thought she knew Nick through and through, although she was aware that there were private glimpses of his life, like his relationship with his father, which informed her that Nick had a very private side.

Still, could she have been so wrong, and the baddest of the bad boys wasn't so bad after all?

She walked over to where Nick was standing drinking wheatgrass juice and eating sushi with an expression on his face that suggested he wasn't entirely sure that either item qualified as food. "How did you do it?"

"What was my score?"

When she told him, Nick set his wheatgrass juice down, his gaze oddly wary. "When do I get my prize?"

Elena's stomach did a somersault as the completely unacceptable sensual excitement that had proved to be her downfall, twice, leaped to life.

Her reaction made no sense, because she had no interest in a slice of the relationship cake—she wanted the whole thing. She wanted to be desperately in love with a gorgeous guy who was just as in love with her.

She wanted to wallow in the attention and the nurturing warmth of being with someone who not only wanted her but who couldn't live without her.

Nick was not that man.

At six, as part of the pamper weekend package, they were all due to go on a sunset cruise. The cruise would take up a substantial part of the evening. By the time they got back there wouldn't be much of the evening left. "Tonight."

Twelve

Nick knocked on her door at six. Feeling more than a little nervous, she checked her appearance. For the first time in her life she was wearing a bikini, a daring jungle print, concealed by a filmy green cotton tunic that fell to midthigh and was belted at her hips. The look was casual, chic and sexy.

Applying a last waft of perfume, she picked up her beach bag, slipped on matching emerald-green sandals and strolled to the door. When she opened it, Nick, still dressed in the dark trousers and polo, was lounging in the small portico talking on his cell.

His gaze skimmed the emerald-green cover-up and the length of tanned leg it revealed as he hung up. "There's been a change of plan. The motor on the resort's yacht is leaking oil, so we'll be taking mine."

Saraband.

Elena's pulse kicked up another notch at the mention

of Nick's yacht. She had seen it moored out in the bay. It was large, with elegant, racy lines.

He checked his wristwatch. "The catering staff is stocking *Saraband,* but before we cast off I need to collect a spare radio." He nodded in the direction of his Jeep, which she could glimpse, parked just beyond the trees that screened her cottage.

Long minutes later, emotion grabbed at her as Nick drove onto the manicured grounds of the Messena family home. She used to visit on occasion when her aunt was working here, but she had never actually been invited.

The house itself was a large, Victorian old lady with a colonnaded entrance and wraparound verandas top and bottom, giving it a grand, colonial air.

Ultrasensitive to Nick's presence and the knowledge that she had agreed to sleep with him again, *tonight,* Elena climbed out of the Jeep before Nick could get around to help her.

Nick strolled up the steps with her and held the front door.

Removing her sunglasses, Elena stepped into the shady hall.

Nick gestured at a large, airy sitting room with comfortable cream couches floating on a gleaming hardwood floor. French doors led onto a patio, a sweep of green lawn added to the feeling of tranquillity. "Make yourself at home—I won't be long. Eva's staying here for the duration of the retreat but, other than her, the house is empty."

Elena stiffened at the mention of Eva's name.

Firming her chin, she banished the too-familiar insecurities. She had committed to spend the night with Nick. She would not lose her nerve or allow herself to imagine that she wasn't attractive enough for him. It wasn't as if they had never spent a night together. They had. Twice.

Taking a steadying breath, she checked out the sun-washed patio with its pretty planters overflowing with gardenias and star jasmine, then stepped back inside, blinking as her vision adjusted to the shady dimness.

She had already reasoned out her approach. The whole idea of challenging Nick to the quiz had been a mistake. She would never in her wildest dreams have imagined that he could score so highly.

Now that he had, it was up to her to create a positive for herself out of the experience. It was an ideal opportunity to demystify the exciting passion that she now realized had blocked her from experiencing the true love she needed.

Both other times their lovemaking had been spontaneous and a little wild. This time she was determined that out-of-control passion would not be a factor. If Nick wanted to get her into bed, he would have to woo her, something she was convinced—despite his meteoric test score—that he would fail at, miserably.

Once he was exposed as superficial, unfeeling, basically dysfunctional and terrible husband material, she should be able to forget him and move on.

In theory....

She strolled to a sideboard covered with family photographs. Idly she studied an old-fashioned, touched-up wedding photo of Stefano and Luisa, and a variety of baby and family photos. She halted beside a large framed color photo of a plump, bespectacled boy in a wheelchair. It was clearly one of the Messena children, or perhaps a cousin, although she couldn't ever remember anyone mentioning that there was a disabled member of the family.

She studied the young teenager's nose, which had been broken at some point, perhaps in the accident that had injured him, and froze, drawn by an inescapable sense of familiarity. A split second later she was aware that Nick was in the room. When she turned, she logged that he had changed into faded, glove-soft denims and a white, V-necked T-shirt that hugged his shoulders and chest. A duffel bag was slung over one shoulder and he was carrying the spare radio he needed.

She looked at the framed photo of the boy in the wheelchair then transferred her gaze to Nick's nose.

The wariness of his expression killed any uncertainty she might have had stone dead. "That's you."

"At age sixteen."

She could feel the firm emotional ground she had been occupying shift, throwing her subtly off balance. She could remember her aunt mentioning that Nick had had an accident, she had just never imagined it had been that bad.

Just when she thought she had Nick in focus, something changed and she had to reevaluate. The last thing she wanted to learn now was that Nick had a past hurt, that he had been vulnerable, that maybe there were depths she had missed. "What happened?"

"A rugby accident." He shrugged. "It's old history now. I was playing in a trial game for a place at Auckland Boy's Grammar and their rugby academy. I got hit with a bad tackle and broke my back."

Nodding his head at the door, he indicated that they needed to leave, but Elena wasn't finished.

"How long were you overweight?"

He held the door for her, his expression now distinctly impatient. "About a year. Until I started to walk again."

"Long enough not to like how it felt."

"I guess you could say that."

Her mind racing, Elena followed him outside and

neatly avoided his offer of assistance as she climbed into the Jeep's front passenger seat.

Her fingers fumbling as she fastened the seat belt, she tried to move briskly past this setback. She thought she'd had Nick all figured out, that he was callous and shallow, but it was worse than that.

He had a nice streak, a compassionate, protective instinct that she could relate to with every cell of her body. When she was a kid, she had automatically protected every other overweight kid. She hadn't been able to help it; she had felt their vulnerability when they got picked on.

Nick shared that trait in common with her because he had been in that same depressing place, *and* with the glasses. "Is that why you stepped in as my blind date, then slept with me?"

Nick frowned. "The reason I stepped in on your blind date is that I couldn't stand the thought of Smale getting his hands on you. And it wasn't just because I wanted to protect you," he said grimly. "Babe, believe it. I wanted you for myself."

Nick maneuvered the *Saraband* into a sheltered crescent bay on Honeymoon Island, a small jewel of an island about three miles offshore from the resort.

He started lowering the anchor. While he waited for the chain to stop feeding out, he looked over the bow.

Elena had spent the first part of the trip circulating with the clients, but for the past fifteen minutes she had been a solitary figure sitting on the bow, staring out to sea.

Nick jammed his finger on the button, stopping the anchor chain from feeding out. Impatience ate at his normally rock-solid composure while he waited for the yacht

to swing around in the breeze. He took a further minute to check line-of-sight bearings to ensure that the anchor had locked securely on to the seabed and that they
weren't drifting. By the time he walked out onto the deck,
the first boat, with Elena aboard, was already heading
for the bay.

His gaze was remote as he slipped a pair of dark
glasses onto the bridge of his nose. No doubt about it,
she was avoiding him.

Not that he would let her do that for long.

She needed some space. He might not be the sensitive, New Age guy she thought she wanted. Over the
next few hours he intended to prove to her that he was
the man she needed.

Two hours later, annoyed with the champagne and
the canapés, and the fact that Elena seemed intent on
having long, heartfelt conversations with the two men
attending the seminar, Harold and Irvine, Nick decided
to take action.

He didn't dislike Harold, though something about Irvine set him on edge. Though both were married, he
wasn't about to underestimate either of them. Harold, at
least, was a carbon copy of the guy Elena was lining up
to be her future husband.

By the time he had extracted himself from a conversation with a pretty blonde, the kind of friendly, confident woman he was normally attracted to, Elena had
disappeared.

Annoyed, he skimmed the beach and the array of bath-
ers lying beneath colorful resort beach umbrellas. There
was no flash of the green tunic Elena had been wearing.
After having a quick word with Harold, who was now
immersed in a book, he followed a lone set of footprints.

Rounding a corner, he found a small private beach

overhung with pohutukawa trees in blossom, their deep red flowers a rich accent to gray-green leaves and honey-colored sand. Beneath the tree, in a pool of dappled shade, lay Elena's beach bag and the green tunic.

He looked out to sea and saw her swimming with slow, leisurely grace. His jaw tightened when he saw a second swimmer closing in on Elena. Irvine.

Out of habit, suspicious of the motives of men who wanted to come on a course designed for women, he had done some checking and received the information just minutes before. Harold had proved to be exactly as he appeared, a businessman intent on trying to please a dominant wife. Irvine, however, had a background that was distinctly unpleasant.

Nick shrugged out of his T-shirt and peeled off his jeans, revealing the swimming trunks he was wearing beneath. Jogging to the water, he waded to the break line. A few quick strokes through choppy waves and he was gliding through deep water.

A piercing shriek shoved raw adrenaline through his veins. Irvine was treading water beside Elena, holding his nose. Relief eased some of his tension as he logged the fact that it was Irvine, not Elena, who had shrieked. The source of the outraged cry was clear in the bloody nose Irvine was nursing.

An odd mixture of pride and satisfaction coursed through Nick as he saw Elena slicing through the waves toward him, her strokes workmanlike and efficient. Irvine had clearly thought he had caught Elena vulnerable and alone—no doubt his favorite modus operandi—and she had quickly dispelled that idea with a solid punch to the nose.

Irvine finally noticed Nick, and went white as a sheet.

Nick didn't need to utter a threat—the long steady look was message enough. He would deal with Irvine later.

Elena splashed to a halt beside him. "Did you see what Irvine did?"

Nick watched Irvine's progress as he gave them a wide berth and dog-paddled haltingly in the direction of the crowded beach. "I was too busy trying to get to you in time."

She treaded water. "You knew about Irvine?"

Nick dragged his gaze from the tantalizing view through the water of a sexy jungle-print bikini and the curves it revealed. "I ran a security check on him this morning. I received the results a few minutes ago."

Nick's hands closed around Elena's arms as the swell pushed her in close against him. "He has a police record and no wife. Did he touch you?"

The question was rough and flat, but the thought that Irvine had laid hands on Elena sent a cold fire shooting through his veins.

"He didn't touch me—he didn't get the chance. It was more what he said."

"Let me guess, he wanted 'sexual therapy' to help him with his problems?"

Another wave drove Elena closer still, so that their legs tangled and their bodies bumped. Automatically, she grasped his shoulders. "That's what's stated on his police record?"

"He targets therapists. Lately he's been doing the rounds of the health spas. Although this will be his last attempt."

"You're going to get him." Her gaze was intense and laced with the kind of admiration that made his heart swell in his chest. Finally, he was doing something right. He stared, mesmerized at her golden, flowerlike irises and wondered how she could ever have reached the conclusion that she had to change those. "I'll sic my lawyers onto him as soon as we get in."

Leaning forward, she touched her mouth to his. "Thank you."

The kiss deepened. He fitted her close against him, acutely aware of the smoothness of her skin against his, the tiny span of her waist and the delicacy of her curves.

The moment when he had realized that Irvine had swum after her replayed itself.

Unconsciously, his hold on Elena tightened. He had let her out of his sight, too busy brooding over the easy way she had shut him out, and Irvine had taken his chance. That wouldn't happen again. From now on, he would make certain that Elena was protected at all times.

Messena women routinely required protection because the amount of wealth his family possessed made them a target. Elena hadn't agreed to a relationship with him—*yet*—but even so, she would accept his protection. There was a small clause in all Atraeus and Messena employment contracts he could exploit if he needed to.

She wouldn't like it, but as far as he was concerned, until Irvine was put behind bars, Elena wouldn't move more than a few paces without either him or a bodyguard protecting her.

When she pulled back and released her hold, Nick had to forcibly restrain himself from reaching for her again. Instead, when she indicated that she wanted to head for shore, he contented himself with swimming with slow, leisurely strokes so she could easily keep pace.

As he waded from the water, satisfaction eased some of his tension when he saw Irvine still struggling in the surf, holding his nose.

When Elena stepped out of the water and Nick got his

first real look at the bikini, he felt as though he'd been punched in the stomach. With her hair a satiny cap, her skin sleek with water, she was both exotic and stunning. The bikini revealed long, elegant legs and the kind of slim, curvaceous figure that made his mouth water, the bright jungle print giving Elena's skin a tawny glow.

He had always registered that she was pretty and attractive, but now she took his breath.

As Elena reached for the towel she had tossed down on the sand, a scuffling sound attracted Nick's attention. Harold, the carbon copy of the sainted Robert, was walking over the rocks, his gaze firmly fixed on Elena.

"That's it," he muttered. "No more men on your weekend seminars."

Elena wrapped the towel around herself and knotted it, successfully concealing almost every part of the bikini but the halter tie around her neck. Her first outing in the skimpy swimming costume had been a disaster. After the unhealthy way Irvine had looked at her, his eyes practically glowing, she was over revealing her new body. "Harold's harmless."

The complete opposite of Nick, who, with his gaze narrowed and glittering as he regarded Harold's halting progress, looked both tough and formidable. "Like Irvine?"

A shudder went through her. "Point made."

She noted that Harold's gaze was riveted on her chest. Her stomach plunged. She suddenly wished she hadn't spent so much time talking to Harold, who seemed to have misconstrued her intentions. "Do you think—?"

Nick said something short and sharp beneath his breath. "You should know by now that if you spend time with a guy, chances are he's going to think you're interested in him."

Elena recoiled from the concept of Harold falling in clinging lust with her. Reinventing herself and wearing the alluring clothes she had always longed to wear had an unexpected dark side. "That hasn't been my experience."

Nick's gaze sliced back to hers. "You've dated. I checked."

"You *pried* into my personal life?"

"You work for the Atraeus Group. We now share a database in common."

"You accessed my personal file." A file that did contain a list of the men she had dated. Working as a PA to both Lucas then Zane Atraeus, she was privy to confidential information and anyone she dated was also scrutinized.

Elena's intense irritation that Nick was poking his nose into her private affairs was almost instantly replaced by a spiraling sense of delight that he was worried enough to do so.

Her attention was momentarily diverted as Harold unfastened his shirt and tossed it on the sand, revealing an unexpectedly tanned, toned torso. "I don't think I'll include men in the pamper program again."

Nick's head swung in Harold's direction, and he muttered a soft oath. "Include men, babe, and you can bank on it that I'll be there."

The blunt possessiveness of his attitude, combined with the way he had come after her to protect her from Irvine, filled Elena with the kind of wild, improbable hope she knew she should squash. Hope messed with her focus. She needed to approach this night together exactly as Nick would—as a pleasurable interlude from which she could walk away unscathed.

Nick's gaze dropped to her mouth. "If you want to get rid of Harold, you should kiss me again."

A shaft of heat at the prospect of another passionate, off-the-register kiss seared through her. "It's not exactly professional."

"The hell with professional."

As Nick's hands settled at her waist, the clinical list of things she would absolutely not allow was swamped by another wave of pure desire. Before she could stop herself, mouth dry, heart pounding a wild tattoo, she stepped close and slid her palms over the muscled swell of his shoulders.

Without the cool water that had swirled around them out at sea, Nick's skin was hot to the touch. Taking a deep breath, she went up on her toes and fitted herself more closely against him.

The instant her mouth touched his, she forgot about Irvine and Harold, and she forgot about the strategy she'd decided upon. Streamers of heat seemed to shimmer out from each point of contact as Nick gathered her closer still, his arms a solid bar in the small of her back.

A small thrill went through her as her feet left the ground and she found it necessary to wind her arms around Nick's neck and hang on. The situation was absolutely contrary to her plan to control her emotions and keep her heart intact, to inform Nick that she was not the easy, forgettable conquest she'd been in the past.

Dimly, she registered that the towel had peeled away and that she was sealed against Nick from thigh to mouth. Long, dizzying minutes later, a rhythmic, vibrating sound broke the dazed grip of passion.

Elena identified the sound as the ringtone of a cell, emanating from Nick's jeans, which were tossed on the sand beside her beach bag.

With a searing glance, Nick released his hold on her.

Stumbling a little in the sand and again conscious of the brevity of the bikini, Elena noticed that Harold had disappeared. She snatched up her tunic.

By the time she'd pulled the filmy tunic over her head and smoothed it down over her hips, Nick had walked several paces away. His back was turned for privacy and he seemed totally immersed in his call.

She caught the phrases "construction crew" and "form work," which meant the call was work related.

Despite the heat that radiated from the sand and seemed to float on the air, Elena felt abruptly chilled at the swiftness with which Nick had switched from passion to work.

Retrieving her towel, she tried not to focus on the pang of hurt, or a bone-deep, all-too-familiar sense of inevitability.

Of course work would come first with Nick. Hadn't it always? It wasn't as if she had ever proved to be a fascinating, irresistible lover to him.

What they had shared was passionate, and to her, beautiful and unique, but it was as if she had never truly connected with Nick. She was certain Nick had the capacity to return love, she just didn't believe it would be with her on the receiving end.

She rummaged in her green tote, found her sunglasses and jammed them onto the bridge of her nose. In the process, her fingers brushed against a book of lovemaking techniques she had bought online. Her cheeks warmed at the research she'd embarked upon because she felt so hopelessly out of her depth in that area. It was part of her general makeover; although the whole idea of planning lovemaking became irrelevant around Nick. It just happened.

She was still reeling from the last kiss and the notion that he wanted her as much as she wanted him.

As if he couldn't get enough of her.

Nick pulled on his jeans and T-shirt and slipped the phone into his pocket. "Time to go."

The searing reality of what would happen when they got back to the resort stopped the breath in her throat. "We've only been here an hour."

"An hour too long, as far as I'm concerned." Snagging her towel and beach bag, Nick held out his hand to her.

Elena's breath caught in her throat at the sudden softness in his gaze, an out-of-the-blue sense of connection that caught her off guard. It was the kind of warming intimacy she had dreamed about and wanted. As if they were friends as well as lovers. Something caught in her throat, her heart, abruptly turning her plans upside down. A conviction that there really was something special between them, something that refused to fade away and die, despite the attempts both of them had made to starve it out of existence.

Nick might not recognize what it was, yet, but she did. It was love.

And not just any love. If she wasn't mistaken, this was the bona fide, once-in-a-lifetime love she had dreamed about. The dangerous kind of love that broke hearts and changed lives, and which she had longed for ever since that one night with Nick six years ago.

From one heartbeat to the next the conflict of making love with Nick when she was supposed to be keeping him at arm's length zapped out of existence to be replaced with a new, clear-cut priority.

Making love with Nick was no longer an untenable risk or an exercise in control; it was imperative.

As crazy as it seemed with everything that had gone

wrong, they were at a crucial tipping point in their relationship. Now was not the time to shrink back and make conservative choices; passion was called for.

By some fateful chance, Nick had taken her quiz and given her an insight into aspects of his personality she would not have believed were there. The kind of warmth and consideration that would make him perfect husband material.

On the heels of that, she had unraveled a piece of his past in the disabled, overweight boy with glasses he had once been.

She had agreed to spend the night in his bed.

Her heart pounded at the thought of the passionate hours that lay ahead, their third night together.

Nick had gone out on a limb to get her back, even if he couldn't quite express his intentions, yet. She was now convinced that the risk she had taken twice before, and which each time had failed, was now viable.

It was up to her to help Nick feel emotionally secure enough to make the final step into an actual relationship. To do what, in her heart of hearts, she had wanted him to for years: to finally fall in love with her.

Thirteen

Nick marshaled the guests back onto the yacht with the promise of free champagne, cocktails and dessert when they reached the resort. The regular manager would probably have a heart attack when he saw the damage to his bottom line on this particular venture, but the way Nick saw it, his night with Elena took precedence.

He had engineered a window of opportunity. He wasn't going to let that time be eroded because clients wanted more time on the beach.

When Irvine stepped aboard, Nick intercepted him and suggested they both go below.

Irvine's expression turned belligerent. "You can't give me orders. I'm a paying guest."

Nick stepped a little closer to Irvine, deliberately crowding him and at the same time blocking him, and their very private conversation, from the rest of the guests. "You also tried to molest Ms. Lyon."

His gaze turned steely. "You can't prove that."

"Maybe not, but we can have some fun trying."

Irvine tried to peer over his shoulder. "Now I'm scared. Elena wouldn't lay charges."

Aware that Elena was conducting a conversation with some of the guests on the bow, Nick moved to block Irvine's view. "Let me see. This would be the same Elena Lyon who has a double degree that she shelved in favor of being Lucas Atraeus's personal assistant for five years."

Irvine's Adam's apple bobbed. "*The* Lucas Atraeus—?"

"Who engineered a number of mining company and resort takeovers and tipped over a major construction company that tried to use substandard steel on one of his developments." Nick crossed his arms over his chest. "Elena might look little and cute, but she orchestrated Lucas's schedule, monitored his calls, including the death threats, and deployed security when required."

Irvine paled. "I don't get it. If she's that high-powered, what's she doing in Dolphin Bay?"

"Spending time with me." Nick jerked his chin in the direction of the two inflatable boats that, on his instructions, hadn't yet been tied at the stern and were still bobbing against the side of the yacht. "I'll make things even simpler for you. If you don't go below, you can stay on the island until I come back to get you. After that, it's a one way trip to the Dolphin Bay Police Station."

After a taut moment, Irvine visibly deflated. With a shrug, he started down the stairs.

Nick followed him and indicated a seat in the dining area, positioned so Nick could keep an eye on him while he was at the wheel.

Expression set, Irvine sat. "Who could know that there would be a police station in a hick town like this?"

"Just one guy—that's all Dolphin Bay needs. And as

luck would have it, he happens to be a relative." A distant uncle, on his mother's side.

Irvine seemed to shrink into himself even further at that last piece of information. Satisfied that he was contained for the moment, Nick went topside and skimmed the deck, looking for Harold. Relief filled him as he noted that Harold had evidently given up on Elena and now seemed to be directing all of his charm toward Eva.

Eva caught his gaze for a split second and winked.

Grim humor lightened Nick's mood as he logged exactly what she was doing—running interference. Somehow, with the scary talent Eva had for figuring out exactly what was going on in men's heads, she had summed up the situation and taken charge of Harold before Nick chucked him over the side.

Minutes later, after starting the yacht's motor, then weighing anchor, Nick took the wheel. A faint, enticingly feminine floral scent informed him that Elena was close. Turning his head, he met her frowning gaze.

"What did you do with Irvine?"

"Don't worry, I didn't hit him. He's in containment." He indicated the glass panel that gave a view into the dining room below.

Satisfaction eased the tension on Elena's face. "Good, I don't want him causing trouble for any of my clients. Bad for business."

"That's my girl."

Her gaze locked with his, the absence of levity informing him that she hadn't liked the situation with Harold or Irvine one little bit. Her reaction was a stark reminder that no matter how strong or efficient Elena seemed, when it came to men she was in definite need of protection.

He had to resist the urge to pull her close and tuck

her against his side. There was no need for the primitive methods he had employed on the beach. Irvine was controlled and he had made arrangements to have him removed from the resort as soon as they reached Dolphin Bay.

As much as he would like to lay a formal complaint againt Irvine, he was aware there wasn't anything concrete that Irvine could be charged with since all he had done was make an advance, which Elena had rebuffed. Besides, police procedure took time. Elena was exclusively his for just a few hours. He wasn't going to waste that time trying to get Irvine locked up.

His jaw tightened at the thought that one more night might be all they'd have. The desire for more than a sexual liaison settled in more powerfully. The thought process was new, but he was adjusting.

Elena crossed her arms over her chest as the yacht picked up speed, hugging the thin fabric of her tunic against her skin. She sent a worried glance in Eva's direction. "Will Eva be okay?"

Satisfaction at Elena's total rejection of Harold, with his smooth good looks, eased some of Nick's tension. He spared another glance for Eva and Harold, and noted the change in Harold's body language. The expansive confidence was gone and his shoulders had slumped. He no longer seemed to be enjoying the conversation. "Don't worry about Eva. She can spot 'married' from a mile off."

"A consequence of being in the wedding business, I suppose."

Nick lifted a hand at the deckhand who had secured the inflatables. "Eva came from a broken home before Mario adopted her. She's never placed much trust in relationships."

Elena slipped sunglasses onto the bridge of her nose

and gripped a railing as the yacht picked up speed.
"Sounds like a family trait."

Aware that Elena was maneuvering the conversation
into personal territory he usually avoided, Nick made an
attempt to relax. "Maybe."

A heavy silence formed, the kind of waiting silence he
had gotten all too used to with his own family.

Elena sent him a frustrated look. "Trying to get information out of you is like talking to a sphinx."

"Seems to me I've heard that phrase somewhere before."

"Let me guess… Your sisters." She tucked errant
strands of hair behind one ear, revealing the three tiny
blue-green jewels that sparkled like droplets of light in
her lobe.

"And the head inquisitor—my mom." He steered
around a curving lacework of rocks and reefs that par-
tially enclosed the bay. "What, exactly, do you want to
know?"

She met his gaze squarely. "What you like to eat for
breakfast, because we've never actually had breakfast together. Why you went into construction when the family
business is banking, and…" She hesitated, her chin coming up. "What's your idea of a romantic date?"

"I like coffee and toast for breakfast, I went into construction because while I was disabled Dad taught me
how to design and build a boat, and my favorite date is…
anything to do with a yacht. Don't you want to ask me
about my relationship dysfunction?"

"I intended to skirt around that question, but now that
you've brought it up, why haven't you ever been in a long-
term relationship?"

In the instant she asked the question, the answer was
crystal clear to Nick. Because he had never quite been

able to forget what it had felt like making love with Elena. Or that she had waited until she was twenty-two to make love, and then she had chosen *him*.

His jaw clamped against the uncharacteristic urge to spill that very private, intimate revelation. "I've got a busy schedule."

"Not too busy to date, at last count, twenty-three girls in the last two years. That's not quite one a month."

Fierce satisfaction filled him at the clear evidence that Elena was jealous. There could be no other reason for the meticulous investigation of his dating past. "That many?"

Her gaze was fiery and accusing. "I thought it would be more."

He increased speed as the water changed color from murky green to indigo, signaling deep water and a cold ocean current. Against all the odds, he was suddenly enjoying the exchange. "You should stop reading the gossip columnists. Some of those so-called dates were business acquaintances or friends."

"Huh."

He suppressed a grin and the urge to pull Elena close, despite her prickly mood. Instead, he made an adjustment to the wheel. With no more rocks or reefs to navigate, and the bow pointed in the direction of the resort's small marina, he could relax more. He found there was something oddly sweet about just being with Elena.

Glancing down into the dining room below, he noted that Irvine was still sitting exactly where Nick had placed him, although his face was now an interesting shade of green.

The conversation he'd had with Irvine replayed. It occurred to Nick that the reason he hadn't been able to walk away from Elena this time was exactly the same reason Irvine needed to back up a step.

Elena had changed over the years, even since their meeting in Cutler's office in Auckland, morphing from the quiet, introverted girl who used to watch him from the beach into a fiery, exciting butterfly with a will of steel.

His stomach tightened. She was gorgeous and fascinating. He could understand why Harold and Irvine had been dazzled, why she could keep a successful businessman like Robert Corrado on ice while she pursued her new career.

If there had ever truly been anything soft or yielding about Elena, like her old image, it was long gone.

Elena turned her head away from him, into the wind, the movement presenting him with the pure line of her profile and emphasizing her independence. After years of single life, it occurred to Nick that she was happy with her own company. Abruptly annoyed by that streak of independence, a strength that informed Nick that, as attracted as Elena was to him she didn't need him in her life, he finally gave in to the urge to pull her close.

She softened almost instantly, fitting easily into his side. Despite that, he was uneasily aware that something important was missing between them. That something was trust.

He needed to come clean about the quiz and release her from the night she had forfeited.

But that was a risk he wasn't prepared to take. If he released Elena before he'd had a chance to bind her to him in the hours ahead, he wasn't certain he would be able to convince her that she should refocus her attention.

Away from Robert Corrado and onto *him*.

Elena, still uneasily aware of both Harold and Irvine, was more than happy to leave the yacht with her clients when they docked at the small jetty.

With satisfaction, she noted both Irvine and Harold being ushered by Nick into a resort vehicle that appeared to also contain their luggage. The driver of the vehicle was one of the gardeners she'd noticed, a burly man who looked as though he had once been a boxer.

Nick strolled alongside her as she entered the resort restaurant. Waiters were already circulating with trays of champagne and canapés. Lifting two flutes from a tray, he pressed one into her hand then began ushering her toward the door.

"We're leaving now?" she asked.

"It is almost eight."

A small thrill of excitement shot through Elena. She had thought they might have dinner and maybe dance on the terrace, but Nick's hurry to get her to himself was somehow more alluring than a slow, measured seduction.

And technically their bargain terminated at midnight. Her stomach clenched at the thought of four hours alone with Nick. "Uh—what about dinner?"

He stopped, his hand on the doorknob. "We can get room service. Although, if you'd prefer to stay here for dinner, we can do that."

His expression was oddly neutral, his voice clipped. If she didn't know Nick better, she would think that eating here and losing time alone together didn't really matter, but she knew the opposite to be true, and in a flash she got him.

Nick was utterly male. Naturally, he didn't like emotion, and in the world he moved, showing any form of emotion would be deemed a weakness. She knew that much from working with both Lucas and Zane Atraeus. The only time they truly relaxed was when they were with their families.

Carla and Lilah had made comments that when their

men felt the most, they closed up even more. Getting actual words out of them was like squeezing blood out of the proverbial stone.

Carla and Lilah had been describing Lucas and Zane, but the description also fit Nick.

Her heart pounded at a breakthrough that put a different slant on some of the starkest moments in her relationship with Nick and made sense of his extreme reaction to his father's death. Nick walked away, not because he didn't care, but because he cared too much. "I don't need to eat."

"I was hoping you would say that."

She took a hurried gulp of the fizzy champagne so it wouldn't spill as they walked. The walkway was smooth enough, but with the shadowy shapes of palms and thick tropical plantings plunging parts of it into deep shadow it would be easy to stumble. She took another sip and noticed the moon was up. "I'm for room service."

His quick grin made her stomach flip. She hadn't thought the night would be fun. She'd thought it would be too fraught with the tensions that seemed to be a natural part of their relationship.

The fact that she was applying the term "relationship" to herself and Nick sent a small, effervescent thrill shimmering all the way to her toes. Finally, after years of being stalled, and just when she had thought all was lost, they were finally in an actual relationship. She felt like hugging him, she felt like dancing—

"Okay, what's going on?"

Nick was eyeing her with caution, which made her feel even more giddily happy, because it was clear he had noted what she was feeling. He was *reading* her mood.

There was only one reason for that to happen. He was concerned about her happiness; he was beginning to *care*.

It wasn't love, yet, but they were definitely getting closer. "I'm…" She suppressed the dangerous, undisciplined urge to blurt out that she was head over heels in love with him and had been for years. "I'm happy."

His gaze slid to the half-empty flute.

Elena took a deep breath and tried to drag her gaze from the fascinating pulse beating on the side of his jaw. "It's not the champagne." She examined the pale liquid with its pretty bubbles and without regret tossed what was left into the depths of a leafy green shrub. "I don't need champagne to spend the night with you."

To make gorgeous, tender, maybe even adventurous love with the man she loved.

For a split second the night seemed to go still, the tension thick enough to cut. "You don't have to sleep with me if you don't want. The quiz was a spur-of-the-moment thing. I shouldn't have—"

"We have a bargain. You *can't* back out."

Startlement registered in his expression. Relief flooded Elena. She had been desperately afraid he was going to release her from their deal. By her estimation the next few hours together were crucial. If they didn't make love and dissolve the last frustrating, invisible barriers between them, they might never have another chance.

In response, Nick reeled her in close with his free hand, fitting her tightly enough against him that she could feel his masculine arousal. "Does this feel like I'm backing out?"

The breath hitched in her throat at the graphic knowledge that Nick very definitely wanted her. "No."

"Good, because I'm not."

He took the flute from her and set it down with his own on the arm of a nearby wooden bench. Taking her hand, he drew her down the short path to his cottage.

The warm light from his porch washed over taut cheekbones and the solid line of his jaw as, without releasing her hand, he unlocked the door and pushed it wide.

Instead of standing to one side to allow her to precede him, Nick stepped toward her. At first, Elena thought he wanted to kiss her, then the world spun dizzily as he swung her into his arms.

Startled, Elena clutched at Nick's shoulders as he stepped into the lit hall and kicked the door closed behind him. Seconds later he set her on her feet in the middle of a large room lit by the flicker of candles and smelling of flowers. Heart still pounding, and pleasure humming through her at a gesture that was traditionally shared by a bride and groom, Elena inhaled the perfume of lavish bunches of white roses.

Nick took his cell out of his pocket and placed it on a workstation in a small alcove that also contained a laptop and a file. The small action made her intensely aware that, for the first time ever, she was in Nick's personal quarters—not his home, because the resort cottage was only a temporary accommodation, but in his private space.

Elena strolled to one of the vases of flowers.

"Do you like them?"

Throat tight with emotion, Elena touched a delicate petal with one fingertip. She was trying to be sensible and pragmatic, trying not to get her hopes too high, but she couldn't *not* feel wonder and pleasure at the trouble Nick had gone to.

Even though the room, with its candles and flowers, had most probably been staged by one of the resort professionals, it was still quite possibly the most romantic gesture any man had ever made. More wonderful than the traditional red roses Robert had sent to her. Even though she had been thrilled to receive the bouquet, thrilled at the fact that for the first time in her life she was being wooed, Robert's dozen red roses hadn't made her heart squeeze tight.

Blinking back the moisture that seemed to be filling her eyes, she straightened. "I love white roses. How did you know?"

"I got my PA to research what flowers you liked." Nick picked up a remote from a low teak coffee table and pressed a button. A tango filled the air, sending an instant thrill down her spine and spinning her back to the steamy tango they had danced at Gemma's wedding.

Determinedly, she dismissed the small core of disappointment that had formed at the systematic, logical way Nick had selected the flowers for their night together. Using a PA was a very corporate solution. She should know; she had done similar personal tasks herself for her Atraeus bosses.

Nick may not have personally known what flowers she liked, he may not have staged the room, but he had arranged it for her pleasure.

She forced herself to move on from the flowers and examined the rest of the interior. Furnished with dark leather couches, low tables and exotic teak armoires, the stark masculinity was relieved by a pile of yachting books on a side table and an envelope of what looked like family snapshots.

The family photos, some of which had slid out of the envelope, riveted her attention because they proved that Nick loved his family, that at a bedrock level, relationships were vitally important to him.

She sensed Nick's approach a moment before he turned her around and drew her into his arms. The tango wound its sinuous way through the candlelit room as she allowed him to pull her closer still and the night seemed to take on an aching throb. Filled with an utter sense of rightness, Elena wound her arms around Nick's neck and went up on her toes to touch her mouth to his.

Long, drugging seconds later, Nick lifted his head. "That's the first time you've actually kissed me properly."

"I've changed." Elena concentrated on keeping her expression serene. As tempted as she was to let Nick take control, to simply abandon herself to sensation, she couldn't afford to get lost in a whirlwind of passion as she had done on the last two occasions. To maximize her chances of success with him, she needed to keep her head and control her responses.

Threading her fingers through Nick's hair, she pulled his mouth back to hers.

Conditions were not ideal for the love scene she had thought would take place. For one thing, she hadn't had time to slip into the sexy lingerie, or the jersey silk dress she had intended to wear. She hadn't had the chance to shower or use the expensive body lotion she had bought, which would have been a more pleasant alternative to the residue of sea salt on her skin.

She couldn't allow any of that to matter. Luckily, she had remembered to pack the book of lovemaking techniques in her beach bag, intending to read it on the beach, so at least she could attempt to be a little more sophisticated than she'd been on previous occasions.

As if in response to the sensuality sizzling in the air, the tango music grew smokier.

Feeling a little nervy, Elena dragged at the buttons of Nick's shirt. As she unfastened the last button, she watched, mouth dry as Nick shrugged out of it, letting the limp cotton drop to the floor.

With his shirt off, his shoulders muscular and gleaming in the glow of candlelight, his chest broad and abs washboard tight, Nick was beautiful in a completely masculine way. The dark hair sprinkled across his chest and arrowed to the waistband of his pants, adding an earthy edge that made her pulse race. He pulled her close for another kiss, this one deeper, longer than the last.

Once again, determined to take the initiative, Elena found the waistband of Nick's pants and tugged, pulling Nick with her as she walked backward in the direction of the bedrooms.

If this cottage was the same as hers, and so far it looked identical, the master bedroom would be a short walk down the hall and to the left, with a set of doors opening out onto the terrace.

She managed to maneuver a step to the right so she could grab the strap of her beach bag on the way.

Nick lifted his head, his brows jerking together when he noticed the bag, but by then they were in the hall and the ultimate destination of the bedroom was clear.

The plan stalled for a few seconds when Nick planted one hand on the doorjamb, preventing further progress. He cupped her jaw, sliding the pad of his thumb over her bottom lip in a caress that made her head spin. "Maybe we should slow this down—"

"You mean wait?" A little breathlessly, Elena tugged at the annoyingly difficult fastening of his jeans. By now, Nick should have been naked.

Fourteen

Nick's palm curled around to cup her nape. "Are you sure this is what you want? I had planned something a little more—"

She found the zipper and dragged it down.

Nick made an odd groaning sound. "Uh, never mind…" With a deft movement, he undid what looked like a double fastening and peeled out of the jeans.

Elena's mouth went dry. With Nick wearing nothing more than the swimming trunks he'd had on beneath his jeans while she was still fully dressed, the sexual initiative should have been hers, a clear message to him that she was no longer a novice at this. But with the golden wash of light from the sitting room flaring over taut, bronzed muscles and adding a heated gleam to his gaze, there was no hint that Nick had registered the dominating tactic. He looked utterly, spectacularly at home in his own skin.

Seconds later, in a further reversal, Elena found herself propelled gently backward into the bedroom. She remembered to hang on to the strap of the bag, which had slipped off her shoulder and hooked around her wrist. Having to concentrate on keeping the bag and the book with her was an unexpected boon, because the sensual control she'd worked so hard to establish was rapidly dissolving into an array of delicious sensations that made it very hard to think.

Nick's fingers brushed her nape. Heat surged through her as she felt the neckline of her tunic loosen. Cool air flowed against her skin as the tunic slipped to her waist, trapping her arms.

Nick took advantage of her trapped arms to bend and brush his lips over one shoulder. The featherlight kiss sent another throb of sensual heat through her, before she dropped her bag and finally managed to wriggle her arms free.

A split second later the entire tunic floated to the floor, informing her that while she had been concentrating on the logistics of moving Nick into the bedroom, his fingers had been busy undoing the entire line of buttons that ran down her back.

A wave of melting heat zinged through her as Nick's hands cupped her breasts through the thin Lycra of her bikini. Dipping his head, he took one breast into his mouth, and for long, shimmering moments she lost focus as the aching throb low in her belly gathered and tightened.

Dimly, she noted that this part of the seduction was not going to plan. She had hoped to keep all of her clothes on until the last moment. Somehow things had deteriorated to the point that she was in danger of being naked first and once more irresistibly propelled into a whirlpool of passion.

Nick transferred his attention to her mouth. Without thinking, her arms coiled around his neck as she arched into the kiss and fitted herself more closely against him. With a slick movement, he picked her up and deposited her on the bed, following her down and sprawling beside her.

She felt a tug at her hips, the coolness of air as her bikini bottoms were stripped down her legs. Her brain snapped back into gear when she realized that for a few seconds she had allowed herself to drift in a pleasurable daze and now was completely naked.

Bracing her palms on Nick's chest, she pushed.

He frowned. "You want to be on top?"

She drew a deep breath. "Yes." The position was the most basic in the book, but it had the advantage of being easy to remember.

Obligingly, he subsided onto his back. Taking a deep breath, Elena began the business of peeling the swim trunks down. With Nick now impressively naked and the trunks in her hand she realized she had forgotten one crucial step: the condom.

Mouth dry, she clambered off the bed and rummaged in her beach bag until she found the box of condoms she had bought earlier in the day. Feeling a little panicked because she sensed the ambiance was deteriorating, she selected one at random. In the process a number of the packets flew onto the floor.

Nick slid off the bed. His light green gaze pinned her. "When did you buy these?"

The sudden grim tension made her freeze in place. "Yesterday."

"Then they're not for Corrado."

"No." She blinked at the idea that she would want to sleep with Robert. Although that concept was overridden by a far more riveting one. Nick was jealous of Robert. "I haven't slept with Robert."

Nick released her wrist, relief registering in his gaze. "Good."

The conversation was blunt and inconclusive, but the fragile hope that had been slowly, but gradually, growing over the past two days unfurled a little more.

With an easy, fluid motion, Nick picked up the box and began shoveling condoms back into it. "These look… interesting."

"I just grabbed the first box I found." And unfortunately, it seemed to be filled with an assortment of acidic colors and strange ribbed shapes.

As she attempted to tear open one of the packets, Nick picked her up with easy strength and deposited her back on the bed with him, pulling her close. The rough heat of his palms at her hips, gliding to the small of her back, urged her closer still.

The foil packet tore across. A black, ribbed shape emerged. Nick made a choked sound—a split second later he kissed her.

Swamped by a sudden sensual overload, she kissed him back. Long seconds later, she surfaced. The condom was still clutched in one hand; she had almost forgotten it. Not good.

Pulling free, she eased down Nick's body.

Obligingly, he allowed her to fit the condom. She had almost mastered the art of rolling it on when, jaw taut, Nick stayed her hand.

In a strained voice he muttered, "Maybe you should let me do that."

With an expert motion he completed the sheathing. Face oddly taut, he pulled her beneath him. Before she could protest, he kissed her, his gaze soft, his mouth quirked. "Sorry, babe. You can be on top next."

Babe. A quiver of pleasure went through her at the easy endearment. Entranced by Nick's heat and weight, his clean masculine scent laced with sea salt, it suddenly ceased to matter that her plan had been overridden, or that she'd had a plan at all.

She was with the man she loved with all her heart. As he came down between her legs in the intense, heated joining that seared her to her very core, she had a split second to log that, as inspiring as the book with its chapters of advice was, in that moment it ceased to have any relevance.

Lost in coiling shimmers of sensation with Nick, she had everything she needed and more.

A rapping at the door pulled Elena out of a deep, dreamless sleep. Nick was sprawled next to her, the sheet low around his hips, sunlight flowing across the strong, muscular lines of his back.

Suppressing the urge to ignore whoever was at the door and snuggle back against him, she glanced at the bedside clock, which confirmed that it was late, past nine.

Another rap had her sliding out of bed. Grabbing a white terry-cloth robe she found draped over a chair, she finger-combed her hair as she padded to the front door.

Her first thought—that it was someone from the hotel wanting to speak to Nick—died when, through a window she glimpsed two feminine figures. Both were casually, if elegantly dressed, which suggested they were guests.

It occurred to her that they could be clients from her seminar who'd decided that What Women Really Want meant some kind of license to pursue Nick.

If that was the case, she thought, becoming more

annoyed by the second, they were about to be disappointed. The days of Nick being pursued by gorgeous young things who thought he was free were over. Nick was no longer free: he was *hers*.

A rosy glow spread through her at the thought. Suddenly, wearing a bathrobe to the door had its upside. She was in Nick's cabin. It was obvious she had been in his bed.

She wrenched the door open and froze.

"Elena?" Francesca Messena, dressed in snug jeans, red heels and a filmy red shirt peered at her. "We knocked on your door—"

"When you didn't answer, we figured you must be here." Sophie Messena, cool and serene in an oversize white linen shirt and white leggings, frowned. "Are you all right? Honey, can you speak?"

Elena clutched at the lapels of her bathrobe, which had begun to gape, but it was too late, Sophie and Francesca had already zeroed in on the red mark at the base of her neck. "I'm fine. Never better."

Sophie glanced at her twin. "She doesn't look fine." Her voice turned imperious. "Where's Nick?"

Francesca gave Elena a sympathetic look. "We heard about the bet."

"What bet?" Elena attempted to block the doorway, but she was too slow. The Messena twins, both taller than her by several inches, and as lithe and graceful as cats, had already flowed past her into the hall.

"It wasn't a bet," a gravelly voice interjected. "It was a wager."

A split second later, Nick, strolled out of the bedroom dressed in jeans, hair ruffled, his torso bare. If there had ever been any doubt for the twins about what they had spent the night doing, it was gone.

Nick's gaze pinned her. Linking his fingers with hers, he drew her close, then casually draped an arm around her waist, holding her against his side. "Let me guess who told you. Eva."

Francesca picked up Nick's shirt, which was still lying on the floor from the previous evening, and pointedly tossed it over the back of a chair. "We're not at liberty to reveal our source."

"You should say sources," Sophie corrected her twin. "Then he gets left guessing."

Francesca lifted a brow. "Hmm. Obviously, you're much better at this than me."

Sophie folded her arms across her chest as if she was settling in for the duration. "I'm in retail. It leads to wisdom."

Nick's arm tightened around her. "Now that you've had your say and seen that Elena survived the night, you can leave. I love you, but you've got approximately…" He consulted his wristwatch. "Five minutes before we start making love again."

"Before what?" Francesca's brows jerked together. "You wouldn't dare."

Sophie ignored Nick and looked directly at Elena. "I heard the wager was for one night. You should leave if you want."

Elena was abruptly tired of the intervention, as well-meaning as it was. "It's not about one night," she said firmly. "We're in love. This is about the rest of our lives."

There was a ringing silence.

Francesca sent Nick a level look. "Then I guess congratulations are in order."

After breakfast, Nick suggested they leave for Auckland and his apartment, where they could be guaranteed privacy for a few days. The seminar was technically finished. There was no need for Elena to go to the main part of the resort, and since she wasn't a guest, she didn't have to check out. Her car was a rental, so it was easy enough to arrange to have it collected from the resort, which meant she could travel with him.

Elena was happy to pack and leave. Ever since the twins had burst in she had felt unsettled and on edge. Nick had been nice. More, he had been charming, but the good manners and consideration were oddly distancing.

She found herself desperately wanting him to revert to type, to be blunt and irritable or even outright annoying. She would rather fight with him than endure this sense of being held at arm's length.

On the bright side, they were going to spend the next few days together, before she had to fly back to Sydney, and Nick had mentioned a sailing holiday. It wasn't everything she wanted, but it was a positive start.

The drive to Auckland took three hours. Exhausted from an almost sleepless night, Elena dozed most of the way and woke as Nick pulled into an underground parking lot.

Minutes later, they walked into his penthouse, which had a breathtaking view of the Waitemata Harbour.

The penthouse itself was huge, large enough to fit three normal-size houses into, with expanses of blond wood flooring and an entire wall of glass.

Nick showed her to a room. Her heart beat a little faster until he dropped his bag beside hers. With relief she realized they were sharing his room.

Feeling happier and almost relaxed, Elena strolled through the apartment and checked out the kitchen before stepping out onto a patio complete with swimming pool and planters overflowing with tropical shrubs.

While she was admiring a particularly beautiful bromeliad with tiger stripes and a brilliant pink throat, Nick's arms came around her from behind.

"I have to apologize for my family. Sophie and Francesca should have stayed out of it."

She turned in his grasp and braced her hands on his arms, preserving a slight distance. "You mean stayed out of our relationship?"

"Uh-huh."

Elena frowned, but Nick had already drawn her close and the feel of his lips on the side of her neck was making it difficult to think. Just before he kissed her, it occurred to her that Nick had carefully avoided saying the word *relationship*.

Elena woke to the dim grayness of early evening in a tangle of sheets. Nick's arm was draped heavily across her waist, as if even in sleep he wanted to keep her close.

Easing herself from the bed so as not to wake him, she picked up his shirt, which was puddled on the floor, shrugged into it and padded to the bathroom.

The reflection that bounced back at her stopped her in her tracks. Dressed in the oversize shirt, with her hair ruffled, eyes still slumberous from sleep and faint red marks from Nick's stubble on her jaw and neck, she looked like a woman who had been well loved.

Her cheeks warmed at the memory of the few hours they'd spent in bed. The lovemaking had been sweet and gorgeous and very tender. While she hadn't gotten a chance to consult the book, mainly because Nick had snatched it out of her grip and tossed it over the balcony, she had gotten to be on top, *twice*.

Elena used the facilities, and washed her hands and face. Feeling absurdly happy, she studied Nick's razor and the various toiletries lined up on the vanity, and gave in to the urge to take the top off his bottle of aftershave. The familiar resinous scent made her stomach clench and her toes curl.

Strolling out to the kitchen, she poured herself a glass of water then walked through the sitting room, fingers trailing over sleek, minimalist furniture. The thought that this could be her home for the foreseeable future filled her with a rosy glow.

Although nothing was settled, she reminded herself. Nick was clearly still adjusting; they would be taking this one step at a time.

A familiar humming sound caught her attention. Nick's phone was vibrating on the masculine work desk in the alcove. Moving quickly, she snatched up the phone and thumbed the Off button. The absolute last thing she wanted now was for Nick to wake up and shift straight into work mode, ending their interlude.

Holding her breath for long seconds, Elena listened hard, but the only sound she could hear was Nick's slow, regular breathing, indicating that he was still deeply asleep.

She placed the phone carefully down beside a file, and froze when she saw her name on a sheet of paper that had slipped partway out of the folder.

Flipping the cover sheet open, she found a note from Constantine Atraeus, her boss, indicating that he was sending Nick materials he had requested.

The materials turned out to be her proposal for the seminar, the quiz she had devised *and a copy of the answer sheet*.

Knees weak, Elena sat down in the swivel chair pulled up at the desk and spread the sheets out.

The tension that had started at Francesca and Sophie's

intrusive questioning, followed by Nick's evasive behavior, coalesced into knowledge.

At some point, way before she had ever gotten to Dolphin Bay to run the seminar, Nick had filled out the quiz, marking every question with the correct answer.

The mystery behind Nick's high score was solved.

He had cheated.

Fingers shaking with a fine tremor, she double-checked the folder in case she had missed something.

Such as a real, fumbled effort at the quiz. Anything that might indicate that Nick Messena had an actual beating heart and not an agenda that was as cold in the bedroom as it was in the boardroom.

There was one final piece of correspondence. It was a memo to the manager of the Dolphin Bay Resort, granting him a week's leave covering the period of the seminar.

Clearing the way for seduction, because Nick had known how weak her defenses had been, that given long enough, she wouldn't be able to resist him.

Setting the letter down, Elena walked back to the kitchen, replaced her glass on the counter and looked blindly out onto the patio with its lengthening shadows.

Her head was pounding and her chest was tight. Why had Nick done such a thing? And why with *her,* out of all the women he could choose?

In her heart of hearts she wanted it to be because, secretly, he had always been falling for her, that he was just as much a victim of the intense, magical chemistry that had held her in thrall as she had been.

But the weight of evidence didn't add up to that conclusion. Three short flings with a man who was known for his tendency to go through women. A seminar Nick had maneuvered his way into, with her accommodation placed conveniently next door to his. The champagne and the carefully staged room, the scene set for seduction.

The fact that he had cheated on the quiz, as hurtful as that had been, was only the clincher.

A bubble of misery built in her chest. She had wondered what the invisible, unbreachable barrier was with Nick. Now she knew. It was his own well-established protection against intimacy.

The twins busting in now made perfect sense. They were his sisters; they knew exactly how he operated. They had been trying to protect her, trying to tell her that despite Nick's pursuit of her, he didn't intend to allow a relationship to grow. All he had wanted was the thrill of the chase, with the prize of a few passionate hours in bed.

She had stupidly ignored the twins and her own instincts, choosing to cling to a fantasy that she wanted, but which had no substance. In so doing, she had allowed Nick to succeed at the one thing she had vowed she wouldn't allow.

He had made her fall in love with him all over again.

Fifteen

Nick came out of sleep fast, drawn by the utter silence that seemed to hang over the apartment like a shroud and the taut sense that he had slept too long.

Instantly alert, he rolled out of the empty bed. The first thing he noticed as he pulled on his trousers was that Elena's suitcase, which he had set down beside the dresser, was gone.

Stomach tight, he finished dressing, grabbed a fresh jacket from the wardrobe and found the Jeep keys. As he strode through the apartment he automatically took stock. Every trace that Elena had ever been there was gone.

The knowledge that something had gone badly wrong was confirmed by a copy of the quiz, and the incriminating answer sheet, placed side by side on a coffee table.

Too late to wish he'd told Elena what he'd done, or that he'd shoved the file in a drawer out of sight until he'd had the chance to come clean. But yesterday, after the showdown with the twins and Elena's quiet statement that she was in love with him, he had been stunningly aware that it was decision time.

Either he committed to Elena or he lost her. But knowing that he should commit—more, that Elena needed him to commit—didn't make it any easier to step over an invisible line he had carefully avoided for years.

Grabbing his phone, he stepped out of the apartment and took the elevator to the lobby. He speed-dialed Elena's number. He didn't expect her to pick up, and he was right.

When the elevator doors opened, he strode out of the building and was just in time to see a taxi pull away from the curb and disappear into traffic. He controlled the impulse to follow her in the Jeep.

He already knew her destination. Elena was smart and highly organized, and as a former Atraeus PA she had a lot of contacts in the travel industry. She would have booked a flight out of Auckland. He could try and stop her, but he wouldn't succeed. She would be back in Sydney within hours.

Stomach coiling in panic he took the elevator back to his apartment and threw on clean clothes. Minutes later, he was in traffic. It was rush hour and took an agonizing hour to do the normal thirty-minute drive to the airport.

During that time he made a number of calls, but every time he came close to making a breakthrough and discovering what flight Elena had booked, he was stymied. Elena, it seemed, had invoked the Atraeus name and chartered a flight. Now, apparently, there was a code of silence.

He found himself considering the caliber of the woman who had started out as a PA, then turned herself into one of the Atraeus Group's leading executives. It was just one more facet of Elena's quiet determination to succeed.

Now she was leaving with the kind of quiet, unshakable efficiency that told him she wouldn't be back, and he couldn't blame her

He had made a mistake. It was the same mistake he had made twice before with Elena. He had been irresistibly attracted but had failed to be honest with her about where he was in the relationship stakes.

He had changed. The problem was that the process of change had been agonizingly slow and the urge to protect himself had become so ingrained that he'd closed down even when he'd wanted to open up.

The quiz had been a case in point. Instead of being up front with Elena, *exposing himself to vulnerability,* he had used his knowledge of the quiz to leverage the intimacy he wanted without exposing any emotions.

Now that very protective behavior had backfired, ensuring that he would lose the one woman he desperately needed in his life.

He picked up his phone and stabbed the redial. When Elena once again refused to pick up, he tossed the phone on the passenger-side seat and drove.

Nick stepped off the evening flight from Auckland to Sydney, carrying his briefcase.

He hadn't brought luggage with him because he didn't need to. He was in Sydney often enough that he owned a waterfront apartment just minutes from the city center.

Twenty minutes later, he paid the taxi fare and walked into his apartment. A quick call to the private detective he had hired earlier on in the day and he had the information he needed.

The tactic was ruthless but, as it turned out, necessary.

Elena had arrived on her flight and gone straight to her apartment. She had stayed in her apartment all afternoon, the curtains drawn. Twenty minutes ago, she had taken a taxi to an expensive restaurant where she was having dinner with Corrado.

Nick's stomach hollowed out at the report. Corrado's name was like a death knell.

He grabbed his car keys and strode to the front door. The mirrored glass on one wall threw his reflection back at him. His hair was ruffled, as if he'd run his fingers through it repeatedly, which he had. His jaw was covered with a dark five-o'clock shadow because he hadn't stopped to shave, and somehow he had made the mistake of pulling on a mauve T-shirt with his suit jacket. The T-shirt was great for the beach; it looked a little alternative for downtown Sydney after five.

Fifteen minutes later, he cruised past the restaurant, the black Ferrari almost veering into oncoming traffic as he saw Elena and Corrado occupying a table by the window overlooking the street.

Jaw clenching at the blaring horns, he searched for a parking space and couldn't find one. Eventually he found a spot in an adjoining street and walked back in the direction of the restaurant.

He was just in time to see a troop of violinists stationing themselves around Elena and Corrado and a waiter arriving with a silver bucket of champagne.

His heart slammed in his chest. Corrado was proposing.

Something inside him snapped. He was pretty sure it was his heart. In that moment he knew with utter clarity that he loved Elena. He had loved her for years. There was no other explanation for his inability to forget her and move on.

Too late to wish that he could have found the courage
to tell Elena that.

His family had termed his behavior a dysfunction
caused by the supposed betrayal of his father, but they
were wrong.

The situation with his father had definitely skewed
things for Nick. He had walked away from a lot of emotions he wanted no part of, but that still hadn't stopped
him falling for Elena.

He had been hurt, but his dysfunction hadn't been his
inability to fall in love, just his objection to *being* in love.

Dazed at the discovery that he had found the woman
he wanted to spend the rest of his life with *six years ago*
and had somehow missed that fact, Nick walked up to
the table and curtly asked the violinists to leave.

The music sawed to a stop as Elena shot to her feet,
knocking over the flute that had just been filled with
champagne. "What are you doing here?"

"Following you. I hired a private detective."

Elena blinked, her eyes oddly bright, her cheeks pale.
"Why would you do that?"

"Because there's something I need to tell you—"

"Messena. I thought I recognized you." Corrado
pushed to his feet, an annoyed expression on his face.

Doggedly, Nick ignored him, keeping his gaze on
Elena. "We didn't get to talk, either last night or this
morning, and we needed to."

He didn't need to shoot a look at Corrado to know that
he had heard and understood that they had clearly spent
the night together. It wasn't fair or ethical, but he was
fighting for his life here.

Reaching into his jacket pocket, Nick pulled out the
original copy of the quiz he had attempted without the

answers and a letter he had written on the flight from Sydney, and handed both to Elena.

The quiz contained the raw, unadulterated truth about how bad he was at conducting a relationship. The letter contained the words he had never given her.

He didn't know if they would be enough.

Elena took the crumpled copy of the quiz and the letter.

Breath hitched in her throat, she set the letter on the table and examined the quiz first.

She knew the answers by heart. A quick scan of the boxes Nick had marked gave him a score that was terminally low. It was the test she had expected from him, reflecting his blunt practicality and pressurized work schedule, the ruthless streak that had seen him forge a billion-dollar construction business in the space of a few years.

It was also, she realized, a chronicled list of the non–politically correct traits that attracted her profoundly. Alpha male traits that could be both exciting and annoying, and which Corrado, despite looking the part, didn't have. "You cheated."

The hurt of finding the sheet seared through her again. "I thought you used it to get me into bed."

A woman from a neighboring table made an outraged sound. Elena ignored it, meeting Nick's gaze squarely.

"I did cheat," he said flatly. "I knew I wouldn't stand a chance with you, otherwise. Things were not exactly going smoothly and the opportunity was there to get you into bed so we could have the time together we needed. I took it."

Elena held her breath. "Why did you want time together, exactly?"

There was a small vibrating silence. "The same reason I arranged to be in Dolphin Bay during your seminar. I wanted what we should have had all along—a relationship."

Fingers shaking just a little, she set the quiz down and picked up the letter. Written on thick blue parchment, it looked old-fashioned but was definitely new and addressed to her.

Holding her breath, she carefully opened it and took the single sheet out. The writing was black and bold, the wording straightforward and very beautiful.

The flickering candles on the table shimmered, courtesy of the dampness in her eyes. Her throat closed up. It was a love letter.

Her fingers tightened on the page. Absurdly, she was shaking inside. She noticed that at some point Robert had left. It seemed oddly symptomatic of their short relationship that she hadn't noticed. "What took you so long?"

"Fear and stupidity," Nick said bluntly. "I've loved you for years."

He took her hand and went down on one knee. There was a burst of applause; the violins started again.

Nick reached into his pocket again and drew out a small box from a well-known and extremely expensive jeweler. Elena's heart pounded in her chest, and for a moment she couldn't breathe. After the black despair of the flight to Sydney, the situation was…unreal.

Nick extracted a ring, a gorgeous pale pink diamond solitaire that glittered and dazzled beneath the lights. "Elena Lyon, will you be my love and my wife?"

The words on the single page of romantic prose Nick had written, and which were now engraved on her heart, gave her the confidence she needed to hold out her left hand. "I will," she said shakily. "Just so long as you promise to never let me go."

"With all my heart." Nick slid the ring onto the third finger of her left hand; the fit was perfect. "From this day forward and forever."

He rose to his feet and pulled her into his arms, whispering, "Babe, I'm sorry I had to put you through this. If I could take it all back and start again, I would."

"It doesn't matter." And suddenly it didn't. She had been hurt—they had both been hurt—but the softness she loved was in his eyes, and suddenly loving Nick was no risk at all.

Epilogue

The wedding was a family affair, that is, both the Messena and the Lyon families, with a whole slew of Atraeus and Ambrosi relatives on the side.

The bride was stylish in white, with racy dashes of pink in her bouquet and ultramodern pink diamonds at her lobes.

Elena did her best not to cry and spoil her makeup as Nick slid the simple gold band, symbolizing love, faithfulness and eternity, onto her finger. When the priest declared they were man and wife, the words seemed to echo in the small, beautiful church, carrying a resonance she knew would continue on through their married life.

Elena's bridesmaid, Eva, on the arm of Kyle Messena, the best man, strolled behind them down the aisle. They halted at the door of the church and the press jostled to take photos.

Elena leaned into Nick, suddenly blissfully, absurdly

happy. "Let's hope they get the wedding story right this time."

Nick pulled her even closer, his hold protective as they made their way toward the waiting limousine. "No chance of a mistake this time. Pretty sure Eva's on record as saying she'll never marry, and Kyle's escorting her on sufferance. They're oil and water."

As brilliant and sunny as the day was, the wedding photos proved to be a trial. The Messena family did what all large families did; they argued. Sophie and Francesca were the worst. They loved Nick unreservedly, but they couldn't resist poking and prodding at him.

Their main issue was that they wanted to know what the aliens had done with their real brother, the bad-tempered, brooding, pain-in-the-ass one, and when would they be getting him back?

Nick had taken it all in good part, telling them that if they had an ax to grind over the fact that he had fallen in love, they would have to take it up with his wife.

Sophie and Francesca had grinned with delight, given Elena a thumbs-up and opened another bottle of champagne.

Halfway through the wedding dinner, which was held at sunset under the trees at the Dolphin Bay Resort, a guest they had all been waiting for arrived.

Tall, dark and with the clean, strong features that would always brand him a Messena, Katherine Lyon's long-lost son hadn't wanted to miss the wedding. Unfortunately, his flight from Medinos had been delayed, which meant he'd missed the actual ceremony.

Nick, who had gone to Medinos to meet with Michael Ambrosi just weeks before, made introductions.

Elena dispensed with the handshake and gave him a hug that was long overdue. After all, they were cousins.

After being thoroughly welcomed into the family fold, Michael took Elena and Nick aside and produced a small box.

Elena surveyed the antique diamond ring, nestled on top of the stack of love letters they had found in Katherine's attic, and finally understood why there had been so much fuss about it.

The pear-shaped diamond was set in soft, rich gold and radiated a pure, white light. The setting suggested that the ring was very, very old, the purity of the stone that it was extremely expensive.

Gorgeous as it was, Elena very quickly decided she much preferred the softness of the pink solitaire Nick had given her. "Aunt Katherine would have been proud to wear it."

Michael replaced the ring in its box. As Carlos's son, the ring was his to give to his future wife if he chose. It was just one of the many strands that now tied him irrevocably into a family that had been anxious to include him and make up for lost time.

As the sun sank into the sea, Nick pulled Elena onto the dance floor constructed beneath the trees. Illuminated by lights strung through the branches and just feet away from the waves lapping at the shore, it was the perfect way to end a perfect day.

A little farther out in the bay, Nick's yacht—the venue for their honeymoon—sat at anchor, lights beckoning.

Elena wound her arms around Nick's neck and went into his arms. "I have a confession. I used to watch you from the beach when I was a teenager."

Nick grinned. "I used to watch you from the yacht."

Elena smiled and leaned into Nick, melting against him as they danced.

No more unhappiness, no more uncertainty, she thought dreamily. *Just love.*

* * * * *

A sneaky peek at next month…

Desire™

PASSIONATE AND DRAMATIC LOVE STORIES

My wish list for next month's titles…

In stores from 21st February 2014:

☐ The Texas Renegade Returns – Charlene Sands

& Double the Trouble – Maureen Child

☐ Seducing His Princess – Olivia Gates

& Suddenly Expecting – Paula Roe

☐ The Real Thing – Brenda Jackson

& One Night, Second Chance – Robyn Grady

2 stories in each book - only **£5.49!**

Just can't wait?

Visit us Online

You can buy our books online a month before they hit the shops!

0214/51